i was broken, now
I Am

A novel

by

SIAN BEZUIDENHOUT

i was broken, now I Am

DEDICATION:

To my amazing daughters: Nadia Simone and Bianca Celeste. For being there.

CONTENTS

BONNIE

CHAPTERS

i was broken, now I Am

ZOE

CHAPTERS

i was broken, now I Am

CARRIE

CHAPTERS

i was broken, now I Am

'It has been said, 'time heals all wounds.' I do not agree.
The wounds remain. In time, the mind, protecting its
sanity, covers them with scar tissue and the pain
lessens. But it is never gone.'

— Rose Fitzgerald Kennedy

BONNIE

i was broken, now I Am

CHAPTER 1: THE TOWNSHIP

DURBAN, SOUTH AFRICA 1979

'When you deal with a country with harsh landscapes, where life isn't really convenient, the nature of the beast is that you do what you have to do.'

The Angel.

My curious and regrettable entanglement with the Ellis family happened when I was just seventeen years old.

Nomthetu, (who I fondly called Thetu) and I had been sitting on our stone, a flattish piece of rock on the side of a wide, open dirt track near our houses that we were fond of. Overhead, the jacaranda trees in full bloom, resplendent in their deep purple floral displays, provided canopies of shade as we sipped cold water and sucked on ice blocks, anything to cool us down from the sickening humidity which characterised the Durban summer. The sky was cloudless and a deep blue despite it being late, much later, the sunset would be an Edvard Munch painted canvas of fuchsia and blood orange, wild, primal and dramatic. What is it about Africa that magnetizes and seduces artists, adventurers, pleasure seekers, world wanderers, missionaries, colonialists, explorers? Despite hysterical rants about crime and danger, they all flock here. It's understandable. I love my country. My continent.

To me, the township was home. I was content, even though others called it the crumbs that the racist government had dished out to us. Everyone knew each other, it was like being part of one big family. I knew that some people called it a shantytown with some dwellings being constructed rather flimsily of corrugated iron pieces nailed haphazardly together. Some families did not have a bathroom or toilet and they had to use communal facilities that were dirty and dangerous. But the sense of a community, that's what kept us going. We were all Black brothers and sisters, we shared a common history, spoke the same language of poverty and limited opportunities. And for me, it was the glue that kept me there. I've been accused of wearing rose tinted spectacles before, of seeing ugliness as beauty, my glass has always been half full. Some of my more realistic friends don't share my vision but I call them out for being bitter and pessimistic. You must believe if you want miracles to happen. And I've always invested emotionally, in community.

There was activity everywhere that day. Kwaito music with its distinctive pumping beat blared out from a boombox. Stray, waif like dogs wandered around seemingly casually but keeping their anxious eyes peeled, anticipating either a scrap of food or a sharp kick; skinny, naked, motherless toddlers took hesitant, tottering steps and then collapsed crying on the red sand, groups of orphaned children dressed in rags played football using rusty tins as goalposts, the clanging of the tins and their excited shrieks filled the air as did the aroma of fried chicken from a makeshift food stall nearby. Young girls like Thethu and myself, sat around sharing sweets, gossiping and braiding each other's hair.

There were deviants too. Knots of teenage boys roamed around looking for trouble. Sometimes this was a thirst for a ruck, or a quest to have sex, evidence of a powerful, dominant, masculine culture in our community. They say that rape is not about fulfilling a desire for sex, it's not a biological imperative. It's about power and, to my mind, hierarchy. Instilling fear in women and children is about driving them out of the public or social world so that they become subjugated and invisible. Masculine prowess becomes default, status quo. Men can then take control of the streets becoming 'kings of the jungle'. This hegemonic masculinity was at the core of township life. Sadly, countless children had been raped and molested in the township, some by their fathers as sometimes fathers slept in the same beds as their daughters, some by gangs of errant boys who regularly patrolled the area.

Drugs and alcohol, the comfort blankets of the poor, pacified us. In front of us, some boys squatted in the dust mulling marijuana with their fingers, they'd separate the seeds from the dried leaves in the palm of their hands carefully so that they could roll and then smoke joints. Some older boys smoked even stronger drugs that got them passing out, their drug infested bodies limp and wasted in ditches were an everyday sight. Girls were never allowed in these circles except as eye candy. Many girls preferred to stay indoors or hang around with other girls to protect themselves. A powerful undercurrent of fear ran like a dark and dirty secret throughout the township much like the open sewers that carried fetid smells. Blood had been spilled here, many times. The blood of sick children with no medicine, the blood of unsuspecting community dwellers caught by marauding gangs late at night.

On occasion, it's been the community itself who has taken matters into its own hands and rallied together to punish a known criminal who escaped conviction or prosecution usually due to corruption or red tape in the legal system. The traditional concepts of law don't work so well here, in South Africa the rich get richer, the poor get poorer. If those at the top were okay who cared about us at the bottom? In the townships, we'd been abandoned and marginalised all our lives. Police took their time on call outs to the township. Why hurry? We were going nowhere. We were forgotten people almost completely out of touch with the evolution of Durban's socio-political landscape. So, we retaliated by turning inward, we did things *our* way. The People's Court in the township is a powerful tool to create harmony and cooperation, usually the elders in the community would preside. As Africans, we're tough, strong and resilient. Our microcosm is complete, we have ombudsman, medicine men, sex workers, racketeers and the best fried chicken in the whole world.

Apartheid has created this urge in us to defend ourselves, to adopt a fierce pride in our culture and customs. It segregated us and moved us away from the city, why? Because our ramshackle dwellings must look like an eyesore. And don't forget our mob mentality. The pent -up fury and rage that we harbour, the venom that spews forth when the mob wants justice, we're not safe in cities. We're descendants from a tribe of warriors. Not poncey eco warriors, keyboard warriors or weekend warriors. I'm talking about civil combat. Buildings, sports centres, schools, hospitals, shopping centres, we rip them apart, burn them or loot from them openly. We target our heartbreak and rage at these structures because we'd all be strung up for murder if we caught the people who *really* let us down, the politicians with the false promises who sweeten us up during elections but after that avoid us or try to get rid of us like flicking dog shit off their shoes. Placatory gestures and dodgy, half- baked excuses as to why the delivery of promised services had not materialised did nothing to quell hungry bellies, sick children and women and girls constantly living under the impending threat of rape, assault and battery.

Poverty can either break you or build character. For me, it did both.

A mangy mongrel came to urinate near us, its coarsened, nude skin cruelly exposed under patches of matted hair. It looked cancer ridden, a large tumour protruded from its belly and swept the ground as it shuffled around, misshapen and heavy. I was transfixed and paused the conversation to stare.

'That dog is dragging itself around like it's cursed,' I said to Thetu. 'I feel like it's an omen, it's a *tokoloshe!*' Thetu's family were Christian and attended an Evangelical church in a huge marquee every Sunday, our family being traditional African were still steeped in Zulu folklore and had not embraced what we saw as a colonial religion, a religion of the White man. We had a paranoia of these little evil sprites inhabiting our bodies leading to sickness, or even death.

'Oh, so that's *more* important!' she retorted, throwing a small stone sharply at the dog which saw it howl then shuffle off in pain. She was trying to tell me something, but I was lost in thought as usual.

It was late afternoon on a Friday, that magical time when I would await my Ma's return from the City as she was a migrant, domestic worker and would come home every other weekend just like the other male and female migrant workers returning to their families. For us motherless children, weekends were always high points unless you had a father who spent his earnings on beer and ended up beating you and your family up in a drunken rage. But this afternoon did *not* feel magical. Something bad had happened.

We were both in the same year at school, being seventeen, we only had one year to go to finish matric. She was going on to nursing college in another town. I wanted to go into teaching not just because I was sweet on her older brother, Themba, who was in the middle of his teaching diploma. I've always admired my teachers. I wanted to be like them. Which other role models did I have? Helping fellow Black students to get qualifications, become professional and upgrade their lives, was my passion, my commitment to my people. At school, I embraced my role as academic coach and peer mentor to other students with something akin to

religious fervour. Supporting with homework or
revision was never a grind, my big picture was my tribe
being able to hold their own on any national or
international platform. But cynics who ridiculed this
zealous approach would point out that doors would
always be closed to us Blacks and upward mobility was
a White's only dream. Apartheid after all, was another
term for institutionalised White privilege. And no
matter how passionately some of 'us' flew the flag for
education, they pointed out, deep in our psyches, we
knew there'd always be a ceiling, an upper limit of
success that we were allowed to achieve no matter how
resilient or talented we were. The upper echelons were
reserved for Whites, we were relegated to the bottom
of the dung heap. Unless a miracle happened, and a
democratically elected government came into power.
And that was a pipe dream or pie in the sky thinking as
Thetu would describe it. No matter how many
sparkling white chickens we slaughtered in ritual
sacrifice, this long- awaited fantasy remained just that.
Maybe, with my half- baked, self- righteous attempts at
being the success champion of the township, it was me
who was the laughing stock. I've always been a
dreamer.

Mrs Dlamini, my lovely English teacher, was heavily pregnant. It was such a pleasure helping her with her colourful displays on the back wall of the classroom, I loved English literature and she was always slipping me school books to take home to read even though it was not allowed. Some students couldn't be trusted to return them, but I was different, I was her favourite and the cleverest, she kept reminding me. Who doesn't like being singled out as 'teacher's pet?' There was no urgency to get home, Ma only came home during weekends and my grandma and aunts turned a blind eye to whatever I did. So, I happily chatted away to my teacher that day, taking my time while we chose the best posters and stuck them on the wall. Miss was going to drop me off at home in her luxury car and I was buzzing with excitement, I loved spending time with her, she had such style, the way she wore her hair and clothes, the metallic nail polish that she used, the smell of her perfume. It was a gift just to be near her! Every man fancied her. I could see them looking when we walked around the soulless, brown brick building of our school where danger lurked in every dingy corner. I've never felt safe there. Us girls chaperoned each other just to visit the toilet. Rapes and gang related violence happened there, some of the perpetrators were not even students at the school yet they walked in and out fearlessly. And it wasn't just limited to bathrooms,

I'd seen a gangster slapping the Principal, Mr Dlamini, once. He's Mrs Dlamini's husband, he bought her an upgrade on her old car when she found out that she was pregnant, he must have wanted a child badly. Unlike others who bring unwanted children into the world.

Sometimes on days like this she would stop at the shop and give me money to get a doughnut and a milkshake, waiting outside for me in case anyone caused trouble which happened sometimes when I went there alone. Jobs were limited for us, we were trapped in that depressing cycle of low incomes, no support and poor role models; many had lost the aspiration to do better. Daily survival for some was tricky. Some delinquent young bucks who had lost their way, hung around the shops looking for someone to rob, rape or assault. We always needed protection or prayer when we went there.

When Themba was back during college holidays, life was different, perfect in fact. Themba is tall, strong, handsome, dignified and intelligent. I know I go on and on about my beau but it's true. I'm considered to be one of the prettiest girls in my school but even I knew that I was punching above my weight when I hooked up with him! A college boy about to become a teacher. Everyone respects him, and therefore they respect me. Simple. Since officially going out with him, guys have stopped stalking me, pestering me for sex or just following me as is their habit with some other girls. I keep myself just for Themba. He has always loved my light complexion, my rosebud pink lips. He keeps teasing me calling me 'Whitey', saying that my father must have been very light skinned as Ma is ebony dark. Or was I adopted? I didn't mind his jokes, but I hated it when he went too far.

Privately, I also wondered whether my Pa had been pale. Everyone in my family is dark, it's only me who is light. I hate it when guys want me just because of that. 'Everyone fancies you,' Thetu would remark in a mock pout.

'They see your skin and prefer you to me.'

'Nonsense!' I'd say. There was a kind of racial hierarchy even here in the township, light skin was preferable to dark. I couldn't work out why. Was it the colonial version of beauty that had been instilled in us? So Themba, being dark, had traded up by going with me? I was uncomfortable with that, it seemed counter - productive to building a solid community. Madiba had wanted a 'rainbow nation,' where we embraced diversity and where we were all one, not a pecking order based on degrees of light and shade. The thought of Themba made me tingle. We'd already discussed marriage. 'Sex every day!' he mused, and I playfully slapped him for bringing up that embarrassing topic. I've had to give in to him, he pestered and pestered and finally I broke. It hadn't been painful or eventful and he was careful to use protection. But Thetu was still a virgin. To be untouched or intact, on her wedding night was her big dream. As Zulus, Durban's largest tribal culture, girls were all expected to be virgins until marriage. Every year, girls flocked to Nongoma, the seat of the royal family, to participate in the reed dance before the Zulu King. They had to be bare breasted, unsullied and prepared to be one of the many wives, if chosen. They also had to be comfortable with polygamy. I wasn't. Monogamy was just fine for me. Besides, I wasn't a virgin and getting me to bare my mosquito bite breasts was like squeezing blood from a turnip. I don't have the required melons to go around flaunting my mammary glands in public, I prefer mine covered up.

That day, Thetu had wanted to rush home as she had just got her period, she was sensitive about things like that, must be something about being the only girl in a house full of boys. So, she left without me, doing the thirty- minute walk alone, en route however, a car had pulled up. It was our Science teacher, a fierce old man who shouted and sometimes slapped the kids so that everyone feared him. He had offered to give her a lift. Now us girls spoke about this all the time. We *knew* how men were and what they wanted. *None* of the girls in our circle had been promiscuous, most had regular boyfriends, some were virgins. Even so, our mothers would have killed us if they'd had a clue about what we got up to when their backs were turned! As the new generation, we were expected to study and focus on having careers. Knowing this, Thetu gave many excuses as to why she did not want the lift, but he was persuasive, telling her that it was on his way and she would be home in no time, so she accepted. After all, it was a teacher. But soon it was clear, that he was going the wrong way. He wouldn't stop despite her pleas and then tears, instead he drove faster and much to her horror, period blood started to seep onto the velvety cream upholstered fabric of the car seat, leaving a huge stain like an unwieldly Rorschach inkblot. Guilt and shame merged into panic. Wracked by this, and stomach-churning pain, a high-pitched wail was emitted from somewhere deep inside Thetu.

Poor girl, I tried to picture her in the car bunched with anxiety, not knowing whether she was more terrified about the stain in that executive car, or about what was going to happen next to her. She must have seen her precious virginity ebbing away, bit by bit. To have guarded that treasure for seventeen years and to lose it in a heartbeat to some decrepit old pervert! I cringed just thinking about it.

Eventually, he had stopped in a seemingly deserted area and had flung himself on her, raping her despite her period. Some men see us as unclean at this time, the dirty blood pouring out is repulsive to them. But we live in a world that is weird and wonderful, other men relish being inside us during our monthlies, in fact we become more irresistible. To them, it's not a curse but a privilege. Thetu said that the teacher had almost worshipped and welcomed it, lapping it up with his tongue first and then penetrating her. Maybe he just cherished the idea of being with a virgin, there were endless numbers of myths in our culture about the healing and restorative effects of bedding a virgin, whether it was forced or consensual did not matter. The Science teacher must have been convinced of this as he drilled into her. Distraught, Thetu had thrashed, lashed out and screamed throughout her ordeal until a few local people heard the commotion and came to her rescue. The teacher had been set upon and beaten severely but he managed to escape in the end. I would have chopped off his head and speared it on a broomstick for all to see, maybe we could have presented it to Mr Dlamini the Principal as if to say, 'Look what your staff is doing to our students!'

Shock had taken hold of my dearest friend and she had to be helped to get home. As soon as her mother saw her and heard of what happened they both huddled together sobbing and wailing joined by many in our community. A communal wail meant that something significant had happened, it was a red alert that things had gone wrong. No one slept that night, least of all me. Every sound rattled me, I felt overwhelmed by fear, as if it would be my turn next. I kept lifting the curtains to peer out, half expecting the shadows of the coal black night to morph into violent, sex crazed monsters. This attack was close to home! My best friend and neighbour! And the Science teacher! I used to love Science. I kept twitching and breaking into a sweat, until auntie brought me sweet tea and sat with me, holding me tightly until dawn, while I reflected on how, if ever, we could move forward after this.

In other households, mothers paced restlessly, pondering what extra layers of protection they could put in place to keep their daughters from similar fates. Outside, vigilante groups prepared themselves, huddling together as they hatched their strategies and plans for revenge. Together with Thetu's remaining brothers, they approached the teacher's house with machetes and other makeshift weaponry, but he had fled with his wife and kids. Clever man, they would have butchered the lot of them! Now, she was not allowed to go to the school anymore, the only secondary school in the district. In fact, there was such outrage and a clarion call for justice, we wondered if the school would still be standing, so many surrounding buildings were burned down as people rampaged and raged for days, demanding answers. It was not the first time that a child from the community had been violated in this way. What was the point of school if you couldn't trust your own teachers?

Death threats were sent to the Principal. A call for action was sent around, someone suggested that the community storm into the school and pull the teachers out one by one to present themselves at our community kangaroo court. Even known rapists were secretly enraged. The sneaky Science teacher had deprived them of a chance to devirginize a beautiful girl, in her prime. Themba would be devastated that his one and only sister could be treated like a piece of meat by a teacher no less! I could just imagine how his blood would boil, how he would want to settle the score when he came back from college.

We were all in shock. How could this happen to my dear friend? Our sweet and placid Thetu who had been overprotected all her life. We knew of girls who had been molested and ended up pregnant or worse, HIV positive. Some of our friends told us about young girls as young as six who got raped just on the way to the shops to buy milk and bread. If they had come of age, some of the girls ended up leaving school and staying at home with babies they never wanted, husbandless, just sitting sexual targets for single or married men in the area who would pursue them relentlessly. There's nothing like a broken woman with a low self- esteem. Men flock to them like vultures over carrion in the Serengeti. Worse- case scenario, the victims died a shameful death riddled with Aids, something that we never talked about, it was so disgraceful, so ugly. Of course, some couldn't live with the memories and killed themselves. If only jacaranda trees could talk! I wondered how many had hanged themselves from those branches.

Thetu and I had been raised very conservatively. Our mothers were best friends. We were not allowed out except to each other's houses or the yard adjoining our houses. Other teenagers we knew took part in protests against the government and were bussed to rallies all over the city. In the community however, there was so much talk about police brutality towards our Black people, so many had been killed off already, whether in custody or just shot in daylight, that our mothers, albeit supportive of the cause, were too scared to let us attend.

There were no men in *my* household, Pa had died at work when I was a baby. There had been a shoot- out and as a security guard he was the first to take the bullet. Ma had received no help. There was no such thing as compensation or financial remuneration from our government. She had been very lucky finding work with a rich White family in the city, they were kind and generous to her and she could come home on the weekends. In the meantime, I was well cared for by my auntie who made a modest living sewing and knitting baby clothes and blankets to be sold in the market. There was also my granny who was so old that she was almost blind, yet she kept chickens in a small coop at the back and toiled in her vegetable patch, taking delight, it seemed, at being able to contribute to the family's food supply. Our modest house was cosy and small but still, it was a life of sorts. We lived for weekends when Ma would arrive laden with groceries and presents, then, the singing and dancing would start and end on Monday mornings when, at the crack of dawn she would board the bus for the city again. Ma was our anchor, our rock, her comings and goings brought visitors to the house, well -wishers and relatives wanting to be regaled about the city and her experiences as a worker there. It gave a structure to the thrum of our inconsequential lives.

Until now.

Thetu's ordeal had spread like wildfire and everyone came to know. The school said nothing despite demands from our community which made her parents even more adamant that she would never return. Outside the school, someone had painted 'Rapist' on the walls and an angry mob had attacked staff in the car park. When the community got this riled up, they wouldn't stop until the school was burnt down or closed for good. My worry was if she did not return how could she finish her matric? We had both come this far, persisting in studying together and trying hard, what future awaited her now with no chance of finishing school? Would she become a maid like Ma? Looking after White people and hoping that they would be kind to her? We heard so many stories from Ma, stories of cruelty and abuse. Our Black women being forced to sleep on floors and treated like sub humans not being allowed to use the bathroom reserved for the White family, sometimes they were given extra jobs to do on top of their contractual duties, like gardening, cleaning swimming pools, cooking and washing their employers' posh cars in addition to other chores which left them exhausted and sometimes sick.

Ma had painted a picture of a different life in her employers' household, she said that she was lucky that they *liked* Black people and were extra nice to her, providing a comfortable outbuilding for her in the garden, giving her time off in the evenings, a decent salary with a bonus at Christmas, even allowing weekends off. She said that they were different and that other domestic workers she knew had *not* enjoyed all this privilege. Black politicians would visit the house sometimes and they ate from the same dishes as the Whites, all this as the family were strongly opposed to apartheid. They were kind, British people. She would never agree to working for the racist Whites who treated us so differently, some of her friends who had worked for these types had been mistreated which filled me with fury. She talked on and on about this and wanting to protect me from the ugliness outside the township.

I could hardly picture Thetu doing this, but a job was a job. Me, I was focused on becoming an English teacher just like Mrs Dlamini my mentor. And nothing was going to stop me.

So, when Ma announced that she would take me with her to the city for a while, I was comforted, wary but happy. Ma *knew* what to do. She said that she would talk to her employers and get advice on how I could finish my final two years in a school in the city, near her work. She was a determined lady was Ma. She so wanted me to become the teacher that I had always talked about. A few days later she made a surprise midweek visit home. She had come to collect me. The Boss had decided that I was to come and live with my Ma and attend a school near their home in Durban. They would pay for my education and give me an allowance, they were keen to support us. The gesture was a kind of liberal largesse and even though I was shy about being suddenly uprooted from my community and thrust into this shiny new world, Ma had clearly accepted the offer, on my behalf. She was so jubilant and filled with gratitude, her eyes glowed like embers, shiny with joy. The Boss would be blessed, he was a good man. For a long, long time, she'd wanted me with her, this was a dream come true for her. Not for me. My place was with Themba, in the township, with my people. But looking at the relief etched on her beautiful face, I couldn't bear to disappoint. Besides, I had to focus on finishing school if I wanted to become someone, and that possibility was looking increasingly slim now that my school could be closed at any point. Granny and my auntie could take care of things at home without me. I was part of the next generation of Blacks in South Africa she said, young, urban, sophisticated, affluent. And she wanted to see her Princess go up in life.

We left together the next morning, at four a.m. while it was still dark.

CHAPTER 2: THE CITY

It was six thirty a.m. when we finally walked into the broad drive of the Ellis family home, huge black wrought iron gates blocking our way until Ma pressed a button on the side and spoke into a microphone. Even *she* was not allowed to know the security code. They seemed protected against all eventualities, this usually meant crimes committed by Blacks. There was electric fencing around the perimeter, regular checks by a private security company and an alarm system linked to the police. Unlike other Whites, the family did not like the idea of having guard dogs, criminals were known for poisoning them and *then* committing burglary. Sometimes, the people were raped and killed in their beds. Ma had heard about these things and narrated tit bits of information as we walked.

i was broken, now I Am

Against the opulent surroundings, I felt dirty and
dusty. That feeling of being overwhelmed had started
just as we jumped off the bus, it was such a visual
assault on the senses. It was sunrise. The sky was alive
with swirls of peach, pink and rose gold, I yearned to
lie down with my arms behind my head and just watch
it. Then the houses on the Berea which is where we
were heading. Giant, squat houses in pastel shades set
back from the broad, tree lined avenues. Ma said that
often only a few family members lived in them,
sometimes even just one. I thought back to the houses
in the township, little, cramped, haphazard dwellings
constructed sometimes from cardboard, rusty
aluminium sheets, rags even, crammed with people, *my*
people. It didn't seem fair somehow. Why did we have
to settle for improvised cardboard boxes while Whites
were living it up in these palatial homes? Our blood ran
red too! So many opportunities had been denied to us
and handed, instead, on silver platters to others. They
must have relished the disparity between the racial
groups, because they seemed hellbent to protect their
privileged positions at the top, all the mansions were
surrounded by high fences and security gates, some had
dogs that reared up when they saw us, openly baring

their teeth and salivating at the sight of us as though we were just pieces of meat to be torn apart in a feeding frenzy.

I was terrified! I wanted to be sick with nerves. My legs had become rubbery and refused to move at Ma's pace. Every so often, I pleaded with her to let me do a U-turn and return to the township, my comfort zone, but she reassured me that the attack dogs were hemmed in by the fences and gates and couldn't eat me. To see so much aggression in them just because we were walking past. I'd heard somewhere that Whites trained their dogs to kill criminals which meant us. Me, my mother, my family, my tribe. No wonder they wanted to lunge at us, even police dogs strained at their leashes when they saw us. A new feeling settled into me from that day. Wariness. I had to watch myself here. There seemed to be back stabbers *and* front stabbers at every turn, just waiting for me to slip up. I felt like I was crossing over a threshold, entering a foreign White land, where my presence was tolerated through gritted teeth. The township dogs had been meek and submissive, these were savage and ready to attack what they had been trained to see as prey. Yet this was *our* land, the land where our Zulu nation and other tribes had co-existed successfully over thousands of years. I was on a steep learning curve. I guess I had never thought about the prospect of sharing territory. I knew that colonialism, with racist discrimination at its heart, had created an us and them mindset. What I had not realised was the extent to which immigrants had fallen in love with my country and I was shocked to hear how Whites, Indians and Coloureds also called themselves Africans and wanted a stake in the country. Everyone wanted a piece of South Africa, it seemed. It had become a sharing platter with many racial and cultural groups at the table, each picking off the plumpest and ripest of the bountiful resources on offer. My mind was exploding with the new insights and revelations. I needed processing time.

I had worn my school uniform because I had wanted to look smart. But suddenly, I felt self - conscious about how I looked and came across. Would they like me? Would they understand me? My English was good, I was confident about that part, Mrs Dlamini had said that my English was better than my IsiZulu! But I was happy about that, not mad, after all the many English books that I had read, of course I was good, in fact I had been the best English student in the school. But would I ever be as good as the others? The school was multiracial with the majority being White. The prospect of integrating with other races shook me to the core. At seventeen, I had never enjoyed opportunities to meet other racial and cultural groups. I wondered now whether I could pull off this jumping in the deep end, face your deepest darkest fear act. Sure, I was excited, but fear gripped me too.

We walked into the garden, with Ma striding forwards and me lagging far behind, shyly. Inside me, a voice whispered, 'Buckle up, enjoy the ride. It's going to be a bumpy one!' I tried to put it to the back of my mind, but my nagging insecurity about my readiness for the integration programme that Ma had signed me up for, lingered.

How could I have prepared for that initiation into the Ellis family? I was entering the garden of Paradise that I'd only come across in books. My jaw dropped! There were exotic, vibrant flowers with magnificent, bright blooms. Some were draped in tight clusters of buds, others were overblown and gaping, revealing centres that were almost vulgar with rich colours and perfumes. There were majestic palms and cycads reaching into the sky, fruit trees like lemon, pawpaw, avocado and mango…I spun about trying to take everything in feeling dizzy and breathless. I half expected to see angels and fairies gliding about, wings spread. It was the stuff of pure fantasy. I knew suddenly, that I had only subsisted in my past life. This was a portal into a new, luscious world that I could never tire of. Someone had sprinkled fairy dust on the world and I was dazzled, I wanted to stay out there just taking it all in, my eyes were wide open and round with disbelief. But Ma just laughed. The gardener had done a good job, she said. Everyone reacted in the same way when the saw the garden. There was a large pond with golden orange fish too, on the other side. Later, I would have time to appreciate it all. She was rushing inside the main house to prepare breakfast for the Boss, Miss Wendy and their daughter who was her second baby as she had been her nanny from young.

Reluctantly, I was ushered into the main house.

Eyes on me straight away. I looked at the three of them and then looked down at my clothes. I must have hung my head, I knew that I became dumbstruck as Ma clipped me sharply on the head, then rushed off into the kitchen.

'Sit.' I was offered a seat at a large table where the honey coloured wood gleamed. I obeyed shyly.

'Tell us about you.'

I had not been used to reading blue eyes. A coldness and a canniness cut right through me, like an X-ray machine. I was being analysed, taken apart bit by bit as if they were examining their investment closely. They stood together, just staring. The mother and daughter duo positioned themselves on one side, the mother's arm around the girl as if shielding her from something unpleasant. I feasted on their beauty, they looked surreal, like two dimensional images from a magazine, their creamy skins flawless. Their soft, silky clothes swished with every movement. There was an elegance and a sophistication to everything here, I wanted to scream. I couldn't do it, couldn't just slot in and learn to be like them. I wasn't a square peg in a round hole, I was a nonstarter. Ma had presented the idea like it was a rite of passage, their support would get me where I wanted to be. But to be honest, I'd have gladly walked on hot coals to avoid the awkwardness of the initial meeting. Ma could have warned me, smartened me up more, helped me to prep, maybe held a rehearsal. But she hadn't and for a moment, I hated her for bringing me to this type of place with no warning, for making me feel foolish. Then the Boss reached out, giving a welcoming smile which relaxed me a little.

'Leave her alone,' he teased. 'Can't you see that she's shy? She'll need some time to get used to us.'

'It's okay, she can take all the time she needs.'

The girl had piped up, she had introduced herself as
Zoe, Ma had said that she was a year older than me so
that would put her as eighteen. She was shorter than
me, her shining white blonde hair fell to her behind. It
was like she had lights in her hair, I'd never seen
anything like that. It cascaded down, silky and straight
like a waterfall, I could have sworn that it was just
above her knees. Like her mother's, her eyes were deep
blue, her mouth a perfect bow in a deep red. She
looked like an angel. I'd never seen anyone that pretty.
When she moved, her breasts and bum jiggled, she
would never last two minutes in the township before
the men descended on her. I didn't think that she could
be safe anywhere.

Ma arrived with food, piping hot black coffee for
them, tea laced with sugar and milk for me. Miss
Wendy had her arm around me now and she seemed
soft and kind. Her skin was heavily perfumed with a
scent that made me feel heady, and her bracelets jingled
as patiently, she pointed out the name of each food
item: croissants, ham, scrambled eggs, fruit salad,
muffins, cheese. She spoke extra slowly to me as if I

was a slow learner which made the girl giggle, but her smile was genuine and kind. I ate hungrily, almost in silence, painfully aware that I was in the spotlight even as I chewed, so when Ma whisked me away to her quarters afterwards, I didn't complain. Whew, I had been waiting to exhale!

What a novelty it was to use a proper bathroom, I had not known that Ma had all the mod cons. Our bathroom on the farm had been a basic, functional affair, most times I wanted to speed up my time there and run out. But Ma's bathroom was designed for lingering and luxuriating, her bath products were creamy and scented, the matching towels soft and fluffy. She had a flushing toilet and a shower, the pale blue and white tiles giving it a modern, clean look. In the room itself there was a comfortable double bed with a large duvet and spare blankets, a kitchen area with cupboards, a hot plate and fridge, even a table and chairs. It was a mini house. With a shock, I had to admit that they had been exceptionally considerate to Ma. I had fully expected these Whites to be aloof and dismissive of our people even though she had reported that she'd been content here. Apartheid in all its evil glory, had kept racial groups away from each other, thereby sowing seeds of bitterness and negativity about other races, stereotypes abounded in the absence of positive interactions, knowledge and experience. I was socialised to believe that they were all cold, cruel and selfish in keeping the best of *our* country for themselves, but here, in Ma's outbuilding, philanthropy stared me in the face and proved me wrong. Maybe I'd become xenophobic as a side effect of the carefully crafted segregationist mindset of the apartheid regime. Now, I was turning against Ma.

I couldn't say it to her face but inside, I was seething with rage, where was Thetu when I needed her? How could I tell Ma how resentful I felt, looking at all her possessions in that mini house that could have accommodated an entire family? How come she never bought colour coordinated soft furnishings for *our* house in the township? She had used baby blue, white and grey here, it looked comfortable and smart compared to our mish mash of things that had been thrown together. We had constantly lived off hand me downs, nothing matched in my township bedroom, whereas she had new stuff. No wonder she wanted to keep this job, no wonder she never complained. When I was little she only came home once a month sometimes, put it all down to work demands. But now I knew that there was a lot that she hadn't told us.

She'd been leading a double life, I could see that now. She was different here. We'd been struggling. She had not. She'd told me that she ate the same food as the family and naively, this had conjured up images of tasteless, uninspiring dishes to me, unlike our mouth-watering cuisine. But even that had been a myth on my part because I could see after the extensive breakfast that she had in fact, been cherished. Everyday meals here seemed like attending a banquet.

She wasn't part of my tribe anymore, this pampered, underhand traitor. The snake. What else was she not telling me? How many new truths would be unveiled in the days to come? I hadn't expected this.

It was midday, but I was exhausted. I wanted to sleep for days, just quietly processing everything. As I lay down, my thoughts turned to the girl, Zoe. Just as Ma led me away, I saw it on the girl's face. The wrinkling of her nose, the rolling of her eyes.

'She smells of the farm.'

'Now Zoe don't be rude,' he hissed. 'Give her a chance, she's going to be like a sister to you. In fact, from now on I want you to regard her as your sister. No arguments about that!' The Boss was my ally, I liked him immediately. I wasn't scared of him.

'A sister from another mother,' she sang. I could hear and understand perfectly. I wasn't there to see the look of menace between husband and wife. If I'd hung around, I would have been able to cut the atmosphere with a knife.

I missed the safety and predictability of my people so much that I cried in my sleep.

School was not a hurdle as I thought. The teaching, resources and support was better than expected. The first week, my learning buddy walked all over the school campus with me pointing out the names and functions of different buildings on the imposing, post-colonial campus. I wanted to memorise every nook and cranny. I liked my English teacher the most, she recognised my talent for writing straight away and nurtured it, offering me extra lessons after school to make up for gaps in my knowledge. I wondered whether some staff had opposed the relatively new initiative of offering scholarships to students of different races, or of letting multiracial staff in. When I joined, the school was heaving with scholarship students of different races and cultures. We banded together in classes and on the playground, little knots of students defined by their skin colour: Indian, Coloured, Black. How South African! They called us Blacks 'coconuts,' Black on the outside but White on the inside. I guessed that this meant that despite our outer skin colours, that we were cultured now that we had access to the opportunities that had been exclusively reserved for Whites in the old segregationist system. Of course, middle class Whites were still the dominant race, with their passion for rugby, hockey and swimming, they stood out, competing aggressively against other schools to put our school at the top of the league tables. Us? We struggled to latch on in English driven lessons, English being our second language not our first. For some, it was also a case of not concentrating and treating school like a big social club which I wished they didn't do, we couldn't let the side down, we were here to show that we could blend in. Most of the non -White students as we were called were bussed in from neighbourhoods far away. During apartheid, they had had to be relocated out of the city to create stress free living spaces for Whites meaning the British and the Boers. After school, they travelled long distances to get home unlike me, in my new life.

The walk to school for me was only a short fifteen minutes. Initially I had tried to walk with Zoe, but she had been aghast at the prospect of walking, choosing to pester her parents for a lift or, when they were away, her friend's parents. It was funny how the tables had been turned. Once upon a time it was I who had to wait to see Ma every other Friday. Now I saw her every day and even slept with her which I loved. They had made a beautiful room for me next to Zoe's in the main house, but I was too shy and couldn't bear to be separated from Ma. Zoe on the other hand hardly saw her parents as they were never around.

Boss Toby was a writer who had produced several books on the history of South Africa, Ma said. He was an important man, travelling around the country giving speeches about his vision of a new, multicultural South Africa. Miss Wendy was involved with charity projects, of which I was one. She too travelled around giving speeches and receiving awards. Both were constantly out, attending dinners and special events, they seemed to have high flying friends. Sometimes they hosted parties at home too. A long time ago, Miss Wendy had been a famous artist but all that stopped when she had Zoe.

So, this was why Zoe was Ma's 'second baby', she had been there to see to her needs from the time she was born. I secretly hated the way she fussed over her, why couldn't she be like that with me? It wasn't just that I was consumed by the green- eyed monster, I had a valid claim, it was *my* Ma after all. Why should I have to share her? In fact, Zoe didn't care whether her parents were present or absent, she was so used to everything being done by Ma. Happiness, they called her. I laughed cynically when I heard it. What an absurd name. How could anyone be called that? It was dehumanizing, couldn't Ma see that and stand up for her rights? Why could they not use her real name Nobantu? It was such a beautiful name and meant 'mother of people.' In lots of ways Ma *was* that figure. The way in which she took care of the homeless and hungry, dividing what little we had to help and support, the help she gave out to those who were infected with the horrible HIV virus, the kindness shown to my granny and aunties who she accommodated at our house. She was a real Community Mamma back home, a true inspiration and everybody adored her.

Now, here, she had been rebranded as Happiness. My name too meant something. Sibongile meant 'we are grateful.' Ma was forever thankful for me, the love child that she had with my father. I was proud of my name, my Zulu heritage. It was who I was. But my name was evolving with my new identity, Bongi was what I preferred now.

I had made friends with a group of Black girls unexpectedly quickly. Zoe had her own friends and seemed to want to avoid me at school. In fact, if it hadn't been for my friends, I would never have survived the stress of starting at a new school. They were warm and funny. We shared food and helped each other with the work. After school one Friday afternoon, Toby gave us a lift to a salon in town where I had my hair braided. I chose black and red hair extensions; the style would be long with a side parting. I hadn't expected him to wait while it was done and to call me 'gorgeous' afterwards. He kept flicking the braids and pestering me to go out for dinner which made me more self-conscious than ever.

I preferred the company of my friends now. We chose new, trendy clothes together and roamed around the malls, shopping. I had money now. Miss Wendy had given me a purse and filled it with notes. Ma said that we would be forever in their debt as they had saved her Princess, but I didn't think they wanted financial payback. The cynic in me raged that they had inadvertently benefitted from apartheid, adopting me now as a charity project helped them to make peace with the universe, in their hearts. I still did all my school work diligently as before but now, with the support of my new friends, I started to really explore my city, Durban. I was growing in confidence every second, and I was falling in love with my new life. Ma said, after a few months that I was unrecognisable. Every day, I could sense her efforts in catapulting me into the new, affluent, urban world that the Ellis family belonged to. And as a new generation Black woman, how could I resist? I was desperate for success and I needed a voice, a platform to help shape my country's destiny. Especially as a woman. I had seen too much of poverty, hardship and cruelty. If I wanted to effect change, I had to start by changing myself.

Often, when Ma would go back to the township, my friends would stay with me in the outbuilding. Then, in the morning we would head for town, picking up food and wandering around eating and talking. The harbour became my favourite place, I loved to stand and watch the ships and the flow of activity around the docks. The first time I saw the sea, my eyes were as big as saucers. Wow! That shimmering sheet of perfect, unruffled blue. There were parks too on the fringes of the harbour where we would picnic with our favourite crispy fried chicken and spicy rice. The beach with its golden mile of sand and amusements became a regular favourite, it was ages before I could summon up the nerve to go on the rides or even eat at restaurants with friends. But still, just walking along the promenade, with the salty air stinging my skin, eating vinegar infused fried chips was a revelation. I could never get tired of Durban!

To me, other students seemed so street smart whereas I was a newbie, a fresher. I had a list as long as my arm to perfect. Small things pleased me, sometimes I was content just to look! I had so much to learn. Sometimes, I resented all the baggage that I had carried with me from the township. I wished that someone could press the reset button and I could start afresh, here, in the city. How different life would have been if I had had that chance. Just seeing the variety of food choices in the city made me hungry, so hungry, I never wanted to stop eating, I wanted to gorge myself on food. I fantasised about tables piled high with resplendent, indulgent food...meat, fish, plump, exotic fruit. I wanted to cram all of it into my mouth.

I was thirsty too, the kind of thirst that can never be satisfied or quelled. I was parched. Starved of culture, art, books, fashion, experiences. Everything.

That's what township life did to me.

Of course, I was grateful for the lifeline that the Ellis family had thrown me, but I'd started to see how township life had damaged me, how it had eroded my self -confidence, filled me with fear, especially of men. Every now and then, I also reflected on the other township kids, why couldn't they be given opportunities like me? It was time for change, a militant voice demanded. We desperately needed a new regime that focused on inclusion, not separation. Secretly, I envied the confidence and poise of my new friends, the way that they blended in and feared nothing. They lived in suburbs but were used to coming into the city by themselves, they knew everything whereas I made mistakes.

Often, in malls, we were chased off by security guards who had come to perceive us as thieves and criminals, just out to snatch handbags or jewellery. But I didn't let this get to me, I learned to run away laughing with my group of friends. I felt like I was finally getting a glimpse into real life, I was becoming relaxed, bold, urban. 'Laughing like hyenas! Coming

here to shoplift!' the guard would complain in fury
when he saw us. But my friends just kissed their teeth
and called him a racist pig. Ma noted the new gritty me
and was proud of this burgeoning confidence, she
actively encouraged it. She so wanted this new life, I
could see the pride in her eyes when I dressed smartly
with my hair and makeup done, 'You're not a maid's
daughter,' she whispered, 'You're a Princess!' I hated
that word, 'maid.' It didn't do justice to the way in
which she nurtured the family, she seemed to live for
them. 'Thank you for giving my baby a chance!' she
gushed with gratitude endlessly thanking the family
who would quickly reply that it was no trouble, that
they should have done this before, when I was younger.
She truly was a Happiness for the family.

One day, she told me that I didn't need to come
to the township on weekends anymore. She would still
go and visit the family, I was to stay in the city and go
out with my friends or use the opportunity to study. So,
I stopped going with her, which meant that I had
weekends to myself. Freedom was what I was
becoming used to, now that I was in the city, the
deliciousness of anonymity and the pleasure of
reflection! In the township people crawled around me

like flies to jam or something nastier, you couldn't get two minutes to yourself. Here, I could think deeply, focus, reflect and dream. Themba was in the midst of exams and had even taken on a part time job in the library at his college, he rarely came home now. I was starting to forget him. I had the world at my feet. Finally.

My identity was changing right before my eyes.

One warm Saturday, I found it so blisteringly humid that I jumped in the swimming pool and splashed around. There was no one home. Strange this family, each doing different things at weekends. Still, it left me free and I loved the space to process all the new developments that were happening in my life so suddenly. Sometimes I felt like a caterpillar who had just turned into a butterfly, I had gone from having a simple life to this luxurious one that anyone in the township would have died for. Often, I felt woozy while processing the changes. Pinching myself wasn't enough, this was a proper 'rags- to -riches' situation. Looking down at my swimming costume, I realised that at seventeen and a bit, it was the first time that I had ever worn one. I was not a good swimmer, I only started learning a few weeks before and my attempts were awkward, still I felt refreshed afterwards and I lay on the sun lounger sipping an ice -cold Coke taking in the beautifully manicured lawn and vibrant flowers. Suddenly I realised that I was not alone, It was Boss Toby, he was standing over me clutching a beer and smiling.

My usual shyness made me sit up immediately and cover my body, the white, one -piece swimming costume suddenly seeming skimpy. It looked now like a thin sheath, highlighting every curve, I'd never displayed myself like that even for my boyfriend. He must have read my mind as he gestured for me to stay put, he pulled up a lounger for himself next to me and lay down with his shirt off. I wanted to run but was scared that it would look like rudeness, so I lay there feeling embarrassed and awkward.

'Have you ever been to a political rally?' he asked somewhat amused at my shyness.

'Rally?'
'A mass meeting?'

Oh yes, I knew about those. They happened all the time. Many members of our family and friends attended them to protest about the government and the various initiatives they kept implementing to make our

Black lives hell and White lives better. But Ma never allowed me to go as the police presence was scary for her, they often used tear gas and batons to intimidate protestors. Some of our Black comrades had been shot and killed in this way in the past, some were arrested.

In the townships, these stories circulated everywhere, Ma was paranoid and flatly refused to let me attend even one. Now that she was home for the weekend, I badly wanted to go and see for myself.

Boss Toby said that there was one in the big sports stadium in the city and that he would take me. I was so happy that I jumped up excitedly and ran to the room to change. As I got up, he wolf-whistled.

'You should do modelling,' he said. 'Look at those legs! You are beautiful! Listen, don't take that off, just put some shorts on over it, it's so hot!'

Shyly I played with my braids wrapping them around my fingers and half covering my eyes. A lot of boys looked at me and even asked me out on dates, but I was too shy to even think about romance. And Boss Toby was supposed to be my new dad. It was weird, even creepy to see his eyes skimming over my body like that. To me he was an aging White man, his body soft, puffy and padded with fat. His stomach protruded large and pregnant looking. He had these small, watery blue eyes bulging out of his fleshy face and they were always trained on my breasts, my behind, the bit between my legs. Once, he may have been good looking. But he had aged badly, desperately even, the few strands of yellowy grey hair on his otherwise bald head carefully positioned to give the illusion of fullness. But he was a kind of father figure to me now and I was grateful and full of respect for him. After all, it was he who had gone out and bought me all my fashionable clothes, okay I had to model for him afterwards but when I saw the price tags I couldn't believe it! He wanted me to swim more often, Zoe had had a pool party and he had got me a designer gold bikini that cost as much as our electricity bill back home! Everyone told me that I should model but I couldn't understand why, maybe they were being extra kind to me to my face, to cushion the blow when there were sarcastic comments behind my back.

But I was warming to Boss Toby, I was submitting to his efforts to be my new father. I was fatherless, why not? He always had a present for me and I knew that I could turn to him for whatever I wanted. It was especially heartening to hear of his involvement in the struggle, something that I had genuinely only imagined

Black people to care about, after all it was *our struggle,* not his. He was rich, White and intelligent, why was he so bothered? He had nothing to protest about, he had to be grateful about his blessings. My friends laughed when I discussed his passionate support of our struggle.

'If he doesn't want his life then fine. I'm happy to take his house, car and servants. He can go live in the squatter camps, we can do a swap.' Gugu said.

'Can you imagine it?' I mused, 'Whites stripped of everything and living in squatter camps, us living in luxury?'

No one could. We just couldn't understand why Whites would protest, for us. Their lives were so cushy, why didn't they shut up and lap it all up?

That day, I sidestepped his prying eyes and rushed away to get ready for the rally. It was so strange getting all this attention from a rich, White man. I hated to admit it but part of me liked the attention, the other part felt like Themba wouldn't approve. I could just imagine his face, thunderous with jealousy. Anyway at least I was seeing and experiencing life like I hadn't before, I felt like I was playing a role in a soap opera.

The outcry was for apartheid to end. The colourful banners and posters adorning the stage spoke of ending

job reservation, police brutality, detentions without trial
and the list went on and on. There were thousands of
people there, not just Blacks but some Indians,
Coloureds and Whites too. Most carried placards. The
noise was deafening, the speakers on the stage shouting
'Amandla!' and the crowd responding with 'Awethu!' as
they attempted to rouse up passion and anger in the
people. Joining in with the toyi -toyi dance, I truly felt
part of the People's War against the racist institutions.
The deafening chanting and dancing were a call for a
revolution, I finally understood the point of the rally.
Some would have called them a mob, but actually it
was an organised protest as they were quite peaceful
not aggressive. When things were in mid flow, the army
arrived. Suddenly, you could sense the tension in the
air. Soldiers in combat gear created a barricade around
the entrance and exit to the stadium, effectively
blocking us off with their huge army trucks. Someone
shouted, 'Casspirs!' and I trembled. They were fierce
looking four- wheel drives made of reinforced steel,
soldiers perched on top, their machine guns pointed at
the crowds, cocked and ready. Adrenaline flowed, some
people looked set to retaliate, there was a new ferocity

in the crowd that scared me, I could see why Ma had refused to send me to rallies.

Some youths nearest to the police barricade started to throw stones at the soldiers, some taunted them openly swearing and shouting out foul names.

Then.

CRACK! BOOM!

The sound of gunfire filled the stadium. Suddenly, bravado gave way to alarm and fear. The crowd surged in every direction to get away but where to go? The entrance and exit were blocked. They had us cornered. We could easily have been crushed but then Boss Toby grabbed my hand and urged me to run. Somehow, we were in the kitchen of a restaurant and we dashed through, followed by some others now, desperate to get away as chaos seemed to rule. Shouting ran through the air, surely the stampede itself would kill or injure a few. The side street was full of people by now, but we eventually made it to the Mercedes and out of the area, many passers by giving us dirty looks registering our skin colours and the fact that Toby held my hand.

I could never forget that day, it was my first glimpse of the turbulent political landscape in Durban, I wished that I had been brave enough to stay and experience what happened afterwards, but I didn't have the guts.

CHAPTER 3: TOBY

As women, we're expected to be undaunted and fearless. No one prepares us for the reality of what's out there. There definitely was a lot to fear!

Back home I was so upset that I was shaking.

'What about those people who got shot?' I was vehement now. 'Or those who got trapped and couldn't get out?'

Boss Toby was angry too. He launched into a scathing attack on the police and said that this was why the whole family had their British passports ready, they could get up and leave at any time if there was trouble. He had applied for a South African passport for me, he said, it would arrive any day, at least it would give me options. I had my own bank account and bank card. We were silent as he parked the car.

'Let's get something to eat,' he said. 'I'm starving.'

Instead of going into the main house, he led me to the outbuilding that they called the annexe, in the garden. It was a stand -alone new build and it was where he spent a lot of his time.

'You will like my annexe babe,' he said, trying to change the topic.

'Is this your home?' I asked, 'why do you live away from your family? It doesn't seem normal.'

He sighed and fixed me with that penetrating stare.

'You ask a lot of questions young lady, you'd make a good reporter.'

That shut me up and I fell silent as we entered what looked like a little self -contained house, tastefully decorated in grey, black and red. It had everything: a bedroom, a small kitchen, even a lounge and office. I had been feeling emotional since the rally, so I sat on the sofa and pretended to watch TV. I could hear him bustling about in the kitchen, so I got up and offered to help. He was heating up two pizzas, my new favourite food.

'Pour us some drinks please,' he said, 'I need something to calm me.'

Me drink? I had already disobeyed Ma by going to the rally. I had never ever tasted alcohol in my life before. I could just imagine her face, the wide eyes, the look of incomprehension. I missed her and suddenly wished that I was with her back on the farm, chatting to relatives over sweet tea. But now I was here, how could I get away?

'Do you have tea?' I asked hopefully.
'Don't be a silly little girl, you're what? Seventeen now, an adult! Enjoy yourself, let your hair down, you deserve it.'

He produced a few bottles and some glasses. He wanted me to taste some new brands that he had bought recently on his travels. The first sip got me choking, the brash fieriness hitting the back of my throat. But then a sudden warmth filled my head and cascaded to my whole body, I started to relax instantly.

Boss Toby had knocked back a good few while I was on drink number one.

'You like Scotch, do you?' I was a source of amusement now. 'Expensive girl.'

Once again, the reference to money. I hated it. Miss Wendy was the worst.

'We paid your school fees for the whole year in advance…hope you like the school!' Her eyes crinkled at the corners when she smiled. Soon after I arrived at the house she said, her voice laced with sarcasm, 'My husband insists on giving you a room in the main house. He's gone to great lengths to decorate it for you.'

'I'm happy to sleep with my Ma.' I said nervously.

'Well he won't take no for an answer. And it's a bit rude to snub him like that, after all he's done for you. He's even got you a bank account and you can draw from your allowance whenever you like.'

I didn't want to sleep away from Ma.

Sometimes it felt like the money was a weight around my neck, that no matter how many times I said thank you, it was never ever enough. I could never repay that huge debt anyway.

The pizza was delicious, and I attacked it, I hadn't realised how hungry I was. But Boss Toby was setting out more drinks, this time with different types of alcohol. While I had to screw up my eyes to taste them, he was gleefully knocking them back. His face, flushed now, loomed above me as he kept replenishing my glass. I was just taking sips, the taste being strange and unfamiliar. My throat burned but I felt loose and warm inside, aware of heat spreading from my face to my body. I kicked off my sandals and concentrated on the TV. The news was on and they were reporting about the rally. If it hadn't been for the pizza I would have fallen asleep, the drink was making me tired. Boss Toby too, had changed into shorts and a T shirt. With his shoes off he looked casual and approachable. I wanted to leave but I couldn't, I had to find something to fill our time until I could leave. A social prisoner. I decided to talk to him about his writing, anything. I tend to over talk when I'm nervous.

'What sort of books do you write?' I asked, 'and how did you start?'

'Aha! A budding writer!' he smiled. 'You want me to share my story?' With the drink inside him, he had started to look me over with greater scrutiny, his gaze moving from my face to my breasts to my legs. I was wearing a strappy summer dress but now I started to feel underdressed. He sensed my discomfort and came close, putting a heavy arm around me. His breath reeked of alcohol and garlic.

'I like you, you know that?'

'I like you too.' What else could I say to my benefactor?

'Is it?' softly now. 'You know, you're old enough to be my daughter, but sexy enough to be my girlfriend,' he whispered taking a swig of his drink. I tried to get his arm off and wriggled on the sofa.

'I asked about your books,' I accused feeling bold, 'not anything else!' But I couldn't get the words out of my mind. His girlfriend! I had never been with this kind of man before. I felt no untrained, so naive. The only boy I'd known intimately was Themba.

'What do you want to know?' he bellowed. I'm a White British liberal, I stand together with all the oppressed in this country, I just live better than them that's all!' His smile was smug. 'We are all the same. Underneath this skin, this outer suit we wear, we are all the same. We all know that, we just try to protect our privileged lives. All this Boss Toby, Miss Wendy…bah!

Fuck that. Just call us Tobe and Wendy. You don't have to treat us like Kings and Queens baby.'

At this he handed me a glass made from intricate crystal. He had poured something red into it, not the Scotch but another drink.

'C' mon!' he roared, not realising how loud he was talking. 'Bottom's up!'

I sipped it watching him out of the corner of my eye, he was unrecognisable compared to before. His wisps of hair swayed in front of his face as he spoke, his eyes were more protruding now and were trained on me sharply. Every now and then he would lick his lips, I couldn't help noticing that they were full and a deep red, they did not look like they belonged on his aging face. They were pretty on Zoe but on a man? I was repulsed.

'Look at me!' he sighed. 'My wife has gone out again to goodness knows where. She's never here! Why we stay married, I don't know. If it hadn't been for Zo I would have gone. I stopped knocking on her bedroom door a while ago, that cold bitch. Had me begging and pleading for it. Never liked it from the start. What do you do with that hey?' His accent usually neutral, had become more pronounced and more like the Berea dialect most Whites used at school now. His voice was slurry.

'No, I'm, not chasing *that* tail. Gave up a long time ago! Zo, well, she's young. Doesn't have time for anyone but her friends and boyfriend now. She doesn't care about spending time with an old man like me. I'm looking,' and he leaned towards me, 'for a girlfriend. Do you think you can be that? You and me together?' He was looking hard at me now, his eyes darting from my eyes to my breasts.

I wanted to run, I couldn't take in his story. Instinct kicked in and prompted me to run. As I got up, it happened. It was quick and totally unexpected.

First, I heard, 'Where do you think you're going?' Then, he grabbed my arm in a vice like grip, pulled me down heavily and climbed on me, his weight stopping me from protesting. With his mouth on mine and his arms holding my hands down, he parted my thighs with his knee, undid his shorts and entered me. Oh! The shock! For the very first time I felt a man enter me roughly. This was not consensual. 'No!' I screamed, 'No! Please!' I bit and hit, kicked and screamed, but he still carried on, hurting me as he drove himself deeper and deeper with each thrust. That's when I realised that 'no' was not a safe word. Neither was 'stop,' 'painful' or 'unfunny.' And the pain of that ordeal! It was sharp and totally unexpected! There had been love, even commitment for my first time. With Themba, I'd felt bonded forever. But *this* was brutal and disgusting! The animal grunts he was making rang in my ears until suddenly it was over, a cold rush filled me, and he sat up, head back in relief.

'Wow you're not a virgin,' he said pointing to the silver suede sofa. 'No red stain there!' And then, seeing me sitting up in total shock and horror, tears coursing down my face, he had the nerve to ask, 'Are you ok?'

I ran out. My legs felt like jelly, but I ran and ran until I got to Ma's outhouse. Inside, my breath coming in rasps, I had a panic attack. My chest hurt, and I was struggling to breathe. I pushed the chest of drawers against the door to secure it even though I had locked it, then I checked that all the windows were closed and the burglar bars secure. Sobbing and wailing I ripped my clothes off and entered the shower, letting the hot water sting my skin until it burnt. Half way through I started vomiting and when all the drink had come out, I showered again. Lastly, I pulled on Ma's long flannel nightdress and got into bed, blacking out almost immediately.

When Ma returned the next morning, she laughed at the idea of barricading the door and closing the windows. She told me not to feel unsafe when she was away and if I had missed her so much then I should accompany her to the township on the weekends instead of staying back. She talked non- stop giving me news of the family and friends. It was Monday morning. I was running a high temperature, I lay huddled on the bed shivering. All attempts at getting me to visit the doctor met with a flat refusal from me, so Ma made me sweet tea and handed me some pain tablets. She massaged my back and chest with Vicks Vapour Rub and asked me to stay in bed for a few days until I felt better. The truth was that I ached down below. The pain was sharp and stabbing, it made me sob and curl into myself. I clung onto Ma like a baby not wanting to let her go. But she soon extricated herself from me, she had to go and attend to the family.

Who could I tell? What could I do? Ma wanted me here to get the education and the life chances that she had never received. If I pulled the plug on these dreams what would happen to me? And what about her prospects? Would she continue to be employed here? A place that she loved, with employers who had treated her fairly and generously from day one? After all it was her salary that ran our household in the township and I knew that she also helped other families. Most of the cast -off items that she brought home, she shared around. One time, they had given her a loan to spruce up our house and they had not asked for this again. And now all their generosity with my schooling, my clothing, my books, my allowance, my passport. Which Black teenager that I knew had any of this? Even at school, I was the envy of my friends. Could I throw it all away now?

Thoughts. They kept circling in my head. Round and round, relentlessly, like a merry -go- round on speed. There was only one option that I liked. I wanted to die. I craved the comfort of darkness.

But I didn't get to die just yet. I got to wake up each morning and carry that weight around with me.

I missed a week of school as I was ill, but Zoe brought back homework and assignments for me, work that I discarded and threw carelessly on the floor. Ma was worried and annoyed. She had never seen this rebellion in me. She put it down to my being overwhelmed by the newness of it all and kept reassuring me that everything would be okay. But I sensed her embarrassment, she was losing her patience with my drama queen act. I refused eye contact when Wendy and Zoe came to see me and the chocolates and biscuits they brought sat unopened on the table. *He* never came. That weekend, everything changed for me. I'd given up. If I wasn't sleeping all day, I would sit and stare into space, never leaving Ma's room even though she scolded me for not getting fresh air and sun in the garden. I didn't care about how I looked anymore. I didn't wash until Ma showered me herself. And I stopped eating, becoming stick thin almost overnight. How can you think about food when you feel dirty and contaminated?

I knew what they were thinking. The dreaded HIV virus had infected thousands of people in the townships and on the farms, Whites too were getting it. Victims wasted away quickly, becoming thin and emaciated until they died. In Durban, where it was becoming rife, there was a shroud of secrecy about the topic, people shunned the 'A' word, almost as if they would get contaminated if they said 'Aids' out loud. But the issue hung in the air like a bad smell and didn't go away. Myths circulated daily, infected men raped virgins as they believed that this would cure them, babies were preferred in their sickening self- healing sprees; syringes full of infected blood were positioned on cinema seats ready to penetrate new innocent victims. Stomach-churning stories about angry, illiterate people.

Ma had not appeared to be sexually active after my father's death and the Ellis's had welcomed her single status, but somehow you could feel that they were expecting news of her HIV status anytime, she was Black after all, a walking time bomb. It was because I *didn't* want them thinking that Ma or I had introduced this ugly disease into their lives that I decided to get up one day and try to get back on track. My Ma had done nothing wrong, she was everything I had. And I wasn't going to let her down. So, I went back to school and tried in all other ways to resume my life there in the Ellis household. It was hard, very hard, but not impossible. He had disappeared on some business trip, so I didn't have to see him. My period came and went so I knew that I was okay. I studied harder than usual and stopped going out. After a few days, everything seemed normal. But *I* was not normal. Inside, I knew that I would never be normal again.

About two weeks later, I was having an afternoon nap after school. The heat of that Durban summer had driven me insane and I often came home and collapsed on Ma's bed. Even Ma felt listless and tired in the heat, I could see old age creeping up on her. How much longer did she have to go? She didn't complain, but I couldn't see her cooking and cleaning, fetching and carrying for much longer. Her movements were slow and sluggish at times which pained me to watch. I resented how she laboured for the family, not necessarily because they demanded it from her, but because she always wanted to go the extra mile for them, even if it meant jeopardising her health. I could hear Wendy ask Ma to get ready to accompany her to the fruit and veg market, Ma had to go to push the trolley and carry the stuff to the car. So, Ma gave a final check on me and grabbed her purse, promising to buy me my favourite fruit, peaches. Zoe's voice wafted in through the open window asking her mother for a lift somewhere. Even the whirring of the ceiling fan couldn't drown out the sense of something ominous in the air. Soon I was alone. I rolled myself in the blanket like a cigar and shut my eyes.

Ma says you get what you think of, so think happy thoughts. My thoughts recently, were of something dark and ominous. It felt like the good times were coming to an end. Even the double layer of bricks under Ma's bed couldn't keep out the tokoloshe. Suddenly, I heard the door open gently and footsteps entered quietly into the room. I twisted around to see if it was a burglar or Ma returning as she had forgotten something. It was him. Dressed in a formal suit, he looked like he had just returned from a business meeting, vanilla and cinnamon scented aftershave filled the small, basic room. Grudgingly, I looked at him, he looked so out of place in our maid's quarters. Then, fear gripped me and made me freeze up.

'How are you? I heard you were sick.'

Silence from me, just awkwardness. I had sat up in bed by now, anticipating something ugly, I could just smell it in the air.

'I brought you a present.' He tossed a bag onto the bed. 'Open it!' It was an order. My fingers had stopped working but I prized them apart and opened the bag nervously. I had stopped breathing; my heart was lodged in my throat. Chocolates, a necklace and a purse.

'Open the purse!' again, a command. He was sitting on the edge of the bed now, staring at me.

Inside, was a bundle of notes, a thick wad of money. I had never seen so much money in my life.

'I thought you could use it to buy books and stuff that you needed.' Embarrassing pause. So, this was a pay- off. Recklessly, I tossed the bag and its contents on the floor, still I would not look at him. Then, I tried to get off the bed. But again, he was fast, heavy and strong.

'You bitch!' he whispered, '*you* do this to me, it's *you*. I can't stop thinking about you. I want you so much. And don't act all coy and innocent, you must have done it lots of times before! You can stop pretending, you're not a virgin.'

He was quick to undo his fly and pin me to the bed, picking up my school skirt with his knee and hand. This time I thrashed and screamed but a sharp slap across my face with that padded, fleshy hand silenced me. I closed my eyes tight and lay there feeling the pain and shame wash over me again as he did what he had intended to do. This time, he was gentler though. When it was over, he rolled off me and for a moment we lay there, side by side. Inside me a little girl's voice pleaded, 'please, please, go away!' But he just lay there. Then, he pulled my face to his and kissed me. After a while I looked at him, his face still suffused with blood and excitement, an ugly leer on his face replacing the kind man I had thought he was. My father, what a joke!

'Can you go?' I croaked, my school uniform wet in places where my tears and his orgasm met. Slowly, he held my gaze, his eyes hardening.

'First kiss me,' he said. 'You kiss me with your tongue and I'll go.' Reluctantly, I slithered over and kissed him. I had to pretend that he was Themba otherwise I would have been physically sick, there was too much mouth on him, his lips were wobbly and loose. He started touching me again and I could feel him get hard.

'Go now please,' I whispered. 'You promised.'

'Go?' He spat as he tucked his shirt back into his trousers and patted down his wisps of hair. 'Listen here, this!' he pointed to the room and to the garden outside. 'It's ALL mine! Do you understand me? Never forget that. And anytime I want, I can take you. Do you know how much I invested in you? Huh? I could have left you in that township to rot! But I brought you here, gave you everything, treated you like a queen. You owe me! Now pull yourself together and put that money away!'

'Oh!' he shot at me as he walked out, 'I want you in that room in the main house that we had decorated just for you. I'll give you a few days, but I want you in there. I'll be sleeping with you every night, so get used to it. I didn't pay all that money for nothing! And make a fucking effort next time!'

And without a further look, he was gone.

CHAPTER 4: SEX WORKER

Time heals some but for me, life had become an open wound. It was a month since it first happened. It was true that with the volume of assignments and homework that I brought home, my Ma's outbuilding was not the most comfortable. She slept early every evening and I needed to study, I couldn't do my work in darkness. So reluctantly, I moved into the room created for me in the main house. It was very pretty, with peach walls and white furniture, like something out of a *Country Life* magazine. It was strange sleeping in a small double bed alone and for the first few nights I missed my Ma. But I soon got used to the space and privacy. Ma would come to visit me, crooning over how blessed I was to have such a beautiful room, in the township, she said, a whole family could sleep in that space.

As Zoe and I were neighbours now, she popped her head in one afternoon when I was just finishing a long History essay. She was a year above me at school and I wondered whether it annoyed her that I never went to her for help.

'Hey' she said. 'So nice to have some life in this house. Even better to have a sister right next door to me.'

I smiled at the word 'Sisters.' We had not been close. Ever since I arrived, she had been busy with school, her Art, friends and her boyfriend. I didn't know if she just wanted to avoid me as she did not like me. Now, it seemed like she was trying to make amends.

'I was wondering if you fancied a sleepover?' she asked cheekily. 'We can do hair and make -up, eat pizza which you love, drink,' she looked around and lowered her voice, 'alcohol. Do sisterly things, you know. I'm sorry I've been neglecting you, I've a lot on my mind right now.'

I knew that she was finishing school in a few months and the pressure was on to pass her exams with flying colours. Of course, I grabbed the chance and that night we dragged the single mattress from the guest room and placed it next to her bed. Wendy appeared with slices of pizza and chocolate muffins and we closed the bedroom door ready for a girls' night in. Oh, it was such fun! Amidst food and loud kwaito music, we messed around with hair products and make up, dancing and singing loudly. At the end, we vowed that we would be friends and family for life. She was a truly stunning girl and once made up, she looked even more breath taking with her long flaxen hair and beautiful features. She reminded me of a princess in a fairy tale. In turn, she complimented me on *my* looks, although I couldn't see why, and after drinking a few beers that she had hidden away in her room, we laughed non- stop and fell into bed happy and relaxed. I couldn't understand why she would take the handful of sleeping tablets each night, she told me that she had to get 'out of it,' each night but I didn't want to spoil the evening with an interrogation of why a lovely young woman with everything to live for, should be so dependent of drugs. Soon, we both drifted off.

Her bedroom was large and painted in baby pink and magenta, the walls were full of pictures of ballet dancers. Maybe it was the unfamiliarity of the space or her snores, but I tossed and turned, struggling to get to sleep. Suddenly, the door creaked open.

No, no, not here, not now, I prayed. But there he was in his pyjamas like a ghost in the night, a Florence Nightingale with ulterior motives. I pretended to snore too, like Zoe, but despite this, he lifted the duvet and started to touch me. I hissed for him to stop and kept hoping that Zoe would wake up, but the girl was out cold. I could not believe what was happening, here he was in his own daughter's room doing ugly things to me with his hand over my mouth. Had he been touching Zoe too?

A new thought presented itself. Maybe I could share this experience with Zoe and then she too could disclose what he did to her, with two teenagers supporting each other, the police would have to do something. I vowed that I would talk to her. But I never got the chance to be alone with her again. This time he took his time, putting himself in my mouth and then performing oral sex on me. When he finished he whispered, 'Thank you baby,' and left smiling in that eerily smug way that I hated.

As always, humiliation set in. And a deep sense of sadness. I felt so alone, with nobody to turn to and no options. The visits happened daily, and I was losing the will to fight them. I constantly felt unclean and ashamed. The shower, with the hot water turned up was my best ally. I started to become reclusive, I didn't have the strength to engage with anything and anyone including Ma.

He had given me my new passport and ATM card which should have been a turning point in my life. But I greeted the package with deadness. Every now and then he would mention that he had deposited money in my account for my studies. So, this was what my life had boiled down to? A paid sex worker. I was stunned at how things had changed for me, I could barely look at myself in the mirror, I was disgusted with myself.

The next weekend, I planned to go to the township with Ma, she was meant to meet me at the school gates after school and we would go together. But there he was, like a bad smell, at the gates in his white Mercedes and sunglasses.

'Get in, I want to talk to you!' Another command.

'No! I'm waiting for Ma.'

'She won't have a job to come back to if you're not careful. It's just talking.'

In the car, he drove a bit so that we were just out of full view. We sat silently, each looking down at our hands. Funny he never wore a wedding band, even the illusion of marriage was not enough. I sneaked a look at him, he looked ashen and sad.

'I don't want you to go.'

Silence from me. Then angrily, I spat out, 'Really!! Why would that be? You want to rape me again?'

He took my hand in his and smiled disarmingly, those fleshy lips wobbling. He was getting careless, Ma would be here any minute.

'I'm afraid you won't come back. I'm going to miss my girlfriend.'

Silence. I took my hand back and fidgeted with my school tie.

'Do you hate me?' I had to turn to stare at him full in the face. This was absurd! Truly ridiculous! And then the bombshell. Or the mother of bombshells. 'I've fallen in love with you. I want to be with you all the time, not just for sex, but for your company too. I haven't been this close to anyone in a long time.'

It was my turn to shout and he had to close the windows.

'You *LOVE* me? I'm seventeen. You are what? Fifty- something. How could you repeatedly rape me and still think that this is love? Your daughter is eighteen, do you do it to her too?'

I shielded my face thinking that he would slap me but there was a heavy silence. Then the tears came. They coursed down his cheeks and onto his clothes, he made no attempt to wipe them off. I felt scared, like I was witnessing a person on the edge.

'No, I don't make love to my daughter', he said through his tears. 'I make love to my beautiful girlfriend because she enjoys it just as much as me. We love each other, age has nothing to do with it. And it's okay to be angry, I admit I was rough a few times. But I will be gentle in future, I promise. I want you in my life. I will leave her one day, I can't take this loneliness forever. I love you so much baby.'

I was floored. This was just insane. He looked so foolish sitting there, uttering this nonsense. Maybe even funny to some.

Then seeing Ma approach, we parted with, 'Okay go, but please come back. Otherwise I will find you.' He handed me a bag. 'This is for your family. Enjoy baby.' In it was a large packet of sweets, biscuits, and a thick wad of crisp twenty-rand notes.

The weekend passed in a blur of love and warmth. Granny, looking as shrivelled as ever, danced and sang when she saw me, she had made a meat stew and putu for us, my favourite in the past. It's a stiff porridge that comes alive with anything with a gravy, it could be curry, stew, vegetables in a sauce. My new food to go with my new lifestyle was healthy salads and relatively low carb food so I was reluctant to eat. But in the end, I had to. This was my culture and there was no use pretending that I was something else. In fact, it was a relief to get away from the city and feel enveloped in the loving embrace of my people. But now that I had been away for so many months, the sheer extent of the poverty appalled me. Babies walking around naked, young jobless people just sitting around on old crates or drums being idle, adults crouching outside squishing flies. I thought of the luxurious lives that the Whites had in the city, there did not seem to be poor Whites there. Why? It didn't seem fair and I was boiling with rage.

I told Thetu about the rally and asked her to keep it a secret. I told her all about my new life but with a few edits…she didn't need to hear about how I got tainted by an old, White man. We were sitting on a grassy mound a few metres away from my house when she turned my face to hers.

'You look more beautiful that's for sure,' she said. 'But you look hard. I know you Bongi. Your eyes used to be alive with laughter and joy. Now, the lights have gone out. You look older.'

That opened the floodgates and I started to sob, becoming increasingly hysterical. Cautiously, she led me to a space behind the houses where no one could see us. Slowly, she got it all out of me. By the time I had finished, I had concluded that I was going to leave the Ellis family and return to the township. Even if I did nothing but wait for Themba to finish college so that we could marry I would do it.

But Thetu had other ideas. 'Let me tell you something sister,' she said, 'here I am doing *nothing* with my life, sitting in this dump, not learning skills, just waiting to get married. I can't even attend school because of the bad behaviour of some people, including my teachers. Now, my parents are getting desperate. The last thing they want is me getting pregnant or getting Aids. So, they are sending me away to my aunt's place in Johannesburg where I will work in her salon and learn about doing hair.'

'So?' I shook my head in disbelief. 'At least that's something. One day you can have your *own* salon. There are so many Black female entrepreneurs. You could *be* something one day.'

'You're missing the point', she lamented. 'All my life I've wanted to become a nurse or something in the medical field. And you. You wanted to teach. Remember our talks? Our hopes and dreams?'

I still couldn't understand what she was driving at.

'Why should you let this White man destroy your future? You only have a year and then you will have finished school and heading for university. You're nearly there! Don't give up now! He's giving you money, wants to take you overseas, you have a passport. Treats you to fancy dinners, designer clothes. Wow! Do you know how lucky you are? What I wouldn't give for that!'

'But, he rapes me,' I whimpered.

'Oh, and if you had lived here in the township? You could have been raped by some HIV positive man or you could just have been used by some guy promising you everything and the next day, he's with someone else. C'mon, stop complaining, stop crying. You're rich. Use the opportunities to better yourself.' She looked scathingly around. 'Don't come back to rot in *this* hole. As for my brother Themba, I'm sure he's got plenty of girlfriends at college, don't you worry about him!'

Her words stung me. I hadn't thought of it like that. But then, she was focusing on the upside of my life. The downside was that I had to sleep with someone who called himself my father, every night. I already had a boyfriend that I loved, Themba. It was the devil and the deep blue sea. Then, she said something that changed things forever.

'Besides, Themba wouldn't want you now. Not after I tell him what you're doing. You're not a Christian, maybe things happened like this for a reason. We want a Christian girl for him. We all want Christian partners in *our* family.'

End of conversation.

Stiffly, I gave her some of the cash that I had brought with me and she was elated, saying that she would use it to travel to Johannesburg. We cried bittersweet tears but inside, I knew that it was time to move on. Granny and auntie too got some of the cash and they too celebrated by singing and dancing. Maybe I was able to do some good after all. In my heart, I knew that I would not be returning often or soon to my home. I hid the rest of the cash in a tin in the kitchen, knowing that they would find it and use it when resources ran dry. There was a lot there. I had sacrificed myself to rescue them.

I left with Ma on the Monday morning with a heavy heart but with my mind made up. I would grin and bear it until the day that I could leave that house and go to university, after that I never needed to think about them again.

And so, the months wore on. We fell into a pattern, he visited me every night, and bought me expensive lingerie that I had to wear for him. I got so used to it that I started looking forward to the look of pure pleasure on his face when I would try different things, I was becoming bold and confident in bed. After, we would cuddle and talk incessantly, he always used me as a sounding board now regarding stuff that he was writing, his life, anything.

His mother was neglectful, an alcoholic, his dad a known philanderer who had left the family when he was young. He had fallen in love with Wendy but after

i was broken, now I Am

Zoe was born she had become a 'cold fish', it was then that he attempted to lose himself in his writing. Sometimes he got drunk and started crying holding me close and saying that I was the best thing that had happened to him. I knew how to calm him now, he loved it when I climbed over him and did unspeakable things to him. I was becoming a pro. I loved his kisses now, those fleshy lips would probe me all over and I knew that I would never have experienced these kinds of orgasms with Themba, this was different. I was with a man now. I think that over time, I fell in love, we both were in love.

Oblivious to the rest of the house, we went on weekends together, dinners out in the evenings, theatre and the ballet. I held his hand boldly now and he seemed proud to show me off. Every evening it seemed I had a new outfit and he would complement me non-stop. In the car, the front passenger seat was mine now. He would run his hands up and down my long legs saying how satiny smooth the skin was, how pleased he was with the expensive beauty products that he chose for me. Sometimes after a show, I'd ask him to book us into a hotel, I wanted to extend the thrill factor, the feeling of being on the set of a soap opera.

Every woman makes a trade somewhere, sometime. We trade our true purpose for the trappings of luxury that only certain men of stature can give us. We trade our integrity, our honesty, our dignity, our self- respect. Because wearing the nice clothes, dousing ourselves with classy perfumes, it satisfies another side of us. The need to be at the top. The need for power and prestige. The need for salespeople to be scrabbling around us, elbowing each other out of the way so that they could be the chosen ones to serve us in shops. Being poor is definitely not glamorous, we all know that. Who wants to be the shabbily dressed Black girl in exclusive shops that store detectives follow around or that staff would not serve because it looked bad for the brand? Not me. Look at the women who go around campaigning about women's rights. Are they poor girls from townships? No, because those types are solely interested in one thing. Survival. The activists are almost always intellectual types, the ones who already sold us out. Maybe they used their men to secure a better education, to free them from the indignity of having to live in a bad neighbourhood, to support their penchant for posh, ethically sourced food.

I had made a choice. Just like any other girl in my position. Just like any other girl in the world.

i was broken, now I Am

Gradually, I was developing a sense of power over Toby, with all his disclosures and his new fragility. I grew distant from Ma as I too grew older, developing a new separate identity. My body was changing. The seasons had changed, and it was getting colder. I had started to eat non -stop. No matter what I had it was never enough. Soup with hunks of thickly buttered bread and sweet tea, stew, roast meats, pies, anything. Ma commented on how cute I looked as my face became chubby and my breasts and thighs thickened. I took to wearing long tops and baggy trousers to cover up as I had put on so much weight.

Nine months into my stay at the Ellis's home, he came into the room which we called our room and fixed me with that penetrating stare. I was finishing my Maths revision as I had a test the next day.

'No!' I said panicking when I saw him. 'I have a test tomorrow. I have to revise.'

'It's okay,' he said quickly. 'I just wanted to show you this.' It was a white plastic stick and he wanted me to pee on it. He couldn't explain why, he was just testing something. To oblige him, I did it, and handed it back to him.

'Shit!' he sighed heavily and fell back on the bed. 'You're pregnant.'

Pregnancy had NOT been part of the master plan for my life at this stage. And in any case, not with an old White man. How could I not have known? I was such a scatterbrain sometimes, I could never predict when my period would arrive, I just reacted when I saw the blood. When it didn't come I had been relieved. But that had been a stupid, childish, ignorant approach.

He took me to a small clinic in another town to get checked over. I was about four months gone so no possibility of an abortion for me. I wanted an abortion desperately, but he said it was dangerous. What could I tell Ma? My family? My school and my friends there? I concocted a plan. With Zoe and Wendy, I could say that I had a Black boyfriend from school. Then when the baby came, Toby and I could run away.

At first, Toby had seemed jubilant and couldn't stop kissing me. When I asked what we would do now he just said that we would find a way, and everything would be okay. Other times he seemed moody and upset. He said, 'Shit!' and 'Fuck!' a lot. He also said that it was what he needed to change his life forever. He spoke about going abroad together and getting married, I tried to picture it but only saw an old man, raising a mixed-race child together. I couldn't see how it would work. Just when I was doing so well at school, this had to happen.

I was devastated.

Like idiots, we did nothing about it. He moved me into the annexe and we were officially living together.

He was careful with me now, and more generous. He bought me bigger clothes to hide my growing bump, drove me everywhere and supported wherever he could. I needed his support now more than ever. Once, he took me to see an apartment along the beach. He said that it was a multiracial area which was a first for me. My understanding of my country was of a deeply divided place. Each racial group had designated areas to live and socialise in, breaking these rules could land you in trouble with the law. That was why us Blacks had to live on the farm miles away from the city, the best parts were reserved for White people. Indians and Coloureds were the next level down. These beach apartments modelled how diversity could work, he explained, it was part of the new inclusive mindset.

The apartment was mind blowing but not for me. Inside, I broke out into a cold sweat, Toby put it down to the pregnancy or the dizzying view from the balcony. The truth was that I felt scared to live so far away from Ma, my people and everything I knew. I just did not want to be a mother to his child and to be cut off from the community, because I would have to abandon them if I chose this. I kept picturing Thetu saying, 'Use this opportunity!' Or 'Beggars can't be choosers!' I *was* choosing. The lights had come on in my head, I would have it, abandon it and run. It was a no deal from me.

At last, exams were over. Zoe had applied to universities in the Cape to study Art. I had a year to go still but with my growing pregnancy who knew what would happen. It was the school holidays. Ma had gone home for a full two-month holiday laden with groceries and presents for the family. Toby had been kind enough to take her. I could not bear to face them with my body looking and feeling bloated and sore. I didn't want to explain how I got pregnant and I certainly didn't want to hang around when a Coloured baby popped out of me. South Africans have racism etched into our psyches. Each racial group with their own culture and values, no space for blurring of boundaries here. We do it to each other, judging and making assumptions.

i was broken, now I Am

When the family spoke about going to Wendy's house in the Drakensberg for a few days to party and celebrate Zoe's transitioning to university, it seemed like a good idea. She was leaving in a few months. I would stay in the house for another year until I too finished school. Wendy and Zoe had gone ahead with boxes of food and wine. Wendy was used to driving there alone, she did it all the time, but this time it was Zoe who was driving to showcase her brash new independent attitude. She'd recently passed her driving test and of course, they had gifted her with a brand new car. Surprise, surprise!

With Zoe often drugged out of her tiny mind and Ma sleeping early, often, Toby and I had the house and annexe to ourselves. Toby explained one evening that the farm as they called it, was Wendy's original home, she had lived there when he'd met her, now, she used it as a retreat to paint and enjoy the solitude. It was set in the Drakensberg, or Dragon Mountains, in Afrikaans, an area bursting with farms, pubs, restaurants and quaint, curiosity shops overlooked by an impressive mountain range and breathtaking scenery. Toby called it the Berg. I had never seen it. I had never ventured anywhere beyond the township before now. He wanted me to drive up in his Range Rover with him and he promised to show me around. To this, I flatly refused. He could go alone. I had become increasingly unsociable with my ever -growing bump. The movements alone terrified me. Also, I seemed to be permanently tired and the rest would be welcomed.

But after everybody had left, he hung around trying to tempt me to go. 'Do you think I would steal something if I'm here alone?' I taunted.

'Well, I don't think Wendy would want you alone in the main house,' he said finally, trying to smile disarmingly. 'What if there was a burglary? A fire? What if we disconnected the alarm and something happened?'

I understood where he was coming from. It was a multi -million -rand house. He could sleep with me, but he couldn't trust me in their precious home which was filled with expensive trinkets. Blood is thicker than water. And a whore is a whore is a whore.

That was another peculiar South African thing, everything revolved around burglar alarms, guard dogs, police. All this to protect Whites from us.

Die Swart gevaar! That's what we were!

i was broken, now I Am

Feeling slightly irritated at the prospect of a long drive there, and the lack of trust in me to be alone in the house, I got ready for the trip, planning to sleep for most of it. The Range was a big car, I could stretch out on the back, or in front with the seats reclined. And so, we set off for the Berg. Now and then I looked at Toby, his fat, pork sausage fingers on the wheel, his slack jawed aging face. I couldn't get over it. How did this happen? Seriously. Why me? Why couldn't I have an age appropriate boyfriend who was handsome and single? Sometimes, if I allowed myself to thrash around in a pool of negativity for too long, I came to the conclusion that my life was doomed from the start. One look at my stomach confirmed that doom and gloom mindset. My body had become firm and rounded, the baby moving often now. I had had many checks in the clinic, crafting a story about my boyfriend abandoning me just to keep them from the truth. It seemed normal to them, expected even. Black men made you pregnant and just left you for someone else. They were infamous for cheating and having a lot of women on the go, that was how they spread Aids. Of course, White men would never stoop to this, and Indians and Coloureds to a lesser extent. With all these thoughts whirring in my mind like the hamster on his wheel, I fell asleep.

Hours later, Toby nudged me as he wanted me to see the house from the approach.

'Wow!' I exclaimed, awestruck. It was perched up on the hill, a solid and substantial farmhouse painted a deep, mango yellow. It was so large and spread out that it almost appeared to squat, with its wrap around balcony protecting it. Excitement stirred in me, I wanted to see it.

But Zoe's first comment after welcoming her father in a great bear hug upset me. 'What is she doing here? She doesn't belong here!' She looked sullen and moody suddenly. I had thought that we were sisters. Well, maybe so when it suited her. Now that she was set to leave soon, she just ignored me. Toby hastily grabbed her arm and took her to one side. I could hear them.

'It's not nice to talk like that Zo! You should be more accepting. What wrong has she done to you?'

Sullenly, I walked away while they argued. Around the house chickens scratched in the dirt. Flies of all sizes and colours hovered and settled wherever they could, including, my face. The red sandy ground calmed me and reminded me of being home, in the township. Of course, it wasn't really a farm where I lived, we just called it that sometimes, as it was rural and away from the city. But this *was* a working farm, the vegetable patch with its scarecrow in the middle looked overgrown with produce, fruit trees dotted the perimeter. I would not have ventured inside if it hadn't been for a kind and handsome middle -aged man who found me outside and approached me to shake my hand.

'Hi, I'm Johan,' he said.
'Hi, I'm Bongi.'

'I know. I heard all about you from Wendy. I own the farm next door and when she's not here we look after this farm.' His skin was golden brown and his eyes a deep green. His short hair was greying at the temples, he sported a small beard. I liked him immediately. He seemed honest and approachable for a White person.

'Come inside,' he said. 'Don't worry about Zoe, she will soon calm down.'

He had the slow drawl of an Afrikaner. I knew about White accents now, there were many Afrikaners at school. I was hungry and exhausted, I needed to sit down. I followed his lead and entered the house by the back door which led directly into a large kitchen.

Wendy sat at the wooden table, drinking whiskey. I had never seen her like this, dressed so casually in shorts and a strappy top, she had no make- up on and her short, spiky hair was uncombed. She had never looked so beautiful and young since I first met her. The transformation startled me. Her lack of greeting too, surprised me and made me self -conscious. I wrapped my long cardigan around myself protectively and sat down.

'Help yourself,' she said rudely, even though she hadn't greeted me first. I tried to make eye contact to thank her, but she was already in intimate conversation with Johan, so I ignored her and focused on the food. The table was laid substantially, and I heaped my plate not caring about who was looking, I was that ravenous. There was honey roast ham, peri- peri butterflied chicken, cold boiled eggs, pork sausages, warm bread rolls, garlic infused grilled queen prawns drizzled with lemon mayonnaise and a large salad. On a separate table their housekeeper had laid out beers, bottles of red wine, Scotch, tequila and mineral water. These people lived in the lap of luxury. Every day was an opportunity to feast! Zoe seemed to have another boyfriend here, a chap called Anton, Johan's son. How lucky, I thought bitterly. To have gorgeous young men in proximity to each of your houses. They were kind, gentle types too, not criminals or old, White, married men.

Later, I realised that this was part of White privilege. Choices.

There was an air of casual comfort here, everyone walked in and out of the kitchen with beers and cigarettes, simply nodding to acknowledge me. All the doors were wide open, the Coloured housekeeper who looked after the house bustled about plumping cushions and filling up the ice so that the beers stayed cold. She was also preparing the food for the braai that evening. Every now and then she would tweak Zoe's cheek or hug her, calling her, 'my precious.' It pained me to see how much love there was for this drug addled, spoilt rich girl. It wasn't fair. The rest of them talked amongst themselves. Zoe, I noted, looked as radiant as her mother, she sat clutching her beer on Anton's lap in a big velvet armchair on the porch, both had locked eyes onto each other and no one challenged this. Her skimpy boob tube top and cut off shorts were so outrageous, I would have said something if that was my daughter, her breasts and bum cheeks spilled out and Anton seemed transfixed even though he had brought another female friend along. I could see how unwanted I was here at this gathering. I could have killed Toby for bringing me, but I kept silent and scoffed my food feeling the infernal baby kicking as if to say that it was enjoying the flavours. Back I went for more of those unforgettable prawns, the succulent chicken. Still, everyone ignored me. Toby was in high spirits, he had joined Johan in a drinking game already and both were joking and laughing loudly as though they were old friends. All this history, I kept thinking, and I'm not a part of it. As the lone Black person, I felt shyness creep over me, like the mist over the Drakensberg mountains. Would I ever stop feeling so damn awkward? When Zoe came in and sat beside me, not looking at me but mouthing things to her mother, I pushed my chair back and asked if I could go lie down.

I could have cut the tension with a knife. 'Where are her bags?' Wendy asked Toby.

'The front room.'

'This is my house and you brought her *here?*'

Silence.

Even Toby had changed now that he was with his friends and family, I was invisible to him now. They all seemed fully absorbed in the drinking games and with music in the background, the party was in full swing. I was told to use the front room, so I crept along the long, dark corridor with its countless rooms, past the huge bubble gum pink lounge and I finally found a small, curtainless room with a bed and cupboard where I lay down, exhausted and emotional now. Flies buzzed around me and I didn't bother to swat them away. I balled up into a foetal position, tears streaking my cheeks, and fell sleep.

I don't know how long I had been asleep for, but my dreams were interrupted by the opening of the door and someone tip toeing, causing the floorboards to creak. It was Toby, drunk now after an evening of partying. I could smell it as he walked in.

'Hey!' he said as if he had only just remembered me. I pretended to sleep. 'Hey babe!' He was sitting at the foot of the bed. Irritated, I sat up. The room was in pitch darkness. Through the window, I could see the moon like a big cream cheese in the dark sky.

'I can't see,' I said. At that, he lurched up and turned on the lights. His leery smile and vacant expression told me that he was now very drunk.

'I just wanted to say sorry. I know it's hard for you.'

So why did you bring me against my will?

I couldn't find the words to say anything. I just sat up in bed staring out at the moon. The room backed onto the front part of the veranda and I could hear voices, laughter, the tinkling of glasses.

'We're having a braai,' he whispered. 'Come see.'

'No, I want to sleep.' I was adamant.
'Please…'

Drunken men reacted differently to women, I had learnt. Sometimes the drink brought out their sadness. *Dronkverdriet,* it was called in Afrikaans. Some wanted to fight and argue. Toby and his kind wanted sex. And now here he was fumbling under the covers, trying to get me to open my legs and hurting me in his drunken clumsiness. I was not having it, not here where his family had frozen me out. I stood up firmly and made for the door. Even if I had to sit outside alone on the veranda under the stars I was not going to give in. But Toby was strong. He pulled me as I got out of bed and ripped my top. The thin cotton gave way and the top tore clean down the middle.

'Stop or I'll scream!' I warned, shrugging off the top and reaching for my suitcase where I had others.

'Five minutes, please my baby.' he pleaded, trying now to roll down my trousers so that he could take me from behind. He had stripped off himself and stood behind me fondling my engorged breasts, my large, round stomach. Somehow, it all turned him on.

'No, no!' I tried feebly at first and then louder.

'Stop struggling you bitch!' his voice when drunk, was ugly and loud.

Suddenly, the window which previously had framed an empty veranda with a mountain and the moon in the distance seemed different, full of something. I tried to focus but shock stopped me from processing it. They were all there, drawn to the window perhaps by the shouting. Wendy, Johan, Zoe, Anton, Anton's friend. All stood stock still just peering into the curtainless room with the lights on showing clearly me half naked and hugely pregnant, with Toby, stripped now to his socks, fondling me from behind.

What happened next seemed to unfold in slow motion. First, there were shouts and screams of outrage. Then Wendy stormed into the room and lunged at us, throwing Toby on the floor and laughing manically at his nudity. Then she looked at me hard, screwing her bright, turquoise eyes to concentrate. I did nothing, I just stood there, frozen in shock. She took me with a resounding slap that twisted my head onto one side and I covered my stomach in shame. Behind her, Zoe tried to get at me. All had disgusted expressions on their faces. I couldn't bear it.

'You scum!' shouted Wendy.' We took you in to help you. Is this how you repay us? Is this how you show gratitude? You slut. You seduced my husband? Your father. Your own, biological father!'

'No.' I whimpered, reaching for my torn top and unsuccessfully covering my body. 'It wasn't like that.' But I kept staring at her. What did she mean my own, biological father? My father was dead in a shoot-out at work. My father had been a Black man.

But Wendy had fallen into a rage, she was seething, her wiry body contorted in anger, her mouth twisted as she spat the words.

'And you!' aimed at Toby who had pulled his trousers back on and was frozen in shock too. 'You bastard! You no good, alcoholic, aggressive, womaniser!' she reeled off the insults whilst raining blows on him, she seemed hysterical. 'I expected more from you! You went with your daughter! Made a baby with her? What kind of man does that? First you sleep with Happiness,' she turned around announcing it all triumphantly to a shocked audience. 'I had just given birth to Zoe, I was sick with post-natal depression. So, instead of waiting for me to heal before having sex with him, he just took up with the servant! Oh, she got pregnant in no time and then we had to think fast, adopt the little girl or send her to the township to live with her family? The latter won. And they didn't stop there, he carried on with her off and on. I pretended to turn a blind eye because I had Johan. If it hadn't been for you,' her voice faltered as she turned to him.

'Why didn't you leave?' Zoe's voice was small now, she looked like a frightened child, her mother's brilliant turquoise eyes staring at me from beside Anton.

'Because I wanted you to have a father, my poor, poor, girl. Besides, imagine the gossip. All our friends laughing at me. I couldn't bear it. I made him move out to that annexe because I just had to find a way to live through it!'

Silence.

'And now you went and made a baby with your daughter. Your grandchild will also be your son or daughter! Filthy scum! Who does that? Someone deeply depraved and perverse that's who!'

Zoe had looked disgusted and aloof, her mouth twisted like she'd eaten some rotten fruit. 'I HATE you,' she spat, 'I hate you both. I never want to see you again. If you come near me,' pointing at me now, 'I WILL KILL YOU! You used us. You took everything from us. Our money, our hospitality, our kindness. You're all the SAME! Selfish!' She spat at me. 'I don't have a father anymore. You!' to Toby, 'You're dead to me!'

In the end it was Johan who restrained Wendy and took her away sobbing. Anton who could barely look at me, took a trembling Zoe away, embracing her and talking in low, loving tones to her. Toby rearranged himself and walked out of the room on unsteady legs, I was left all alone. I found new, fresh clothes in the suitcase, got dressed and sat on the bed. In the morning at first light, I would leave. A kind of clarity tempered with white, hot rage took over me. Ma never said a thing! The bitch! Was this why she never came home some weekends when I was little? Oh, I could have torn her face off, that lying, conniving bitch! I hated her now. It was all her fault. If she hadn't slept with him then I wouldn't have been born to this ugly, cruel world and this shameful thing would never have happened. When the baby kicked, I punched and pummelled my stomach in revenge and then, all movements stopped.

This was what I had to do. I would go back to the house somehow as all my stuff was there. I would pack up and leave. That was that. I wanted to walk off the planet and never ever return.

At some point that night, the voices receded, and the house became silent. I was desperate to use the bathroom, so I traipsed along the dark corridor again, finding no one home but Toby. He was in the kitchen, drinking more Scotch but out of the bottle, his swaying body and half- closed eyes an indication as to how very drunk he was. He never even noticed me. I finished in the bathroom, closed the front and back doors and switched off all the lights. I slept deeply, my dreams full of monsters and dark demons trying to possess me.

The cock's crowing woke me up. It was a glorious, sun drenched morning. The distant mountains surrounded by trees and scrub looked majestic. I packed quietly and made up the bed again. In the kitchen, I found Toby slumped in an armchair, the empty bottle shattered on the floor. I had to shake him repeatedly but eventually he woke and tried to remember who I was. I helped him to the phone where he placed a call to the local taxi service. When it arrived, I helped him find his wallet so that he could prepay the exorbitant fare to the city. I also took his house key. In the car, I sat stony faced and tight lipped while the Coloured driver bopped about to pop music from the radio, I dared not sleep as I could not trust that I would be safe. A few hours later, I was in Durban outside the house. It only took me about fifteen minutes to get inside, shower, change and pack one bag of my stuff. I made sure that my wallet with my passport and bank card were at the bottom of the bag. I had plenty of cash hidden under the mattress and in the cupboard which I retrieved.

In no time, I was on my way out of there. A new life beckoned.

CHAPTER 5: CARAMEL

The Lodge for Lovely Ladies must have been an impressive family house or hotel in its time. Now, it had been converted into something very different. Situated on a wide, sweeping avenue lined with jacaranda trees, it had an ornate, pinkish, flesh coloured façade fronted by a long veranda filled with white chairs and tables. The building was not designed to be a brothel. Clearly, it was an ode to Durban's rich, colonial history. In the evening, it came alive. The polished brass plaque next to the door announced its name, and under it were the words in italic: *A Relaxing*

Haven for Men and Women from All Walks of Life to Mingle.

I had seen it many times while driving past with Toby and he had often remarked with a sigh how 'the area had gone to the dogs under the rapidly developing new South Africa.'

'But I thought you are a political activist,' I would tease, 'You of all people should welcome change. You lobbied for this right?'

'You're getting too cheeky!' he would laugh, 'of course we all want change but not this! This used to be a decent White area, now it's full of brothels, drug dens and gangsters. A paradise for criminals really. You can't walk here at night anymore, they've taken over. No one wants this in their backyard, it's like a glimpse into hell.'

By *they,* he meant Blacks. Maybe Coloureds and Indians to a lesser extent. Once he parked the car on the side of the road and said, 'look, let me show you. You are a new generation Black woman, you need to see for yourself, hopefully, you young people can drive change in a more positive way.' He pointed to a clutch of scantily dressed women standing on the side. They looked beautifully made up, some seemed to lean in and chat to drivers who had been cruising along looking at them, some just beckoned to passers -by.

The drivers were of all races, most of them seemed to be White men. Toby in his white Merc did not stand out. Further along, past the women, the street looked like a market: there were pop up hairdressers in tents, makeshift stalls selling anything from fruit to batteries to plastic toys. Many young Black men hung around, some smoking weed, some selling it. Toby knew about all of this and he was eager to discuss the before and after effects of the changing South Africa.

'What we don't want is this!' he said vehemently. 'Change means just that. We want decent people and a safe environment. This is just deplorable. Our lovely streets are now filled with lowlifes. I suppose this is what apartheid tried to hold at bay.'

I was speechless. This road led to the town centre and I often walked along it with my friends. To us it was perfect. It reminded me of the township. The stuff at the market stalls were affordable. Thandi had had her hair braided here for much cheaper than in town. I liked to sit on the side eating fruit and watching the goings on. No one attacked us. If anyone spoke to me they would address me as 'sister,' which I loved. We were one. I preferred this area to the smart shopping malls where often I would get chased out if the security guard was in a bad mood.

'We think differently,' I said at last. 'I don't know if any healing *is* possible between the races in South Africa. Maybe too much has happened. We live in different worlds. Anyway,' I challenged, 'how do you explain the Whites who are coming here for these Black hookers? I thought they're meant to be racist. I know that you're not,' that with a cheeky grin.

'Well young lady, sex is sex. Maybe they too have cold fishes for wives. Maybe they want something different, who knows.'

I'd heard the saying from an Indian boy at school... 'Why stick to chicken curry every day when you can have lamb, vegetables, prawns, fish, duck, anything. Variety is the spice of life.' He'd been boasting about having several girlfriends and had used the food analogy to justify his departure from monogamy.

'Another way of looking at it is, why buy a book when you have the whole library to choose from? You take out one that you fancy, and then just return it if it turns out to be disappointing. You haven't paid for anything. Just use and return. It's the same with people!'

These snippets of conversation played again and again in a loop as I approached the lodge. It was the only place that I knew that could potentially help me. The door was open but as soon as I stepped in an older, smartly dressed Black sister appeared and asked me what I wanted. She eyed me, my large, round stomach and my bag suspiciously. Feeling calm and confident (oh the power of money!), I explained that I wanted to rent a room for a few months. I had a little money, no need to tell her the whole truth, and I could pay. If she couldn't help me, could she recommend somewhere else. At the mention of money, she relaxed immediately. In no time, she had shown me around the house and to my room which was on the top floor, not perfect for a heavily pregnant young girl but still, I didn't complain. Downstairs was a communal kitchen and lounge with a TV. All other rooms were taken. She talked about the need for discretion, about dressing smartly, and advised against skin to skin contact with clients, there being a large supply of condoms in the bathroom. Rolling my eyes in mock horror, I tried to explain that I was not a hooker, that I was there to birth my baby, I was homeless.

'Whatever!' she said smiling, waving her painted pearly fingernails in my face. 'I don't want to know the details. If you pay up on time you will have a safe place here with all the girls. Oh, and that,' she pointed to my bump. 'We ask no questions here. Just let us know if you need anything.'

I quickly paid the three months' rent up front and she tweaked my cheek smiling, 'I love you already, beautiful girl. I'm going to call you Beauty.' Did that mean there was a Beast lurking somewhere waiting to fall in love with me? Or had I experienced that already?

The room was not small. The double bed dominated the space, in the corner was a sink, next to a small table and a cupboard. A red lamp sat next to the bed. Everything seemed clean and welcoming. I was exhausted. I had bought food on the way there, so I locked the door, sat down heavily on the bed and started to eat. I started with the meat pies, then the bananas and finally chocolate. I had certainly ballooned. I had about two months to go before I could get rid of it and get my life back. And I planned to spend that time hibernating: sleep and food was what I craved now. Not people. I couldn't bear the thought of connecting with anyone, only to be let down later. No, that was not for me. I lay down and fell asleep.

i was broken, now I Am

Two months went quickly, and Lady Luck was on
my side. I made a good friend called Tanya who had
the room next to mine, she was a stunning Black sister
who had come to the city out of desperation as her
family were struggling financially. Now, she had regular
clients and a special friend, Niall, a middle -aged White
guy. Tanya was my salvation at the lodge. Every day
she would check in on me, bringing me food and
organizing lifts to and from hospital. Niall was at her
beck and call so that helped as I had no one to turn to.
I could see that he was besotted with her and even
referred to her as his girlfriend, little did he know about
the string of customers she had after he left.

Did it bother me that I was living in this sort of
house? No. When I looked in the mirror, I could see
that I had changed. I was no longer the quiet, shy rural
girl from the township. The city had hardened me, even
my face looked angular, my huge stomach a daily
testament to how my life had been transformed.
Against my wishes I might add, but then, I just
accepted it all. Initially, the yearning for my Ma, granny
and auntie was so strong that I cried myself sick, my
eyes would become raw from crying. Often, I
pummelled my fists into my stomach, trying to end the

torment, thinking that it would stop moving, stop reminding me of what happened. And it did stop for a time. Then, it started again, reminding me, always reminding me. My dreams became full of little babies with blue pug eyes, flat noses and sparse yellow hair in wisps. Later, the memories faded into the distance and I stopped missing anyone. I was alone in the world, a person with a brand-new identity. A new person in the new South Africa. I had no mother, no father, no community, no context or definition. I was a nothing. In the township, I'd been the bright, beautiful belle of the ball. We were respected. And now this.

I have always had a very good memory, not quite photographic, but graphic enough. Now, my time with the Ellis family played out in my head again and again and again. From those early days when I was fresh and green, to the sharp city slicker whore that Toby had groomed me into becoming. I interrogated myself, blamed myself, pointed the finger at Ma. It was mental torture. To stop it, I filled my time with sleep. Most of the time I was tired anyway, so sleep seemed a reprieve. Sometimes in the afternoons, Tanya would help me walk down the stairs and we would stroll to the nearest mall to get ice cream and cold drinks. I didn't want to invest in maternity clothing. I had not planned or wanted this. So, I protested by squeezing myself into my larger clothes and wearing my long nightgown indoors. During those seemingly endless days, I hatched a plan.

I'd asked Tanya to introduce me properly to Niall, there were things I wanted to ask. We met in her room one afternoon, he seemed like a nice, older man who liked a drink or two. And he had a big thing for young, Black women so he was happy to help and support. I told him that I wanted to resume my studies and I had a passport already, could he help me get a ticket to England after the birth? His interest piqued, he wanted to know all the details, who was the father of the baby? How did this happen? Why the secrecy? Why was I here? Clearly, I was not a hooker so why the lodge? I was beautiful, educated, a wordsmith even, and very intelligent so why why why why??? I liked listening to him speak in his lilting Irish accent which he had kept despite living in Durban for twenty years. In a low voice, as calmly as possible, I told him the bare bones of the story. I had been raped by a White teacher at school, I had to run away as I couldn't take anymore, now I was pregnant and couldn't wait for it to be all over so that I could abandon it and move abroad. Once in London, I would complete studying and eventually become a teacher, something that I had always dreamed about. Toby Ellis was such a famous figure in Durban. I didn't dare mention his name.

He was impressed. He said that it was rare to see a young woman with such vision, such determination and strength. He also admired my grasp of English and how confidently I spoke. I think if it hadn't been for Tanya hovering he would have wanted more from me, so I was grateful for her presence. I could see his eyes on my breasts, full now with milk, my lips, my eyes. My hair was in long braids but other than that I had done nothing to enhance my looks. I hated his leery stare, it reminded me of someone…

He said that he knew people who knew people and he could get me a study visa, but I needed money for this. And my plane fare of course. In London, he had friends and family who could help if I paid enough. As for the baby, he could help there too, there was a church nearby that helped with adoptions, maybe I could go and see the church people with him? I agreed, and we set the plans in motion. He seemed surprised that I had the funds to pay him and started to question whether I had stolen money, then he quickly changed his mind and stopped asking questions. He said that I had been through a lot for such a young girl, that I was brave.

i was broken, now I Am

When the pains came, and I lay writhing on my bed
screaming for my Ma, I had no wish to speak to the
church. I wanted it out and I wanted to disappear.
Tanya and a few others helped to deliver her into the
world at home on my bed. I heard her crying as soon as
she was out and turned away when they wanted to
show me my 'beautiful baby girl.' She was White, they
said. 'White and strong. A fighter.' I had bought a few
basic pieces of clothing in neutral white. They bathed
and dressed her and tried again to present her to me to
breast feed. But I had already bought the tablets to dry
up the milk supply and planned on taking them that
day. I refused to see her. In tears, Tanya handed her
over to Niall who had agreed to approach the church
for me. He had brought a baby carrier and he made
ready to take her away forever. As they left, I stood up
feeling weak but relieved. I caught a quick glimpse of a
light skinned child with a penetrating stare, those huge
brown eyes boring into me.

'Why are you giving me away?'

I shuddered and turned my back. Even as they
walked out of the lodge, I sneaked a look through the
window. She *was* beautiful. Such a fat and healthy

baby. Ma would have loved to cuddle her, help me with her, granny would have knitted clothes for her, a blanket in rose pink.

But *not* for a Coloured baby! Mixed race, mulatto, of questionable racial origin, with no proper identity.

'What were you thinking child? How could you bring this thing home to the farm? Which self-respecting Black man would touch you now?'

On and on, the questions. The stares in the street, the hostility. The gossip behind my back.

'She's not one of us anymore, maybe she never was. She always had airs and graces, the way she kept herself to herself. The outcast.'

'To be single forever because no one wants you now.' Thetu's face. 'You stupid! I said use the opportunities not get yourself into a mess. Brainless. That's what you are. Why throw away community, family? You think Themba will want a Coloured baby? Ha! Grow some sense. Your head in the clouds as always, all those books you read, filling you with nonsense.'

And Ma, what would she say? 'You slept with your daddy. You did things with your own father. Filthy slut! Sorry I didn't fill you in on the truth, I thought it was better to keep you from my rotten history. But I never dreamed that you would stoop to this! I don't know you anymore. Dirty whore! You're nothing to me now. Take that thing that you made with him and drown it, just like we drown unwanted animals. And drown yourself in the process. Granny and your auntie, they're waiting for you, with stones in their hands. Just try coming back to the township, just try. If you have a death wish, you come here. Themba's waiting too. We're ready. The People's Court is ready.'

Her incredulity and judgements would be both understandable and yet so cruel.

'A whore is a whore is a whore. You can dress it up in different ways. It's still a whore!'

I could just see her, crying in anger and utter disappointment, then resolutely walking away, turning away from me, the monument toppling from its great height. I had gone from her Princess to a bitch in no time.

I had stared impassively at the white wall with its paint peeling off in patches while Niall asked about a name. At first, I didn't respond. Then I made up my mind.

125

'Caramel,' I said. 'She's Caramel.'

'You sure you don't want an African name? A Zulu one? Nandi sounds perfect,' suggested Tanya. 'Means sweet.'

'She's not Zulu. She's a Caramel. That's it.'

'Okay, it's cute too,' Tanya chipped in. 'Like an ice cream. It suits her.'

And what Tanya wants Tanya gets. So, Caramel it was.

Two weeks later, I boarded a South African Airlines Boeing 747 jet plane destined for Heathrow Airport, London. It was the beginning of a brand-new chapter in my life. Abroad. I loved that word, it was better than 'overseas.' I never heard from Toby again.

CHAPTER 6: LONDON 1980

I had landed in London as winter approached.
Even my long, brown, duffel coat and grey cardigan
had not prepared me for the biting, cold wind and
constant rain. The skies were slate grey, the taxis black.
Where was the colour in this place? No wonder it was
such a serious place. Marley, a friend of a friend of
Niall's, met me at the airport. My legs had felt wobbly
and shaky like a new born foal after the long flight and
there, to my surprise, was a young Black man with long
dreadlocks carrying a board saying simply: Bongi. I
shuddered with my usual self -loathing, I needed to

change that name. He drove me to his flat talking incessantly about arrangements. I could stay for a few nights, but really it was important to approach the universities and colleges in the area asap, if I left it too long I wouldn't get in as there were strict deadlines. He knew a student who could advise on this. He knew a lot about me already, I was here to study, I needed help. He would help me with getting a bank account and all the basics.

Once inside his tiny flat, I felt awkward. Do all rape victims feel this awkward around men? Straight away, he rolled a joint, the flat filling up with that decrepit smell that I had always hated. So, Londoners smoked too? Just like the guys back home. No changes there, I thought. 'That's why they call me Marley,' he grinned when I asked if he smoked every day. His humour and cockney accent were lost on me. I decided that I would keep a low profile and move out as soon as possible.

In a week, I had found a shared house close to the university that I was registered with. I had to sign up for catch up courses even *before* I could start the foundation year, but I was ready for that. I had qualified for financial help so all I had to pay for was my room. Again, Lady Luck. Rajesh, whose father owned the shared house, said that it had recently become vacant after a Japanese student moved out. And it wouldn't be vacant for long. Again, a room on the top floor. To me, it was huge. It came with its own little en suite and sink, I could even create a small living and eating area, he was quick to point out, and still have plenty of space for the bed. Of course, the bed was part of the package, but I could get second hand furniture cheaply and he was prepared to help. All the inhabitants of the house were foreign students and he would introduce me to them in time.

I took my time taking everything in. It was such a welcome change from Durban. The people. It blew my mind to see so many cultures and races walking around freely, not judging or being hateful. Blacks from all over the world walked around freely and worked in all areas from banks to offices to government. Under job reservation in South Africa, only Whites held these positions. I was dumbstruck as to how short changed we had been all this time, imagine if *we* had enjoyed such life chances! All that protesting and the senseless deaths. And we *still* hadn't come to this level of equality and acceptance! The area was vibrant with cafes, pubs and small supermarkets selling curry powders, goat meat and fruits of all kinds. On the top shelves, magazines with pouting, naked women, some with their legs spread wide open shocked and teased me.

Everyone seemed to go about their business without making eye contact or asking questions. I relished the freedom of London, absorbed it all like a sponge, even kicked myself as I couldn't quite believe that I was here. On the bustling streets of Durban or in shopping malls, we always felt like we were under surveillance. Blacks were perceived as being either murderers, shoplifters, muggers, rapists or some other type of criminal. Women moved their handbags when we approached. Most people got antsy when they saw us around. Even if we hadn't committed a crime, we had the *potential* to do it, it was in our blood. The word 'native' became associated with an uncivilized, tribal person, a savage who could never be rehabilitated. Prisons were full of us. Now, my elation at being free was tinged with anger and sadness. We had been boxed in and stopped from developing, for so long. Whites had creamed off the best of our country and left us with the dregs. I noticed bitterly that Indians seemed to thrive here in London. Their restaurants popped up here, there and everywhere on the streets emitting tantalising aromas of grilled meats in spicy sauces, garlicky breads, fried rice. They seemed to thrive everywhere.

i was broken, now I Am

They say that South Africans tend to racialize everything, their perceptions deeply tainted at the subconscious level by having grown up with institutionalised racism. It was the first thing I learnt in my Politics class. It was true. We could never process stories without first referencing the racial identities of the protagonists and other characters, for example. We had to know who we were dealing with, after that everything made sense. And we had a thing about gossip especially on the topic of crime. It was like we were virtual victims, feeling that empathy for people who had been robbed, raped or shot. Maybe it made us feel better. We got to live another day free of that kind of horror.

Everything that I saw and experienced was set against the backdrop of South Africa, the undignified lives we had been forced to lead while others flourished. I realised how bitter I had become. I felt jealous of people who hadn't grown up with poverty and hatred. I tried but I could never forget.

I soon acclimatised to the cheerless weather. A pair of jeans, thick socks, low boots, a warm top and a heavy coat became my daily uniform. I had found simple, surprisingly inexpensive furniture from a charity shop around the corner. A navy blue two- seater with a small rip at the back, a faded red armchair, a small, scratched, teak table with two chairs, new red bedlinen, a two -plate stove and a small fridge that fitted under the worktop. I could see Rajesh's face change when he saw the room a few days later.

'I could have charged you more.' He said smiling, 'you don't have just a room, you have a whole apartment here.'

It was perfect. At last, I thought. I had my own place and I could shut the door behind me each day and be at peace. The grant I had, helped to pay for things. I had cash hidden away too. Niall had really come through for me, he had money transferred to my London bank account too so financially I had nothing to worry about. I settled into my studies and tried to forget the past.

It would take me around six or seven years to get the qualifications I needed to teach English. What lay before me *after* this was the big question. Would I be allowed to stay in the country and work? Or would I have to go back, my tail between my legs? In the end, Tiana, a stunning Nigerian housemate intervened. I'd seen her around and often tried to make eye contact, but she seemed too busy or unwilling to talk. Then one day over a cheese and wine get together at the house, hosted by the delightful Rajesh, we met properly.

I introduced myself as Sibongile. 'Uh huh,' she said looking me over, 'I'm Tiana.'

'Where are you from?' I asked anxiously trying to place her, noticing her shiny, ebony hair worn long and straight, her immaculate make up and glamorous clothing. Her long nails were blood red.

'Here, there and everywhere,' she said, in a strong London accent.

I felt like she was teasing me.

'I mean which part of Africa? Which tribe do you belong to? I'm trying to picture you in Africa, but I can't.'

'Tribe? Lord, you are such a newbie,' she laughed, 'it's cute. But not practical. To survive here, you need to move on.'

'On from what?'

'That whole who are you, where are you from, do we know each other's families etc. You need to recreate yourself, invent a new identity. Then you can embrace all the changes properly. You have a golden opportunity here, to be someone different. Leave the shit behind. Start afresh.'

I was awed. I wanted her as my mentor. She seemed so super confident, the way she spoke and moved, the way she sipped her wine instead of glugging it down like me, she epitomised elegance and sophistication.

'Take me under your wing,' I pleaded, gushing. 'You're so amazing! I never had a sister, but if I did I would want her to be like you.'

'Oh, how sweet!' she was touched. She plonked me down on the deep sofa next to her. 'I'm no different from anyone else', she said, 'London is full of survivors. We made it here, we are heroes and heroines, the struggles we had to get here!'

'You could say that again! It's been so difficult especially for me. I've been through hell back home, sometimes I wonder how I made it here!' I thought I had found a partner to share things with, someone to disclose to at last.

'See that!!'
'What?'

'That attitude right there, that please feel sorry for me cos I'm a victim thing you got going…it doesn't work here.! Cos here, no one gives a fuck! Everyone,' she gestured towards the other students milling around in knots, 'has a back story, a history of something shitty. But we all need to move on, right?'

Her words hurt and stunned me. I hadn't realised how others perceived me, I had thought that my life was low key, unnoticeable.

'I'm sorry to rub it in honey,' she soothed enveloping me in a hug. 'But listen, if you're up for it, I will help you. In between my Business degree and my social life, I will see what I can do.'

'I'm ready!' I said firmly, 'Please, I need your help. I have stuff I need to forget.'

'Good, good, good!' she said. 'Let's catch up tomorrow. Must dash!' And with a conspiratorial wink, she was gone.

The next evening after class, I hung around anxiously waiting for her. I had tidied up my room and prepared a few nibbles: ham and cheese sandwiches cut into triangles, chicken pies, orange juice and white wine. I was quickly getting used to the taste of wine, I liked how it made me feel. When I was drunk, I could forget. Eventually, she knocked on my door.

'Whew! What a day!' she said, taking in the food and furniture.

'Would you like something to eat?' I offered.

'Don't do bread!' she looked disgusted. 'Too fattening. Just pour the wine!'

And so, she spoke, and I listened. She had plans for me, big plans. First, I needed to change my name. Sibongile or Bongi was way too ethnically recognisable. I had to change it to Bonnie or Sibbie, even Sib would work for her. I preferred Bonnie. She wouldn't even entertain my Zulu surname. I needed to change that too.

'You can start using Bonnie straight away,' she said. 'But as for your family name, you need to get married girl. That way you will have a brand -new name.'

'Married???' my eyes widened. 'I didn't know anyone in London to marry.'

'Don't stress,' she said, 'everyone does it here. And later, you get divorced. That then leaves you with a new identity. It's a starting point. And what you make of your life afterwards, is your business.' I wondered fleetingly what her transformation had been like, picturing a traditional, tribal girl with curly hair in corn rows melting into an image of a sharp, urban, fashionista. Who had *she* married?

'I'm just waiting for my divorce to come through myself. You have to be relentless. Everything must be about starting anew. If you keep harping back to the past it's never going to work. It will be like old wine in new bottles, do you see?'

I saw.

'Let's do this,' I said. She seemed so smooth and confident.

'Cool. I'll put a few feelers out. Are you free Sunday?' Of course, I was free. During the week I studied hard but during weekends I liked to walk around a bit, familiarising myself with the area, the red double decker buses, the underground, trains, I was still discovering all these new delights. She looked thoughtfully at my clothes.

'Let me bring you an outfit,' she said, 'you need to look the part. Now, let's polish off that vino.'

The Helpful Souls Fellowship was held in a musty hall with high windows that had never been opened. Oddly, the Pastor and elders waited to receive the congregation on the street. First you had to be vetted it seemed, then you could proceed up the narrow stairs which led eventually to the hall where a choir lined the stage and the rest of the crowd sat in rapture. Dressed in the red lycra dress and black heels that Tiana had brought me, I felt out of place among the families that had gathered there. Some wore traditional African robes and headscarves, others shiny gold or silver dresses or waistcoats with matching shoes. The clingy lycra fabric made me look sexual. I felt like a predator.

'You have a delicious figure,' Tiana had said, 'Sticky out African bum, small firm boobs, tiny waist, long legs. What's not to like? Stop hiding and start celebrating girl!' I had lost weight since giving birth, but I could never see myself as delicious. She had done my make- up and hair expertly, I could hardly recognise myself. Still, the pointy shoes hurt my feet and I couldn't wait to get back to my room.

I could see that I was turning heads as we approached, Tiana herself had dressed down for this occasion as it was me who was meant to have the spotlight.

'Hello Pastor,' she beamed as he shook her hand, 'let me introduce you to Bonnie, she's new in London.'

As he turned to me, I squirmed uncomfortably. He was the oddest-looking Black man I had ever seen. It was his eyes that unsettled me the most. I kept trying to look away as he took my hand in his, but he seemed to like me and started to talk. His eyes were rheumy and very bloodshot, they dripped a steady stream of tears down his sunken cheeks. His skin was scaly and dry, the nails on his fingers long and dirty. He took my hand rather than wait for me to offer it, then he covered it with his other hand. I felt like I was being courted by a reptile. All the while, his eyes searched mine, interpreting my squirming away as shyness. I was repulsed.

He asked us to occupy the front row. 'I think you will inspire me,' he said, gently stroking my hand as his eyes wandered over my body and lingered on my chest. The theme today is 'Appreciation and Gratitude. Sometimes we need to take a moment to just say thanks for the Lord's bounty. In you of course, we see perfection.' I shuddered and withdrew my hand in sudden recoil, conscious of a growing queue of people waiting to greet him. He sensed my discomfort and disgust. Tiana was busy chatting to the elders.

'What we need to remember,' he hissed sharply now, in a low, menacing tone, 'is that one good deed deserves another. Here at the fellowship, we help many, many people, but first they need to accept and want help. You've heard of quid pro quo?' His accent was perfectly British. I knew. I knew. This was familiar territory. Every time I thought I had turned a corner I was back to square one. Back to this. I had a sudden flashback of Toby with his leery, disarming smile.

'I understand,' I said, smiling sweetly, searching for his name tag.

'Call me Father,' he said. 'I welcome you to the flock.'

The afternoon wore on, the songs and prayers executed with evangelical fervour took my mind off the initial meeting. Then, afterwards, when the crowd thinned out, he approached us. Tiana took him to one side and spoke to him in hushed tones. They seemed to be in earnest discussion for a long time, she spoke, and he just nodded curtly. Then he approached me while Tiana signalled that she would wait outside. This time he sat next to me and took my hand again.

'We need to get you married as soon as possible,' he said.

'What?' I tried shocked and confused.

'No buts!' he said too sharply for my liking. 'Believe me, you need that here in London. Support and a loving community await you. Just accept as I told you before. You're lucky you found us. Some people fail here and are forced to go back to their country, I'm sure you don't want that. Or do I read you wrong?'

'No!' I was adamant. 'Please, I want to stay.'

Ma's voice echoed in my head, 'The People's Court is waiting for you. You slept with your father, you must be punished.'

'Good!' He seemed more relaxed now. 'So, we have good cooperation from you? Flexibility? Openness? I can work with that!' he smiled without waiting for my agreement. 'Leave it with me, I will contact Tiana when I'm ready. It will take a while, months even to get everything in order. But we can do something. By God's Grace, we will do it!'

On the way home, I begged Tiana to stop at the pub, I had never been in alone before and just needed the company. Words had failed us. There seemed a sisterhood between us, a kind of glue that bonded us now. A new understanding. We didn't talk much, she ordered as I was conscious of being underage, I just sat in the corner and drank whatever she handed me. I wanted to get drunk, really, really drunk. As if to obliterate what had just happened. I could feel in my bones that another turning point was about to happen.

I was eighteen, but I still had to wait a few weeks for them to prepare. Eventually, my wedding day approached. I didn't have to do anything, just turn up at the fellowship. My passport had already been handed over to the Pastor. I was so nervous, I had a ton of questions to ask but Tiana found this trying. At the last minute, she bailed on me and complained of too much work, so I went alone. A woman from the team greeted me and took me into a little changing room. She stripped me down to my underwear and then made me step into a long, white bridal gown and matching shoes. With my braids twisted and piled high into a knot and discreet make up, she said that I looked every bit like the blushing bride. Then, I stepped out into the main hall and saw my groom for the first time. He was a Jamaican man in his thirties, his name was Ronald Collins. Ronnie and Bonnie, I giggled nervously. The whole thing seemed like the theatre of the absurd. But one hard stare from the Pastor and I stopped laughing. Collins, my new name thrilled me. Bonnie Collins.

'The Lord works in mysterious ways,' said the Pastor. 'We all made a big effort for you.'

'Thank you,' I said not daring to look at his face.

A few people had gathered, and the ceremony took place. The photographer demanded all sorts of poses afterwards, and I played the part to perfection. In the park, we strutted and smiled, held hands and even kissed. No longer did I resist. The possibility of being Bonnie Collins. Wow! Tiana was a genius. I loved my new name. I didn't care to find out more about Ronald, he looked like a normal, quiet man. He was not really my husband, I knew this. This was all a piece of theatre and we were the lead act. He'd even gone to the trouble of putting food on afterwards. It was just finger food but still. I nibbled at a few sausage rolls and tried a piece of our wedding cake. Then, feeling tired of the constant attention, I was keen to take off the clothes, get back to my jeans and go home.

'Where are you going?' The Pastor looked surprised when he saw me in jeans again. My husband had disappeared by now.

'Well, I'd like to go home,' I said. 'I have a test in a few days' time. I must revise.'

'Oh no!' He laughed jumping up to take my hand again. 'You just got married. This should be the happiest day of your life. You're officially Bonnie Collins now! You are a brand, new person. Just like a new, shiny coin. Fresh and clean.'

'Clean?' I felt insulted.

'The slate!' he exclaimed, 'It's been wiped clean. Ready for you to write a new story!'

'I know,' I said, 'and for this I sincerely thank you. Really,' I added for emphasis, 'I'm truly grateful.'

'How grateful?' his eyes twinkled now, tears still coursing down his cheeks making tracks along old, dry patches.

'Very grateful,' I said slowly. I wanted badly to go home. I wanted Tiana to be here with me. The hall had emptied, the flowers, food, photographer had all disappeared. The stage set now dismantled, he asked me to go for a drive. I could hardly refuse.

He took me to a new estate not far away from the fellowship, parked outside a house and led me in. The bland, magnolia décor with plain carpet did not feel welcoming and the small fist of fear in my chest started to bang against my chest cavity. The house was empty. There were two double bedrooms, a lounge and a kitchen, all in the same magnolia. Again, I felt like I was on stage, only the set design had changed. He pulled me into the bigger bedroom and pushed me on the bed. Standing above me, he unzipped his fly.

'Really, we should be having our wedding night,' he murmured. 'After all, we're on honeymoon officially. But I have things to do, family commitments. This will be quick.'

His cock was long and thick. It tasted, mercifully, of soap. It was his gnarled fingers that I fixated on, I had perfected the art of being disengaged at times like this. Afterwards, I had to run to the bathroom to wash out my mouth while he rearranged himself. When I re-emerged, he held out his hands for an embrace. This time, his voice was low, and he spoke directly into my ears.

'You did very well, my dear. My beautiful wife. I'm sorry that was so quick, next time we will take more time, okay?' he tilted my head by lifting my chin.

'I thought I had married that other guy,' I said wildly, trying to process everything, it was all happening so fast, I was confused.

'Well…' he smiled slowly, 'let's say he was standing in for me for the day. He already has a family and commitments. It's me who will take over from now.'

I had a lump sum to pay but he was happy to accept instalments spread over a few months. Tiana, unaware of my healthy, overflowing bank balance, arranged for me to teach English to foreign students in my spare time, the cash I earned, I carefully stashed away. The payments were easily done. Twice a week, I had to stay over at the house. Sometimes he stayed the whole night too, sometimes he hung around after for a few minutes and made his excuses. He had applied for my new, British passport and I had to wait until it arrived. In the meantime, life went on. Seasons changed. I changed. Inside of me, something had died. I became disaffected, cynical and disconnected. I drank often and ate junk. I was short with people and stopped socialising with my housemates. Money dripped steadily into my bank account and I lost all sense of reality.

I never really saw Ronald again. Some of the money I paid went directly to him, I knew that. The rest was collected by the Pastor whose name was Frank. I refused to call him Father, it seemed so perverse somehow. So reminiscent of that dark episode that I'd been trying to forget. Everything else, I obliged in every way. I had to. It was the deal I'd signed up for. There was no going back now. And it wasn't all bad.

There was a tenderness about him, I discovered. An old man with a thirst for young girls. My destiny, it seemed. Autorepeat. We tried different positions and angles, always looking for what was most pleasurable. I realised quickly that if I went along with it, it was easier, quicker. The more I resisted, the more he insisted and the more it hurt. Lessons learned. Over time I learnt to cope. I learnt to kiss that tearful face, welcome his exploring tongue with his smelly, rancid breath and open my legs wide enough for him to feel pleasure. Sometimes I wondered whether my desire really was fake or whether I had grown to like, even love, him. He was certainly a good lover and he was rapidly educating me in all the areas of lovemaking.

And, true to his word, he *did* help. Every now and then he took me away for weekends. We did the English countryside, city breaks and sightseeing tours.

He loved driving and didn't mind if I slept in the passenger seat while he swayed to the sounds of gospel music on his six CD multi changer. When we had exhausted most of the popular places, we drove to Wales and then took a train up to Scotland. My knowledge of the UK deepened in direct proportion to our deepening relationship. He seemed to know where to stay, where we would be accepted with no questions. He always introduced me as his wife which I was now. He complimented me on my beauty often, insisting on buying me clothing, make up, shoes and handbags as he liked me to dress up for him. I soon got used to the attention, I even wore the lacy underwear he picked out in different colours and which drove him wild in bed. I was used to this, it came easily, like a script that I'd perfected in a previous role.

For my part, as per the quid pro quo agreement, I cut his fingernails so that they were less gnarly, massaged his skin with shea butter so that it glowed, picked out the most effective eye drops, and advised on clothes, shoes and aftershave. He'd insisted on paying for a weave, so I surprised him by picking out a long, straight style half way down my back, in a golden brown. In a bed and breakfast in the Lake District one weekend during a Sunday lie in, after spooning vigorously, he told me that he loved me. And to my surprise, I was happy, as I loved him too. I told him that I wanted to live with him every day as a normal husband and wife and that I wanted a real wedding ring, not the cheap plasticky one that Ronald had given me.

That weekend, we were intertwined with each other, stopping to kiss and cuddle at every opportunity. We were late for our hike up the mountain, so we laughed it off and stayed instead in the bedroom drinking tequila and making love. With Frank, I had developed a thirst for sex. Often, it was me unzipping him, me climbing on him or me stripping off first. For a fifty something man, he had a surprisingly muscular body and was a much more agile and adept lover compared to Toby. He loved biting me on my neck, leaving huge purple bruises that I had to cover while back at university.

Tiana had moved out. She had stopped answering her phone and we lost contact. I was grateful though that she had introduced me to this new life. Frank helped me to perfect my British accent. He was there at the drop of a hat whenever I called. I introduced him to my housemates as my husband, much to his shyness and slight dismay.

When I kept asking if we could live together as a normal couple, he refused saying that he had other commitments. But I was curious about what he did when he wasn't seeing me, jealous even. I had fallen deeply in love with him, so much so that I craved his company, his clever conversation, and his body when I didn't see him. One day, I teasingly asked if he had another wife that he went home to. To my utter disappointment, he said that he did.

She was a White, British woman who had helped him a lot since he arrived in London some years back. He owed her a lot and couldn't or wouldn't divorce her. No, she was not young and sexy like me, she was his age. But she had given him a free home, introduced him to the fellowship where they made him Pastor and set him up in the UK at a time when he was needy, clueless and penniless. For Frank, those acts of kindness were unforgettable. She was understanding too. His work, including, I presumed, offering a higher tier of service to certain individuals in his flock such as myself, a platinum service defined by attention to detail and continuity of care, kept him away for several days, nights and weekends. Holidays even. She had accepted this and had turned a blind eye to his frequent absences from the bedroom which is what had endeared her to him even more. Later, I reflected on this and realised that perhaps most men would find this quality attractive and desirable in a wife. For all these reasons, she was a keeper and I was not, I could see that. I'd never let my man do that!

I had been with Frank for two and a half years, but we had hit a point of no return. I was now ready to slowly disengage from this married man, unfurl my wings so to speak. When my new passport arrived with my new name, I started to slow things down and he knew that things had changed. From time to time we still spent a few nights together, but it was him doing the chasing now, him unclasping the belt of my jeans in haste, him initiating it all. I suppose he got tired of this after a while and gradually he stopped contacting me.

On my twenty-first birthday, at a Frank-less party with my housemates, I realised that I was free. Really free for the first time ever. He'd arranged for my divorce and the paper work came through as a sure sign from the heavens that it was over.

CHAPTER 7: NEW IDENTITY

I hit a lull after Frank. For a while, there was silence in my head. I still had three years to go to finish my studies and my tutoring on the side was as busy as ever. The restlessness inside me however, had died down. With my new identity, came a new consciousness, I felt like I had been rebirthed. My dreams became full of giant, mutant red lips opening and closing like a clam, eventually spitting out a mini me, a creature that unfurled itself and then grew to monstrous proportions, embracing the world with huge, open arms. My name, Bongi, abbreviated to

Bonnie, paired well with my new surname Collins, I
thought. In one fell swoop, I had erased the past and
created a new me. The excitement that this caused in
me was so intense that I felt dizzy sometimes. Sibongile
had died, I buried her in style, even performing a little
ceremony with a few grams of the white stuff to
commemorate the event.

Transformations are therapeutic at times.
Especially if you're on the way up and are running away
from your past. I was desperate to have my lips
reshaped, God how I wanted it done! They were way
too big. As soon as someone at university
complimented me on my 'blow job' lips I made a
mental note, scheduled the surgery after consulting a
plastic surgeon in London's prestigious Harley Street.

'I want a more reserved, bow shaped mouth,' I
requested when he asked me what I wanted done. I had
even brought some pictures with me.

'But these are all White mouths,' he said shaking his
head. 'Why do you want to be White?'

Silence. What do you say to that?

'What I see in front of me, is a stunning Black woman who doesn't need anything doing. Maybe some therapy if you want to work on some issues around your identity but really, you don't need work. You're young and perfect!' he said smiling. He went on to explain that people of all races were using lip fillers to create fuller lips, I already had the full, sensuous mouth that they craved. It was reckless to change my mouth when it was perfect.

I was silenced by this sensible man.

Then, stupidly, I did a U-turn. I found another plastic surgeon who jumped at the chance to change my features for a hefty price tag. I explained that I had been raped and that I needed to change my identity in order to heal. I got my pert, aquiline nose in the end, I also had a cheekbone reduction which effectively changed the shape of my whole face. Now, I had the slim, gentle, contoured look that I had coveted ever since I had moved to the city, I was unrecognisable. I kept my prominent behind of course, I'm not that silly. At last, Toby's money had been put to good use. I was never to see him again and couldn't care less what happened to him, but at least I had payback. I could never think about this man as my father. And incest? What an ugly word. Who'd want to have a conversation about that? It was best kept in the taboo category and secreted away, somewhere remote.

My identity change worked wonders for what was essentially, my healing journey. I liked, even loved what I saw in the mirror, the new, sophisticated Western woman surprised and enthralled me. I took to speaking to myself in the mirror in my newly acquired London accent. I experimented with hairpieces of various lengths and styles, settling on a blonde crop which I later got my hairdresser to create as a weave. I changed my clothing to sexy, fitted short skirts, figure hugging jeans and cropped tops that outlined my pert breasts. Tiana had left her legacy on me and had taught me well. Now, when I stepped out I got appreciative looks, wolf whistles and phone numbers on slips of paper.

One day, a handsome European guy with short, blonde hair and intense blue eyes, handed me his number on a bus ride home after I had been shopping in the city. His name was Milan and he wanted to take me to dinner. It was the start of a new adventure. In eye candy ratings he was up there, and I fell for him almost immediately.

'You're so beautiful,' he would say in between bursts of passionate love making on my bed. My dark skin, brown nipples and curvy body excited him, he said that he was sick of the 'fried eggs' appearance of White women's breasts and had fantasised about a Black lover for ages. Of course, I loved the attention, the massages, the little simple, pork -based meals that he would rustle up, the small tokens of love that he bestowed on me. Slowly, we fell into a relationship that would last a few months.

Milan was highly educated it seemed. He talked extensively about politics, psychology and law. Sadly though, as an illegal immigrant who had risked everything to come to the UK, his university degree was not recognised and so he was resigned to do cleaning jobs that earned him cash. Through him, I realised how little of European History, Geography and culture I knew having been obsessed with South African politics all my life. Those politics had crippled us, forcing us to take stands, dividing up our communities, killing our youth in violent protests and altercations with the racist police...it was all consuming. Now, here I was with a White guy who was a cleaner, where would I have found that in South Africa?

Never! Just that alone would have been a tasty morsel of information for Thetu and I to chew over as we sat on our stone exchanging gossipy titbits, that is if I had her contact details which of course I hadn't by now. But I still thought about her constantly. Sometimes, I would hold up a new dress against me and picture her face, I could hear her voice wherever I went, in fact thinking about her grounded and energized me. Other people turned to agony aunts for advice, me I had a mini Thetu inside me constantly monitoring, commenting and approving or disapproving.

'So,' I could picture her saying, 'overseas there are Whites who get treated like Blacks and Blacks who are higher than Whites. Big learning curve!'

'Overseas' is what we called anyplace outside Africa, it referred to anywhere out there and symbolised freedom and escape from the daily tyranny of our lives in South Africa. If you went 'overseas' you had 'made it.'

But hotness aside, Milan had some habits that I was finding hard to ignore and, on these days, I missed my Frank. To start with, he was extremely tight with his money. We would go to a restaurant and he would not order food, saying instead that he was not hungry. Then when my food arrived, he would lean over and snatch only the plumpest prawn or juiciest piece of steak from my plate, always commenting on how good it was but never paying. Sometimes, he decimated half of my dinner in this way to my utter frustration, *my* food was *my* food, I felt violated by this and knew that it would be the final deal breaker. I understood that his wages had to be sent home every month to support his family, I was sure that he had a wife and child even though he tried not to disclose information about his life back in his country. I had even accepted his heavy drinking and drugging, which, once recreational had become almost a daily thing. But his tight stance on paying for food and constant plundering of my dinners were too much. The writing was on the wall.

One evening while lying in his arms in his room in a shared house which was small, dark and stank of goat due to the previous tenants who had one tethered in the kitchen, (oh, the joys of London life! Thetu's face again), I told him that we could not go on, that I needed time to focus on my studies which in its final throes were demanding more and more of my time.

'I get it!' he spat in broken, heavily accented English. 'Don't call me I'll call you.'

And then he pushed me angrily off the bed so that he could find his drugging paraphernalia.

I was single again.

What people do for a British passport! I had started to meet many, many people in London who had arrived looking for streets that were paved with gold. Sarcastically, my inner voice told them that there was no pot of gold at the end of the rainbow. I knew. Well…I had made it out of South Africa, that much was true. I had changed my life. Check. But I had sold my soul in the process that too was true.

Ludo, my next boyfriend was another beautiful man. In bed however, I discovered a series of burn scars covering his shoulders and chest. The welts, now old but still thick and raised, seemed so inconsistent with his city slicker's appearance that clearly, he had been careful to cultivate. When I ran my fingers over them even lightly he had squirmed and then dressed himself hurriedly, refusing point blank to talk about his past.

There were others. Hassan, Altran, Taj, Raj, Kris, Pierre…the list went on. Each shared their narrative about how they came to be in London, it was almost an opening gambit in conversation, a starter to the session that followed. We always ended up in my bed as I couldn't trust the dodgy, dowdy backrooms that most of them rented, they were inevitably in shared houses with no heating and basic facilities.

'What are you doing, you fool!' Mini Thetu would chide. 'Pay attention to your studies!'

'Gap fillers,' I would mumble, just silly fun.' Then my guilty conscience would kick in and I would do extra work on my essays and assignments. My teaching practice came and went uneventfully. Finally, I had to produce a series of essays on my experiences in different school settings. Of course, I passed with flying colours and knew that I'd easily secure a teaching job in a good school.

About eight months into my first job, I met Sunil. An 'unexpected pleasure,' I called him.

'Rather, an exotic treasure,' he quipped, smiling with those sexy dimples showing, knowing how they melted me. Those initial honeymoon days passed in such a blur of happiness, we went on weekend city breaks, discovered a common passion for restaurants and theatre, and walked in the forests and parks. When South Africa held its first democratic election we celebrated together by visiting an iconic South African pub in London and got drunk on lager. Of course, I had to say that I was simply interested in South African politics, that kind of thing. I could never just come out and disclose that I *was* South African! No! That would involve getting into a long explanation about how I came to escape my past and end up in London. I couldn't open to anyone about that. He loved chatting about race and culture anyway, he would reference India when we were on these subjects, a culture I was just starting to appreciate.

'Black is beautiful!' he would say, staring at me.

I had found the One.

CHAPTER 8: SUNIL

4 YEARS LATER

My plants are dying. I left them on the windowsill and the heat from the radiator is killing them, it's a slow, painful death. I move my money plant to give it a chance of survival, I can't afford for this to die too. I drown it with water and hope for the best.

Sunil is late as usual. I wonder fleetingly what the excuse is this time then the worry is gone, to be replaced by some other preoccupation of mine. I'm always thinking, doing. Even when he speaks, I tune him out. I come home early. Can't bear the thought of staying on at school for an extra minute. Funny, how in the rest of the world British education is held up as being exemplary, the standard that all other countries aspire to, yet when you teach here you realise that it's more about taming feral behaviour than about imbuing young people with values, morals and the tenets of academia. High standards are a joke here. Why do you think us teachers spend our lives trying to massage data so that our departments look successful on paper? Every year, kids seem more and more messed up. We deal with paedo parents, druggies and alcoholics, even parents who just disappear on holiday leaving their kids alone with no resources, no support. Yup, the great British paradigm. Not so perfect is it? It never fails to fascinate me how some people here struggle with the most basic of things, like parenting. You wonder how they can clean themselves after a shit. Yet they sit in armchairs going on and on about and national and international issues, venting and ripping into other countries, cultures, nationalities. Look inward, I want to shout! Sort the basics out. If you have kids, look after them!

Still, a job's a job.

The empty, lifeless afternoon yawns before me. There is no one to visit, no one to call on. I don't know people anymore. My people are in another continent. These are *not* my people.

But who are my people? I've lived here for so long, I've lost touch. In all my years here in the UK, I've never been back.

My nap on the sofa has not given me that deep rest, my dreams are constantly full of death and doom. Familiar themes recur. This time, it's the mountain episode. We are clutching onto sparse shrub and bush on the mountain peak, then he falls first, sidelong, his screams and shrieks shatter the still air, piercing the silence. Large rocks and boulders roll off and accompany his descent, landing on top of him as he lands curiously doll like in the valley below. I watch nervously, relief flooding me, I am safe. Safe because he is finally gone. I scramble up and fan my body out so that I lie spread-eagled on the flat rock, warmed by the golden sun. Nothing stirs. A sense of deliciousness overwhelms me, such peaks and troughs I think. One moment feeling like everything is spinning around me, the next, this sheer, luscious joy. Then, something wakes me up prematurely from this nap, I'm tired and groggy.

i was broken, now I Am

The apartment is dark. Through the sheer curtains, I see that the sky is charcoal, and the rain is pouring down in sheets, beating against the windows and balcony tiles. I slide open the balcony doors and breathe in the intoxicating blast of cold air and fresh rain. It's the ferocity of the beats that have woken me. I know that it scares some, but I love it, after all I am African, I'm used to dramatic thunderstorms and brilliant sunsets, this is tame. The beats are welcome, comforting and regular, soothing, like a kind of rhythmic drum pattern if you listen hard. I want to put on Sunil's Kenny Gee but not yet, the rain provides a natural soundtrack, takes me back home in a way. I keep the doors open, relishing in the moment.

It's time to check on my stash of white hidden in a book on the bookcase. I know how to enhance the mood, lighten the atmosphere, I'm an expert. Sunil's not home yet, I have time. How to keep disintegration at bay? How indeed. Within minutes I've transformed hard lumps into neat piles that look like a glistening mountain range with high peaks, funny how it reinforces my earlier dream. A few sharp hits and it's gone. Shiiiiit, it hits me hard this new batch! I'm rushing, my heart pounding, I feel euphoric! Energized,

I wipe away the mess, check my makeup and decide to freshen up, I always get paranoid about traces of white on my face. I'm suddenly horny, I only have to rub my thighs together to orgasm, when I'm like this. But I'll wait for him. Masturbation sometimes brings with it the troughs of self -loathing afterwards. I'm not in the mood for more censure or self -sabotage as my therapist puts it.

The chicken tikka masala garnished with chopped coriander, is ready, there's a green salad and garlic naan for the sides. I'm always super organised. I'm just waiting for him to get home and then I'll warm the food and dress the salad, I've got the jazz on now and I am sashaying sensuously to it as I taste the food. Seema doesn't approve of my food, her original recipe called for double cream and orange food colouring, but I prefer just Greek yoghurt to give it creaminess, unctuousness. Miss Bossy won't appreciate my tweaks that's for sure, but she doesn't understand how we are. Why pile on extra calories? We're both trying to lose weight. Sunil's a foodie that's for sure, for an estate agent he is extraordinarily well read on food and wine and I have had to learn new skills, a whole new cuisine, but I don't mind, I want to please him. Being submissive fills a gap, gives me a role to play, occupies me. Of course, he thinks that I'm a 'good woman,' and I like this reference to one side of my personality.

When South African women commit, it's for life. Really. Must be all that crime which is a constant backdrop to life there, knits people together. If you have that rare thing, a husband or partner, you cling on like shit to a blanket. That right there is your protection from what's lurking outside, peeping in your windows, looking for a way in. Even if he does not have a gun stashed away somewhere like many, just his arms around you at night is strangely reassuring. Gives that illusion of safety because of course you're never safe. In South Africa, you live moment by moment, always giving thanks that you get to live another day. You'll read in the newspaper that so and so got murdered and you sigh and weep in horror, but deep inside you're filled with relief, you're really saying, 'thank you, thank you, that it isn't me or my family!' I know these things now, I'm Black but I've lived among many racial groups and heard the different perspectives on crime. And I get it, I'm not thick. I'm a mother myself, well, in a way. A mother with a twist if you like, a twisted mother, ha ha, funny. I'm curiously creative when I'm on coke, opens the brain for me. Dilates my pupils too!

Better calm it down before he arrives, don't want to arouse suspicions.

Seriously, back to my recurring dreams, I need to make sense of them somehow, they taunt me, always challenging, forcing me to reflect, ask questions. Why does he always have to die leaving me feeling safe in a resplendent kind of way, joyous and dazzling with light? What do they really mean? Is there a symbol there? An element of foreshadowing?

Sunil asks why I take texts apart, he moves on to ask why I take people apart as well. He means that I dismember or butcher texts, people, situations, I micro analyse everything. I've lost the knack of seeing things as wholes. He says cheekily that it's lamentable that he fell in love with an English teacher, a grammar Nazi, especially given that his spelling is so poor. He minds when I try to read into things. Before we met, I used to spend my Sundays in antiquarian bookshops searching out books on topics that I'm studying: hermeneutics, semantics, semiotics. Now, he comes with me. I've trained him well, he can hold lucid conversations on the meaning behind texts now, well sometimes. But then he lapses into cheeky chappie estate agent mode, just give him a large Scotch and a view of a rounded derriere and he's content. I can never share my dreams with Sunil, I can just imagine how he'd look, the eye roll, the impatience with anything non-literal. And he wouldn't like that it's always him who's falling from the mountain and being crushed to death underneath.

Anytime now, he will walk in with his heavy camel wool coat and sharp black suit underneath. He tends to leave his wet umbrella in the hallway, I have had to put down a special rubber mat for wet shoes and brollies as I don't want the cream carpet marked. It's not my apartment, it's his even though we are co-habiting, but I still help him look after it, the old quid pro quo. After all, he's given me a leg up in buying a little two bed flat for myself so we're all okay, I know that I have the tenant from hell, but I don't want to dwell on that tonight. My blood pressure has already taken a battering around the issue of this tenant. The girl pays the rent whenever she feels like and still gets to stay on! She's lucky that I'm Black too so she's a sister in a way, of course she milks that fact though. I'm trying hard to understand her financial issues, to show empathy. Pretend that she's a long lost relative. But she's nothing to me, she's not from my country or my tribe. Still, it wouldn't be right if I didn't show support. I've come a long way since I arrived in London. Sometimes, I look around at everyone getting on with their lives all harmoniously and think: Rainbow Nation! It's here, in London. Look how we can all coexist as one! But under the pretence, I know what people think, the looks of alarm when they see us congregating in places, no one wants a noisy Black mob in their area. White immigrants they barely tolerate, Blacks now that's a different matter. As soon as they clock that the area is going Black, you see 'For Sale' boards going up. Time to retreat to the country. Or overseas. Spain is calling! It's all water off a duck's back to me, we stick together, I'll always be partial to helping my own kind. I know how we struggle.

The food is not a surprise for him, he's gotten used to my high standards, I have perfected Indian food I think. I want to be his domestic goddess. Good home cooked food, great sex, it's all a man wants really. He deserves it too, after all, he's a keeper, a rare breed these days it seems. Of course, I hadn't dabbled with Indian food before I met him, but I've learned quickly, Sunil loves it. It took me a while to get used to it at first mind you, it's a far cry from my own traditional African cuisine. The flavour profile is so different...but I have learned to appreciate the different notes: a hint of cumin, freshly grated ginger and garlic, a garnish of coriander, crushed chillies. Nowadays I have become such an expert that I can tweak ingredients to bring out the delicate flavours. My lamb biryani, for instance, is a winner. Sunil gets me to make it for special occasions at the office. Picture melt -in -the -mouth lamb off the bone, layered with fluffy rice and topped with sliced lemons, crushed pistachio nuts, caramelized onions, cardamom and coriander. It's the lemons that take it from bronze to platinum, I think, slice them thinly and scatter them intermittently while layering, then a whole layer for the top. Brings out the succulence of the meat and adds a welcome tang to the dish. Usually, I cook roasts, pasta or posh pub grub: fish, chips, mushy peas and tartare sauce is my favourite. I am the guru of the twice cooked chip which is crispy on the outside and soft inside, the fish is often cod, thick, white slabs of it, dipped in foamy beer batter and flash fried. I'm not such a fan of heavy African food, but every now and then I still love a good meat stew paired with *putu* and sweet tea of course.

I've been lucky. He's taken me to all the best restaurants in London and I've watched and learned. The South African one in central is my favourite, just the décor of faux animal skins, rugby pictures and topless African girls with grass skirts gets me nostalgic, not that Sunil is aware of my identity. I love him with all my heart, I would never put my relationship in jeopardy. Some things are better left unsaid! No, there's not a wall of silence between us, the whole secrets and lies theme that some couples have and try to minimise, we are very much alive with love. I mean after four years together we still leave love notes for each other. From what I overhear in the staffroom, nobody goes the extra mile for relationships anymore! Of course, *he* never cleans or cooks even on nights when I'm late from Parent's evenings, study group or some function at school. He's spoilt, my man, he reminds me of a petulant boy sometimes. On those nights it's a takeaway but I don't mind those every now and then. At least I'm coming home to a hot meal and a hot man, not like some, to an empty house. Or the sight of your man wrapped around some woman in your bed. That would just kill me.

Footsteps in the hall! I quickly pour the opened wine into fat, balloon, crystal glasses. We have a collection of decent reds, this one is a silky Cabernet from Down Under with lots of fruit. Suddenly, he is here. He enters, moaning about the traffic and weather as usual, then stops abruptly and sniffs the air, catching a whiff of the food, noticing the fat, lit candles, soft lamps and jazz. I'm cocooned in a big bear hug and we kiss passionately. He's been smoking, the little shit. He thinks that he has disguised the smell carefully with mint chewing gum and extra deodorant, but it's still there as a background note to the kiss. Normally, I am repulsed but today I am celebrating, and I don't care. I have finished my big assignment and sent it off successfully. I'm working on adding courses to my existing degree, layering myself up academically. That way, I can be promoted easier. I'm ambitious all right, there's nothing to be gained from remaining as a bog-standard English teacher forever. There's just so much crap that one can take. I have my eyes fixed on a headship one day or maybe a deputy position, that way it's you who gets to dish out crap and troubleshoot problems. Ma would be proud, her little girl finally in management. Well, I'm not doing it for her, I can't even imagine her these days. I'm doing it for me. One day, I'll get to the top, don't we all want that?

Tonight, I want to relax with my man and spend a quiet, romantic evening. When he showers, I impulsively strip off and go in behind him, it's his favourite thing this and I want to give him a happy ending. I need this too, takes the edge off my day. When I hear people saying that they do it once a week I shudder! I'm a once a day and all-night person myself, pleasure is my right, it's not a luxury! Again, I cannot fathom other people and the lives they lead. Why would you wait to do it once a week if you have a man in your bed? After, I soap him all over, loving his cuteness, his little round stomach, love handles, hairy chest and smooth bald head. He is forty, more than ten years older than me, but he has light, hazel brown eyes with long lashes that I adore, a boyish smile and of course a thick, ever ready cock that keeps me from complaining. In fact, sometimes I can hardly crawl out of bed, he's so good.

Sunil has shared some scraps about his past life and quite frankly, I don't want to hear more. After dating a string of Seema's friends and finding them lacking, he paid an agency to set him up with the ubiquitous Russian bride. She was all blonde hair, green eyes and long legs and for a while his life had seemed perfect. Then off course, the inevitable happened, I know I'm cynical but how could he not see it coming? He'd walked in one day to find the so- called Russian beauty stark naked and sitting atop another man in his bed no less, a well-endowed Black man. He'd been in the throes of ecstasy and had trouble disengaging from her, that's how Sunil knew about how large he was. What a story! Just picturing his shocked, conservative face taking in the scene, the size of his rival's package and the pleasure on her face, makes me snigger. The rest is such a cliché, she made a quick departure out of London, cleaning out the joint account and taking their child with her never to be seen again. This is the part that makes him still cry sometimes and I hate seeing him in such pain. He keeps talking about it when he's had a few drinks and I try so hard to comfort him. In the pictures, I see a fair child with lots of soft curls, green eyes, a red smiley mouth. I'm of a different race and culture, I can't give him that if that is what he is after. We could write a new story though. Co-create. Start a new journey.

'You'll die when you see my daughter!' he says to anyone who will listen, 'she's like an angel. Blonde.' He thrusts her picture in their faces proudly, his tears streaming into his drink.

We all have sons and daughters Sunil. They are all precious angels to us, whatever their colouring.

I cringe inwardly when he makes a point of reminding us that this is *his* child, this blonde, green eyed vision. As if he can't believe his luck. He touches his nut- brown cheek and places a manicured finger next to the child's face as if attempting a virtual comparison. He was right to feel this disbelief, she was nothing like him, was she even his, I ask myself spitefully.

I'm not apologizing for being me, he *chose me*. I have explained repeatedly that I don't want any children yet, well *any more* children yet to be exact but I didn't say that. My studies and work are all important to me at the minute and he respects this, sees me as more credible I think, because of it. I am an Ebony Goddess who is NOT out to ensnare a man or live off Child Benefits. He says that he can't believe he met someone as decent as me and this makes me hold my head up high. I sense that when his divorce comes through, he will pop the question. I'm so ready to be Mrs Sunil Singh. To be swallowed up in his arms, to never feel alone, to be an 'us' not a 'him and her.'

For various reasons, I have tried to forget the past. I have cleaned and disinfected that whiteboard of my mind so many times, trying to forge a new life, new connections, a fresh history. But every so often it still comes back, like a scar that shows up when your make up has faded, it's all still there, and the pain never goes away. I know now that part of my world will always be sunless. It feels somehow like the devil had come knocking at my door and I had let him in, that's right, *I* am to blame, I must be! I don't care to actively dwell on what happened between my father and myself, *that* issue has never been on my dissecting table in the past and never will be in the future. I don't think I'm interested really. I have put that to rest.

But I don't know why I'm not right. After all these years. Will I ever heal? That is the question that I constantly ask myself.

Sunil and I had met at speed dating, a fun, modern concept where you dress up and get to talk to lots of guys for a few minutes at a time to gauge whether you were compatible or not, then I guess you just took it from there. He was my number six I think, but I could see him look appreciatively at me all along. I had not wanted to go, I'm not exactly shy of men, just that I had had a basinful at that time and was on a break. But my housemate needed company and at the end, I gave in to her nagging. We downed a fair few cocktails one evening and stepped out together, me in my pulling outfit: a tight pencil skirt emphasizing my rear end, tiny waist and long legs, she in her little black dress from a charity shop. She looked good though if you could see past the missing sequins and buttons.

We had hit it off right at the outset. Those sexy hazel eyes and dimples, I had never dreamed of dating an Indian before, they just seemed to stick with their own kind really. I had bedded a few hirsute types who were quite a revelation in bed, must be all those spices in their diets! But I was beginning to think that they were undatable. They never seemed to want to go places after the initial shag. I'd get a phone call suggesting another furtive hook up in my bedroom but no dinner invite, no promise of a boat cruise down the Thames, no tickets to the theatre. See I *liked* that, no, correction, still *like* that extra mile stuff. No woman just wants a wham, bam, thank you ma'am. And it's rude to always fuck in the girl's house, why do London men always ask: 'Do you live alone?' Sometimes, a change of scenery is refreshing and may contribute positively to the act, like the change of a theatrical backdrop. Unless of course the guy is married which, I suspected was the status of most of my lovers. Why are married men, who give out a semblance of dignity and respect, always on the lookout for something on the side, usually something that they quickly want to make regular? Are their wives just palate cleansers then? They love to talk dirty and try out new things. 'I just want to f.. ** you into oblivion,' 'bang you til you're unconscious,' 'smother you with honey and squirty cream and eat you all night...'

The script had become, well, a script. Familiar. And promises had failed too often to deliver. I had not experienced oblivion yet and I'd become tired of being urinated on or coated in baking ingredients from our communal student fridge. My mattress had become stained and dirty after such encounters and seeing it tarnished like that, (always *my* mattress never *theirs*), made me furious enough to want to put the brakes on. But there we were Sunil and I, laughing and joking together on our speed date, totally oblivious that we had exceeded our time limit and still relishing in each other's company, until the organizer approached us angrily to spell out the rules. Giggling like teenagers in trouble, we left the venue, ending up in a dimly lit Italian bistro where, over spinach lasagne and bottles of Chianti, he confessed that his sister had set him up with the speed dating ticket and effectively turfed him out of his own apartment bossily. That would be Seema's style, I could just picture her complaining.

'How you going to sort out your life if you don't get *out there*? You can't grieve for a woman who has left you. They *not* coming back!'

She can talk. Having been married and divorced to an abusive cheat of a man, she was ready to hang up her dancing shoes forever. Now, she concentrated on her health food shop, a thriving business in London's East End that made her enough money to buy her small Victorian house and still leave something for her to make those frequent shopping trips to Mumbai. She was a stunning, exotic creature, slim with Sunil's hazel eyes and straight, shiny, liquorice black hair that ran down her back, I couldn't imagine anyone not wanting to bed her. But she was elusive, the little snake, she never let on if she had a lover, always taking the moral high ground in conversation and pretending to be ultra -religious. I can smell bullshit from a long way off.

CHAPTER 9: RAINBOW NATION

At first, we made love in my room, the clutter of books and papers in disarray everywhere seemed to get him going. Maybe it was such a sharp contrast to his obsessively compulsively tidy apartment or luxury mancave as he called it. He said that he had grown weary of his place, having lived there all alone since she left. That and my behind. He was a butt man, most men are. He loved to look at me while I cavorted in various strips of lingerie. 'Luscious,' he called me. And then, he'd fondle me, I felt quite the Queen. It was funny doing it on a bed strewn with students' essays, some with marking in red and some unmarked. Once when he pulled out early to cum on my face, he just missed a pile of assessments on a Shakespearean sonnet. Handing them back to the students was sure to summon interesting memories, I giggled with irresponsible delight. I'm not indecent really. Just a rebel sometimes.

I loved the shared house that I lived in, but it was never quiet. Out in the hallway you could always hear the footsteps of my four student housemates and their various friends in tow, coming and going. I hadn't moved out of student digs, it had just grown on me. I was the late student of course, making up for lost time. I never seemed to stop studying.

The decision to go into teaching was a no brainer. Those endless summer holidays on full pay. Weekends off. Besides, I liked the work, I always had a thing for English literature. Weekends if I didn't have a shag, I spent drinking coffee or wine, visiting bookshops and poring over books or latterly, lesson plans. Now, I had Sunil, my first proper boyfriend, I say proper because *he* had not been a boyfriend despite what he had tried to get me to believe. And the others had just been ships passing in the night. With Sunil, I felt a *real* connection, the kind of man you could talk to, the kind you wanted to spend your life with. I had finally come home. By way of explaining about my past, I had created a little white lie about having been born in Jamaica and having wanted to study abroad from the start, my parents, both lawyers, had supported this. Now, having finished one degree and starting another there was no going back there and besides, we had lost touch. There was no mention of my accent, as I was losing that quickly, I had spent days perfecting the London accent. No mention of any other family issues, friends, nothing. I kept myself to myself.

London seemed to be a haven for anyone wanting a new life…we were all escapees from an old, traumatic life and we all had the scars to prove it. Seriously, everyone here seemed to have some back story of how they came to be here. Sunil too, had summarized his passage to London from the north of England in a few words. His parents had left India when he and Seema were young children, his dad was a doctor and his mum a stay at home housewife who was known for her mouth-watering food. Then the tragic car accident and both parents were killed on the spot. The children, in their teens by now, had basically had to fend for themselves with some help from distant relatives in London who had reluctantly taken them in, that is until

Sunil started working and providing for them. And boy did they do well, his rise from lowly paid jobs to becoming an estate agent, then owning his own franchise, that huge, squat, building with a black and gold façade on the High Street in the next town. He bought his stunner of an apartment far away from work deliberately, he said, when he first showed me around. He loves driving anyway, sitting there looking smug in his black BMW with tinted blue glass. Of course, I'm not allowed to drive it, he's old fashioned my man, thinks that all women are dangerous drivers. Hello, have you seen the driving in India! So, we have our own cars. Privacy is important to Sunil. I read 'hide away.' And that is fine by me, we are a perfect combo, always hiding, but together. I want it to stay like this, I want this desperately, I have never felt this connection with anyone before. Sunil my sexy soulmate, I call him when I'm feeling passionate.

I remember times when I would look at Indian couples on the street or in the supermarket. They would look so absorbed in each other, so bonded for life. Even the mundanities of shopping seemed like an opportunity for close contact: they held hands, patted each other on the shoulder, wiped smears of fast food from each other's faces with their bare hands. I once saw a woman lick remnants of sauce from around her man's mouth as she seemed to be out of tissues. That nesting instinct…I was jealous of them. I coveted that feeling of safety. I was sick of the constant ache of isolation and hollowness which stemmed from being in a strange country surrounded by desperate people. There were no South Africans in London, maybe some Whites but no Blacks, how would a Black person come here? I'd heard of Black political activists hiding in London but where? I never met them or heard about them. Madiba had been released from jail and everything seemed to be changing for the better in South Africa, but I still couldn't go back.

No, I'd never be welcomed there again. They probably had people in passport control looking out for me at the airport.

Whores are not allowed to enter the country, sorry.

So, I was effectively trapped in the cultural vacuum that was London. Sure, there were art galleries, museums and theatres but they were interesting to other people. I longed for my African culture, African food, African music, African dancing.

'Don't be like the others,' Mrs Dlamini, my English teacher, used to drum into me when I stayed behind after school to help her with her display boards, 'Do something with your life, you're an *exceptional* child. A bright star in a sea of darkness. Step into your Light!' I had a lot of respect for Miss. It was she who had instilled in me a passion for English Literature.

Well, I was miraculously in London. Who would have thought it? And that's because I got lucky in a twisted way, I got out through the back door. Again, the devil and the deep blue sea. When I left to gain my freedom, I left my people and my child behind. But I'm not a masochist, I don't feel that pain, I just move on, let it all wash over me.

When I first started teaching I became friends with this young Indian teacher who interned with me. I would joke with Pawan, suggesting that he hooked me up with an Indian doctor to marry. The reasons that I'd cited were class, commitment, intelligence, money, status, food … Oh and those sexy sarees that could be ripped off baring naked flesh underneath. Pawan got serious much to my amusement.

'I need to know your background dear,' he said over a coffee in the English department, 'so that I can create a profile for you, market you so to speak. Prospective grooms will need that information, they won't want to marry just anyone. What's your family history?'

What's yours, darling, gay Pawan. Do they know how you came out as soon as you hit London?

'Matrimonial issues are complicated in India,' he said with a camp flounce. 'There are preparations beforehand, arrangements. We talk dowries, sarees, bridal packages…'

'I'm a Black woman, what are my chances?'

'Well….it will be difficult, really difficult. Maybe a doctor who lost his wife, or who got divorced and lost everything. Maybe in desperation for company and sex. You do know that we have a caste system? You would almost be categorised as an untouchable.'

'Really? Why?' Some people don't realise how offensive language can be. How language can impact mindset. Why would anyone want to tolerate that cruel term, 'untouchable?'

'You know what trading up and down means don't you?' he smiled uncomfortably, 'in your case it would be like trading down. Your skin colour coupled with a lack of history and family. You would not be a bonus ball or a jackpot. Rather a last resort so to speak.'

Thanks, Pawan. I was fine. I was not into Indian doctors anymore. There seemed to be far too many hurdles to jump if I wanted to go down the doctor route. In any case, said the cynic in me, I'd love to see who Pawan ended up with, he'd probably settle for a pretty, White, professional woman and then do his back- door bits on the side. Then, after a few unhappy years pretending, he would tweak this ratio, come out openly (or more openly), as a gay man but still do his duty by visiting his kids. That way he'd have everything. Biological, fair skinned children, an ex, a gay partner.

I'd seen too much in London, the Great Rainbow Nation. My head has been stuffed with noise.

The next day he'd returned to the topic in the staffroom, this time over complimentary tea and pork pies, someone was celebrating a birthday. 'You have a UK passport?' he asked, his eyes twinkling mischievously, 'maybe we can do something based on that! It's quite an attractive feature. Do you want me to put out some feelers? Lots of Indians want to come to the UK without the hassle of work visa applications.'

I'd heard him say once that he was not allowed to eat beef or pork, yet here he was cramming jellied pig in suet pastry cases into his mouth. The layers and lies in people's lives. Freud would be like, 'told you!' wagging his finger gravely and nodding his head with a smug smile.

That had been a few years ago, now I had my Indian estate agent and I could stop looking for my Indian doctor. I was content. And he went beyond the others, inviting me to move into his flat very soon after we met. Keeper!

CHAPTER 10: MIMI

LONDON 2008

I've put up with bullying here for so long, I've lost count of how many incidents there have been. All over the school, we have Anti Bullying posters plastered on walls, doors, classroom notice boards. Yet staff bully each other every day and there is nobody to turn to.

I've been Head of the English department for five years, it's been a difficult ascent to the top, but I did it. I've gone on training courses, upgraded my skills, built a team, instilled competence in that team and been a positive role model. I've only had a few days off in the five years, I even go in on weekends. Yet what do I have to show for it? A teacher who worked at the school previously has only just returned to our team after doing a stint in the Middle East, she's been fortunate as the Headteacher has kept her job 'open' for her. Wow, what a perk! Note, I don't call it White privilege. Just a perk. I'm trying to stay away from the old racism discourse. You'd think that she was this hotshot, outstanding teacher who was able to secure the very best results, like someone who could support a student to go from a D to an A grade in a year. No! Mimi does very little. She ponces around the school gossiping mostly, she hardly attends my meetings, and she does not allow herself to be micromanaged by me the way I'm expected to with all the rest of my team. I am her team leader after all. But the headteacher's 'golden girl' has immunity. This allows her the licence to be the uber bitch and I can't take any more.

I'd established a tradition of taking cakes in every Friday, it was meant to be a treat from me to my team. Sometimes, I baked them myself, sometimes I bought them. Usually the team would descend on them hungrily, (have you seen teachers attack free food?) But on the first Friday with Mimi around, I heard her say tartly, 'Ooh type two diabetes food. Come on all, let's head down to the salad bar, I'm treating you!' Of course, they followed her, like sheep, the carrot cake that I'd stayed up baking much to Sunil's annoyance, sat untouched and unloved. He hates it when he doesn't have me all to himself of an evening. Even when he watches boring sports, he likes me to curl up with him, with a drink. He says that we spend the whole day apart, the evenings are for bonding. But as an English teacher how can I promise this? Marking takes over my life! Then there are reports, and endless form filling. I'm absolutely out of it in the evenings, on the nights when I hit the gym, I'm literally wiped out. Sex is something that I just acquiesce to nowadays, I lie prostrate and let Sunil do whatever he likes to me. I hate being called a sack of potatoes in bed but to be honest that's what I feel like sometimes. On weekends and holidays its different.

So, they rejected my cake that I compromised my relationship by baking.

The next Monday, I wear a fitted, red pencil skirt that comes down to just above my knee, a cream chiffon blouse and black high heeled sandals. I think that I look suitably smart, lots of staff compliment me as I walk in. But not Mimi. I have my back to her in the office as I am busy photocopying, there are only a few of the others in the room.

'My you're a bit of a sex siren, aren't you?' she says, eyes skimming all over my body, 'that skirt just screams out sex.' She stands there in her loose cotton dress that looks like a tent. Is she wearing her curtains? She's make-up free and bites her nails so short that her fingers are just pads of flesh with random bits of nail attached. With her thick glasses and thin lips, it's no wonder that her husband left her. She rants and raves about any self- respecting, well dressed woman with a good figure. Next time, I'll bring a saucer of milk, I make a mental note. Catty and oozing jealousy.

'It wasn't my intention,' I say tartly, 'I think it's very smart.'

Just because she's huge, freckled like black pepper on feta cheese, and clumsy, doesn't mean we're all not allowed to wear fitted clothes. I mean she literally ambles about, I call her 'elephant,' in my head. But then even elephants have that 'je ne sais quoi' quality and I love their unique emotional literacy that they're gifted with. She's just plain nasty.

'You know, when male students say that they can't focus on their work cos their teacher makes them get horny every time she turns to write on the board, we can't blame them, can we? And when that teacher is a head of a major department, well, what can I say?'

Silence. Everyone puts their heads down pretending they're busy. You can cut the atmosphere with a knife.

'I think you should go home and change. I really do. That will show that you're willing to take positive feedback on board.'

'You've got some nerve talking to me like that,' I retort, my back up now. 'How dare you? That's not a professional approach. Besides, I'm your manager, have some respect!' Insubordination. I'll get her for that.

'Ooh attitude!' she's loving the negative attention of this. 'How come *all* you Black women have it? You flip from one to ten in a heartbeat. Insolence is a sign of bad manners did you know that? Why do you have a chip on your shoulder? You must all be hardwired to be like that! It's all that meat that you eat.'

'I don't believe what I'm hearing! Racism *and* insubordination! I'm going to have to speak to the headteacher about this. You love your little stereotypes don't you!' I'm fuming!

i was broken, now I Am

'Pete? Please go ahead. He's my brother in law. I've already mentioned a few concerns about *you* over dinner last night. Our family's very close, we get together every couple of nights. And recently, we're talking a lot about *you*.'

The penny drops. There's an elephant in the room. I'm the only Black member of staff in the school. Well a few cleaners and admin staff are Black, but not one person in a higher position. Why? I had wondered. Imagine the trouble I'd be in if *I* said something back, like the fact that she was a fat pig and a bully at that? I'd be out on the streets with my P45 in my hand. Racism is ingrained into systems and structures here, I was a fool to think that I had left it all behind in South Africa.

White privilege. It's everywhere.

But I'm *not* letting her break me, I have worked too hard for this. I walk out knowing that she's turned everyone against me.

Every day is the same. She walks in with the headteacher now, they share a car. And that stupid, jubilant smile on her fat face! It's a triumphant smile, she's scored one up on me now. I haven't done anything wrong, just worked hard and kept my head down, but no, it's not enough sometimes. Was she jealous? A few times, she's said in meetings that if I can't do the job, she's happy to step in. Step in? She can't do her basic job! I've done lesson observations and found her lessons wanting. She's not interactive enough and the kids sit there like zombies, not learning anything. But Pete, the head, won't let me reflect this on the form.

'Keep the peace please!' He warns, glaring. 'I know she can be a handful but it's down to your professional skills to manage the situation. Otherwise it will reflect badly on you. What support are you providing? Maybe it's not good enough!'

'Pete, I *don't* want her on my team!' I say crossly.

'Well, it's *my* school and *I* make that judgement call!' he says and walks off.

You mean she's your sister- in- law and you have a soft spot for her. Nepotism. Don't think it just happens in the third world. Oh, it's everywhere, it's just that some get away with it. I don't want to make it a race thing, I don't. I think that they're just waiting for me to scream racism just so that they can say, 'Oh no, not the race card again! Not that old chestnut about White privilege as soon there is any sign of competition.'

But let's face it, if I were White this wouldn't be happening. It's not happening to others on the team, they're all White. Why me? I don't have a history with this person, I never met her in my life. I can't bear it. Nowadays, I can't sleep, can't concentrate, it's eroding my life. I have tried to talk to Sunil about it, but he holds his hands up rudely.

'Babe, no offence but I don't have the time or energy for these rants. When you asked me to come to bookshops, I reluctantly went along to please you. When you asked me to meet your colleagues over dinner, again I said okay when, to be quite honest, I was knackered and wasn't in the mood for teacher speak. But this is an everyday thing and I don't want to hear it. Okay? Go ask her to fuck herself or something, I don't care. I just want my sexy girlfriend back. Can we have proper, sociable evenings and normal sex now please?'

What do you say to that?

We had a bring and share in the department the other day. I bought into their new healthy eating agenda and made a huge salad, cost me a bloody fortune getting all the bits from an organic deli but never mind. As I was rushing to the office, the head saw me and beckoned me over.

'How are things now? Settled down?'

'Not really, I'd like to schedule a meeting with you,' I say, surprised that I had started to tremble. 'I'd like to know what my rights are. I mean when someone is steadily chipping away at you, daily, trying to undermine you in every way, even picking on your race.' I'm tearing.

'Listen Bonnie!' his sharp tone frightens me, 'there's no one like that at my school. And if there were, they wouldn't be working here, do you hear me? I hate trouble causers, rabble rousers. That's why I employ highly professional people who don't rock the boat. We have enough on our plates just getting these youngsters an education, do you hear me? Or are you saying that it was a mistake to promote you?'

We were at the top of a stairwell and there was nobody present, I wished that someone could overhear this. Or maybe they did but would pretend like it hadn't happened. What was happening to me? I had begun to unravel. I thought about the days pre- Mimi and how I used to love going into school. I walked into the office both shaken and stirred. The party was in full swing, why had they started without me?

'Have you tried the salad?' I asked retrieving it from the fridge.

'Is it bought or home -made?' piped up Mimi who had established herself firmly as the centre of attention by offering sugared doughnuts to the eager takers. I thought they'd gone off cake!

'Home made,' I said. 'I made a lovely vinaigrette to go with it.'

'Eew in that case no thanks,' she said.' It's not very sanitary, we don't know how many times you rinsed the veggies and so on. Some of us are very cautious about these things you should know that.'

'Anyone?' I ignored her. I'd brought plastic forks and paper plates.

A murmur of no thanks goes around the table. Okay, I will eat it myself. No one wants to talk to me. She sits with her chair angled to exclude me, talking softly to the team so that I can't hear. She is regaling them with tales from her time in the Middle East. A tear trickles down my cheek mid forkful of salad. No one says anything. I want to run out, climb into my car and drive home, never to have to go back. I dump the salad in the bin and everyone notices.

Next chapter.

I call my teacher's union. I had been paying into the service for fifteen years.

When the preliminaries are over we discuss the case.

I'm being bullied. There have been race related comments thrown at me. I feel ill just thinking of work.

Do you have proof of this?

Well it's a member of staff with nasty, verbal digs at me.

So, no proof. Sigh. Have you discussed it with your line manager?

My line manager is the headteacher. She's his sister-in- law. He's not supporting me, he's supporting her.

So, you're officially telling me that your headteacher is not taking a complaint of a racist allegation seriously? Why do you think this is the case?

I just told you, she's his sister- in- law.

Could it be that it's NOT racism? Could it be that you imagined that it was? You have no witnesses, no proof.

What? That is ridiculous! Can you help me or not?

Are you getting angry? Would you like us to continue this at another time Miss Err?

Well, after waiting on the phone for twenty minutes, no I don't want to come back to this, I need support, answers.

Well, I choose not to continue this Miss Err, we are not punching bags and I will not be on the end of a line of someone just venting and shouting non-stop. We are also bound by codes of conduct and...

I hang up and lie down. I'm done.

There's a meeting for all heads of department on Monday after school. It's a strategy meeting to discuss our planning for an upcoming visit from government inspectors. As I get there, I sense an awkwardness or is it just me again? I'm second guessing myself at every turn, my confidence is at an all-time low. And then I see why. Mimi is at the meeting.

'Oh, I didn't think you're coming,' She says to me, 'I was going to help you out and attend in lieu of you.' She socialises regularly with people from the meeting.

'Why wouldn't I come? I'm confused, I'm Head of English right?' Coolly, I take a seat.

'No need to turn aggressive. Again! I just thought I overheard that you were tired or wiped out by all the marking, I'm sure I heard that. You're always complaining about the school eating into your relationship. I thought I'd give you the chance to go home early and rest.'

'Wow, you're lucky,' the Head of Maths turned to me, 'you have proper team spirit in your department.' The deputy head chairing the meeting wanted to start.

'Sorry, I'll go.' Mimi.

'No don't *you* go! You've always got some valuable insights to share, particularly from your last experience of an inspection. We need and value your expertise,' says the deputy.

'Value, that's nice,' says Mimi, 'it's not often that one feels that in the school anymore. I've come back from the Middle East and I feel like a stranger in my own school. I'm happy to share any tips, I'm happy to help in any shape or form actually.'

'Thank you, dear Mimi, we really appreciate you!' someone else pipes up.

I want to be sick. Have I missed something here? A halo perhaps? I'm supposed to be professional and strong but how can I get past this? It's sickening how they all collude against me. She talks all throughout the meeting, strategically sticking her oar in every time we talk about school improvements, she has a long list about how the English department can improve, I'm sure she left one out. Replace me with bloody her. I'm floundering. With no one to talk to, no one to turn to, it feels like an impossible job to do.

Why aren't there more independent, impartial structures to prevent workplace bullying, I ask myself. In management meetings, we spoke with hostility about colleagues who had taken months off on stress leave, they were drawing a salary yet were taking chunks of time off. Also, we were struggling to recruit good teachers, this was the pattern all over the UK. Schools were participating in costly recruitment drives simply to attract good staff. But I knew why teachers did not flock to the profession or took time off. It wasn't just about pay, workload, kids' behaviour. Poor management often ignored the needs of bottom feeders like ordinary teachers. Those who had been bullied by others in their teams never got to disclose or report this. Our management team was full of old, White people with a distinctly top down approach. They had a hit list of staff who they considered were suboptimal: Tina, a lesbian in the Art dept was there, Tim, a single parent who took time off for his sick son's medical appointments was there. In fact, I was pretty sure that anyone who deviated from the so-called norm was there: staff with tattoos, anyone from the LGBT plus community, anyone with a life- threatening disease like Suzy who had cancer, staff whose English was not as fluent as they wanted. And of course, I was on it. I was Black, unmarried and co-habiting with my partner. I wasn't an ordinary teacher anymore, but I was still treated like I was. As a Black person, maybe it would always be this way, even here in 'Rainbow Nation' UK, I thought bitterly. And to think of all the extra time I'd put in, all those unnoticed hours. For what? I would never ever be good enough. I'd compromised my sanity, my relationship and my social life for this job. And now, I wondered whether it had all been worth it.

Keep your friends close but keep your enemies closer. After the meeting, I saw Mimi in the car park. I praised her for her useful ideas and asked if she wanted to go for a drink. But she scoffed at my proffered olive branch.

'Sorry,' she was as cold as ice. 'I'm very fussy who I drink with. Besides I have a son with ADHD who needs me.' At that, she sped off.

I am trying meditation. It's the only thing I can try to calm myself down and save my relationship. I sit in the lotus position and focus on an imaginary candle, I have lit incense and am playing the mantra 'Om' on autorepeat. Thoughts about Mimi dominate my mind, then I picture myself at work. I'm tip toeing around in the corridors, my shoulders hunched, my eyes cast down. I'm a picture of gloom. I feel like I've aged recently. Funny how I start thinking about the township where I was born and unexpectedly, I start to cry. Warmth, human warmth and support. That's what I had there. And empathy. Sure, life was tough there, I didn't have a fraction of what I had now: Wi-Fi, smartphones, computers, smart clothes, my own property that I rented out, top notch food, an executive boyfriend. Yet I was so happy there. If Ma had not asked me to come to the city, where would I be now? I could have been happy with Themba and the rest of my tribe.

I'd heard about positive changes in South Africa under the new Black government, things have improved for my people there. And if they didn't then at least we had each other. Even criminals would band together with us, if push came to shove. But here, in so called democratic UK, people were nasty. They were shockingly in your face when they discriminated against you, I'd heard people make no attempt to conceal their dislike of Black people on the buses and trains, the 'n' word, something that I had never ever heard in South Africa was used here, 'monkey,' too. Alarmingly, I'd also heard of 'poor White trash' and 'chav' to indicate a White working- class person. Why had I not heard these terms in the circles that I lived in, in South Africa? Maybe we were so attuned to the notion of race that we would consciously pussy foot around the harsh, derogatory nicknames and slurs. I felt short changed, disappointed that I'd chosen this country as my home.

A Nigerian man befriended me when I took the bus into town on the weekend sometimes, he must live near me as I always saw him at the bus stop. I loved taking buses, it gave me a chance to mingle with the public and to glimpse the reassuring routines of everyday life. I needed that after the stresses of school and the yawning gap between Sunil and myself. Mothers, babies, pensioners. They were all there.

I asked Michael, the Nigerian man what he thought of the UK, over a cappuccino at Costas.

'They treat us like shit here,' he said. 'Xenophobia is everywhere. I've been called the 'n' word too many times here. Sometimes, I want to fight them, other times I let it slide. I'm getting too old and too tired for conflict.' He smiles, showing pearly White teeth.

'So why are you here?' I know I'm being provocative, after all, he could ask me the same question.

'Aaah Sister, it's the million- dollar question,' he sighs. 'Really, I should have gone to Canada with my brother. He's happy there, feels welcome.'

'But surely here you can approach your local government, your MP,' I say, struggling to find a solution. 'Surely as a tax payer, they have a duty to make sure that you are safe.'

'It's all lip service,' he says smiling now. 'As soon as you complain or ask for answers, they see you as a

rabble rouser. I told you, I'm a lover not a fighter.
What we need to do is: Keep calm and carry on!'

Our joint laughter cut the tension that day.

I wanted to leave work. Enviously I stared at the
barista making the coffees. She seemed so content, just
going about her business doing her own thing. Why
couldn't I have that? Even if I took a pay cut, wasn't
that worth it for peace of mind? But another side of me
firmly said no. I was a brilliant teacher. I'd worked and
studied so hard to be where I was, nothing was going
to deter me en route to senior management. The haters
could continue to try to yap away at my heels, but they
wouldn't bring me down. Not when my wings were
poised for flight. Eagles don't mix with sparrows, I
once heard someone say at a motivational conference. I
needed to get away from sparrows.

I applied for jobs elsewhere and quickly got
snapped up by a rival school. They too had been slated
in the press for not demonstrating diversity as all their
staff were White as well. They wanted to address this
by hiring me and a few other key staff. I never got the
warm send off from my old school, no, I was not beige
enough for that. Of course, they slotted Mimi in
immediately as my replacement, in fact they had her
installed even before I left, I doubt she even had an

interview. She'd moved me out of my office a week before my departure, placed all my possessions in a black bin bag and left it near the bin. If it hadn't been for the kind cleaner who had looked inside, I would never have been able to retrieve my books.

'God says love thine enemies,' Michael says over a hot chocolate. 'You should have bought them all gifts to say thank you. Wasn't it Mimi who inadvertently catapulted you to a new position?'

Really, sometimes Michael with his happy-clappy approach took things to ridiculous heights.

As usual, I worked like mad and within two years, I was deputy head.

CHAPTER 11: BIRTHDAY BLUES

Where are you, Little One?

I'm here Ma, still here. But I'm old now. I turned forty-five yesterday. I celebrated with no one.

Hush little baby, don't you cry,
Granma loves you and so do I.

They say that time flies when you're having fun. Define 'fun'. I've learned that it means different things to different people. I celebrated my birthday miserable and alone the night before. As I sat in the Headteacher's oak panelled office on his dark Chesterfield, nursing a raging hangover and coming down off a little pill that gave me relief a few hours back, I tried desperately to appear composed. I mused that I was in the middle of a new decade of my life and I had never felt more fragile. Basically, I felt like shit. Why had I come in? I could have been at home, sleeping or sitting on the balcony with a big glass of cold water with a side of paracetamols and codeine. Teachers and the guilt trips that schools put on us. If we're away it incurs cover, someone who *has* bothered to make an appearance now has to give up that precious free period to cover a lesson for someone who is usually the worse for wear at home, after partying and having no self-respect the night before. Well that's how we're made to feel. That moral high ground thing again. Not that I teach many lessons now that I finally made Deputy Head. Still, I keep my hand in and teach the odd English lesson to seniors, it looks good to management, makes me seem more committed to my students than I really am. I'm worn out.

Since I met him sixteen years ago, I'd celebrated every birthday with Sunil and most times, Seema would be there too. I'd felt safe, this was my family now. Colleagues would ask, 'Are you off somewhere special tonight?'

I'd wanted them to ask this, even encouraged it, because I wanted to shout it out to the rooftops about how blessed I was, how pampered, how much of the Queen, the Goddess.

I was safe!

'My man has planned a weekend away,' I'd say triumphantly. Or, 'he's booked at that new fancy restaurant that's just opened in central.' Or, 'he's flying me to Paris for the evening!' Technically, it was the pilot of the cheap low- cost airline who would be flying us. But my man has paid for it so that, in my book justifies the phrase 'my man is flying me to Paris!' This always got the administrative staff in a flutter resulting in 'oohs', 'wows,' and 'lucky you!' Once a colleague asked tentatively, 'so is your man your colour?'

She meant: Why don't you Black girls like to go out with your own kind? And stop taking our sons?

Interracial relationships were all over London. Almost every Black person was accompanied by a person of another nationality. Again, another dialogue that I would have loved to have with Sunil, but here in diverse London, liberal politics muzzled us and silenced debate. There were so many unspoken, untackled issues hanging in the air, unresolved. We were meant to tactically avoid discussing certain truths. But why, in the great so- called democracy of the UK? It ate away at me, made my therapist unhappy.

'It needs out,' she'd say sternly, 'stop pushing things under the carpet.'

'Me???' Oh of course, it was all me. Most times, I would lie on her zebra striped chaise longue, playing with my fancy, long, metallic nails. The mute approach works for me. She doesn't really give a monkeys, she still gets paid.

Back in the day, there was always something special for me on my birthday. Even the fall back was a seven - star affair, an invite to Seema's restaurant which was at one end of her shop. With the blinds pulled down, the lit candles twinkling in the dark and the scent of sandalwood and rose wafting from the incense, we'd sit sipping champagne cocktails and feasting on her gourmet food which she would create just for me. Every dish on her menu would be characterised by her love of super healthy, fresh food in season. Sunil would feed me the little triangles of vegetables encased in the lightest of pastries, I would offer him the tiny balls of fish and crab dotted with chillies and dipped in lime juice. She even managed to make the mains into cute, fun sized parcels, almost playfully serving them on beds of various sauces and salads. Her signature dish was kulfi, the luxurious Indian ice cream flavoured with fruits or nuts, I always opted for the intense infusion of mango and coconut. Seema had been hailed in the local press as a chef who had 'revolutionised the Indian culinary experience,' her modest health food shop was now a Wellness Centre with a bustling restaurant attached, someone was even holding yoga classes in the offices above, which she had taken over now.

But where was Seema now? What had Sunil shared with her to have caused her to have grown so distant and aloof? I'd stopped at her shop many times over the last few months to try to rekindle that family connection. As a non- Indian, she had very reluctantly accepted me into the family fold and I had loved her instantly as a sister. She'd dressed me in sarees, taught me to appreciate a chai masala strongly brewed, and treated me to several cooking demonstrations. On a giggly girls' night out, she'd shared Kama Sutra tips. But something had happened, and she had turned her back on me, refusing even to meet my eyes when I visited the shop on the pretext of picking up spices. I'd stood there stupidly staring at her lithe body with her deft movements, her silky hair, coiled away from her beautiful face, which invariably uncoiled itself and snaked down to her perfect bottom…I'd always drooled over her, she seemed like the perfect woman who never aged. Sometimes I'd even wondered if I'd turn for a woman like her, but I quickly banished the thought. Seema had stopped being hospitable towards me. She had stiffened when she saw me at the shop the last time, and then darted out to the back. Charming! Clearly, I had passed my expiration date.

I'm a mess. There's no one to talk to, no one to listen. There's just noise in my head.

Barry, the headmaster, had a thick wedding band that gleamed shiny and gold every time he gestured during meetings. The photo of him, his blonde wife and their three kids looking weather beaten on a camping trip, sat proudly on his desk encased in a vintage gold frame, there were separate portraits as well. Each child had the iconic blonde hair and blue eyes that seemed to run in his family, they were all slim and poised unlike their heavy-set father with his swollen fingers that reminded me of something unpleasant in the past. Barry made me feel unsafe, I had no idea why. Queasy even. I hate hypocrites. Despite the trappings of contentment and marital bliss, he was doing the new, young PE teacher, Dee. We all knew this because she was always around just before lunch checking to see if he was free to step out for a 'bite to eat'. I was pretty sure it was not food she was after but why would she choose a man with a physique like Barry? She was so hot she could get anyone for herself, she didn't need a fat, bald man with a protruding belly and broken thread veins on his face. Maybe it was something about extra pay or the promise of a promotion.

I couldn't do it, not with Barry. All the staff gossiped about it constantly, sniggering as they walked by together, pretending to be in earnest conversation about improvements to the PE Department. Barry, of course, was oblivious to this or careless. With his usual bullish manner, he just seemed to steamroller his way through life, not looking right or left, just forward, the thinking with his dick and not engaging his brain mentality. One phone call to his wife and his house of cards would come crumbling down. As his deputy I believed that I had to support, even cover for him, but the blatant display of his unrestrained behaviour was unconscionable. I made a mental note to call his wife.

i was broken, now I Am

I felt rough that day, I should have taken the day off.

We had just finished a meeting about raising standards, another one. I was bored shitless, and she was there, in his office, helping herself to the remaining sandwiches and shards of iceberg lettuce that we were too polite to polish off. She gestured with her head towards the door signalling to him that she was ready to step out and I felt incensed as I knew what was coming.

Don't play me for a fool Barry! Don't joke with the joker! To think that I came in for this!

'Miss...' he said with a cheeky lilt in his voice. I ignored him, pretending to collect my files. Would you lie for me again?

'Err Bonnie.?' His voice was low but urgent, he sounded annoyed with me, it must have been his raging hard on prompting this. Dee was walking around the office giving him a view of her perfectly toned behind or perfectly pert front. I have always campaigned against PE staff wearing Lycra, but I have always been outvoted by male management or lesbians on the staff, who never saw those things as an issue. I was forced to look at him.

'I...we're just popping out for a few minutes. Hold the fort, will you?' This with that conspiratorial wink that was just not cheeky anymore, it was disgusting. I resented being part of his charade.

Sure, I'll just call your wife, maybe she can keep me company.

It was my fucking lunch break too. I seethed inwardly while smiling graciously on the outside. A few months into the job and what was I? A glorified holder of the fort. A keeper of secrets. I'd waited so long for the promotion, I'd studied and stood by patiently. For what? The work, mind numbing as it was, just kept accumulating, most of it was his! Of course, he was otherwise occupied and never seemed to do anything properly. Yet he got away with it!

I had thought that being Deputy Head meant that you stopped taking crap, no such luck. My life had descended into a nudge nudge wink wink affair, you scratch my back, I may scratch yours sometime.

Fuck you Barry!

'No problem! Have fun!' I said breezily resisting the urge to glance at his erection. I was such a cynic.

I needed time to myself in any case, time to think and process what happened the night before. I waited for him to leave then marched into my office and kicked the door shut sliding the 'DO NOT DISTURB, MEETING IN PROCESS' sign into place. Fuck it, who cared?

It was not every day that you split up after a sixteen-year relationship, on your forty fifth birthday. I was still in shock, the alcohol numbing the pain somewhat, but the pain was still there.

He had walked in unexpectedly early from his so called 'golf trip with the boys.' These trips had been happening almost every single weekend and I had stopped caring. I had to develop this thick skin, I could hardly sit there every night crying for what I had lost. The downhill had happened gradually, not overnight. When we'd first met, he'd insisted on commitment. 'Fuck friends!' he'd said bitterly, 'I've had enough of them to last a lifetime! It's a good woman like you that I'm after now, need to settle down and that kind of thing.' I'd felt myself buzzing with the attention, so much so that slowly, I'd allowed him to erode my own social life and at the end, I had no one. He'd whisk me off in the evenings and weekends, he booked time off on my school holidays so that we could go travelling together. It was so perfect that I hadn't needed anyone to confide in.

But over time, the very thing that he had rejected, was what he had started to crave. 'Me time'. Trips away with 'the lads'. Team building sessions with the office staff that took him away for days on end. Then, work projects: opening branches in other towns, acquiring new properties for his portfolio. Nothing was about us anymore. When I complained, he justified it by saying that it made his time with me more special, added more quality to the relationship. How could I argue with that?

It was supposed to be us against the world baby! Where did that go?

One day, when the suffering became intense and he could sense that I was becoming withdrawn and moody, he grabbed me in his bear embrace and suggested a fun trip to Florence during my half term. A whole week of Sunil to myself! It had seemed so romantic and special that for the few days building up to the trip we had rekindled our passion again. Then, when I saw with my own eyes what he had really descended into, the scales were lifted, and I grew up overnight.

Florence is warm in May. In the golden embrace of those sun- drenched days, I wore skimpy shorts and tight, halter tops, my bra-lessness causing a flutter with waiters and men in general. 'Bellissimo!' they would shout as they walked by. I felt beautiful too, my gym membership finally paying off as I admired my own toned but curvy body in the hotel mirror. The only person who remained quiet on the subject was Sunil.

In fact, you were otherwise occupied, my love. Eye raping those Italian women!

We'd sit sipping beer or wine on the pavement cafes outside and he would stare at *every* woman passing by, his eyes boring holes into them not just undressing them. Often, he would look them up and down and then back up again, sometimes they would lock eyes and there'd be a playful, flirty smile. I half expected him to jump up and request their phone numbers. And the irony of the situation, the absurdity of it all was that men looked at me! So here we were, on a romantic getaway in the city of culture, but there was nothing remotely romantic about it as his eyes were reserved for other women and I was making eyes at other men!

How pointless to have gone away together!

It took me a long while to process this and each time I tried to defend him I just felt more and more outraged. I could have killed him right there. Stabbed him through the heart with my fork. Or used a sharp steak knife to drill through the soft tissue of his brain. The fool! How he had used me. Led me to believe all that crap about commitment and monogamy. This, this was what he had been about all along.

I had to do something. So, I switched.

Don't joke with the joker. Don't fuck with me Sunil. You want to play? Let's roll that dice. I'm ready now. I see you and I'm ready. I wasn't ready all those years ago when he raped me. But boy, I'm so ready now!

So that holiday, I started to create my own diversions and amusements. Meeting men for sex in Florence, no, anywhere in the world, is 'piss easy.' You have a range of options from personals in the small ads, to internet dating. You can advertise yourself as someone seeking fun, intimacy or just pure pleasure, depending on how dirty you felt. Once, I advertised myself as a 'good ride' and I got about four thousand hits in a few hours, many from professionals such as doctors and dentists. Many of them were married men on the lookout for a saucy diversion. Alternatively, if you want to pick up someone quickly in an un-virtual way, you go to a pub wearing suggestive clothing, short skirt, tight top, fuck me heels, red lippie, it's pretty much in the bag. Just stand at the bar smiling at anyone and everyone blandly like those blow up dolls…men love that vacant look! Nurse your glass of wine or shot of whiskey but do not, repeat, do not pay for more than one drink, that's their bit coming in. (In fact, if you do have to fork out for more drinks it's a sign that you have failed to conquer the territory. Just go home love!) If you heed my advice, half the men there will be clamouring to explore your nether regions. I can't remember exactly how many paramours I have had but there were quite a few, I think they run into hundreds. That's just during my relationship with Sunil. Game set and match.

I started with the waiters who had been ogling me non-stop, some trembled just to serve me. A young hottie kept tempting me with various desserts from the cake stand all of which I refused, preferring instead to push a slip of paper with my hotel name and room number into his shirt pocket. I had not challenged Sunil or given him the silent treatment. I didn't want the full scale what are you talking about woman? What's going through your head, scenario of denial. I was passed that, I had seen more than enough. If he could eye rape other women right in front of me, I could just imagine how much fun he was having when I was *not* there!

No baby. Let's just roll that dice, I'm tired.

So, I encouraged him graciously to go for that afternoon stroll on his own, I had a headache, a migraine really and I needed the darkness of the hotel room. He was welcome to step out after breakfast alone every day really, I knew how much he appreciated art, no sculpture wasn't my thing, he was free to explore. He could check out the 'David' statue all day and all night, he could stroke it or do whatever he wanted to it. A red mist had come over me remembering his beady eyes all over the other women. I morphed into passive aggressive mode, speaking to him not through gritted teeth but with a smile and a reassuring promise of a sexy night later. I would take the time to catch up on my reading, that way both of us could use our time productively. He had accepted these offers willingly, too willingly in fact, the cunning swine! Of course, he set off diligently every morning, like a dog on heat. And, true to my gender's track record of dealing with scornful men, I did the waiter, a good few times, fresh young buck he was, and then I proceeded to meet other willing participants.

Then, it became addictive, especially after we returned to London. I had to have a lover every weekend, it just kept the loneliness at bay. Time passed quickly that way. Sometimes it was a rewarding experience which left me feeling vindicated.

'This one's for you Sunil,' I'd whisper each time. But sometimes I drew the short straw, like the bloke with the super tiny penis who kept trying to push his balls *and* penis into my mouth to be sucked at the same time. After what seemed like hours, he allowed me to come up for air, at which point I made a dive into the shower and emerged saying that I felt ill. I knew how to kill the buzz.

Before my birthday, Sunil announced that he would be going away for a few days on that golf trip, on my special day. Who plays golf on his girlfriend's birthday? Did he think I was stupid? The insensitive bastard! It was Sunday, I got out my little black book and picked up my phone. I called a cute, young guy, some kid who had chatted me up in the supermarket a few days before, probably turned on by my butt in its sheath of tightly fitted skirt as I navigated my way around pushing a trolley. I know how to work it.

Within minutes we had exchanged numbers and there we were setting up a meeting on my bloody birthday. Downing tequila, in the throes of getting ready, I felt excitement and arousal in equal parts, all thoughts of Sunil had vanished. Half a day it had taken me to get ready, thankfully it was a Sunday otherwise I would not have been able to deliver my usual high standards.

There was the hair mask that I had to use prior to washing my weave which was now shoulder length and jet black, then depilating the unwanted hair from certain key areas of my body. I liked to do it in front of the mirror pre-shower, that way I could be careful and thorough. Next a walnut and apricot kernel face exfoliator to slough off the dead skin to get that glow. No one understands how much us women prep for these events, only us. After the shower which took ages, it was a case of drying myself and my hair, brushing my teeth and tongue, (I don't like smelly breath), moisturise my face and neck, perfume my body generously including those naughty bits, a bit of make-up: smoky eyes, highlights on cheeks, lip gloss. Last, nail polish, they love them long and red. We had only been together twice so far, but I knew his type. He loved me to claw his back, made him feel like he'd been with a black panther type, a wild woman. His very own cougar. He would probably take his shirt off in front of his flatmate nonchalantly...show off those tiger stripes proudly to say, 'Look at me, I'm sexually active.' Young guys and their eagerness to show off! Especially about sexual paramours.

Then the clothes. I had pre-selected them carefully, a silk short sleeved dress in paprika red with a wrap over frontage, an old birthday present from Sunil. Easy to get into and out of... he would find that sexy. And the pleasure of him fingering the soft fabric, his coarse landscape gardening fingers calloused and ripped by thorns, negotiating the opening of the dress, the ties, the buttons.

This one's for you Sunil. Wherever you are, whoever you're doing...this one really is for you.

That is always my constant mantra every time I did it. Stiletto heels and more perfume finished the preparations. Then he arrived. There was the usual greeting, the offer of wine but he had refused. His eyes had looked a tad glassy, was he high? I wanted some of what he was on, but the selfish pig had pretended to have run out. No matter, I had gulped down several glasses of Sunil's prize South African Shiraz and downed a few whiskeys too for good measure, so I was ready. In no time, we were on the bed, Sunil's and my bed not *her* bed, doing it. Doggy, he had asked for, they always do when they see my behind. Or anal of course. Gripping my tiny waist and large buttock cheeks, he shuddered into orgasm less than three minutes into the session, much to my disgust. Last time it had been longer.

'Sorry babes,' he sighed,' I was horny. 'His dick had shrunk by now and the condom had come off.

'It's okay darling,' I said, 'we can always have round two, can't we?' I snuggled up to him and cuddled his thin, pale, pimply, uncuddly body.

Where are you right now Sunil? How did this happen to us?

'Nah,' he'd shoved me away rudely and got dressed. 'Maybe another time. Gotta go. Things to do, people to see.' His eyes had darted around the room. 'Nice place. Any chance of some water?'

I'd dragged a silver satin dressing gown from its peg and wrapped it around me shivering in anger and disappointment. Half a day of prepping for *this*?

Seriously? It had been an outrageous waste of my Sunday.

'Here's your fucking water,' I'd said in the kitchen later, handing him a glass then flinging it in his face as he approached.

'What the fuck?? You're mental you know that? Really fucking cuckoo!' he'd spat as he dried his face with a tea- towel.

'Mental? You didn't call me that when you tried to get me into bed!' I'd shouted.

'Oh, I could see it from the start,' his voice had dripped sarcasm. 'I'm better off with my Missus.' And with that parting shot, he'd bolted out the front door.

'Please!' I'd screamed suddenly seeing the empty afternoon stretch out in front of me, realizing I'd be alone again on my birthday too. I'd beseeched him to stay, promising all sorts of things now, while standing at the top of the stairs …a blowjob? A hand job? Anal? What would he like? 'Come back, come back, I'm sorry,' I'd sobbed to no one because he had gone. Left the building. I watched from the window, his van moving off at top speed. I didn't know what I was sorry for, but I still felt sorry.

'Have some dignity!' my old neighbour had spat as she saw me sitting on the steps, imploring him to come back. 'Just look at the state of you! You know this used to be a decent building before you came here!' She hid just inside the locked security gate firing barbs at me because she feared that if she emerged with that kind of crap, I would murder her, like she deserved. She'd hated me from the start. Sunil had been like a son to her when he lived alone. As soon as I'd moved in, he stopped going around for dinner, she had no one to cook for then and no handyman either. Her children lived away and only visited occasionally. Seeing the pair of us together, lovely, smart, Asian Sunil and then me with my weaves and big behind, it must have been a real affront to her conservative Asian sensibility. I knew. In her heart, she must have been hoping to introduce him to someone more culturally appropriate. Besides, there was the issue of danger. At any time, I could erupt and attack her. Was this why she always spoke to me through the slats of her locked security gate?

'Fuck you, old nosey parker. Stay out of my business!' I had been vicious, and she'd slammed her door in my face.

i was broken, now I Am

Sadness had engulfed me, so I set about finishing his whiskey. There hadn't been much in the bottle but then again, I hadn't eaten anything. I had also finished the wine. Sunil was only due back very late, I knew his weekend routine now. The dog. Player, bastard, hound. I hated him nowadays. Couldn't even bear to sleep with him in the same bed. Often at night I would sit up and watch him sleep. Those hands, those ringless, manicured fingers. Who had he been caressing? That full mouth that I had loved once, where had it been recently? Not near me. Every woman who has been cheated on has some kind of inkling. Call it intuition.

It was the way he avoided eye contact with me, that new jauntiness in his step as he walked around making absolutely no effort to cover up love bites, new suspicious looking bruises and marks on his back, even whistling tunes from new pop songs on the radio. At first, I did try to challenge him, and he'd bit back in defence. *I* was going mad. *I* was overreacting. *I* should get out a bit more. All that paperwork from school was tipping me over the edge. Where had the trust gone?

Of course, it was all my fault! He always had to rationalize it.

Why he hadn't left first and then started this I didn't know, it was baffling. That would have been logical. Maybe this way, with the added danger of me finding out increased the thrill, added to the excitement. A friend had confessed once over a late-night shag that when he was single, he could go for ages without sex. But when in a relationship he almost always cheated, it turned him on, that cloak and dagger type of life. Disgusting really.

I'd walked back into our bedroom to rearrange everything, put everything back in its place. Take down the set and return the stage to normal. That's when I found it on the floor, a soggy, saggy, deflated condom on the cherry carpet, where I watched the gardener's cum ooze and dribble like over-melted brie. It had started to catch on the wool pile, setting in stubbornly, determined to stain. I'd been fascinated. Of course, I had seen used condoms before but today there was a difference. My senses were heightened by the drink, the anger and loneliness, my stomach growling. I'd wanted to look closely at the condom lying there somewhat sadly. I was mesmerized somehow. A poem formed in my mind. I had wanted a pen and paper but didn't have the strength to get up, so I just lay there on the carpet beside it, forming the words of the poem in my mouth.

He had walked in suddenly, unexpectedly. A coldness had entered the room with him.

'It's a prop, don't move it!' I'd screamed in drunken abandon.

I'd been lying on the floor reaching out my tongue carefully, trying to taste. Multisensory ...that's how you write poems. I knew, I was an English major. He had looked down on me, a disgusted expression forming on his aging face, that familiar habit of screwing up his eyes in disbelief, his mouth curled in a sarcastic twist that he reserved just for me. Condescending and bitter. I had always felt utterly degraded by that stare, reduced at once to a whimpering mess.

He'd packed a small bag. How long had he been there? I had lost track of time, but then I saw that he had taken out the bigger bags and was cramming suits, shirts, jumpers, willy-nilly into them, muttering under his breath about wanting to get out, wanting to get away from the crazy bitch.

I had stood up.

He mustn't see the other room, mustn't see how I had completely transformed it, how I was even sleeping in it now. He wouldn't understand anyway.

I ran to pull the door shut but he had followed me there, given that sarcastic sneer reserved for underachievers and beggars on the street. How I hated him!

'What's going on in your head woman?' he'd barked, 'You need help!' This while packing frantically now and calling up someone on the phone, someone to give him a hand in moving his stuff out of the apartment.

'Please,' I'd pleaded trying to shield the condom from his view, 'I'll try to help you understand, I'm writing a poem. Listen, it's called:

i was broken, now I Am

YOU LEFT YOUR CONDOM ON MY CARPET

Now it's oozing pus

like a ripe brie melting in the heat

Thick and fishy

Should I taste

The creamy saltiness?

I want to roll it into small, glutinous balls

    and   play with it.

Fling it

    around,

        feel it.

For,

    if I understand your cum

Then I can understand the mystery of

Birth and Death

Creation and Destruction

Pleasure and Pain

And I will find peace in my heart.

See? I'm good right?'

He knew about my passion for poetry, he knew. It was not his cup of tea exactly, it was *my* thing. I had started writing in earnest a few years ago, it was a cathartic release for me, my therapist had recommended it. I already had volumes written but they were never published. All in good time. He'd stared at me, eyes wide.

'I'm trying to find stuff to write about, didn't want to tell you until the collection was finished.' I'd tried to sound bright and hopeful. I had quite a good voice for poetry recitation I thought. The kids in the few English classes I still taught loved it when I read aloud.

'Good? Good?' he spat, 'You are *not normal!* In fact, you are so fucked up! What did I ever see in you?'

He had started laughing now, the patronising bastard. Strange how, when it all goes to shit, you see your lover differently, like scales falling from your eyes. Suddenly to my mind, befuddled with drink and sadness, he looked like some old, washed up, travelling salesman, someone who would never have interested me if I hadn't been so fucked up when we first met. There was nothing literary about him. I looked at his growing paunch, his receding hairline, his scowling face wrinkled in mirth. I didn't fancy him anymore.

'Do you know what? We should have ended this a long, long time ago! *You are an effing joke!* That security camera out front has picked up loads of images of men coming here to visit you at all hours at times when I'm out, *you think I don't know?* Mrs Patel next door has told me that she is worried about security in the building recently as there are so many undesirables entering to see fucking *you!* Mr Ganesh says that our lives are more entertaining than any soap opera! You think I'm happy about that? I have tried and tried, oh what's the point, I'm living with a looney tune, a drunken one at that! Thanks for finishing my best Scotch you bitch! I'll send you the bill!'

It was a wonder I hadn't picked up something heavy and bashed his brains out. A marble ash tray would have been an ideal investment. But wait, he didn't smoke. No need for an ash tray. Unfunny, lying cheat! He'd been lying for years, deceiving me about his smoking, affairs, who knew what else? But hey *I* was to blame for everything. *I* was having a breakdown.

Exasperated, he'd grabbed his bags and started to usher himself out of the apartment moving his stuff bit by bit as he'd shouted and yelled. Mrs Busybody next door was having a field day listening to our drama.

'I want you outa here asap!' his voice had been cold as if he had never known me. 'This apartment is on the market now and I want potential buyers to feel free to visit without condoms and strange men in the house, do you get me? Go and move into *your* fucking place, kick that piece of shit tenant out. I want this empty!'

Silence from me. My head had started to spin. He was selling up? Since when? Nobody told me anything. That 'For Sale' board outside, was it referring to *this* place? Then the door had slammed just as I had been trying to focus on processing that latest piece of information and he had gone. Fear had filled me and made me sink to my knees. Where would I live? How soon could I find something if my tenant decided to be difficult? Fuck it, I'd thought. Bastard. I'd wanted to vomit suddenly. I stood above his prized Italian leather sofa and barfed my head off, brown liquid sprayed onto the cream surface in a projectile, the smell alone had made me pass out. I wanted to get a knife and rip into the soft leather. I wanted to rip into his flesh, anything to hurt him. I stepped into the shower and afterwards, sank into *her* bed.

i was broken, now I Am

Thinking about the state of my life, in my shabby, undecorated office at school, I started to sob, my head was throbbing with a mother of a hangover and I ached all over. I couldn't keep up a straight face anymore let alone hold the frigging fort. I would inform Barry's secretary that I had to go home, something about a gas leak, some fucking excuse who cared? Nobody. The celebrated, exorbitantly paid headteacher who had taken the school from substandard to successful in six months had his dick in the PE teacher's arse in some grimy carpark nearby, later he would go home and put it in his wife. Me? I was done for the day, it was *my* turn to leave the building. I knew where I was headed, it was a no brainer. It was my favourite place in the world, the only place that offered me a scrap of comfort.

CHAPTER 12: THE SHRINE

It had been a two -bed apartment after all and if
he hadn't gone out so much and left me all alone,
maybe it would never have happened. A few years into
our cohabiting journey together, a time when the
frantic coupling at any opportunity, the groping and
kissing, tearing off of clothing etcetera had sort of
subsided, I'd realised that what was left was a routine, a
script. We would do it only on certain nights and we
even planned for it, we called it date night but really it
was 'Try to Get Our Sex Life Back on Track Night.'
After a quiet dinner that invariably *I* cooked, we'd
knock back a few drinks and make our way to the

bathroom separately. I'd wash, brush my teeth and tongue and perfume myself, he'd just gargle with mouthwash, (only because I'd insisted), and strip down to his socks on his side of the bed. *'Patronising bastard,'* Thetu's voice inside my head would say, 'he's taking you for granted. See how he doesn't try anymore. Most times, he's drunk!'

'Shut up! I love him!' I'd reply. And I would smile at him, hoping to look sexy and bewitching. Then he'd hover over me, entering me from the top or from behind. The kissing and other bits of foreplay had gone it seemed. The magic, the sparkle had gone from our romance. Most times he didn't even look at me as he did it and when I tried to talk softly and lovingly to him, he just asked me to shut up as if I was interrupting some sexual reverie. I refuse to talk dirty but I'm sure he would have responded warmly to that, they all did.

'Give it to me big boy!'

'Hurt me baby!'

'I've been a naughty little girl! Punish me!'

I'm not reducing myself to that!

The lack of proper lovemaking was not the only sticking point, he had not proposed yet. Was Pawan correct? Did the lack of family pedigree matter so much? I was the proverbial 'good' woman, did that not count? Okay, I said to myself, resigning myself to cohabitation, after all many couples did that in the UK, it was fashionable and quite the modern thing. Maybe he was working this hard and these long hours to create a future for us. Okay, the apartment was his investment alone and he made me sign that ghastly contract to that extent. But still, I was well provided for and could easily spend my not insubstantial salary on anything I wanted. I could say, send some home to Durban if I knew who to send it to. But I had lost contact with everyone. Niall was he alive still? I used to write to him regularly at first. I thanked him for all his help and support, told him all about my university courses and what good progress I had made. Once, in a moment of semi drunkenness, I filled him in with the truth about the baby's real father and what had happened to me. Then suddenly, we stopped corresponding. I couldn't get in touch with anyone anymore. Ma, granny…how I would have loved to help them financially now but how? I was the disgrace of the family, the child who had simply disappeared. How much had Ma known about what happened? I shuddered, just imagining the shame and torment she must have gone through, a seemingly decent, upright Zulu woman like her.

Maybe for the sake of her good name in the community, it was best to stay away. The other thing was that I now knew her secrets. Clearly, she had had an active sex life while working for the Ellis family. I didn't want to think of Toby being my father and Ma never telling me anything about this, my mind just would not let me process this. It was best left alone. To think that I had a child with my father. Maybe I too should be hanging from a jacaranda tree. It was sickening how it happened. I couldn't find a place to process it all in my brain or my heart.

So, it came to be that Sunil sat me down and spoke gently but firmly to me, he told me that I *had* to find a hobby, a pastime. It could be anything, he said, but the thing was, that he was entering a very busy period in his work and I had to be much more supportive, not grouchy and miserable every time he came home late or went away for days on end.

'Qualify anything,' I had teased, tears rolling down my face. I so missed him when he was not there. My six- week summer holiday was long and tedious without him, even weekends alone seemed to stretch out. Of course, later, I turned to other distractions, naturally. Now, I saw that I was a stone around his neck, dragging him down.

'I trust you baby,' he had whispered, 'go have fun. Go on a mini break with one of your friends…go out more…visit my sister …do something! Hey why don't you make that second bedroom *your* project? Decorate it…pick out fun colours and get some soft furnishings to match. That can be *your* room, it can be an office…a sewing room…a gym, anything you want.' In other words, just go away and leave me alone, stop prying, stop pestering me.

Sold. We had parted happy again and I had set off to the DIY store with a renewed energy.

Once in the store, the feeling came over me again. This was something I could never tell him about, in fact I could never tell anyone but my therapist, it was that dirty, sad and disgusting. The memories never leave me, of course they hound me day and night. Once, in the privacy of my office I found myself picking at my skin, I'd started on my thighs as hardly anyone noticed them nowadays. Gouging out bits of flesh and skin, I flicked them on the threadbare carpet, then I covered the open wounds with saliva to heal again. Later, I'd googled, 'What to do when you're feeling anxious?' and the names of several therapists had come up. I was supposed to be preparing documents for an impending school inspection, but I dialled the first number furtively from my phone. They got me in straight away which was not surprising, the money they were charging!

'Tell me about your mother,' he asked in the opening session.

Oh fuck! After all this time, I had to talk about you Ma! You've done nothing bad. Just had an affair with a married man then kept me in the dark about who my real father was. I went on and had a baby with my own father Ma!

'No, I don't want to go there.'

'Ok.' He made notes. *Let's try a different tack.* 'Tell me about you.'

'There's nothing to say,' I'd panicked, 'can I have a refund?'

The next one had a sign outside, it said that she specialised in 'Victims of Abuse.' Was that me? I'd stood stock still, staring at the sign. Here was the truth staring me in the face and the truth hurt so much. The therapist, a young girl, was patient with me. She talked about enabling me with the tools to work through what had happened, and finally even accept it. Accept it? I'd jumped up, incomprehension making me aggressive. 'You mean let that pig off the hook?'

'No dear,' she was gentle. 'It's about releasing you. It's all about *your own* healing.'

You mean my sanity. Yes, I'm worried about that.

I started seeing her reluctantly but after a few sessions during which I'd totally clam up, she suggested hypnosis to relive what happened, or starting a journal. Hypnosis! No way was I ready for that! I told her how much I loved poetry and she said that it was a great idea to let it all out. So, I started writing and promised to rebook an appointment when I felt ready. But Sunil's idea got me thinking…maybe creating a room for her was a step in the right direction re: healing. He wouldn't know the real reason, and I got to create a safe space to reflect, something that I badly needed.

I'd walked past the lighting section and seen the Barbie lamp pendants. I had paused in my tracks. I had never been privileged enough to have my own bedroom, my bed had always been in the corner of the

sitting room as we called it. I had to sleep with my
hands over my ears as my relatives talked into the
night, their voices raised in competition with one
another. Africans are loud. And we seemed to have a
lot of relatives living with us from time to time. So,
there'd been no children's theme for me, to a poor
family like ours it would have been an indulgence, a
Western thing that Whites did, not Blacks, not in those
days in South Africa.

Would she have liked that one or this? Pink or
yellow for girls? Hmm yellow. I liked yellow for her, in
fact lemon. It was light and fresh, just like I imagined
her, my own little perfect daughter. The one I had left
behind, not quite a dustbin baby mind you but still. Just
handed her over as soon as she was born, couldn't even
bear to look at her, then last minute I turned to her as
they were wrenching her away. I refused to even feed
her, and she knew, that little, round face, with its
piercing brown eyes wide open, staring at me, the fists
bunched as if in readiness for battle. Our eyes locked, I
felt her accusing me just with that sharp, penetrating
stare.

Why are you giving me away? What could I do?
What? An eighteen-year old with no life, no home. And
she was *his*. Every day would be a reminder of this, as if
I wasn't already being tortured by the fleeting
memories of her, the questions about whether she was
safe wherever she was. It had left an ache inside me
that no one and nothing could fill.

By the time I approached the paint section, I had
decided. It was going to be *her* room, a full-on nursery.
I would not just pay homage to her, I would stock it
full of toys that she would have loved, books, clothes
even, why not? I had never had a chance to be a mum,
Sunil certainly did not want more children after the
Russian took his daughter away, why shouldn't I create
this precious space, this niche for me and her to
connect….? Of course, she was imaginary to me, I had
no idea what she would look like now at what...twenty-
four? I was sure that Niall had done his bit after all his
promises to me. And I trusted him, you had to start
somewhere with trust. Maybe she was married by now.
Or dead. You never knew. Still, I'd felt so energized by
the project.

I picked out a lot of stuff that day and started on
the room straight away, transforming it from a dull
white guest bedroom with a grey carpet and wooden
cupboards into a little girl's playroom, bright and sweet

in tones of lemon and white. The shade of the walls
was lemon sherbet, the curtains a cheerful sunshiny
gingham and the rug a delightful butter yellow. Later, I
added a white wooden headboard for the single bed,
and white furniture followed: a low bookcase, a desk
and wooden chair, beanbag floor cushions to squish
into when reading together. I was an avid supporter of
reading for little children, you had to make literacy a
priority. Then various girls' toys and books suitable for
different ages from six to about twelve. Something in
me had taken over. It was *my* room too. The bedroom I
never had as a child. I could picture my therapist.

'Symbolically, you're trying to return to the womb.
To shut out the harsh outside.'

It *was* a kind of sanctuary, a refuge especially when
the sadness came over me and I needed a safe zone to
stay in while it passed. Sometimes, it took a few hours,
sometimes less. Usually, it would wash over me like a
tidal wave of memories, making me stagger and sit
down and cry of course, that's how powerful it was. It
was never fleeting. Sometimes when I could feel it
coming, I could put it off, like forcing down the urge to
vomit or fart until you had a safe space to vent. But

then it only gave me a reprieve of a few minutes and then it unleashed itself on me. And when the torrent hit, I would lie there and feel it drench me, ending up in sobs and wails, sometimes I wanted to scratch my face with the pain of it all or pull my hair out. Violation, anxiety, guilt. I'm a walking gift for any therapist, a screw up of unsound mind and body.

That room once completed became the room that I slept in when he was not there, the room that I read in, wrote in ...basically it was *my* room now, and our bedroom became his.

He'd given a low whistle when the room had been completed.

'Fuuuck! A proper Alice in Wonder-fucking-land room,' he'd said in condescending wonderment. 'Who in their right mind would want this as their study babe? What were you thinking? Are you broody or something?' Nervous laugh now.

Don't worry, I don't want your kid! Insensitive fuck! I needed this. It made me sense her, made me feel like a girl again too...the childhood I never had.

'No! I'm not broody.' Gritted teeth. 'I'm writing these days. Poems mainly. It helps me think, like a muse you know, helps me focus. And I'm studying too as you know, it helps me.'

'But *this* whacky yellow?? Turmeric yellow!' he'd giggled and his wine, a Pinotage with black cherry and pepper overtones, wobbled in his balloon glass. 'Reminds me of India! Why couldn't you have chosen neutral, modern shades?'

'You mean shitty magnolia? Hey, I thought it was my room? To decorate as I pleased?'

The room had come between us.

'Don't be spilling that on the new rug!' I'd glared and ushered him out quickly, protectively switching off the white lamp with yellow daffodils before closing the door. I loved it and that was that.

But from that day, a new nervousness had come over him, I felt like he had started to watch me carefully all the time, especially when he thought I was not aware, looking for signs of what? Madness? Losing control? I had become a curiosity to him. And secrets. They lay heavily now between us, like a thickly stuffed doorstop, wedging us apart. I was adamant that I would keep that room for me. Funny really, at school we had a reflection room, a place for students to consider carefully their negative actions, an isolation zone. Now,

I had created one at home for myself as if I'd been a naughty girl.

One weekend, soon after the room was completed, it happened. Sunil as usual had escaped to wherever he usually went on weekends, the possibilities were endless, I knew because I constantly played with them in my mind: a brothel, his mistress, a strip club, a friend's place to watch porn movies… etcetera.

I had become disillusioned and tired of games, I honestly didn't care anymore, I hadn't put up a fight, not now that I had my sanctuary. I loved being in it, I relished every minute in fact, I even slept in *her* bed, a baby doll serving as her. I would clutch her to my breast imagining how it would have been in a normal situation. I would breastfeed like this, or maybe do it like that…the doll was the colour of sand, that would be right wouldn't it? I had searched for the right colour, it had to be right. After all she wasn't completely Black, was she? Caramel, I had named her. A luscious name, it rolled off my tongue and I imagined a rich, soft fudgy toffee. It made me happy, this name. I wished I had a photograph but no. Just memories and deep regrets. I wished sometimes that I had the guts to sit on that therapist's chair and just spill all. Someone to fix me, make my head right, make the hurt stop. But I didn't. And with my senior position at school, I couldn't jeopardise my career, what would my team say if they knew that I was harbouring *this?* It was hardly the conversation you had in the staffroom. No, firmly no. Trust me it was not worth alienating colleagues. As a Black female in leadership, it's hard enough to be accepted in the first place, I've gone through it all. The worst is when they flinch when they accidentally bump into you, as if brushing against Black skin is contagious. The profuse apologies that come after.

I didn't mean it to look like a push, would I do that? I'm liberal, I'm on your side after all.

Stiff upper lip and all that. Nothing, nothing must emerge. I've been professional to the letter, it's what the management love about me. No personal crap hanging around like a bad smell. No enemies, nothing to complain about. Yup that's me! Sunil, school, no one must know. All of it must be a secret. *All.* I was not ready for the men in white coats, not yet.

But *I,* Sibongile Mbale, *I* could feel it, taste it, touch it almost, it felt as alive as if it were fresh, as fresh as a newly opened scab that was never allowed to heal and crust over. And all the pain, the hurt and shame came with it in a great whoosh that overwhelmed me. It was a Saturday afternoon. I had cleaned the apartment and drank a few whiskeys to comfort myself, the stinging effect in my throat giving way to a soft mushiness as I gave in to it. There was no food in the house, the planned trip to the supermarket had been put off in rebellion, it was just whiskey that I needed now.

I lay in her bed, my baby's bed, snug under the heavy, crisp, cotton covers, reliving it all. A movie in my mind on autorepeat. A movie about how I had an incestuous relationship with my father and birthed a little, caramel coloured daughter that I gave away.

The truth is that I will never push a buggy with a little baby inside, never baleta my own child, never croon and sing hush a bye baby to anyone but a doll. My breasts will only ever know mens' fucked up groping hands or searching mouths, will only be stared at in lust as someone crumples, screaming or sighing into orgasm. I'm sick with myself knowing this. Can hardly bear to think …I walk into Mothercare touching the cute little dresses…velvet in the winter, cotton in the summer, finger the little toys dreaming always dreaming …

CHAPTER 13: DECISIONS

NOVEMBER 2004

I should have read the signs better, that's for sure. There were things that I could have tried to keep him. Frank's wife had kept him. Lots of other women had kept their partners despite all odds such as playing away and giving them the cold shoulder. At work, I sometimes overheard my female colleagues talking about their partners visiting massage parlours and strip clubs with the 'boys.' These shared secrets were often accompanied by the rolling of the eyes and sighs of 'Men, what *are* they like?' The next day the same women would revert to complaining about domestic trivia like the fact that he never took the bins out or that he had not put the loo seat down, as if that and the visit to the strip club were in the same category. The crucial point was that they kept their men and didn't seem to care less whether he was getting a lap dance or a doner kebab. *I cared.* Sensitive me. I would become distraught at the mere hint that Sunil was doing something untoward with another woman. My mind reeled with the possibilities of everything I could and should have done to keep my relationship intact:

- I should not have become side tracked with writing my anthology of poetry even though, looking back, I was proud of my work;
- I should not have wanted to climb up the career ladder so quickly;
- I should not have wanted to study further, maybe just being a housewife type would have worked for us;
- If I hadn't been obsessed with my baby that I had abandoned, maybe we would have stood a chance. Maybe having that nursery decorated in

that theme was over the top. But then I had to do something to cope with that huge loss that I had felt. I should have consulted a counsellor earlier, but the timing had never felt right. And there was the issue of trust, who could you trust these days with your private information?

- I could have had more plastic surgery done, bigger boobs for example. They all seemed to prefer them plumped up and prominent these days, like tennis balls stuffed inside one's bra, not chicken fillets anymore.

I had gone and messed up the one relationship that had meant *everything* to me. I had known for some time that his love for me had waned. There was that ill - fated holiday in Florence…where he had literally undressed every woman passing by with his eyes whether she was a teenager or middle aged. Then, the week in Amsterdam where we had walked around the infamous red-light district in a non-stop loop, Sunil's eyes had been out on stalks of course, his nose glued to the windows of the booths where prostitutes cavorted tantalisingly, in flimsy underwear. Of course, I dragged myself around with him to start with, feeling like a limpet, knowing full well what he was thinking and feeling. Subconsciously, I begged and implored him to pay attention to me. Many of them were trafficked, I informed him.

They're not begging for it, from you. Look at the fear in their eyes, washed away, temporarily, by drugs. This is abuse.

But, he just blanked me, and stared slack jawed at the women in all their shapes and sizes. It's embarrassing to see your partner descend into that creepy perviness that we all find repugnant in a man.

Please baby. Don't throw me away, not now, after all these years.

After all, the Amsterdam trip had been another last-ditch attempt to *save* our relationship. No one wants to feel despised, excluded. And he wasn't paying attention to me. So, feeling quietly rebellious, I left him to his own devices for a bit and walked around the art galleries alone, focusing only on the genitalia of the naked, male statues and paintings. I'd paid a sneaky visit to a coffee shop beforehand and snacked on weed brownies, so, stoned as a goat, I'd floated around the galleries in a bubble of chemically induced euphoria. To my surprise, I felt quite aroused. I tried to channel this horniness when I got back to the hotel room, by launching my naked body onto Sunil, but he brushed me aside rudely in favour of raiding the minibar and watching porn on TV. I'd overheard a snippet of his phone call to his friend back in the UK when he thought I was in the shower. There was something about, 'The best fifty euro I've ever spent!' I'm not stupid. I'd seen the prices being advertised in the seedy red-light district. That red mist came over me when I realised that he'd played me for a fool that afternoon, I should have walked out right at that moment, should have headed straight back to the coffee shop!

But I didn't. I channelled my anger towards myself. I was such a fucking mess, who in their right mind would want me? Maybe he needed a halo around his head just for maintaining the cheap pretence of our so-called relationship. Even amongst the hundreds of men that I'd revenge fucked, not one had asked to go to the next level with me. What was the universe telling me? Was I a bad person? Would I ever know a deep, pure, sustained love with anyone?

I'd fucked my father and gave away his child.

There it was, in the open. I had committed the cardinal crime. Taken the Elektra Complex to a whole new level. And unsurprisingly, I was yesterday's news.

A true untouchable, in the judgy eyes of the frigging Universe.

Inwardly, I seethed with anger constantly. My mind was a boiling hot mess of self- loathing, mixed with obsessing about how badly he was treating me. So, the Florence trip hadn't been the only time that he had dismissed me like that. He had done it in Amsterdam, publicly staring or drooling at women, especially women whom I did not consider to be competition. It was beyond acceptable that he'd hooked up with a prostitute while out on a city break with me! Where was his respect for me? What about hygiene standards? Did he use condoms? Come to think of it, Sunil disrespected me more than I cared to point out, in supermarkets, shopping malls, on *every* holiday. In Spain, on a beach full of topless women aka totty, his eyes had darted everywhere under his dark glasses, his towel poised strategically to cover his erections. In revenge, he'd pushed me to exact payback. I'd have romps with anyone with working genitals! Young, sexy waiters, bar staff, random guys from the street, hotel staff, tour guides, tourists. With my eye for an eye mindset, payback should have been sweet. But each time I felt dirty, rotten and guilty as sin. I positively detested myself. I'd seen blogs on self- harming where they actively demonstrated how to go about doing it. (Why were these even allowed on the net?) But apart from a brief spell when I was gouging out my skin, I couldn't bring myself to cut. It wasn't really an African thing. Emotional self- flagellation, that was more me. Beating up on myself again and again and again.

I'd also started thinking about horrible ways in which to end his life. Should I poison his food? Lace his whiskey with something? Bite his dick off during foreplay? No, that last one would not work I knew, as we skipped those sexual starters a long time ago, not necessarily in order to jump to the main course. Often there was nothing between us, the passion had fizzled out. I had read somewhere about a woman who had applied poison to her vagina and then, when her husband had gone to perform oral sex on her, he had gagged and died. But how to ensure that the said poison would not enter me leaving *me* dead in the process? In any case, Sunil had started to give me a very wide berth months ago and wouldn't perform anything on me if I'd paid him.

Now, all alone in his London flat and having been given my marching orders, I had come to a decision. I would end it all. I knew that it was a cowardly way out, but there was no point in fighting it, I had nothing to live for anymore. I had grown weary of hoping, trying, fighting even. I had no family, no community, no real friends. Everyone had become slowly excised along my journey this far, leaving just Sunil. Excised or exorcised. I had been reckless and immature in running away. Now, I had nothing.

Stupid! I could picture Thetu. You put all your eggs into one basket. Now see what you are left with. You don't even own half of his apartment. He's left you with nothing after all this time. You never learn, do you? You could have taken him for half of his money, instead of signing away your rights!

I had already asked my tenant to vacate my flat in readiness for my occupation and surprisingly she had accepted this. Perhaps they could have my funeral there? It was a lovely modern flat which I had decorated in neutral tones. I had gone to see it and found it to be relatively unscathed and intact, but I still asked a decorator, (an ex fuck buddy), to refresh the paint work and install new, dark wooden floors. As to my demise, my exit from this world, I planned it carefully. A few trips to the doctor every now and then,

complaining of insomnia the one time, depression the
other, severe headaches the next, and so on. I had to be
patient and do this over time so as not to arouse
suspicion of course. Armed with a cocktail of sleeping
pills, tranquillisers and codeine not to mention Sunil's
pain medications that he had left as well as over the
counter painkillers, I had enough to knock an army out,
I hoped, especially washed down with bottles of cheap
whiskey. Why waste money on the good stuff? My
completed anthology of poetry in its well- thumbed
leather -bound journal sat proudly on the table,
hopefully someone would do the decent thing and send
it to a literary agent. So, with Sunil abandoning me and
my feeling morose and very alone, I took a whole
handful of pills one Saturday afternoon.

It was quiet in the flat without his music and sports
programmes on telly. I had dressed simply in a short,
white, cotton nightie. Maybe if I simulated an angel, I
had a better chance at whatever awaited me in the
afterlife. I had cleaned my teeth, but the swigs of
whiskey had made me reek. Placing the rest of the pills
on the small nightstand next to the bed, I climbed in,
clutching the bottle. I didn't need a suicide note. Why
bother?

Who cared about what happened to me?

Who would find me dead in bed? Prospective buyers for the flat? Sunil's agency staff who had threatened to visit to get the place ready for the sale? Old Busybody Mrs Patel next door? Sunil perhaps, on his way to collect a few more things that he had left behind? The delicious possibility of him finding me, cradling my dead body in his arms whilst regretting deeply the cruelty that he had shown? Maybe he would keep my ashes forever in an ornate urn on his mantelpiece. I hoped that he would not think to scatter them somewhere in Jamaica. With a bitter laugh, my mind flitted back to the township, maybe someone would stumble upon my identity and take my ashes home. No, that was not possible. Outcasts or the remains thereof were not welcome there.

I didn't care anymore.

I grouped the pills into several lots, downing each quickly, feeling them slip down my throat in the fiery liquid. As the whiskey emptied, the room started to spin.

Then, I heard it.

Rat a tat tat.
Rat a tat tat.
Rat a tat tat.

i was broken, now I Am

Insistent.

Someone was rapping hard at the front door. In my drowsy state, I struggled to focus. It couldn't be Sunil, he had a key. So, who was it?

Couldn't a person even die in peace? Fuck.

The second bedroom faced the internal corridor of the block of flats directly, in line with the front door. It was always the reason that we had to keep the curtains drawn there whereas in our bedroom, which faced the green, we could leave them open. I woke up slowly, feeling my legs turn to jelly. Carefully, in slow motion almost, I reached for the curtains and wrenched them apart. My vision had become blurry, but I could still make out the shape of a young White woman with long, curly hair, standing at the door. She was tanned, with broad cheekbones and a sweet face that reminded me distantly of my mother.

Unexpectedly, I began to cry thinking of Ma.

How had my life come to this?

'Yes?' I asked shakily, opening the window a fraction. Quickly, she approached the window and stared hard at me. She must have taken in my bleary eyes, my whiskey breath as she stepped back, making a face.

'I'm err looking for someone, my mother,' she said slowly, her brown eyes boring into me.

Your mother?

'Yes.' She had a piece of paper, but she must have memorised that name as she did not look at it.

'Sibongile. She's an African woman, do you know her?'

Do I know her? Not really my love, you see I buried her a long time ago.

The drowsiness was really overtaking me now, I could feel my speech slurring. I wanted to close my eyes.

I could see her taking me in, my sharp un -African nose, my thin un- African lips, the stench of whiskey emanating from my mouth as I spoke with difficulty. Her face was expressive, hope giving way to frustration.

'What's your name darling?' I asked.

'Well.' impatient now, 'I'm not just going to give you my name. Do you know her or not? I was told that she lived here.' Clipped London accent in an educated voice, irate now.

i was broken, now I Am

'Carrrrameeeel?' The word jumped out of my mouth with no difficulty. 'Is it you?' I reached for her through the small opening of the window. She did not take my hand. But she jumped at the name, stared at me aghast.

'Carrrrrrrmel.'

'Say that again, slowly!'

'Carrrrrmmmmel.'

'What? Sorry I can't understand you. Mum is that you?'

The 'M' word at last! I'd been yearning to hear it all my adult life!

'Let's talk… we have so much to talk about darling,' I say, a lightness, like a gentle breeze lifting me now, making me smile, darkness at the edges of my consciousness closing in now, reminding me of a concertinaed camera lens I once had.

Fight, I said to myself, fight to keep awake. This Angel is here to save you, go to her, embrace her. Look when she made her arrival! Just when you needed her! Your prayers have been answered.

'Okay,' she said, her hands deep in the pockets of her trench coat, what a pretty girl she had turned out to be. Caramel. My Caramel.

Look at what mummy's done for you, do you like your room, my baby girl?

'I'm coming to the door,' I said shutting the window. I moved to the hallway steadying myself against the walls. I almost got to the front door, excitement tinged with lightness flooding me. I was floating.

Wait. How did I look? Damn, I hadn't prepped myself, I looked a mess. I couldn't greet her like that! Did I have time to put on a bit of lippie? Maybe a quick contouring with a bronzer, a spray of perfume…

I could hear her again at the door now.

'Are you there? Hello.' Impatience now. How long had I left her standing there?

Then another droning voice. Mrs Patel from next door.

'You're wasting your time dear. *She* won't open the door, most times she's drunk or out of it. Or she might be with a client, she's a prossie, no use talking to that thing! It's no use waiting out here, come inside, I 'll make some tea, fry samosas, onion bhajis. Who did you say you were? Chicken or veg?'

'Don't go, I'm coming!' I tried to shout but my speech had become very slurred, I could hardly hear myself, there was just that awful drumming in my temples. I could think the words, but they just didn't come out right anymore. My tongue had become thick and swollen, irritatingly, key words that I wanted to get out were getting stuck in my throat. I start crawling as my legs had stopped working.

Finally, I was at the door! Then I thought quickly, my nightie. Damn. What a poor impression I would create! Ma had always taught me to look my best, to be smart. What would she say?

Put some clothes on, where's your decency? How could you open the door in a nightie?

Did I have time for a quick change? I could just nip into the bedroom, the closet was just in front, a few yards away after all. Yes, I could do it. I would put on something nice, that floral print dress, or the red one, or...

I was finding it hard to think. In the bedroom, I sat heavily on the carpet. If only I could sleep for a few minutes, then when I woke up I could get to the door. Then I would be fresh and receptive to whoever it was standing there…it was becoming very blurry as to who had been knocking. The figure had totally receded now in the great blackness that was overtaking me. Maybe it was all in my mind after all.

I lay back against the soft pile feeling it cushion and embrace me. It felt so good. Somewhere I could hear knocking, frantic and urgent. I crawled to the door, inched my way along the polished floor. Just a few more paces. She was there, my baby, come to get me. Oh, it was so hard to crawl when your legs feel like rubber! I tried to pull myself up using a chair for support. Could I reach the lock? My fingers were jelly. No, I couldn't do this. Everything hurt, my head, my stomach and my heart. Then. Nothingness. Just beautiful, velvety blackness.

CHAPTER 14: MAGDA

'It's no use going back to yesterday, because I was a different person then.'

Lewis Carroll, Alice in Wonderland

Magda, my carer does not pull any punches. If I don't cooperate, then I don't get to do my favourite things. I love a decent latte from the new coffee outlets that have mushroomed in the area. I ask for chocolate powder sprinkled on the top and a blueberry muffin on the side, if I'm allowed. Being pushed around the

271

library is fun too, just because of the sheer energy and activity there. All those books that I would never read now. But my favourite is when she pushes me to the park where I can sit in peace eating my sandwich while watching the children feed the swans, ducks and geese. Their excitement and the various efforts of the birds in outranking each other to get to the food, energizes me. I am still not allowed certain things, so she frowns when I ask if I can get out of the wheelchair and walk around.

'No! Knowing you, you will run away or jump into the water,' she says in her heavily accented attempts at English. I simply nod. Too much talking tires me now. At home, she prepares my dinner and lays out my pills carefully next to the plastic cup of water. I'm not allowed cutlery, or glassware, just a plastic spoon and plate. By the time she leaves, I'm exhausted anyway, I nibble a bit of the food and take the meds and sleep. Mind you, she says that I have made great progress, and therefore I have been allowed to come home, to my flat. As soon as I start talking about certain topics, like baby daughters, boyfriends or dying she gives me that look.

'Do you want me to go away?' she asks, 'Put you back in the hospital like before?'

'No. I'm sorry Magda, it won't happen again. I don't want to go back there, most days I just sat in an armchair feeling woozy and out of it, I told them the pills were too strong, but no one listens there. Besides, I really don't want to see those other patients anymore, I've seen enough of old men stripping off and running around the wards screaming their heads off. It's not sexy.'

'Good!' she smiles.

I find her sexy. But I can't just come out with that, can I? I just keep it inside me. She's beautiful. And clever. She's taught me so many things. In her country, she says, she used to be a psychologist. Now, she must pass some ridiculously difficult exam to convert her qualification to UK standards. She uses some of her skills on me even though strictly speaking she's only meant to care for me.

'Imagine your mind as a whiteboard,' she instructs, 'It's full of little marks. Now take the eraser and clean everything off until it's sparkly clean again. There's nothing on it anymore, it's empty. Can you do this?' Who told her that I am a teacher?

I clean my mental whiteboard.

'Now repeat after me: I am an amazing person. I am successful and healthy. I am confident and joyful.'

I have to say this mantra hundreds of times a day. I'm so used to it, I even say it when she's not there. I say it when I'm on the toilet and when I'm in the shower.

Each week, she comments on my progress and records the milestones in her little book. When she can trust me, we walk slowly together into town, heading for the park again, as a reward. They serve delicious coffee in that little restaurant on the side. I know that she watches me keenly and I am grateful for her presence, her support. I want her with me every day, but I fear that soon, as I get stronger and healthier, she will move on to help someone else. It was a gift just to have her in the first place. I'm uncommonly fond of this lovely woman.

'I love the NHS!' I had said appreciatively when she first met me and told me that she would be my carer. At this, she had smiled in that sly way of hers.

'Oh, I don't think the NHS pays for people like me!' she laughed, 'that really would be a luxury.'

'So, who sent you then?'

'Never you mind. Just be grateful that you had a knight in shining armour come to your rescue! Let's concentrate on getting well,' she said and that was the end of the conversation.'

'Whoever it was, had a lot of money,' I said, 'can't I even thank them myself?'

'I will convey your thanks.' And then she was tight lipped again.

I have every hope of going back to work one day. I never realised how missed I was. The flowers they sent, the cards. How very thoughtful and kind. And I would do things differently this time, not do extra work for a start. Maybe just half days. That would be nice. Then I could still come out here and watch the children.

Today I see something out of the corner of my eye. It's a man who looks vaguely familiar. He is tall, slim and light brown. I know him from somewhere but can't quite place him. Those dimples, that smile. He is holding the hand of a little boy with blonde curly hair; his light brown cheeks are rosy from laughing. They sit with their backs to me at the far end, but I can see everything if I look intently. When their order arrives, the man is given a teapot and a cup and the boy a tall ice cream sundae. As the man brings his face near, the boy traces an outline in the cream and then places his finger on the man's nose. They both laugh, I know that man, did I work with him? He looks leaner than before. Younger. Then I steal a glance at Magda, she is following my gaze, she can see them too.

'Next time we go to a different place okay? Change the scene up a bit, it's better for you', she says.

I tear my eyes from the man and the child.

Psychic fatigue.

I'm ready to go home.

I've been ready for a long, long time.

'Okay Magda. I am an amazing person. I am successful and healthy.'

'Nice one!' she laughs. 'Excellent! You are getting well. Don't rush it though. Just take one day at a time. Be present in each moment. Breathe deeply.'

'Stay with me Magda. Forever,' I implore, and she does that laugh again. I'm serious. I can't imagine life without her now. She's my rock. If I'd had a Magda from day one, I'd be on top of the world by now, not a simpering wreck.

'Move in with me.' Half smile. I'm begging, I know. I have a back bedroom which is half decent in size, she keeps muttering about London rental prices. I need her, even the accent, I don't care. Just someone to connect with. Just a young woman who is alive and full of energy, I like that. She reminds me so much of......

See? It's gone. What was I saying? Can't remember.

'I'm a lesbian,' she says. 'You think you can live with someone like that?'

'Of course!' I like her even more. I'm starting to think that I'm falling for her. Except, if I got with her, I'd be bloody clueless.

'I was the champion of diversity at my school!'

We laugh. She says that if I'm serious she will consider it. The rent at her shared place is killing her.

The next week she moved in.

CHAPTER 15: CIRCLE OF LIFE

Magda took me to watch The Lion King musical in the West End of London, to celebrate the progress I made. I sat enthralled and teared when 'The Circle of Life' song was sung.

'It's my song,' I explain over champagne, during the interval. I just feel that connection to it, like it's asking me to rediscover my African roots, go back, give back. Be part of Africa again. She holds my hand and impulsively kisses it. Is this our seventh date? No, we went to a Mexican place last week. And before, it was that Turkish place. And that magical weekend in Paris. We love food. This is a slow journey, like a slow cooked lamb shank in red wine, rosemary and bay leaves.

I have had seven months off and on my fourth week back I must present at a year eleven assembly. I'm still off timetable and most days I go home after lunch but I'm getting there, slowly. I have joined a Pilates class and am practising mindfulness, my new hobbies are colouring and listening to spa music with soft candles dotted around. I'm eating organic food and use only natural products. Magda's made a clean sweep of the flat. Even our cleaning products are natural.

I've done a heap of reflection. In many ways Magda has been the driving force behind my recovery, energizing me when I felt like giving up, encouraging me to get back into my passions: reading, cooking, bookshops, coffee shops, Pilates, writing. In turn, I've tutored her before her exam, helped her with her English accent, and refused to take any money for rent. I mean after all she did for me. That went way beyond a professional relationship. She saved me. Literally. When she first moved in, I asked her to live a full life and to bring her lovers over for dinner or to stay over occasionally, but, she didn't do that. Oh well, whatever I thought.

I spend a lot of time thinking. What I think about will shock some people, I know. But it's not what *they* want. It's what *I* want. And I think about her and me together.

I'm not the same person I was.

In many ways, I've been living a life as a fraud. That's why I came unstuck. Karma got me in the end. Truth. So now, I'm putting it right. It's going to be a challenge, an adventure. But my people are calling me now. And I need to do what's right.

Magda wanted to come to watch my assembly. It's a one- hour presentation which consists of my speech then the awards. These students are leaving school today, it's their final assembly. In a few months they will hopefully be enrolled at colleges in the local area. I want to leave them with something memorable.

'Today I want to talk to you about something that is very close to my heart,' I say, adjusting the microphone. My voice is not as clear as before so hopefully they can hear properly. Staff line the sides and back of the auditorium, listening. Magda, is standing at the back, smiling with thumbs -up for good luck.

i was broken, now I Am

'In a few hours, you will leave the school for good, to embark on a new venture. Many years ago, I too had a new adventure, I came to the UK. You see, my real name is Sibongile Mbale. I was born in a township of Durban, in 1962. It was a terrible time for us Black people as we lived under a racist government who wanted to segregate us from everyone else. We were trapped into poverty and had no jobs, a poor education and no presence in the country, we were nothing. Somehow, I survived. I got a sponsor who gave me a chance to attend a good school and a chance to network, he put food in my belly and bought me clothes, looked after me. I was in a position to then leave the country that had oppressed me for so long, and come to the UK as a refugee, looking to further my education.'

I had his baby too, but decided to leave her behind.

Silence in the room. The student body sits in the middle, all two hundred and fifty of them and you can hear a pin drop. Some staff look mildly amused, some look as if they're about to tear. I can sense side eyes too.

I thought she said that she was from Jamaica!

I dare not look at Magda. Those ocean blue eyes, bright with pride.

'The rest is history. I graduated with a Masters in Education, earning a distinction. I became Head of English, then Deputy Head teacher. I gave back to thousands of youngsters who were in my care at the different schools that I taught at. How? How was I able to transcend the bitter pill of my experiences as a Black stigmatised person in South Africa who had no rights, whose brothers and sisters in the community had been raped or shot or murdered by the police or by gangs?

We often hear the word 'resilience' these days. What is resilience? When one looks forward without even sneaking a peek over one's shoulder, that's resilience. When a person becomes so filled with optimism that he or she can stride ahead and ignore negative, ugly put downs, that is resilience. Resilience is facing your fear head on. It's about saying yes, I've been through the mill, but now it's time to bounce back, get my act together, get out there! It doesn't matter what my obstacles are, they could be discrimination about my gender, my race, my class, my religion, my sexual orientation. And believe me, I've experienced just about everything there is! But, that is not going to stop me. I'm still going to forge ahead. Ordinary people *can* do extraordinary things. And, as an ordinary person, *I will do* extraordinary things. So, will you. We can win at anything we want to.

And that is my message to you. You can do it! No matter where you are, which college, which apprenticeship, don't let anything stand in your way!

I'm going back to where I came from. That's right. Finally, my heart has healed, and I'm determined to play my part in my country's healing. As you know, South Africa has gone through a long and painful transition towards a democracy. We're still ironing out the creases and I have now chosen to return to my country, to play a part in its transition. So, this, guys, is my final assembly at the school, and it's fitting that we leave together. After all the work that I have done with your year, the revision days, the holiday programmes. I shall miss you. But I hope in your heart that you will never ever forget the words in today's assembly.

There's a song that I want to play for you. It is a song that is very special to me. You may know it from the show 'The Lion King.'

The 'Circle of Life' plays on the screen.

The standing ovation and clapping are so loud, it drowns me out. I have the certificates ready to hand to

Barry, he is presenting them to the kids one by one. He beams at me then impulsively gives me a peck on the cheek. He can see that I'm crying.

'Miss! That was awesome! Your swansong!' he says.

It's taken months of do we, or don't we? Now, our bags are packed. The flat is empty, we sold everything in no time. It's just the bed, that will go tomorrow morning, the flight is an evening one but still I want to get to the airport early, settle in so to speak. I'm cooking our last meal in the flat, a seafood paella. I couldn't resist it. The champagne has been uncorked, the two fluted glasses will be left behind along with the kitchen stuff. I'm not taking all this with me on a long-haul flight.

I'm placing the tiger prawns at the top carefully, like the spokes of a wheel. Then I'll wrap the whole thing in foil and steam it in the oven for a bit. My fingers are stained with saffron. Who would have thought that the stamens of a little flower could colour you with such intensity? Suddenly, a sound behind me. She'd been the last one to pack, the decision had been tough. Here, she was a hop, skip and a jump away from her parents in Poland. But who knows, maybe they can come out, see and appreciate a new country? A democratic country in the southernmost part of Africa where a Black government is at the helm. I'd got the Principal's job easily. It was going to be strange, being Principal of my old school in the township, but with my wife's support, anything was possible.

Magda puts her arms around my waist and nuzzles my ear lobe. I think she's signalling that she's impatient for the food. I'm smiling as I admire the shiny gold band that I bought for her. Mine has small stones and looks more elaborate. She pulls me into her embrace, my wife.

And I let her.

ZOE

'Books always speak of other books, and every story tells a story that has already been told'

- Umberto Echo, The Name of the Rose

i was broken, now I Am

CHAPTER 1: BLOOD

Scritch, scratch. The razor blade danced across my milky thighs, delivering pearly drops of precious blood, which I licked immediately. I am not a blood fetishist, but some believe that I am unnaturally drawn to blood in all its gory splendor. I have used all shades of red in my work: paprika red, ox blood, vermillion, crimson, rosy red, wine. Blood is what I prefer. And eating it when I cut makes me feel so alive in an otherwise numb space. For generations, people have been drawn to consuming this prized substance, whether as part of a religious or pagan ritual, cultural norm or just as a source of nutrition. Blood is a conduit of energy. Look at those who devour the placentas of their offspring for example, others who prefer their steak rare and succulent sitting in a pool of blood which is the jus to the dish. The delicacy beef carpaccio is essentially about eating raw meat. On an international spectrum, I can think of others: blood tofu, a nutritious dish to some, is simply cooled and congealed animal blood; there's blood sausage, blood pancakes, blood sweets, and of course drinking raw blood as a tonic. Ever had cold red wine with chopped fruit and brandy aka the refreshing summer beverage Sangria? Did you know that 'sangre' in Spanish is the name for blood? Yup think about this next time you take a jug to the barbecue or reach for your Bloody Mary cocktail. Catholics eat the body of Christ and drink his blood at the altar. Menstrual blood is used in many pagan ceremonies. You don't have to be a Satanist or a vampire to enjoy the taste and feel of blood on your tongue. I should know because I'm a cutter not a vampire, and I love it. The richness of the colour, the way the drops make tracks against my creamy skin and then stop to congeal. The immediacy with which it seeps out on the first cut. Blood. Bleed. The sound of it is pleasing to me. I have never painted with menstrual blood, but I believe that others have, with success. It's the stuff of life. Look at how we use

the word in everyday English phrases: 'blood thirsty',
'blood is thicker than water', 'hot blooded', 'blood lust',
'it's in his blood.' When we kill, isn't it just a thirst to
see spilled blood? The satisfaction of it. A reminder of
our biological roots.

We are hard wired to be obsessed with blood,
whether on a conscious or unconscious level. The
primitive instinct is a common denominator in all
humans and animals. Look, just look at the power of
the colour red and what it is associated with: power,
sexual predation, danger, confidence. It's the most eye
catching colour out of the spectrum. You could stop
traffic in a red dress. I have. All my work is about
blood. All. Even when I change course and say that I'm
focusing on faces or narratives on race, it's still about
blood, the essence of what binds us together. I'm
always looking for it. Because skin colour is only what's
on the outside but what truly drives us comes from
within.

My thighs are perforated and punctured with cuts,
short sharp, long and deep. I love the look of old cuts,
how the silky scars flash pink against my whiteness.
They give me a history, a narrative. You can date me if

you follow the trail of scars and stretch marks, I'm like a tree with growth rings. Except that trees speak a whispered language and have a certain beauty. I'm ugly.

To some, I'm a Neo Nazi, a White Supremacist, purely on account of my looks I might add, not because of anything that I have done. To others, I'm a sad little liberal Brit, an expat creaming off the best that South Africa can offer while making lukewarm, pitiful gestures about appreciating diversity. To others, I'm British 'scum', a spoilt little rich girl, a hypocrite who says one thing about wanting equal opportunities yet lives in the lap of luxury, in a way that is out of reach of other deserving citizens in the country. And the far left would hate my grandparents for choosing to leave the UK to settle in South Africa in the first place, the land of the exploited and the oppressed. Then of course, there's the Far Right who just see me as 'die Rooi Gevaar' meaning Communist, a 'Black lover', or sellout because I do not support racial segregation in their twisted eyes.

If you're White in South Africa, in fact it's not just South Africa it's the whole world, you can't do anything right. You're wrong just for being on this planet. There! I said it. You're not current or relevant. Power, prestige, privilege. It's the trio of burdens that Whites carry around. This is known as middle class guilt, it's the curse that defines conscientious liberals according to some angry individuals, just ask educated White South Africans, they'll know exactly what I mean.

If you want to study race, go and live in South Africa. This amazing country is so fractured by racial tensions that have been created by bad politics and ordinary citizens consume this venom and vent by killing, raping, maiming. There are crimes targeted towards certain racial groups and crimes within communities. An implosion of hatred and spite fuelled by politics. And politicians the world over have not stopped messing with people's heads.

I know what I am. I'm none of the above. And I don't need anyone's approval, especially not people who don't understand me. My heroes are community leaders who stood up to fight *against* apartheid not those who created it. Nelson Mandela, Albert Luthuli, Desmond Tutu, Ahmed Kathrada and many more, many were incarcerated simply for wanting change. I felt pain over this, I wanted to sit at their feet and listen to their eloquent speeches as free men and women. But some people, riddled with residues of hostility and fear of change will never let me have them as my heroes, no, I'm just too White to deserve them, many just wanted us booted out, handing over our homes and property to the 'true victims' of apartheid, as if that would make everything right again. Madiba would not have wanted this constant warring, he wanted a true 'rainbow nation.' Yes, black is beautiful, but so is brown and white, all the colours of the rainbow are beautiful! I want to shout it out, but no one listens.

That's why I stopped speaking, at age thirteen. Not stopped completely as in elective mute. Nothing as dramatic. Just that I stopped believing that there was any value to speaking at length about anything. We all know that no one takes any notice so why bother? They all have their preconceived ideas. Media Muppets. Sure, I could answer questions and mumble my requests. But sitting there going on and on about a topic, no that's not my style. I'm not a wordsmith either, I have no patience for writing. I'm much more interested in pictures and that's how I communicate, so you can call me a picture-smith, I'd accept that if there were such a thing.

I remember at age six or seven, I was sat in my class in primary school. My teacher was explaining something about science and she kept asking for our utmost concentration, well that was not for me. I had

zoned out earlier on, her voice just drifted up to me
every now and then, in the background. I was busy
drawing on my book, not writing, which at some point
I was meant to do. After a while, I could hear amplified
footsteps coming closer and closer. That's another
thing with me, I'm highly sensitive to sensations, this
includes colour, sounds, tastes. I can't abide the taste of
alcohol, for example because it tastes gross, that's why
I need so much mixer in my cocktails. And sometimes
I just need to lie in a glacier white bedroom with no
sound, just silence. Anyway, I heard the teacher
approaching me, she seemed angry. 'I'm talking to you!'
she yelled, 'are you even listening? Are you following
instructions?' Without looking, I knew that every head
was turned to stare at me. Then, she picked up my
book, 'This is your Science book and you're...' then
her voice tapered off. Silence filled the air. She stared at
my drawings, then as if in slow motion, she turned the
page to find other drawings. Stunned, she started
flicking madly, her eyes opening wider and wider.

Finally, in a small voice she asked, 'Did you draw
this?' See, I hate giving answers to dumb questions. Did
I draw that! Duh. I wanted to retort but I bit my lip
instead. The class was silent, in fact you could hear a

pin drop. 'Come with me,' she said finally, 'leave your stuff and come with me.' The teaching assistant sprang into life where she had been arranging things for the Science experiment on the side. They looked at each other meaning that the assistant had to look after the class while I was marched into the Principal's office. I followed her down the corridor, not hurrying or lagging behind, my head held up, a deadpan expression on my face. I'm not arrogant even though some call me that. They just don't get that sometimes I block it all out. Anyway, it was funny what happened next, I felt sorry for the young, naive teacher.

She knocked timidly on the door and was asked to enter, she seemed agitated, I observed. She was shaking. 'Zoe produced this,' she said, her voice trembling with that nervous energy, 'she did this in class today while we were doing Science.' She lowered the book onto the desk like it was a precious document retrieved from an ancient archive. The Principal smiled at me and gestured for me to sit down. Together, they pored over the drawings, going so close to the pages at times, I thought they were smelling the work. I was bored already and wished that I could curl up on the big, squishy chair and sleep. Gradually, I started to zone out, hearing only fragments of conversation.

'The detail!'

'The intricacy here, look!'

'The shading, it's perfect,'

This from the teacher. Then the Principal's voice. 'We shouldn't be surprised really, given her background, it's just amazing that we're seeing it from such a young age.'

'What do you mean her background?'

'Didn't anybody tell you? Gosh, I meant to, so sorry.'

'Tell me what?' she whispered now. My eyes were half closed, and I had to strain to hear, I wanted to hear.

'She's Zoe Ellis…you know. The daughter of Toby Ellis and Wendy Low.'

I wanted to open my eyes for this. I didn't care if I looked smug.

'Y… You mean…the Toby Ellis?' And Wendy Low duh, I wanted to rub it in. God knows dad can't draw to save his life, write yes. But mum, now that's a different story.

'That's right!' The Principal is not always patronizing, but I could sense her impatience.

'She's a genius! A child protégé!' the teacher turned to me, her eyes wide as if she had seen a ghost. I know I'm white but not *that* white. 'We're lucky to have her here!'

I couldn't stand anymore. Attention, sycophants, media whores. They bore me, make me feel uncomfortable.

'I want to go home,' I said to the Principal. 'Ring my mum, I want to go home, I'm not feeling well.'

'Darling you're not in trouble,' the teacher said softly, kneeling in front of me as if to show submission.

'I know,' I said still talking to the Principal. Go straight to the source. Cut out the middle man. 'I still want my mum.' I was tearing with anxiety. Hate being in the spotlight. Now it was the Principal who rushed over to my side. 'If you're ill or tired, you can go home angel. I'll ring straight away okay?'

Mum had come out of some business meeting, she wore a white power suit with a gold vest underneath, her hair and makeup flawless. I had half dosed on the chair, suddenly the room was full of her perfume and presence. Then the gushing in soft voices reserved for visitors, the teacher wasn't trying to upset her, she's new to the school, didn't understand, just awed that's all, incredibly talented, needs her own exhibition, must be so proud, we're honoured to have her here, if we need special resources to nurture such talent we can accommodate that here. Background noise to me is like a soundtrack. I half digest it all. Mum carried me despite my tears staining her suit and the Principal followed, clutching my school bag and lunch box all the way out to mum's sports car, where I collapsed into the bucket passenger seat and curled up, falling asleep almost immediately.

Afterwards, things changed. They built me that studio and supplied me with huge canvasses, Happiness watched me round the clock, mum was around more and worked intensively with me, teaching me how to mix colours, about brushstrokes, symmetry, lines, texture, perspective and most of all about using light. Most times she stepped back in wonder looking at a painting I had finished saying with wonder in her voice that it was I who was teaching her, that I didn't need her. But I did. I did need her. *Who doesn't need a mother?* I flourished when she was around, I ate more, especially when she cooked, I swam with her, read books with her, played my piano to her. She kind of got me, didn't over talk either. Didn't fill beautiful, perfect space with just noise. Strange that I look like dad's side of the family mostly, yet I have inherited mum's talents, we speak the same language. In fact, she was so tuned into me that I didn't have to ask, one day I was attending school every day like any primary school child, the next I just went in for half of the week, on other days, teachers came out to me. When I was eight, I had enough work for a first exhibition and all my paintings sold out in a few hours, some sold before they hit the exhibition and we had to borrow them just to fill up the venue. It was strange to see people drool over my pictures, to me painting has always been a natural and organic process, something that I did not always intentionally do. I just play with a paintbrush and a palette. Pictures burst out of me like the flesh of overripe fruit exploding through the split skins. I've always had a kinship with trees, we share such an unspoken language. The mango tree at the bottom of my garden in the heat of the subtropical Durban summer is where I love to sit most when I'm outside. The black spots, cruelly marking the peachy, rosy skins, the sudden brightness of sweet flesh exposed in the overripe slits, the milky sap congealed on the stalks, the gangster wasps feasting on the fallen fruit, resenting my presence. My work is visceral, guttural. The heavy drops of tears, blood, rain, milk. They all create a three - dimensional narrative on the canvas, it's my distinctive style I suppose, except I wouldn't offer this in an interview. I don't do people.

Then suddenly one day, I didn't feel like painting anymore, my brain cells had dried up like tired, autumnal leaves.

CHAPTER 2: JAMES, 1977

When I was thirteen, not long after I started
secondary school, I stopped talking. That day is etched
on my mind as clear as crystal. It had been the funeral
of some influential Black political activist, a big affair.
He had been detained by the police indefinitely without
a trial until he allegedly *'slipped on a piece of soap in
the shower and died.' Dad had been on the phone for
days in the build up to the funeral, I'd tried to engage
with him but often in those days he gave short, abrupt
answers and expected me to disappear. Or he would
give vague answers, for example when I asked him
what was wrong, he tearfully said that the police were
murderers and that they were killing his friends in

detention. Detention? 'What's that?' I asked. He said that the police were arresting anyone who rebelled against the government, and they had the power to keep you in jail for a very long time, sometimes, they killed you there. I started to cry, it was so upsetting. Visions of the police taking dad to jail and killing him popped into my head and I didn't want that, so I couldn't stop sobbing. Mum blamed him straight away, telling him that I was too young to understand these things, that he was killing my childhood.

Killing my childhood. I liked that immediately and several images sprang up immediately begging to be painted onto canvas. But dad had worked himself into a frenzy that day and his voice was louder than usual.

'You're *never* too young to be aware,' he said firmly. 'No child of mine should walk around in a fog of ignorance! She needs to know!' Then he downed the rest of his Scotch, I was sure that he had had several already as the bottle was empty and his eyes looked bulgy, the heavy bags under them seemed more pronounced. These symptoms were all too familiar now and I chose to do what I always did on these occasions, retreat to somewhere quiet.

I loved to eavesdrop when my parents were having so called private conversations because the truth is that my parents have never really communicated deeply or shared anything, they didn't even share a bedroom. I found this unusual and worrying at first, everyone's parents at least had that. I knew as I'd asked my friends and done the research. So, I lived under the constant anticipation of an impending announcement about a divorce, wondering idly where I would live and what would happen to us.

I'd have chosen mum if I had to, neither of them was around much but at least she didn't shout or throw things when drunk. But they never mentioned divorce. No, they just carried on leading separate lives and I pretended not to notice, I'm a master at pretending now. Sometimes, he would go into her room and there would be an argument. I can't stand raised voices, it achieves nothing. Tantrum-throwing or social posturing is on my list of things that I despise. Maybe it's because I'm an only child and they are all I have in the world. Very occasionally I would hear the creak of mum's bed and low, male laughter and then I'd know that mum had too much to drink the night before or that he'd slipped her recreational drugs to get her into bed, well, he needed something to get her into bed.

Look at her and look at him! It doesn't take a genius to work it out!

That afternoon, dad was adamant that he couldn't possibly take me along to the funeral, he hinted that there'd be police there and people protesting about the police presence at such a significant event. This meant that armoured military vehicles, guns, rubber bullets and teargas would be used to defuse the angry crowds. I still desperately wanted to go. I wanted to experience it all for myself, I didn't want to be like one of granny's China dolls in her glass cabinets. Mum had looked so pretty in her short, black dress with her long, tanned legs encased in pretty stilettos. Dad looked suitably smart in his dark suit and dark glasses to disguise his bleary eyes. Auntie Penny and her kids were back in Durban so that was kind of exciting. I overheard that she had to divorce Uncle Leo and leave him in Johannesburg, that coming back to Durban was the best way to get over him. She smoked constantly and seemed to ignore her kids as she complained about being camped out in granny's house until she found her own place, so I knew that inside, she was still hurting.

She clearly didn't want to stay behind because she quickly went and put on her black dress too, so I had to make do with old granny who was bedridden, and James and Tarryn. I felt shy around my cousins. I hadn't seen them in many years, they were so much older now, at seventeen and sixteen, where I was only thirteen. The last time they'd visited, I was a little girl, now I had little breasts that you could see through my dress and my periods had arrived a few months ago making me awkward and shy like I was harbouring some new, dirty secret. I hated the cramps when they came, the smell of animal on me. But the blood on my panties, that held me spellbound.

Sulking about being left with my estranged cousins, I decided that I would lie down on the spare bed in granny's room and read a book. Granny had lots of books in dark, shiny bookcases with glass doors that creaked when you opened them. In fact, I loved her big old house in Morningside with its polished Oregon pine floors, the beautiful antique furniture filling every possible space so much so that we had to climb over some pieces when running and playing. The dark wood, heavy rose velvet curtains and faded rugs helped to create that air of mystery for me, sometimes it felt like I was in a museum filled with ancient artefacts, that feeling of curiosity mixed with dread, as if the exhibits would come alive and jump out. But I felt wary around my cousins, I barely knew them these days with their new bodies and prying eyes. I couldn't sleep with them around.

The adults disappeared quickly, we had all been fed and granny wanted to rest so us kids started looking for something to do. Tarryn suggested that we play hide and seek, and I let myself melt into the game. Oh, how we laughed and giggled that afternoon, first crawling around on the floor in hushed silence brushing against dead insects and dust, then waiting to be found, barely allowing ourselves to breathe for fear of being discovered too early, then screaming when we got found, pounced on and pinned to the ground. When Granny banged her walking stick from her bedroom at the front of the house to signal that she wanted quiet, we stopped for a refreshment break, talking in whispers now for fear of being told off again.

James had shot up. He was tall enough now to reach the long glasses on the top shelf and we scooped chocolate powder generously into them, adding milk, vanilla ice cream and sugar, mixing frantically, wanting bubbles and froth. We sat outside on the stone steps drinking these sweet milkshakes and eating slabs of fruit cake, almost trying to rekindle our childhood again. We'd been close when I was younger, but they lived in Johannesburg and long journeys used to make me car sick, so we didn't visit them for ages. Tarryn had changed the most, she had spots and there was a mean look about her when she narrowed her eyes which I kept trying to ignore. Inside me, a small knot of fear had started to form. I could feel the tension in the air, something had changed. Earlier, they had been whispering to each other and I felt excluded, now they kept looking at each other. It was time, their eyes signalled. We were to play a new game. It had to be conducted in silence due to granny's illness and recent request for silence. All that build- up of mystery and suspense! I never realized that Tarryn could act so well.

She made us creep into the house again and head into the living room, not the bedrooms with doors and private spaces, not the courtyard outside or the garden, it had to be the living room, strange, just inches away from Granny's room, so near yet so far. What was the game I asked, but she refused to say. All would be revealed in time. It mainly involved me. I had to follow her instructions carefully, she said, narrowing her eyes. A deep feeling of dread filled me up, it was like something was eating away at my insides and there was nothing I could do to stop it from consuming me.

On one end of the living room there was a long wooden sofa, well it was more of a mahogany bench with arms on either ends. Tied to the back and bottom of the bench was a thickly padded upholstered cushion with a scene depicting a hunt, there were men in red jackets and black boots, little dogs, black and brown horses and somewhere, a little red fox but I couldn't find it. I had been concentrating hard on the hunters' uniforms and how vibrant they looked, every detail including the shiny buttons on their jackets worked into the fabric so that if you looked hard enough you felt like you were there. I know because I looked hard without crying. Crying is for losers, Tarryn said so I refused to cry. It was mainly the long cushion covering the back of the bench that I stared at because of course I was lying on the bottom cushion with my panties off and my dress pushed up to my stomach, Tarryn held it bunched there to prevent it from falling and, with her other hand, she clamped my mouth shut so that granny could rest and not be disturbed. Granny almost never emerged from her bedroom these days, her illness confining her to her bed. Still, she must *not* be disturbed under any circumstances. And there was James, his long thin brown hair clinging to his neck with was covered with sweat as he worked up a rhythm, he kept his T shirt on but nothing else as his tongue slid into my mouth heavy with the sweetness of sugar and chocolate. Down below, his penis, slimy with Vaseline that Tarryn had placed on it met my Vaseline coated vagina, first the shock, him pulling down his pants like that to reveal his penis and walnut like balls. My eyes had widened, and I had turned to run or call out to my granny, then Tarryn, firm and hard as stones, gripping me, pulling me down, locking her hand onto my mouth.

They worked together, my panties were removed, Vaseline applied, the cold jelly like nature of it feeling odd against my vagina. James mounting me, his breath quickening as he kissed me and insisting that I kiss him back. Tarryn hissed the instructions and hurt me when I moved my face away, so I lay still for James and opened my lips slightly to meet his probing mouth, the jolt of pain as he entered me and the surprise to see what pleasure and relief looked like on a boy's face, especially as it hovered just above me. He moved inside me again and again, experimenting, long and short strokes, unsteady at first, Tarryn guiding, always guiding and whispering, then his whispers turning to soft grunts getting louder and louder until a gush of cold liquid and it was over. He lay on me for what seemed like ages, no clamps on me now, I had given up, there were no words, no sounds from me. I knew then that nothing would ever be the same.

With James, finished now, lying on me, kissing my face and neck, telling me that I was beautiful and that he loved me, and me with my eyes open and glazed with shock, Tarryn stood up finally and left us. We must have looked like an odd couple, me frozen cold and disbelieving, my lover passionate and gentle, our sexes fused still with the wetness of his orgasm and my virginal blood. I could picture us from above, my pale body with my flaxen hair in a long plait, so long that I had to lie on it while he lay on me with his long hair, skinny body and deeply tanned skin. He has the same dark colouration as Auntie Penny and mum and for a minute, I hoped that it *was* mum, cradling me, cuddling me, telling me that I was safe. But it wasn't mum. It was someone else with a hard, wiry body that smelled of salt and stale fish.

He didn't want to stop kissing and moved to my neck then back to my mouth, instructing me to give him my tongue, then pulling on it and tugging on my lips. Tarryn had disappeared and I lay under James in shock but submitting now, obedient. He had taken off his top and wanted my arms around his neck, forcing them back when the embrace went slack. I found myself concentrating on my breath, imagining scented leather, musk and chocolate smells, not this ugliness, thinking how and why this was happening, the unfamiliar stirrings now filling my body, feeling him stiffen again and harden, his mouth now exploring my breasts which were sharp and pointy. I gave a scream as he bit my nipples, but he would not stop until he saw me staring at something behind him. She was back. She had been watching for a while, her eyes giving nothing away. She was armed with tissues and water. James reluctantly peeled himself away from me when she insisted that she wanted to wash me. In hushed tones they discussed what was to happen next, Tarryn leading as usual, directing the scene. Suddenly I was 'her' and 'she', not Zoe anymore, not their cousin, their mother's sister's little girl. I watched them both play out the scene, spellbound. It was like a new awareness had descended upon me, like I wanted to memorize every moment of this episode. Later, of course, I painted it. Set it down to partially erase it from my memory where it had been clogging up my brain and eclipsing any possibility of joy.

i was broken, now I Am

As he dressed, he seemed different, there was a new jaunty, brazen look in his eyes, he kept meeting my gaze and smiling conspiratorially, even whistling a tune as he used the tissues to clean himself not even turning away to dress but looking at me the whole time. This was James my first cousin, I had loved him like the brother I never had, now this. I wondered whether Tarryn had seen him like this before, if she had she did not show it. His penis, shrivelled now, looked ugly and wrinkled against his balls. In fact, I couldn't stop staring at him while Tarryn cleaned me and I submitted reluctantly, parting my legs when she asked me too, my vagina not mine exclusively anymore but something to be shared with other people. It was the beginning of a new awareness. Maybe that's when I learned to stop feeling shame. I'm not me anymore, I'm a public product, ready to be probed, defiled. A thing. I mean look at my track record: nudist beaches, promiscuous encounters, one nighters, strings and strings of lovers. All delivered in my trademark deadpan way. I stopped feeling that day, couldn't allow myself to. Then, she made me get up and unexpectedly my knees gave way and I buckled, falling heavily on the wooden floor and crying out pitifully. I called and called for granny, but no one came to help.

It was then that this huge, deep sadness mixed with anger began to pool up inside me. Why me? Without realizing, I started to sob loudly, wailing like a dying animal, a delayed reaction I suppose. But oh, she was cruel that Tarryn. With a vicious narrowing of her eyes she set her face into a snarl and marched me out into the yard, pinning me against a wall and telling me to stop blubbing or she would slap me. 'Shut up! Shut up!' she hissed like a feral cat, her face so close to mine that I could see angry pus-filled pimples and little blackheads strewn across her forehead and nose that previously, I had mistaken for freckles. But the sobs came against my will, and the pain down below was constant, then the sharpness of the slap on my face and I stopped, the sting colouring my pale face a deep crimson. It was James who took me away from her, ran me a warm bath with bubbles and sat on the toilet seat watching without saying a word while I washed him away.

Later, mum said that dad had to carry me sleeping, into the car. They had got back late, and I had fallen asleep in one of the bedrooms, weirdly, with my thumb in my mouth, a childhood habit I had stopped some years ago.

i was broken, now I Am

It was the beginning of my stutter or sudden onset stuttering as my speech therapist put it. Everyone seemed bewildered by this sudden change in my development. I could have told her if I'd wanted to. Trauma.

CHAPTER 3: PANDORA'S BOX

'She did not know the nature of her loneliness. The only words that named it were: This is not the world I expected.'

Ayn Rand Atlas Shrugged

When I saw James again, a few weeks from that day that I will never forget, his mum had popped in for a visit, Tarryn was in a private school now as they'd moved back to Durban permanently and she was revising for exams. James had received his letter about military conscription and would leave any day to join the army. This was an inevitable duty of all young White South African men, the government seemed hell bent to fight the 'Communist threats' to the country

but dad said angrily that they were preparing for
warfare against their own Black people. Auntie Penny
raged about it to mum, smoking furiously through her
anger. Many White boys suffered the torment of being
separated from their families and luxurious lifestyles
only to be thrown into the bush clad in unflattering
camouflage gear, rifles in their delicate hands. And
while some rationalized that it would build character,
they knew that some of the more fragile boys would
simply perish or suffer psychologically under the harsh
circumstances. Furious, Auntie Penny went on and on
about the likelihood of her golden boy, James,
becoming unrecognizably butch and messed up over
life in the army barracks, but she also knew that it was
no use protecting him forever. She'd already explored
the idea of forging a psychiatrist report stating that he
was mentally unstable, this had worked in some cases
and boys would be excused from military service on the
back of such reports. But for James, his call up was
final and there would be no negotiating with the
government, after all he did not want to be thrown into
prison for refusing to cooperate. He had come to say
goodbye, for a while at least until his first homecoming
visit.

I was in my treehouse at the end of the garden. Perched there, even as a teenager who was too old for teddy bear picnics gave me a chance to escape, to reflect. It was my favourite place. When I lay down, I felt like I was in the clouds, the embracing, emerald green world above me offered umbrella like protection and gave me an escape from the sharp cruelty of the humanity that I'd seen, heard of and experienced. A world without hurt, pain and spite. I loved to reach out, pull the branches towards me and nuzzle my face against the coolness of the leaves, isn't there something unearthly and magical about trees? Sometimes, I'd take a book of poetry with me and lie back on the rough, thick blankets, savouring each word like nibbling indulgently on my favourite chocolate cake.

Suddenly, a mop of lank, brown hair appeared followed by a skinny, taut body. James had crept up on me. This time he whispered that I was his girlfriend now and that this was what girlfriends and boyfriends did together, even mummies and daddies. Well no that was a lie I corrected him, his parents were divorced, and my parents slept in separate rooms mostly. That made him laugh and call me a 'cheeky bugger.' At seventeen, with large brown eyes and deep dimples, he was not unattractive; as karma would have it however, he lost his hair later and accumulated a tyre of fat around the middle which I put down to Nature's way of dishing out consequences for what he did. He hadn't just stolen my virginity. No. It was far more than that. That day, he'd broken me. Killed something deep inside of me. He'd stolen my voice, my spirit and rendered me lifeless. I was a walking corpse. Some people naively and optimistically believe that we are more resilient than we make out. Human beings have the capacity to bounce back after trauma, they argue. Whether this is an attempt to rationalize vicious crimes against the person, (it's okay, she'll heal), or to justify government cuts of mental health services, I don't know. But I can say for certain that the torment of that day will be recorded in my brain forever and everything I did from that day on would be referenced against the darkness of being violated, in that way. By my cousins. People I had grown up with. People that I had trusted and loved. They were strangers to me now of course, I could never feel safe around either again. I could never feel safe around anyone.

Rape. It's such a loaded word! How differently we react to it. Some walk away in a 'bury your head in the sands' way as if it's too painful to discuss, others offer that placatory smile as if to say wow what an intense aka messed up person you must be to even broach that topic in polite circles. I've been called 'intense' many times and I welcome it, who wants to be called 'lukewarm' or 'dumb'? Especially not 'dumb blonde,' I hate that phrase. I'm not a 'pop' which means 'doll', a brainless plaything, in Afrikaans. 'The family stink,' was a phrase perpetuated by my granny, it meant keep a stiff upper lip or, don't wash your dirty linen in public. Was this why mum was never allowed a platform to say that she hated her marriage? And Auntie Penny had to keep her divorce hush hush too. So, I would never get the chance to say that I had been raped. My own cousin raped me, and I would have to keep this in a secret box, locked away in my brain forever, all for the sake of family unity and a peaceful life. Oh, I could turn to drugs and alcohol to self-manage, all the teenagers were doing that, it was par for the course, but sharing that information about the 'R' word, no that was strictly prohibited in *my* family and in the highly literate, liberal world that my parents belonged to. *That* topic was just too undignified to grace their cocktail parties and charity dinners. Police brutality, crime, conditions in the townships or prisons, we could discuss all these hot topics but that 'R' word…awkward. Especially family on family.

Come to think of it, even my friends would walk away from this kind of discussion. 'Jeez can we just chill?' they'd say, rolling their eyes at each other. 'Is this going to be another Zoe pity party? No! We're not unfeeling. It's just not the right time for this monologue! Just get fucking wasted okay?'

I see them getting mentally prepared when I arrive at the parties. Not her again. Fuuuuck! Give me a break. Awkward.

No one wants to talk about it. Including those who have been date raped or raped in their marital bed or raped by family or friends of family. Or strangers. As a largely patriarchal, misogynistic society, we have made it so that this topic is conveniently taboo. Only weak, drama queens people bring it up. Resilient, strong people don't, they deal with it and move on. And victims have bought into this mindset as we are socialized into this kind of thinking from the get go.

Family honour. Dignity. Respect. These are aspirational words that are carved into our consciousness. Disclosure, no that doesn't have the same ring to it.

Well I call time on this kind of bullshit thinking. The script for social conversations that we are meant to stick to about how successful we are at our jobs, our relationships, school. It's all a pack of lies and I'm not lying down with the wolves that created this mindset of shame. Because pain must go somewhere and if we're constantly muzzled then it will come out somehow. Look at the world. People kill wildly, recklessly, using guns, knives, their bare hands. Look at how we abuse alcohol, drugs, food. Pain. We must find a way to accept that we feel it and we must give people the space to talk without judgement. We need to start now.

Cutting helped me when I thought that maybe I should walk across the road in heavy traffic and lie down, willing cars to hit me. When I focused intensely on the cuts, at least I was in control. I didn't just cut though. I carved out words on my skin. A whole narrative written disjointedly but clearly, all by a razor blade. I hate me. Ugly. Pathetic. It was all there if you got to look at my thighs. Over time, the scars healed somewhat and, covered by my blonde leg hairs, you could hardly notice them. But I knew, and I loved that part of my body. My scars have referenced what no thirteen -year old should know. It's not something I ever want to forget or work through.

But I'm smart, I bide my time over these things. I get mad *and* even. I once stored the intestines of some animal in the fridge as I needed it for a still life painting. It made Happiness almost jump out of her skin when she opened the freezer. 'Miss Zoe!' she cried out in horror, 'what's this?'

'They're for my painting,' I said calmly, thinking about how I would arrange them in amongst lace fabric and silk underwear taken from mum's closet to create a piece called 'Whose Reality?' I'm beyond shock. Nothing, I repeat, nothing is beyond me.

This time I was in shorts, my long, platinum blonde hair plaited to the end to stop it swooshing around. Still, it bobbed and bounced against my behind when it wasn't curving around my neck and falling into my chest. I had backed into a corner when he burst in, shocked and horrified at the sight of him, repulsed by his suppressed excitement to see me. But he held out his arms, and enveloped me in a hug, while I stood shyly, then he kissed me not accepting my pursed lips but probing through with his tongue, forcing me to give him my tongue too. Gently, he pushed me on the blankets and lay on top of me not taking his mouth

321

away. I wanted so badly to scream out and I tried a few times. But the words stayed frozen and dead in my throat and James just laughed at the sight of me stuttering. I've never been a heavy person, but I pushed as hard as I could to get him away from me. Even these seemingly feeble gestures turned him on. He took my fists in his and kissed them muttering, 'Feisty! I like it.'

I could feel his erection drilling into me through my shorts and again I pushed against him, wanting air and escape but, as I stood up, he pulled down my shorts and placed his mouth there, his tongue flicking into me, in and out, oh the syrupy sweetness that flooded me! Unable to move, I stood still, gripping the wooden struts of the low roof for fear of fainting while he crouched in between my legs, his mouth on me. He kept looking up with that new jaunty confidence I had seen that day, registering the pleasure it gave me, noticing my arched back and soft moans and so we continued like that until I felt a surge of pleasure hit me like a wave, then wetness. This time when he kissed me, I tasted my own juices on his tongue. Next, he lowered himself into me, teaching me how to hold him and grip my thighs around him, how to surrender to him until surprisingly, the waves came again. I was speechless as I dressed myself, shocked at the changes in me, the new stirrings in me. Who was this new person in my body? I didn't recognize me anymore. I felt guilty, ashamed and violated at the same time. I'm a child, I wanted to scream. I shouldn't know this pleasure at my age.

I hated myself.

Then, he pulled out a thin, foul smelling cigarette and lit it, inhaling deeply then offering it, no pushing it into my mouth and showing me how to suck deeply. After a bout of coughing and spluttering, I learned how to drag on the joint and started to love the reckless lightheadedness that followed. Sitting on the top step of the ladder with his arms around me, I found things to laugh about, my new stutter which he playfully imitated, the clouds scudding like sheep across the sky, the clumps of bushes and flowers dotted around in the garden, the pond with its bright orange and gold flecked koi carp. Everything seemed funny, but at the back of my head, I knew that this day too, I would not forget. Deception and secrecy enveloped us, like a forbidden shroud. I'm sure that this was when self - loathing set in.

It was certainly the opening of Pandora's Box, the start of my sexual adventures and forays into the murky world of drugs, that dark, demonic release that I craved from now on, becoming addicted easily and quickly.

Anything to take the edge off and to stop me overthinking.

I have always followed in mum's footsteps, I love painting, it's in my blood, I was destined to be an artist. Dad encourages me to write, like him. He's already written several books about the politics of South Africa and his profile features regularly in the media, they call him things like an 'icon of White resistance' or an 'ideologically influential figure in the build up to transition,' 'British liberalism at its best.' He would eagerly pick up the newspaper after an interview with a journalist and tut tut about how he had been misrepresented, he is never content with the accuracy of their statements. Once, he went into a rage when he was called, 'the great White shark,' referring perhaps to his aggressive streak and his 'boep' or growing belly. Sometimes I feel like we are second to his politics. He's been arrested, placed under surveillance and interrogated. The Far Right hate him for siding with the Struggle and he's received death threats, but he soldiers on, lobbying furiously for the release of prisoners, for equal rights of all people.

To me, words don't come close to the power of pictures, I've always preferred the thickness and ooziness of oils on canvas to writing, that hypnotic smell, aroma even, of linseed oil in studios. It's like playing but with color, texture, dimensions, light and shade. During that period which I called my 'Red period,' tongue in cheek, I started to work prolifically again, mum assisted whenever she could, my two-dimensional paintings soon graduating to three dimensional. In my work, objects jutted out of the canvas, they included simulated dead babies, knives, Venus fly traps and AK 47 guns, referencing the high crime in South Africa. I worked from a range of stimuli: memory, the news, real events. Everything inspired me, I was on fire. When they pulled Auntie Penny out of her BMW, threw her to the ground and stole the car, I painted. When a Black child sat on a 'Whites Only' bench in protest in the middle of the town centre and had to be arrested, I painted. When an angry mob attacked White students at our local Whites only university, feeling disgruntled and marginalized, I painted. My Art was hailed as inspired, valid, current and moving. It was disturbing and disturbed. Someone called the big, complex pieces installations and some other journalist hailed me, at fourteen, as the creator of

'Total Art', a testament to the convoluted social struggles present in all aspects of life in South Africa.

My favourite piece at that time was a painting of thick, iridescent bluebottle flies fattened from feasting on rotting meat. I called it 'The State of the Nation.' Critics described this series as demonstrating 'psychological fragmentation,' 'rawness,' 'inner turmoil,' and 'trauma.' Dad called it 'visceral,' and said that I had captured the corrupt government perfectly. Apparently, I had a 'tenacious grip on humanity.' I took no notice. I ran with ideas, painting with my gut rather than my mind. You see, I am unflinchingly faithful to myself, I'm not an investor in others around me and their perceptions of my work. As painful as it is to admit, people have always, always let me down. Take my cousin Tarryn's complicity in my ordeal that day, how could a girl do that to another girl? Where was sisterhood and sharing a bond? To me, everyone seemed to be complicit in dark deeds, when I looked around me, there was no safe place to hide.

Often those days, I was so absorbed in my work that I picked at food and should have been skinny but by fourteen, it was clear that I was not going to be slim and boyish like mum. My body was becoming womanly and changing daily ...blonde pubic hair gave me a golden triangle, my hips thickened, my breasts grew

every day and got me noticed, the areolas large with
hard, round nipples that gave me pleasure and pain
when I touched them. Everyone commented on how
like my dad's side of the family I looked. This was not
flattering to me and secretly I longed to look like mum.
Picture luminous turquoise eyes, thickly fringed with
long, dark lashes, perfectly shaped brows, tanned,
glowing skin and a full, bow shaped mouth. Then,
there's the high cheekbones, the aquiline nose and the
luscious dark hair, worn in a spiky short style that just
seemed to accentuate her beauty. When she dressed up
for cocktail parties I used to want to touch her pretty
designer dresses, her careful make up but she'd quickly
hand me over to Happiness saying that I would ruin
her clothes.

By contrast, dad was pale with insipid blue eyes that
protruded when he was drunk, this happened often
when he was speaking to friends about politics mainly.
Sometimes, they were blood shot which made him look
scary. His hair was blonde once but at forty- nine, he
had lost almost all of it and his bald head looked round,
pink and shiny now, his tummy too was large and
round. From the side he looked absurd with his thin
legs and great, bloated belly, a testament to his love of

rich food and of course, the drink. There was never enough in my house, whether it was mum with her penchant for champagne, or dad, with his red wine or whiskey. I could have been a drug addled, closet alcoholic and no one would have known, they were either so hammered at night or just busy with other things to focus on me.

With my body changing, and the constant ideologies floated in front of me through my parents' work, I poured my new discoveries and stirrings into my Art, working energetically and single-mindedly into the night. New canvasses were constantly put up for me and I immersed myself in that studio, using palette knives to layer red upon red in different shades: oxblood, bright crimson, carnelian, soft terracotta and rose, vibrant vermillion. Then, deep ebony black, charcoal, metallics. My stutter was so debilitating that it became an excuse to not speak so I became almost silent, until my teachers suggested therapy and I started attending twice a week then daily after school, until I could speak fluently again. Still, I remained wary and quiet. A crouching tiger ready to spring. I've never been an orator. Even when quizzed about my work, I remain tight lipped.

Work it out, I want to scream. Process it, interact, engage.

i was broken, now I Am

It was not a loud house. There was only me, my parents and Happiness. Every weekend we hired a gardener and a guy to clean the pool. Otherwise, things were quiet. Most days mum and dad attended fund raising events. Everyone seemed concerned about the spread of HIV Aids in the townships, my parents wished to raise money to help fund research. Then, there were the Animal Conservation projects that they were involved in, and the project Free Nelson Mandela.

Dad had published several novels with South Africa's political landscape as a backdrop and he'd written books lobbying for change, many regarded him as a catalyst for a transformation in the political system.

He had built an annexe to the main house, especially for his writing. Later of course he added a king size bed and a kitchenette, a bathroom and a sofa, signalling unsubtly that he had moved in, away from us. Can you imagine the devastating blow this felt to me as an only child? A child grappling with all the inner torment that James had put me through? Voiceless, I digested dad's news in my deadpan way, but my innards twisted and turned.

In the main house, mum's suite is way down the passage, so I have all the space in the world, I have so much space that I am lonely in that vast, cavernous house. Happiness has raised me from a baby, if it had not been for her I think I could have been officially classed as neglected. Abandoned. What was her original name? I forget now. She has been with us right throughout my childhood, her warm, brown hands lovingly bathing me, plaiting my long blonde hair, dressing me for my parents as if I were a doll, preparing food for me, spoiling me with my favourites: cheesecake, milk tart, chocolate cupcakes. We called her Happiness not due to an inability to pronounce her Zulu name. It was the name she had given herself when she first came to us, that's what she told me when I asked. And stupidly, I thought that she had been called that due to her sunny personality, but of course she had diluted her authentic Zulu name to something that we could pronounce. She's my second mum. I'd love her no matter what. She has her room in an outbuilding at the back of the garden, it is medium sized with a double bed, a wardrobe and a kitchen area. She has her own bathroom and toilet attached to her room as well, I don't know why but she never uses our bathroom indoors, it's just never been discussed.

i was broken, now I Am

As a child, I used to love to hang out in her room. Often my parents would leave me in her care and go out for the day or night. I would arrange her skin whitening creams and hair straightening lotions on her dressing table while she plaited her own hair singing softly, in her native language, Zulu. Or, she would cook the Zulu food that she loved and preferred to our food: a stiff porridge with a delicious, meaty stew. I used to eat it with her, relishing every mouthful as she fed the food to me. Even her simple pan-fried cabbage eaten simply with thickly buttered bread, was delicious. Later as I got older, my mum told me not to go to Happiness's room, when I asked why, she said that it was not appropriate and besides, I had my own enchanting bedroom that was filled with toys, and a house filled with beautiful things, why would I prefer a maid's room? She said that I was growing quickly and that I should stop eating the heavy Zulu food that Happiness made for herself and the other staff, I had to swim regularly, eat salads and go shopping with her to find flattering clothes, especially for our dinner parties.

But to me, she's not a maid and I still whispered,

'You're my second mum,' to Happiness, much to her amusement. I hugged her tightly, visited her secretly in her maid's quarters when I was all alone, slept in her bed and ate her food regardless of how mum felt about it. Dad used to find it funny and once when he was drunk, he lashed out at mum saying that Happiness was more of a mother to me, than mum. And more of a wife to him than mum. I could never understand my parents' relationship. What did that mean exactly? How could an employee be a wife?

Besides, who could replace beautiful, elegant mum? I really hated it when they argued, sometimes I held my hands over my ears to stop having to listen.

I saw her coming out of your room. I thought all that nonsense stopped a long time ago!

I don't give a fuck what you think. Leave us alone.

No not under my watch! One bastard child is enough, how many more do you want?

That's my concern not yours! I told you I'd take care of it. Or do you want me to go? Leave you to bring up our child alone? Tell me, just tell me what you want of me? You don't want to be a real wife, what do you want? I'm still a man you know.

But Happiness. Our maid? You couldn't find anyone else?

i was broken, now I Am

We fell in love Ice Queen! Why don't you go back to that igloo you call a bedroom? Hide, that's right, hide. That way you don't have to face the truth.

I should have left you a long time ago. If it hadn't been for...oh hello baby, go back to sleep.

I can't because there's too much shouting. I'm afraid.

Sometimes they left me alone and returned late or the following day. On those nights, Happiness slept on a spare mattress in my room, but she never showed her indignation. In fact, our evenings were filled with laughter and light; her English was fluent, and we joked and played, she called me her baby. She told me that she had a baby at home in the township that she visited every other weekend but that I was her baby too. She plaited my hair and made me cocoa with cream and chocolate sprinkles with a side of her chocolate cake that I could eat all day and night. Oh, she was a feeder alright. And I've always loved eating, so we were a marriage made in heaven, me and my second mother. When I ate, I'd offer half of it to her. One for me and one for you, I'd say, but she'd refuse to accept. 'My other baby doesn't have this,' she'd say, 'so I shouldn't.'

Then, she'd get sad. Still, upbeat or downbeat, I knew where I stood. I was only safe with Happiness really. When I tossed and turned, struggling to find the peace to sleep, I called out for nobody else, just her. I loved to nestle against her warm, heavy chest, breathing in her scents, funny how she always smelled of lavender. Was it the lavender floor polish or the lavender pot pourri that she put in the bathrooms? Or maybe it was her deodorant. It comforted me, that smell, like an old shoe that was predictable and warm. Call it a child's instinct but I knew that she genuinely loved me. In fact, she cared so much that she wanted to protect me from evil spirits. One day, I found four large bricks on each corner under my bed creating a strange, elevated effect but the covers were repositioned to hang low and no one could see them, just me. The tokoloshe or devil, she said was the evil that stopped me from sleeping soundly. If I were high enough, it couldn't get me.

When I was little, I used to have the most terrifying nightmares. I was that skittish, nervous child who was afraid of everything. I'd cry out for mum or dad but only Happiness would come. Those days she must have slept next to me on that mattress, not even in her own room, that was how protective she was of me. She would belata me by strapping me onto her back with a

i was broken, now I Am

blanket and her body heat, slow, rocking movements and scent of lavender would send me to sleep.

When I got sick, she would rub my forehead with Vicks Vapour Rub and croon my favourite Zulu lullabye:

'Thula thul, thula baba, thula sana,
Thul'ubab uzobuya, ekuseni.

Thula thul, thula baba, thula sana,
Thul'ubab uzobuya, ekuseni.

Kukh'inkanyezi, zi-holel' ubaba,
Zimkhanyisela indlel'e ziyak-haya,
Sobe sikhona ka bonke bashoyo,
Bayathi buyela. Ubuye le khaya.

Thula baba,
Thula sana'

It meant hush, hush, hush-a- bye little man, but I didn't know different, it was my favourite song.

She has taught me a Zulu word that I will never forget. 'Ubuntu'. I have checked it out and I love it, it means 'Humanity towards others.'

That's why whenever I can get my hands on my own money from the sale of my work, I take a generous chunk of it and hand it to her on the Friday afternoon when she is on the verge of leaving to go home to the township.

'Help others with this, please,' I whisper. Not that I needed to hide it, mum and dad would have given me a standing ovation for this act of charity. But I wanted to keep some things private. And when she reluctantly took it saying that now she could buy medicines for so and so or sweets for the orphans or blankets for the old people, it made my heart sing.

Ubuntu.

CHAPTER 4: DEON

Night bleeds into day. The dark seems to control
the skies until the morning when the harsh, golden
glow of the African sun rises high into the heavens and
then there is no stopping the relentless heat and
humidity from unfolding, like an unbearable
punishment, around the city. By lunchtime we are
rendered listless and wasted, hydration and napping
being a must in our attempts to cope. Some take this to
mean lolling around the pool clutching cold lagers,
some drink tea and enjoy their siestas on the sofa. If
you walk around at high noon, you are a sitting duck
for sunburn which gives us that crepey, prematurely

aged skin here. No one uses sunblock, we're not on holiday, this is home. We are in Durban, the largest city in the province of Kwa Zulu Natal, known for its sub-tropical climate, palm trees, Indian curry and long stretch of glittering beaches, hotels and restaurants called the Golden Mile, attracting anyone interested in sun, surf, and spices. This city is ethnically diverse with a community of Indian immigrants, Blacks from the dominant Zulu tribe and then the Whites, most of whom are British, like us, but some are Afrikaans speaking, descendants of the Dutch settlers of centuries ago.

My boyfriend Gideon is Afrikaans but since coming to Durban which he called the 'party capital of South Africa,' he changed his name to Deon. I've heard women call him 'Big D' which unsettles me, but he challenges my moodiness and says that he is sick and tired of my jealousy, so I stopped questioning him for fear of losing him. His parents are retired farmers in the Cape, another of South Africa's four provinces, and Deon had grown up in what seems like an oppressive racist family with strong orthodox Christian leanings. All of this is almost diametrically in contrast with my liberal, privileged, middle class upbringing. Being young and hungry for new adventures, he had grabbed the first opportunity to run away and found himself hitching a lift to Durban's beachfront, where he found work dealing drugs in the city's many nightclubs and eventually got settled in a studio apartment on the twentieth floor overlooking the pier.

It's Sunday, ten a.m. and I wake covered in sweat. Deon, next to me, is snoring and equally sweaty. We came back or rather lurched back in the small hours of the morning after an amazing club night where he had handed me my usual cocktail of pills. I remember tiny pinpricks of colours swirling around me as I danced nonstop often by myself, under the watchful eye of our friend, the DJ. Deon of course had to make the rounds, by trying to sell off as many pills as possible. Being his girl, I get in easily but it's not usual for eighteen -year olds to enter the clubs, you had to be twenty -one. I know that I look older with my makeup and clothes. I always try to look my best for Deon who is ten years older than me and breathtakingly good looking with his muscly frame, shoulder length white blonde hair and luminous green eyes. He is charming and funny, addictive in fact. Women love him and are always finding excuses to talk to him but whenever I complain that he is being too flirtatious he says that I am insecure and that there are no grounds for my jealousy...I *am* his life and he wants to marry me. I want that too. Ever since I met him at a party three years ago, he's become my whole world, my sanctuary against my parents and all the tension around me. I know what my friends think. He's also supplying me daily with pills and smoke but that's not the only reason that I need him. I was a mess when I met him, and, in many ways, he's brought me out of myself, I changed overnight from the protected and pampered only daughter of the so-called celebrity couple Toby and Wendy Ellis to the sociable and confident party lover that I am now. Mum and dad have no clue what I am doing these days on the weekends, but they trust me, and I feel old enough to handle my own life independently, I have been doing it from a long time. I don't need them anymore.

The boy is waking up and grunting for cold water which I promptly hand to him, we are both coming down and feel alternately hot, cold, even nauseous. It's horrible, my skin crawls! But, Deon has a remedy for this and soon my baby is hand rolling a joint which will help to make me feel less ill, it's the best remedy for a come down I know.

'What time is your mum coming to fetch you angel?' he asks gently while scraping my long hair off my sweaty face and neck so that he can kiss me. The truth is that I do not want to leave him and, gazing into

those liquid green eyes, I want to be there with him
forever, like holding the moment and not wanting to
breathe in case it went. We kiss passionately and then I
start getting ready as mum is due in thirty minutes.

I have school tomorrow and a heap of matric
homework that I have not even tackled, it's my final
year and I want to study Art at the beautiful University
of Cape Town, I have seen breathtaking pictures of the
ivy clad campus building set amongst the foothills of
Table Mountain and am determined to study there. I
have a phobia of planes and hate overseas holidays, so I
have refused even to visit Cape Town before. To be
honest, I've been nowhere. Panic attacks come thick
and fast when I travel. But maybe on a coach or in a
car if I'm knocked out? I'd need a bong before
travelling of course, maybe a few joints at the ready
during the journey and sleeping tablets too. Imagine
waking up and you're in a vehicle in the middle of
nowhere! No way am I doing that without chemical
assistance! Anyway, anything is possible now that I
have Deon. He cruelly jokes that my life is all about
'getting high and then coming down' but that is not the
truth, I still love my Art and spend all my free time in
the Art studios at school, finishing my work. He never

understands that side of me and often jokes that when we're married I would have to turn into a housewife. These Afrikaans boys, they are hard wired to expect all women to be passive and submissive. 'I want you barefoot and pregnant, in the kitchen,' he jokes, quoting a familiar stereotype of Afrikaans women. I still love him, no matter how thoughtless or cruel his jokes are.

'Marriage!' my friend Maddie gasps when I tell her that we are serious about each other. 'Darling, he's a drug dealer, a thug. You sure you want to end up with that? Besides, you're eighteen, he's twenty -eight!'

She's so blunt sometimes, it really hurts me. I only have two close friends, we are the three musketeers at school. There's Maddie who is mixed race and Indira who is Indian. Both want to become doctors, it's only me who wants to become an artist. They are so super clever, I pinch myself sometimes. So, I get expert help with homework, projects and assignments as we do all our subjects together, except for Art. In those periods, they do extra Physics. Both are single so that they can focus on their straight 'A' aspirations, and both are academic scholarship students meaning that they live in suburbs so far from the school that they get four buses each day. Still, they never complain and are always fun to hang around with. But, as friends go, there are things that I cannot share with them. That thing with James for instance. The state of my thighs. Sex with Deon. And all the shit we got up to on the weekends, the pills, the smoke, the drink. They would do backward somersaults if they knew about half of it. Anyone would. I'm only eighteen but sometimes I feel like I'm going on fifty with all the toxic rubbish inside me.

But they're not stupid and they've seen me in my 'blue period' when I'd walk around in a cloud of despair or skip classes to sit in the toilet with a razor as my only company. Both have suggested that I see a private counsellor, there was one just across from school and I had my own money so that part wasn't a problem. The problem was how long is a piece of string? Could anyone fix everything that was broken inside me? I couldn't see how. When I refused, both had called me a 'self- indulgent little White girl wallowing in my own misery,' and both had stormed off. They just don't get it.

Maddie's family are super conservative and evangelical Christian, she's anti- drugs, anti-drinking and sometimes, it seemed, anti -fun. But she just doesn't know the half of what I've been through. I hate super judgy people with a passion especially the type that thinks they know you but have not walked that mile in your shoes! And I especially hate it when she rants about Deon not being an appropriate boyfriend for me. She has no clue about what we have together.

'You know in your heart of hearts that he only wants you for a passport Zo, he's Afrikaans, he can't travel anywhere without visas. But marrying you and getting a British passport could open doors for him. How do you know that he loves you for you?'

Hello! I know my own boyfriend, it's been three years not three days.

And Indira, well where do I start? Even after three years, she still rolls her eyes when I mention Deon, so I don't anymore.

'You mean that druggie who came to the school gates selling ecstasy pills?' she asks sarcastically. 'The one who stared at your big boobs and asked you out to a party? That one? The one who knew that you were underage yet still wanted to do hanky panky stuff with you? Zo wake up and smell the coffee! Do you know that you're going out with a gangster? He's just using you for one thing!'

She can talk. She has a loving family, a brain that produces high grades effortlessly and a face and figure to die for. I am the opposite, it seems. I've been to her house on weekend sleepovers. How can I put it? There's chalk, that's my house. And then there's cheese, that's her house. She has a stay at home mum who cooks and bakes every day. Contrast that with my mum who chews ice cubes instead of food, whose mantra is 'Does this body look like it's made for food?'

And her dad is normal too, just like Maddie's.

'Would you like more roti?' Auntie Kay, her mum, offers smiling.

'Yes please! You don't have to ask.' I swear she thinks I'm malnourished, she keeps feeding me.

I make myself a fool, drooling over their food, it's just delicious.

'Mum sent you this parcel of samosas,' Indira says at school and immediately I open it up and scoff the lot.

'Mum sent you these roti rolls wrapped with a curry filling.' Into my mouth they go. I'm a sucker for spicy food.

'You lucky thing,' she says laughing at the way I devour her food. 'It all goes straight to your boobs. How can you eat all of that in one go and still have a surf board stomach?'

I love them really. In fact, we are all planning on going to the same varsity, we made a pledge to stick together, the three musketeers, vanilla Zoe, happy clappy Maddie and brainbox Indira. But I do want them to stop hating Deon, and to stop trying to stage interventions. If I want to make an appointment with that counsellor, I will. I have swung by her office a few times just to check out her details mind you. It's a converted house with a gold plaque outside, she has all these credentials, but I wonder whether she'll see me. Alone that is. Well I'm not taking anyone with me in case she asks for a responsible adult. I've never had a chaperone before and I don't need one now. Rape. It's what I want to ask her about.

In Deon's flat, the clock is ticking, and I step out of my reverie. One, two, three, I quickly knock back glasses of cold water and then splash my face and neck with it, checking the time. It's almost time for mum to arrive at our meeting point downstairs, I told her that Maddie lives here which is why I am a regular visitor at weekends, she bought the story and is happy to drop and collect me. I almost never ask dad, he's usually sitting in his annexe with his drinking buddies pretending to savour the delights of an oak aged whiskey when we all know that he'll down paint stripper if he had to. The chasm between my parents has grown, most days they avoid each other completely. And now, from the balcony, I can see the sleek, platinum silver Mercedes pull into a parking bay downstairs and I must go.

Then, unexpectedly, I start to cry, it's so ugly when it's all come to an end. Deon is only half dressed, but he pulls me to him and holds me close, we are both still shaking. 'I don't feel good,' I moan, 'I feel ill. I don't want to leave you.' He kisses my face and starts licking my tears which makes me laugh. 'I promise to take you out somewhere nice next week,' he says, 'take this if you need it.' He hands me a few white pills with faces on them and leads me towards the door a little too eagerly.

'Okay,' I agree, hastily putting the pills away in the back pocket of my shorts, somehow, I just feel calmer that they are there. Outside the apartment, we share a lingering kiss then the lift arrives and we part, in a few seconds I'm stepping into cloying humidity. It feels like

I'm in an oven, I am thickly coated with sweat just from the short interval of being outside. Mum greets me and tries to read my face for signs of what I have done the night before, but with my dark glasses I am satisfyingly inscrutable, and I stretch out on the camel coloured leather seat, refusing to engage, preferring instead to enjoy the soothing wafts of cold air from the air conditioning while she drives home, Michael Bublé playing gently in the background.

'You need your own car,' she nags. Drive? With my panic attacks? She doesn't know anything about me. I'll sit her down and fill her in someday. It'll be *her* getting an attack then.

CHAPTER 5: FAMILY

When dad was once interviewed for a celebrity magazine, they took pictures of the house, the garden, the pool, the family and the cars. We had to pose in different outfits and it seemed fun and theatrical at the time. Then the story was published calling the house 'a mansion, an exclusive piece of prime real estate on the ridge in the heart of the Berea.' I knew that the Berea was an elite area filled with mostly White millionaire families, but I was old enough to resent the implication that we were over indulged remnants from the country's colonial past, lots of girls at my school came from huge houses, some with sweeping driveways and immaculately tended gardens. I didn't want to stand out as the daughter of a famous writer and artist, both political activists. I wanted to disappear into nothingness, void. I hid in the Art studios from that day on, shrugging and walking faster past girls who would recognize me from the many pictures in the magazines and who pointed or sidled up to me to ask questions. What was it like to live with a famous writer for a father? Did my mother give up her painting now for good? Did she help me with my own work? Who did I want to emulate? Did I believe that it was a shame that my mother had stopped painting to concentrate on me and the house, after all she had been a famous South African artist in her own right before she had me? How much did I make from my own work? How many staff did it take to maintain that mansion? The questions went on and on, teachers too whispered about me, especially if a new story appeared in the press. Many fakers wanted to befriend me much to my self- conscious disapproval and I developed a small but trusted group of friends who hung out or skulked rather in the Art department during breaks and after school.

My Art teacher constantly hovered around me as I worked, fussing, primping and priming. I was, after all,

his prima donna, destined for a dazzling career in the
Art world. I slopped paint on canvas, but he was quick
to describe this as 'textural narratives'. He singled me
out exclusively, speaking about my work with reverence
and respect, I was a 'new generation South African
artist' he said, my work was not White Art or Black Art.
It was South African Art. And that kept my spirits up
at times when loneliness and darkness engulfed and
overwhelmed me. Top marks in Art was my passport in
getting the hell out of Durban and once I got to Cape
Town, I didn't have any plans to come back.

Back home, I rush out of the car to avoid questions
and head for a shower. My face in the mirror looks like
it belongs to a different person. I have changed
dramatically ever since I met Deon, I've become thin
and gaunt. My cheekbones are more defined as I've lost
weight, my body is still shapely but there is a deadness
in my eyes. And I feel tired constantly. My parents put
it down to over studying and over working in the Art
room, all students in their final year of school looked
drained and exhausted surely. But I knew that there
were too many projects now that were not completed,
homework that was unfinished. I skulked in the
shadows of the school, afraid to meet some teachers,

afraid of having to answer questions. Sometimes, I sat in the toilets for whole lessons, just staring at a spot on the wall, or trying to figure out a quote that someone had scribbled on the door, then I would suddenly realize and come back out of this daydream. I craved the comfort of Deon, being physical in bed was part of it, it helped me to forget. He loved my curves and long hair that I had been warned not to cut, he called me his 'Platinum Wife' and made me feel beautiful and protected. We took all manner of chemicals together and there was a feeling sometimes that we were united against everyone in the world.

But he's not here now, in fact he wouldn't ever be welcomed in this house, I know how my parents feel about Afrikaners. But why? The Anglo Boer war is long over! It's petty all this fighting. And I need him desperately! Since I discovered 'chem sex' there's no turning back, I constantly crave it. I must clutch onto the cold sink to steady my nerves, I count one to ten as I savour the coldness. Breathe. In. Out. Breathe again, I remind myself. It's hard when you're coming down. The icy water is refreshing slightly, and I wash away the sweat and the stale smells from the night before. But how to stop my hands from shaking? My pupils seem dilated, how to appear normal? I slip on a pretty, strappy summer dress in strawberry pink and plaster on the make -up. Then, with my hair newly washed and brushed, my eyes doused with brightening eye drops, I spray on fragrance and go to join my parents on the veranda, a covered terrace where Happiness is about to serve us lunch.

Every Sunday, we have guests over and it's our family tradition to host it together. In the summer it's served on the terrace, thus showcasing the lush Mediterranean garden and glittering swimming pool, in our mild winters, we used the terracotta dining room which was heavily decorated with Ndebele and antique Zulu art while still being modern and comfortable. 'How colonial!' I heard someone say once, gasping at the thick carpets and heavy furniture. 'You could host a party for a President here!' Oh, the Sunday ensemble is always interesting, even I must admit it. We have had eminent writers, politicians, artists, social climbers, surgeons and mercenaries over. And the conversation, especially after a few bottles of the finest champagne, Scotch or wine, is never dull. We all talk endlessly about the future of South Africa, it's a perfect 'Out of Africa' scene every time.

At lunch, this time with Aunt Penny and her new man, who is the president of something or other, I cleverly brush over the questions about the event that I had attended the night before. I try to focus the conversation instead on the succulent roast lamb studded with garlic, and delicious buttered vegetables, followed by strawberries and cream. Mum drinks too much champagne as a pretext for not eating much as usual, her slim body is not meant for food, she says. 'Slim? You mean ironing board?', dad jokes and adds her food onto his own. Waste not, want not. After the initial attempt to engage me, there is a silence as we concentrate on the flavours of the food, the only sounds being the sound of cutlery against the plates, the chink of wine glasses, the soft brushing of Happiness's skin against mine as she hovers around me in her immaculate, starched uniform, neatening my hair and tucking my strap back in, as it slips over one arm.

Aunt Penny excuses herself to sit by the pool and smoke, her man has taken a walk to check out the koi carp. Both my parents are somewhere else, lost in their own worlds. What a family! I grab the chance to turn my focus onto the pills that are sitting in my shorts still, now safely tucked away in my room. I plan to pretend to have a headache which would be a good excuse to go and lie down, maybe for the whole evening, one pill would be enough surely, or maybe two just to be safe. The thrill of the trip ahead of me! I can scarcely finish my dessert I am that excited. I want to run out of the stiffness of the lunch, the silence, I want to run to my room, lock the door and swallow the pills, maybe all four. Water, I'll need that.

'Handle!' Deon whispers when he thinks I'm on the verge of losing control. 'You have to pretend, handle yourself!'

I've made up my mind and I push back my chair. 'I'm going to lie down and rest,' I say calmly, 'I have a headache.' I am already walking away when my parents call me back. 'There's something that we want to discuss with you,' says dad. 'We,' and he indicates mum and Happiness, 'have been thinking about it for a while and we want to talk to you about it.'

CHAPTER 6: SIBONGILE

March 1982

So now they want to bring Happiness's daughter Bongi to come live with us. A sister from another mother and father who would be company for me. She's going to have a bedroom inside the house, next to mine, not near her mother's which is outside. She's going to attend my school and be given all the chances that she missed out on so far, to make sure that she could go on to have a successful life in the New South

Africa. 'It's our duty to help her as the Change is coming.'

I'm in no mood for one of dad's political rants and I am too overwhelmed to listen to any more. Mum puts it differently. She relates the story calmly: Happiness has been a loyal servant now for eighteen years, visiting her own home in the township only on alternate weekends. Her husband, a security guard, had been shot at work years ago and Happiness had been left with her disabled sister, her elderly mother and their child Sibongile who they called Bongi, a daughter who at seventeen, was now a year younger than me. Mum said that Bongi seemed like an intelligent young lady according to what Happiness had reported, why should she not have the help and support from my parents to achieve something more with her life? Trapped into poverty by the callous government's system of racial segregation, many destitute young Black girls were forced into becoming housemaids or slipped into prostitution or other forms of criminality. Some got pregnant from a young age and ended up repeating the cycle, some even became HIV positive through rape or relationships with unsavoury men. I could see why mum was a great fund raiser for her charities, she spoke eloquently and passionately. It was impressive.

Happiness had been concerned for a while about violence in the township. A lot of girls got raped or sexually molested, it was not safe for a pretty and sensitive girl like her daughter. She wanted Bongi with her, in the city. We, she looked at dad and he nodded in approval, choking up for some strange reason, wanted to protect and care for Bongi. Meanwhile, her other aunt would move into her house in the township, they would help to care for her sister and mother.

News alert:

White girls get raped too.

White people also become HIV positive.

When mum gets fired up about a cause, it's all she thinks about. Anything to take the focus away from scrutinizing our lives!

It seems that everything has been discussed and planned for several weeks and I am the last one to know!

The new bedroom is getting a makeover and Bongi would arrive in a few days when Happiness went home to collect her. I can feel flutters of excitement. So much change! Who is this Bongi? Would she fit into my school? Our school population was predominantly White with a few Black, Indian and Coloured students who were starting to finally trickle in. It was lame this pitiful gesture of tolerance and diversity. We should have been fully multicultural from the start. What would my friends think of this sisterhood idea? Would we even get on? Then I see the decorations for her room and feel a pang of jealousy. I have a single bed, she has a double. Everything in there is new and fresh, she even has a desk and a swivel chair so that she can study. It looks like a proper teenage pad while my room is a hangover from my childhood, stuffed toys, baby pink walls, even the lamp shades have ballerinas in various dance poses. I know I never wanted change before but now I fear that she might laugh at me, call me a Peter Pan type, forever trying to reclaim a lost childhood.

My parents, both beaming now, ask what I think about it all and I give all the politically correct answers, how can I not? I am genuinely proud of their initiative, but I just don't get why dad keeps getting emotional about it. Is it because she will be the trophy adopted Black child? He can use her to prove his liberal allegiances, perhaps. It seems odd that he has sprung to life ever since they brought up the subject of the girl. Even his familiar Scotch is nowhere to be seen. Instead, he fusses about checking and rechecking her room saying that he wants things to be just right. As for me, I will try to get on well with her and certainly my friends will embrace her so that she will not feel left out, she will feel like a normal school girl. Then, facetiously, my eyes twinkling, I go on to promise that it will be like we have washed out her insides and replaced all her memories of township crime, race related poverty, malnutrition, lack of a proper family life, all with new memories. I explain that she will be a 'coconut' in my school, a new type of Black person who was Black on the outside but White on the inside. They certainly were growing in number, there were many already in the previously exclusively White schools like mine. Dad frowns at the idea of the label 'coconut' but sighs with relief that I have accepted the grand idea.

In many ways I am starting to relish the whole prospect of having a sister, especially on days when I did not see Deon or my parents. It's no fun being an only child, Sibongile would help change that. We'll be partners in crime. Finally!

It's the second Saturday in March and Happiness has gone home to bring back her daughter. I am not allowed to go out until I accompanied mum to the mall where she is set on buying clothes, bedlinen and a range of presents for the daughter. Oh, I'm in a foul mood as I am missing Deon for this! We have not seen each other for days as he has been working the clubs. I know that he is saving to get us a car and later our own apartment. His parents have cut him off financially since he ran away from home with a supermarket trolley full of their prized possessions which he had to sell to raise money to keep him afloat. I wished sometimes that he had a different job, or that he was at university, at least then, I could tell my parents about him, even bring him home, pretend that he wasn't right wing. As it stood, I shudder at the thought of him visiting my parents, what would he say when they asked what his job was? Or how old he was? Surely, they'd put two and two together quickly and realize that a grown man of questionable politics was having sex with their golden angel. Chem sex at that! No, I couldn't risk them meeting! But I wish mum would finish shopping so that I could go out to meet him.

We stop eventually, and she insists on buying me lunch, fussing over me as she thinks that I have lost weight, it's always a weight gain or loss that she's absorbed in, that and getting my hair off my face. She orders a green salad and pushes it around her plate, pretending to eat but she's not, she just drinks a lot of chardonnay. It's okay, she drinks and drives all the time, most people did it and got away with it. I'm tucking into my steak covered in mushroom sauce, with a potato bake on the side. We seem stuck for conversation, then she asks about my recent painting that I have been working on for my exam and her eyes brighten again, this is her topic, her safe zone. Having wolfed down my food, I want to leave and not talk about my project, but she won't leave me alone. Does she feel guilty at never spending alone time with me? I examine her carefully, I know how she feels about dad, she's even engineered his move to the annexe. Once when he was in the middle of a drunken political rant, she walked away in mid flow to her suite saying that she wanted privacy. His room she said was to be in the annexe where he could enjoy *his* privacy away from her. That night, in front of my speechless father, she got Happiness to move all his stuff out of their marital bedroom and their split was finally official.

Now, I throw a few key questions at her, perhaps because of my pent-up jealousy over the attention that Bongi is getting, also because of my intense need for Deon. It's funny, I'm an only child and I should *know* my parents, but such is the state of affairs in my house that we are all just ships passing in the night. The question that bugged me was why did she stop practising as an artist, even though it was her passion? She'd lived in her idyllic, rustic farmhouse in the Drakensberg Mountains when dad had met her, a sort of hidey hole where she could retreat from the world. She kept it on and regularly made trips there on weekends, it was our holiday home too. It was for the sake of a huge exhibition in the city that she'd travelled down for a few days, her work was being displayed together with some of her contemporaries. What had changed since I was born that stopped her career? Why did she slip away to the farm for weekends at a time without taking us? Why the secrecy? And why was dad living separately in an extension to our house?

To my horror, my quick- fire questions cruelly blurted out are met with first a quiet but stiff smile, then, as they continue, her beautifully made up face crumples and she starts to tear then sob. It's good that we are in the corner of the restaurant, she would not want anyone to see her having a melt- down. After all, she's Wendy Ellis nee Low, of minor celebrity status due to her work and her famous husband. Panicking, I quickly settle the bill and shepherd her and the shopping trolley that is laden with bags, into the elevator. Once in, she seems to gain composure. Using the mirrored wall as a guide, she quickly and carefully mops her eyes and refreshes her make-up, dabbing concealer frantically under the eyes.

I'm shaken by this episode and how it has unsettled her, shocked at how fragile she is despite looking so poised and elegant. I don't feel like being my usual nonchalant self today, this is my mum in distress and I love her more than life itself. I hug and kiss her reminding her of how beautiful she is to me, I apologize for asking so many questions. For a minute, glancing in the mirror at her hunched, bony body in my embrace, it feels like I am comforting my child and in this moment I'm certain that there is a narrative behind her demeanour, the false cheer, the physical rejection of dad, the disappearances for weekends, the hiding behind bottles of champagne, chardonnay and charity work, her constant lack of appetite. Does she have an eating disorder? I vow silently that I will get to know the truth and that I will protect her fiercely from today onwards.

i was broken, now I Am

CHAPTER 7: MATRIC, MY FINAL YEAR

When Bongi first entered the house, I could smell her. It was the smells from the farm, earth and wood and a faint trace of urine. What I wasn't prepared for was how stunning she was. With her physique and face, she could have been a model gracing any catwalk anywhere in the world, and I immediately felt a sharp stab of discomfort thinking that this poor beauty had been living an impoverished life in the township all this time. Apartheid had deprived these people of their rights, I didn't feel guilty, but I still wanted to reach out to her, this was my new adopted younger sister. I wanted to paint her just the way she was, the way she held herself stiffly and shyly, the innocence and unspoilt nature of her. At seventeen, she was makeup free, yet she radiated a glow, almost a halo of brightness around her. It was all there in her golden brown, soft Afro hair, her large brown eyes, the full mouth. She looked mixed race, unlike Happiness who looked Black. Was her father light skinned then?

She was taller than I imagined, her long legs ended in school shoes that looked half broken and covered in dried, reddish mud that stained the polished floors. Her old school uniform looked much too small as some of her buttons strained to contain her breasts, she was clearly braless. My friends would call her a 'freshie' or someone 'green,' and new to the ways of the city, but this to me was an advantage. I loved her straight away and rushed to hug her much to her embarrassment. We only made brief conversation as much of her gaze was directed at the floor, but I could see that her English was very good, I was told that she was intelligent.

So, we decided to give her space and we left Happiness to show her around the house and eventually to her new room. Dad's reactions were unexpected though. He had to be literally pried away from her, he just couldn't stop hugging her and mum stopped him in his tracks with her sarcastic remarks about him having work to do on his new book. How embarrassing for him to have an emotional meltdown like that! I never knew he had it in him to embrace his new 'adopted daughter' so affectionately. I had never known such warmth from the man! Was it the adopted token Black child that would allow him to prove his liberal allegiances? Many celebrities were doing it, so I could see him jumping on the bandwagon. I didn't know him anymore. This was a man who hardly spoke to me let alone anyone else in the house. I put it to one side and got on with the day.

As I was busy with exam revision, I only saw Bongi briefly that first week. Mum too seemed suddenly preoccupied, it felt like she had spent her energy on getting things ready for Bongi but now that she was here, she just couldn't cope anymore. Apparently, the housekeeper at her farm in the Drakensberg had called her to report a leak in the roof; although Johan, a neighbouring farmer and close family friend could help supervise the repairs, she still needed to get over there for a few days. She felt that she was letting Bongi down by going but Happiness assured her that she and dad would get everything under control. I could have sworn that she'd sniggered at that, but nobody would believe me if I pointed it out, my house is just bulging at the seams with secrets and lies. It's not surprising that most days, I'm out of my head.

Months pass. Bongi's transformation has happened almost overnight. I'm happy for her, it feels right that she now has the appropriate support from all of us to thrive. But the whole Project Bongi has been mega frustrating too. Take the day of my first mock exam for instance.

I was sitting in the car, late for school because the Diva was still getting ready. Happiness had tried to talk to her but apparently, she was still in the bathroom and had not even touched her breakfast. Dad was unusually quiet and patient that day, he'd barked at me to stop complaining so I stopped talking to him and started sulking. Thankfully, my exam was in the afternoon but still, I wanted to get to school to do more revision. On my neck sat a cluster of huge raspberry and aubergine coloured love bites which, when I touched their slightly raised shapes, triggered all the memories of the lovemaking from the night before at Deon's place. I was trying, unsuccessfully, to cover them with my blazer collar and my hair. It comforted me, gave me something to focus on, otherwise I could have killed dad that day. I hated his car. It was a huge White Mercedes with red leather seats that he called ox blood. To me, it was the colour of period blood. I wasn't seeing eye to eye with him and on these occasions, I loved to hurt him with words. I hated his shifty eyes, his thick, fat fingers on the steering wheel, his girth. Mostly, I hated how he had started to blank me totally.

That week was the final deadline of my Art assessment, I'd titled my project 'Convergence.' For once, I was exploring how Nature worked synergistically, almost mirroring how the fractured strands of my own life were healing and developing as I matured. There was a painting of a single blade of grass against the backdrop of the lawn, the context was the park opposite the school, the imposing trees in sharp relief in the background. Another was a single raindrop splashing into a small, rippled pool of water. Nature had always soothed me, and I was passionate about this new series that everyone predicted would get top marks. It's hard generating work just for marks. As an artist you want your work to have integrity and grit, it's the artist's language if you like, you don't just churn out stuff to earn an examiner's favour. Yet, I badly needed to get into university, Cape Town was all I thought of, day and night. Bongi had arrived at a rough time for me and I just couldn't afford the time to play hostess. She herself had exams and was just one year away from matriculating so she needed to focus on revision and fast track transition issues. Look, I'm hardly a cold bitch. It was just that getting away from the pressure cooker that Durban had become, was an increasing priority to me.

She had tried to put on this big celebrity act. Her face when she finally emerged and sat in the front seat hence upstaging *me*, was sullen. Sure, she looked the bomb. Dad had taken her out to get her hair braided in long dark and red plaits and he'd waited for a few hours until it was done, then he even took her out for dinner afterwards, we had heard. Thankfully, he hadn't asked me or mum to accompany them, if he had, I would have thrown the dinner in his face, called Deon to collect me and stormed off. She had a whole new wardrobe now courtesy of dad, a bank account, a passport application in process, designer shoes, fancy handbags, perfumes…When last did he buy clothes for me? I was practically bursting out of my clothes I was growing so fast. When last did he try to spend time with me? I was fuming as we drove in silence and when we reached the school, he didn't even wish me good luck!

Deon has a little VW Golf now and that evening, he picked me up, our favourite place was the beach where we could park amidst the trees and make out.

'You're a nympho!' he panted as he moved my panties to one side and slid into me. 'Such a horny girl, like an Eveready battery. You never say no. I love that about you.'

It was true, I loved it. And I basked in the deception that I had created at home, my parents were under the illusion that I was a virgin. But here was I, very much the opposite of that. The only thing that made me uncomfortable was his refusal to use condoms and the birth control pill and I have never really gotten along. My constant fear was that I would carry his child, a junior Deon. Frightening prospect. A throwback to the first, racist Dutch pioneers that set foot on the shores of the Cape, that was his heritage. I would have to give the baby a brain transplant if I wanted my liberal family to get along with him or her. So, each sexual episode was laced with the possibility that it could lead to a pregnancy and each time my periods arrived, it was greeted with huge relief.

Deon had turned twenty-eight, but I was not invited to the party, all his friends there were older, he said. He wanted to protect me and keep me all for himself, I understood that now. And it made sense. Everything else that he constantly talked about made sense too except that in our politically correct circles we didn't quite put it as bluntly. We thought it, but in articulating our concerns, we chose fat, meaningless, impressive but idealistic words. Joining hands together. Partnerships. Humanitarian agendas. Positive, new projects. And dad's favourite buzzword: decolonization. The undoing of the past. As though you could do that easily!

Deon was desperate to leave South Africa. To him, the crime was escalating daily, the newspapers were full of reports of rapes, murders and burglaries even in our affluent areas where security was a priority. We had dogs, burglar guards and alarms that were monitored by private protection companies and yet criminals still found cunning ways to outsmart the systems. Dogs got poisoned, electric fencing got cut and security agents got shot in cold blood. It made him so cross. Everywhere he went, he had to check who was walking behind him in case he got pick pocketed or attacked.

i was broken, now I Am

On the beachfront where he lived, he'd already been mugged countless times, it was pointless wearing designer watches, he said, in fact any jewelry meant that you were a magnet for thieves operating in the area. And it wasn't just our citizens who were doing this. Nigerians and Zimbabweans had started to pour into Durban, their lack of skills meant that they couldn't get proper jobs and lived by being pimps, drug dealers and muggers. People had to stay indoors in the evenings or, when going out, they had to stay in large groups, or stick to well -guarded areas. Crime was at a record high.

In my heart, I echoed what he was saying although I was loathed to say it. My parents defined themselves by their high levels of political activism and left -wing leanings, they would have cut out my tongue if I had sided with racists. I knew how exhausting it was to constantly keep a check on my handbag when I was out in public. It was like being forced to have eyes at the back of your head all the time when you were out and about. In Toronto, Perth, London, Paris, things were different we'd heard, people were safer. Many of my friends whose relatives fled there out of total frustration, talked endlessly about it. Every South African is obsessed about being safe, it's the one

common denominator that knits us together. Because
unless you were one of the uber rich and could afford
bodyguards, you were never safe anywhere. Liberals,
racists, tourists, township dwellers, politicians…no one
was immune. Oh, it didn't matter if you helped them in
the past, Deon said, you could still be murdered in cold
blood. And they were all in it together, maids often
schemed behind their employers' backs, aiding and
abetting criminals in the hope of getting a lion's share
of whatever they took. There were cases of maids
stealing, looting and killing their employers themselves,
you just could not take the risk of trusting anyone.
Deon ranted and raged, plotting and planning his exit
strategy from the country that he had once loved.

I appreciated his brutal honesty, he told me from
day one that he needed a British passport, it wasn't his
fault that he was Afrikaans or of Dutch extraction and
had no way out of the country. Once, before he met
me he'd applied for a visa for London, but the
application got refused. He didn't want to discuss this
at length, but I guessed that it was the time when his
parents had reported his theft of their stuff to the
police and he needed to disappear quickly. So, he
decided to go dark and live underground so to speak,
until they stopped searching for him. I had no clue
what he stole exactly but it seemed, by his shifty eyes

that it was something major. Which parent would want to prosecute their own son? To add fuel to fire, he had escaped from doing his national service in the army, he simply ducked and dived until no one knew where he was. If the police found him, he'd he frog-marched to prison he said. He didn't think that he could bear that, sharing a cell with other Black men.

I wanted him to stop going on about it, seeing him was meant to be a therapeutic sexual relief from exam stress, instead all he seemed to focus on was getting me to marry him. He explained that when we were married then he too could get a British passport which meant that he could travel anywhere in the world without having to think about returning to South Africa. It was every White South African's dream, he said, to get the hell out, to avoid the genocide which was looming, as sure as the sun shone in the sky, it was going to happen. It would be the systematic genocide of his ancestors, the Dutch Boers, in a similar pattern to what was happening in neighbouring Zimbabwe. Land grabs, murders and pillaging would be the order of the day.

He painted a bleak picture of things to come but I had a much more optimistic vison. Mandela was our salvation, I reassured him. When the Rainbow Nation came into reality, there wouldn't be the pent -up anger and resentment that underpinned crime. We'd all have an equal stake in the country and we could join forces to help develop it. But, listening to me, Deon creased up. He had the most beautiful, emerald green eyes, clear for someone who ate and drank drugs for breakfast, lunch and supper. I loved the way the sides crinkled up when he laughed.

'Hear yourself, naïve British idiot! It was good while it lasted, but you must recognize when your days are numbered. If you don't want to leave, it will be your head on a stake one day, your beautiful house occupied by a criminal. Do you really think they will want to join forces with a White person? Grow up! They'll kill you for the price of a piece of fried chicken! First, they'll rape you, then, they'll take you out with their bare hands! There will never be any rainbow nation here. Never! Instead, they'll hold it against us forever. Instead, there will be slums full of Whites. Racism from the other side, Black on White as payback for apartheid. And I won't be here to see it.'

In my heart, I was mortified but I didn't say anything. I had always wanted to participate in a South Africa free from racial segregation, not just as an artist but as a member of society. It was our family's big dream that Nelson Mandela would be set free one day and that everyone would finally have the chance to be free from the sickening scourge of racism. That utopia had been my fantasy. And now, he wanted to use my British ancestry to flee with me, like thieves in the night. I didn't want to leave altogether. Cape Town yes, but not leave South Africa, the land of my birth. Just the idea of it made me feel panicked. I didn't know the side of my family in England, in fact I knew no one there. But I couldn't say anything yet, Deon flipped out easily, going from one to ten in a heartbeat when he was not getting his way, so I just kept my opinions to myself.

I love that he supports my studies especially now that I'm in my final year, the home stretch, he calls it. He begs me to study hard and to pass with distinction, how else would I be able to get into the uber prestigious UCT? He plans to come with me and from there, once I finish my degree well, the next stop was London. I nod in confused agreement, we can always talk about settling in Cape Town later. But I'm upset too. He says that he is busy nowadays, business has picked up since he bought the car, he is not always home on the weekends and sometimes he is not able to see me. I can't bear this. When I cry he says that all his efforts are for me, I am his golden angel, he is saving for our future and when he's ready we will plan our wedding, the dress, the honeymoon, the ring. I have always wanted to study Art in Cape Town, Mum went there before me and it's always been a dream to relive her legacy. But for Deon, I would just about do anything, heck, I'd move Table Mountain if I had to. I love him so much, sometimes I feel like I would break without him. Each time he sees me he hands over more pills nowadays to help me get by, and sometimes even other stuff too. I accept it all, I'm in need. So, he wants me to study hard and I will. Anything for my baby.

I owe him so much.

It's Deon who's convinced me to stop cutting. And for that, I owe him my life. I know that mum and dad will never see what I see in him but when we're together, it's like someone sprinkled magic dust over us. I melt into his cocky, confident alpha manliness. I have all the money, *I* am the spoilt little rich girl as he calls me, but see, when we're out, *he* pays for everything. He really does treat me like a queen. I forget to cut, forget to whine, forget that that thing ever happened. Love, it's the best form of therapy. It doesn't surprise me that loners are messed up. They don't have anyone to validate their perceptions of the world. But I have! And I'm so grateful for that. I know I'm young for him, but I seem to please him in bed. 'I can turn you into just about any position and you obey,' he says proudly. Of course, how could I refuse this solid hunk of gorgeousness? I look at him sleeping and pinch myself that I have him all to myself.

It's only when I'm by myself that I know the truth. Often, I can't feel a thing. Just dread. Without his compliments, I'm ashamed of me. I'm so ugly. My breasts are too big and I'm not curvy anymore, I feel fat. I stare at skinny, dark girls envying their svelte figures. Bongi has a better figure than me and I'm eaten up with jealousy.

Exams, exams, exams. Everyday there is a different assessment, a different deadline for an assignment.

Regarding Bongi, there seems to be so many teething problems with getting her settled in, most of the time she does not talk to me she just goes over my head and finds dad instead. As she eats with us I notice the changes in her, it's like a before and after transformation on those TV makeover programmes. She's a little beauty. With her new smart hairstyle and clothes, she's blossomed into quite the fashionista.

Despite this, she hardly says a word to me, she tries to make herself invisible around me. Why? I'm almost her age, I can't be that intimidating. Strange, she's like a frightened mouse, tip toeing around. Once, I heard crying, so I knocked and went in to find her lying on the bed, her whole body heaving with some deep sadness. But as soon as she saw me she withdrew into herself, her body going rigid with self -control, she has adopted this weird smile that doesn't quite reach her eyes, it's to placate us, to make us feel that she is okay even though she is clearly not. I tried to tell dad that maybe she is missing her township and maybe it's not possible to make coconuts out of all Black people, but he asked me to shut up and to stop talking nonsense.

It's strange being called 'racist' by my own father. That's how much he knows me! Some people just use that term willy-nilly and I hate it! They effectively stop having a dialogue with you and shut you out. It's like the boy who cried wolf, after a while no one takes you seriously anymore, even when the situation does warrant the term 'racist.' I'm so shocked that dad has resorted to this approach, he raised me, does he not know me at all? I'm not justifying myself to this man. I have decided that I will not talk to him while he is in these foul moods. I miss the presence of mum in the house and wish that she didn't spend such long stretches of time at the farm. I miss Deon too.

A few weeks in and Happiness too seems to have changed, she is not as attentive to my needs anymore, I am no longer the 'golden angel' in the house. She has a new preoccupation, her daughter. Now we all have to eat *her* favourite food, I don't mind a slice of pizza or two but not every damn day! And around the table, the conversation is all about how *she* is settling in, and which new friends *she* has made. A few times I saw her get really dolled up ready for a night out, it's dad, her champion, who takes her out in the Mercedes to concerts, restaurants, theatre, I know I see the tickets stashed away in his office. It's insane! It's like she is like a long-lost daughter and that I, the real biological daughter, is dead to him. He even seems more animated when they are going out than he used to be with us, a few times he asked me to accompany them and I sensed that it was not a heartfelt offer, just lip service. Maybe he wanted to enjoy her company alone. I once saw him invite Happiness too, but she refused and turned away when she saw me looking.

What's going on in my own house?

Anyway, I'm busy with exams and I can't afford to go gallivanting all over Durban like a social butterfly. No, he can focus on his charity project alone. Frankly, this whole thing has started to bore and irritate me. I am content with studying, then taking my pills and falling into a blissful sleep.

CHAPTER 8: THE ABYSS

July 1982

The months roll on, seasons change. In Durban, winter is settling in. It gets dark early now and we rush to get inside when we get home from school. Bongi is wearing a baggy, woolly cardigan under her school blazer, I have a V neck jumper and a scarf, I am that cold. It's a rugby scarf of course, Deon and I are passionate Springbok supporters, they're our national team and the best in the world we think. That's if we could play overseas which we are not allowed to due to international protests about the government. Of course, I wholeheartedly agree with other countries freezing us out, but I can't say it to him. Deon bought me that scarf a while back to apologize after one of our fights and even though we are not together anymore, I still treasure it. School is almost over for good. I've done my mock exams and after the holidays, I have the real exams then, I will be free forever. It still upsets me to think about how we ended it.

Sadly, it got to the point, after three years of dating, where he seemed to be working constantly and never made time for me. One evening, out of desperation, I got a lift to his apartment to make an impromptu visit, maybe even a booty call. I had rushed to his door and pressed the buzzer excitedly, what would he say when he saw his golden angel? To my horror, a gorgeous Black woman opened the door, it was just a fraction, but it was enough for me to see that she was wearing only a short skirt and heels, her breasts were exposed, and she seemed to sway to the rhythm of the slow and hypnotic Latin music playing inside. There was a strong smell of weed from the apartment, so I knew that Deon was in. It was *his* type of music. *His* weed. The Golf was parked outside, he was in. But the woman denied knowing a man called Deon, I tried the name Gideon and the answer was still no. She said that she had just moved in and that I needed to leave, or she would call the police, then she banged the door in my face.

Incomprehension, disappointment and hurt flooded me and I sank to my knees outside the elevator and started to weep. I knew instinctively that something was wrong, what though? I couldn't piece it together. The blackness was closing in again. I could have passed out right there, but something in me made me get up and take the elevator to the ground floor where mum's friend was waiting patiently in the car. Back in my bedroom, I took three pills straight away and fell asleep, sobbing on my pillow. 'Deon,' I moaned sniffing one of his T shirts that I'd stolen a while ago. His after shave still clung on, what a hypnotic, sensual smell of pine and leather and fragrant wood! It made me feel close to him even though things were not right between us.

In the morning I felt groggy and still drowsy when Happiness woke me for school. It was cold and dark outside, and I settled deep into the bed and announced that I was not going to school as I had flu. Dad came to check on me for a change, but I locked my door, so he would not see my puffy eyes. I was fine I lied, I just needed to sleep. Happiness promised to look after me which she didn't as she was busy with laundry, and dad took Bongi off to school.

Sensing how lonely I was, I lay back in bed, letting the darkness engulf me. Tears came every few minutes and I needed something to stop the pain. But what? Who could I ask? I had isolated myself from a lot of my friends due to studying intensively or shutting myself in the Art room. And of course, the pills made me tired throughout the day, sometimes I could barely keep awake. Now, I needed some badly as I couldn't get Deon out of my mind. I was convinced that he was avoiding me, but why? What had I done that was so wrong? Who was that woman in his apartment? I had seen sex workers lounging around inside and outside the block before, it was a multicultural community who lived in the beach area, but I had not expected my boyfriend to be involved in that! Especially when he had a doting girlfriend like me! When the house was quiet I crept out of my room and called him, I must have rung about fifty times that day. No answer. I sat on the floor and sobbed my heart out.

How are we expected to trust people when they treat us like shit on their shoes?

Maybe it *was* true and maybe I just had to accept it. Maybe it was normal for some people to want to marry you one day and then blank you the next. Maybe he had moved out and forgot to tell me. I went back to my room and lay there thinking about false promises, and about people with evil in their hearts, all my past pain seemed to come back in a loud whoosh and all I craved was thick, velvety darkness. I allowed it to envelop me, like a blanket of grief.

Then, suddenly, a horrible thought hit me! What if he was hurt? Murdered? Drug dealers got attacked all the time, that's why he carried that knife around. I sat bolt upright running through the scene in my head. That would explain his failure to pick up the phone! But the woman...and his car, his music, was it possible? *My* Deon? My brain wasn't letting me release him. Memory can be a tricky, cruel thing, it can hold you prisoner, trapped in an episode so that you relive it again and again. And Deon who had been a kind of saviour from my pain had been everything to me, replacing my apathetic, absent parents, friends who were often on a different wavelength, and a non - existing therapist. That was the truth staring at me now. I needed that counsellor.

But to go to that cobwebby, musty, evil place again? I had packed it all away deep in the recesses of my consciousness. He/she would want me to unpack it all, open it up for scrutiny, maybe even blame me for it. Was I wearing a bra on that day? Did I act provocatively? How come both cousins had turned against me when previously things had been okay between us?

It had to be me, it just had to.

No. I couldn't bear it. I hated myself already, some days it was enough for me to function like a normal schoolgirl whatever that was. For if I really allowed the darkness to sweep me up, I didn't know if I could bear it. The prospect of dying has always been tempting, that sharp screech of car tyres, the feel of metal ripping open flesh, the crunch of bones breaking and then the sweet release of life ebbing away. But in reality, how many of us have the courage to give in, to stop clinging on, even feebly, to life?

It's so easy for me to relapse to that dark place that excluded all love and light that I experienced when I was thirteen. I've tried running from it ever since but inside, I'm exhausted from trying to escape it. I'm so sick of being lonely, it's a vulgar, evil thing gnawing away at my sanity, making me feel hopeless. I can't share this with anyone even a therapist, counsellor whatever. Can't trust. I've isolated myself from everyone for fear of being hurt again, everyone except Deon and now look at how that's worked for me.

Don't put all your eggs into one basket! When the basket drops look at the mess those eggs make when they crack open and break.

People are inherently selfish. If you let them in, they break you. Truth.

Watch your back. And your front. There are backstabbers and front stabbers, either way you're fucked.

I had just one friend left. My trusted razor. Scritch scratch, it danced across virgin skin that day, I put my lips to the blood and gorged myself.

That winter I must have lost a few kilograms in weight. I refused to eat and just slept all day and all night. Even when I didn't feel sleepy, I still lay in bed. Maddie and Indira came to visit me. Indira brought her mum's fiery chicken curry to lift my spirits, but it sat next to my night stand, untouched. Maddie brought cheesecake and that too hardened and grew stale. The budding GP in her looked me up and down critically, pointing out carefully that my body was reacting to the drugs that I had fed it for all the years that I'd been

389

using, this sickness that I had was actually my body cleansing itself. 'You've become an addict, and now, you're detoxifying!' she said sharply. But I didn't believe her medical nonsense, I knew it was just a ruse to get me clean and to never use again. Maddie said that she believed in tough love, it was the only way to support me.

Lucky me to choose conservative, sermonizing, judgemental friends! As usual, I zoned out and returned to the blackness. I *did* get flu in the end and I was under my GP's orders to rest and recover. Happiness tried to tempt me with home- made soup, dad stepped up eventually and bought me chocolate and magazines, mum returned from wherever she usually disappeared to and read excerpts from my favourite books every day, stroking my hair when she stopped; sometimes she'd cry softly, praying for my recovery. I never knew her for a religious person, but I saw her broken, then. She was at home all the time now and I could see worry etched on her lovely face, she too had stopped eating altogether and she said that she would resume when *I* started to eat again. I knew it was another of her excuses not to eat but I needed her love and care, devoured it like a Venus fly trap with an insect, I kept her ball of love locked safely inside me willing it to overpower the darkness. I tried everything. I could feel my soul fighting for me.

But in the house, something felt strange, even wrong. With mum at my side, even sleeping next to me on a small fold up bed during the worst of my flu, it felt that something was incubating inside the house. There was a quietness, an eerie silence. Dad, in his annexe was cut off from us, Happiness was in her room outside. Bongi was sleeping perhaps, she was always sleeping. Mum and I lay in bed in that huge house, waiting, waiting.

CHAPTER 9: MARNIE

September 1982

One day I found myself at the black wrought iron gate in front of a daffodil yellow house. On the side wall flanking the gate was a fancy pants gold plaque that said simply 'Dr Elaine Robson. Psychiatric Services.' Underneath was a simpler, pared down wooden panel that said, 'Marnie Marie. Counsellor.' It felt absurdly like the gateway to the fun factory, I half expected red and white spotted toadstools and fairies peeping out, but I summoned up the courage to press the buzzer on the wall. Instead of asking what business I had there, I heard a click and the gate opened.

i was broken, now I Am

Curiouser and curiouser. Half-heartedly, I stepped onto a terracotta tiled veranda and stood in front of yet another security gate which was magically opened again from inside the recesses of what I was beginning to call the funny farm. I stepped inside a cool, dark passageway which led almost immediately into a large, modern living room on the right. Ignoring the other closed doors in the passage and the security gate that had shut by itself behind me with that decisive click, I drank in my surroundings. This was not a clinic, there was no receptionist, no patronizing posters or propaganda on the walls. Just a large fan blowing refreshingly cool air, some dark leather sofas and a wooden coffee table. I felt flustered. Where was this Marnie?

Then, I heard voices, goodbyes, a door opened but it was not a white rabbit that emerged, instead, it was a beautiful woman. I explained that I was there to see Marnie and that I had made an appointment by phone. I was ten minutes early, I explained.

'She's great,' she said in a faltering voice. 'I've been seeing her for two months now, helped me so much to reframe!'

She sat down on a two- seater and fumbled inside her bag, indicating a seat for me next to her. She looked Indian, with dark skin and light, almost caramel coloured eyes thickly lined with kohl, her black hair was bunched high in a ponytail like mine.

'Sorry, I'm just looking for my car keys, I'm Zubeida, Zubbie.'

Her hand felt slightly damp in mine.

Zoe, Zubbie. It was the beginning of a friendship. I wanted to walk out with her, go to the mall in the next block and swop stories over coffee, there was something warm and needy about her, I could see as she searched my eyes trying to read me. I know the type, I do the same. Broken people. We need to predict who we're dealing with. We started talking, I still had time. After the what are you here for? question, I unexpectedly lifted the hem of my dress, my thighs told the story, it didn't need words to garnish it. But she didn't flinch like I expected. Instead, she sighed a long, deep sigh, then ran her long, smooth fingers over my scars. Touched, I watched as she turned her back to me and asked me to lift her top. Just like that. There was no one around. I half expected someone to barge in with white coats coming to lock up the crazies, but I did as she had asked and then it was my turn to stare, even tear.

Her whole back with its beautiful, silky brown skin was traversed by three dimensional welts, there were so many that they criss-crossed each other and ended just above the waistband of her jeans. Some were angry purple, others paprika red, some almost dark mahogany, all had the same strap- like thickness.

'He did it with a belt. After I complained about the pain of anal sex. I didn't want to be raped in my bed every night. If it hadn't been for Marnie's advice,' her eyes misted up.

I felt numb. Everyone had been right about me. I was a spoilt, self-indulgent little brat! God, I had believed that the world had ended because I had been raped by my cousin, but here, here was this lovely, delicate creature who had to endure this! Night after night. Not like *my* ordeal which had effectively stopped since James had gone to the UK. There was a yearning in her to connect, to reach out. Poor woman, she must have sensed some pain in me too, to be able to trust me like this. We swopped numbers and arranged to meet up at the mall to talk, hugging each other as we parted.

Strange how connections with perfect strangers happen, I now reframe situations like these as little lifelines, lines of support. If you look for it, it's there. I suddenly knew that I was *not* alone, that this lovely lady who had been tortured so much, was meant to come into my life for a reason. Then, a voice called out my name and I stepped into Marnie's office.

She was a surprisingly small, older woman. Not that I had had any past experiences with counsellors before. As she emerged from behind a tower of books and files on her desk to sit in the armchair in front of me, I took in the solid shape, the simple, linen trousers and patterned shirt, the flat sensible shoes, the gold rimmed glasses and short grey hair. I was looking at my gran's sister. Immediately I relaxed and helped myself to a glass of cold water from a tall jug in which sliced lemons floated prettily at the top. Once the form filling was over, she asked if we could record the session and we started.

I'd lost that urge to cover and hide, after the shock of seeing Zubbie. I was there to heal. So, I pulled up my white dress high to gauge her reaction. No frowning, no laughter from her, just a nod as she leaned over and first looked, then softly touched the scars. Her face was soft. Gran had died a few years ago and I had hated the house so much that I had not attended the funeral or the wake there. Everyone put it down to my grief coupled with that ivory tower, artistic temperament and they left me alone. But this lady was as loveable as gran had been, I could sense it. Even when she spoke, it was soft and unhurried. She never took her eyes away from me, she just listened or spoke. And I found myself opening to her like a flower that turns its head towards the sun, I told her everything. I must have spoken for at least an hour, but we had a two- hour session booked, she explained that that was how she liked to work, initially. Block bookings. She wasn't going to ask me to open and then just leave things. I liked her already. She told me that she was a counsellor not a psychiatrist and that her methods were somewhat unconventional. Her prices were disarmingly cheap. But she would help me.

'You see, at the end, it's all about love. Love for yourself. If you don't have it, you can't set boundaries, you don't have any way of showing others how you wish to be treated, what you can or cannot accept. I'm not talking about aggression or narcissism now. I'm talking about how developed your sense of self- worth is. It's a common theme for many.'

Wow! So, I didn't have that self- deprecating thing, an 'issue.' She was going deep, digging into my psyche, not fixing me but almost teaching me. Where was this charming lady my whole life? I was glued to her every word, sitting bolt upright on the long sofa opposite hers, straining to catch every droplet of wisdom until she reminded me to relax as it was all on tape. If I could have folded her up, put her in my bag and taken her home I would have, and I told her this. I hadn't even realized that I was crying. At this point, she moved over, sat next to me and took my hand.

'I'm here for you Zo, I'm here. I'm not going anywhere.'

She said that I had been having a psychic breakdown for years, but I had tried to ignore it and soldier on. My Art had been a therapeutic outlet and of course, the cutting. But the panic attacks showed that things were not okay and that the unresolved stuff was resurfacing each time. It would not stop by itself. I had to stage an intervention. On myself. Rescue myself? Who talks like that? No one in my circles. No wonder she had called herself unconventional. I wanted to know more. I wanted to stay with her for the day, the week. And as she spoke, it all made sense. My parents who had never parented me, the cold vacuum between them that I'd been forced to witness for eighteen years, the distancing, keeping me at arms-length, abandoning me in favour of charity dinners, my father's physically moving out into the annexe outside, mum's disappearances to the farm, dumping me on Happiness, my life as an only child, my lack of social integration with other children when I was home schooled and now the ultimate snub, adopting the child of our maid and emphasizing the hierarchy between us, she was at the top of the love pyramid, I was relegated to the bottom. I was always at the bottom of the heap. White, privileged, spoilt. So, I *had* to be punished. And if they hadn't punished me by the wall of apathy, then it was me punishing myself. She was Black, underprivileged, misrepresented. She'd lucked out on opportunities from the word go so now it was her turn. Payback. Deon too had won my trust, then totally abandoned me, dropping me like a hot potato for no reason, creating no closure. She said it was a miracle that I was here in her consulting room instead of lying in a coffin.

Rape was a crime that we heard about daily in Durban. Burglars, invariably Black, would break in and rape you, *then* leave. I wondered now whether that was down to them venting that pent- up anger over having been marginalized by a racist government for so long, that they wanted to leave you with that legacy of psychic pain as payback. It just seemed that this hate fuelled act was driven more by revenge and wanting comeuppance, that the burglaries too were not done just out of a financial need. The other ugly truth for me was that some people had become habituated to crime. Criminals saw it as a way of eking out a living as work opportunities, in better jobs, were largely reserved for Whites. And everyone else accepted it as the default side effect of living in the paradise that is South Africa. At one stage you knew that it would be your turn to be raped or assaulted or car jacked or mugged. Or killed. It was like playing the game dodgeball, you could run, dance or skip to avoid getting bashed by the ball but at some point, it would get you, especially if you took your eye off it for a moment.

But then, I thought about children being raped by their fathers or family members, wives by their husbands, patients by doctors, kids by their teachers. Even religious leaders did it: swamis, priests, vicars. Politicians, the police, people who were on committees *against* rape. They did it. And they were *not* all Black and underprivileged. So there had to be more than revenge as the driving force. Maybe it was about a lack of impulse control, a lack of self -control. To say that someone was horny didn't cut it for me, we all have biological needs. But taking something by force, there had to be a reason why it was done. There just had to be. So many of us were broken because of it. My mind went to an image of a baby doll that I broke as a child, its lifelike body eerily haunting me as it lay separated from the head with its glassy, open eyes, limbs scattered carelessly around. It was a symbol of how I felt inside. Fragments of me dissociated and scattered, trying to be whole again. Was that how others felt?

At that point, she had to stop the tape as I was wracked with loud, gut wrenching, primal sobs, my whole body heaving and trembling. It wasn't a pretty sound, but I didn't care about anything, I just couldn't go on. I didn't feel safe. I had never felt safe.

There were no quick fixes now, no weed, pills, alcohol. Nothing but a kind soul whose warm arms were embracing me in a hug. We had to take a minute, she said. In the end, she brewed some rooibos tea with honey for both of us and took me into the small courtyard outside where we sat in the sun drinking it in a reflective silence.

When we went back, there was twenty minutes left and she broke the impasse by bits of chit chat. She had retired last year but greatly enjoyed her work, purely to support a handful of existing clients, she came in for two days in the week using someone else's practice for this. She asked me to trust her and said that she had supported many clients through more extreme trauma. I knew, I had seen the state of Zubbie's back.

There was an awkwardness now, I felt spent. I wanted to go home, lie down and process it all. I knew that my eyes would be swollen and red, I had cried myself out. I looked and felt like a mess.

'Zoe, is there anyone that you communicate clearly and effectively with?' Silence. She knew that the answer was a no.

'Then I'm going to teach you to use your voice to speak your truth. Instead of using your precious body to set down your story, I want to encourage you to talk. The more you let it out, the more you will heal yourself. You are a young woman, you deserve to be happy and joyful.'

Joy. What did it actually mean? I had blocked out emotion for so long, I had forgotten the word. She went on to broach the topic of James. Reframing the situation as the act of two unstable teenagers who did not exhibit normal, expected behavior, she painted a picture of James as a sicko, someone who would have trouble having normal, fulfilling relationships with other people as he had a twisted urge to get pleasure out of coercing his partner. He was a paedophile. And before I had a chance to take this in, she said that I had the option to report this crime to the police. Finally, totally unexpectedly, she said that our future work would be centred on letting everything just go, to embrace and accept that the past was the past and to forgive myself.

She suggested that I eat healthily, not binge eat and do exercises like swimming and yoga.

I think I ran out of there, after thanking her profusely.

In the days that followed, I felt shell shocked and craved silence and space. But I had started to regain my strength much to everyone's relief. Breakfast was a bowl of fruit salad and herbal tea, beer was replaced by fresh juice, smoothies and water. I ate salad, swam and read. I sat in silence in the garden, listening to the sound of birds. I watched the gold flecked koi carp glide effortlessly through the water in the pond. I could sense raised eyebrows all round and thumbs up signs. People were noticing.

On the other side, Bongi didn't seem to be doing as well. Usually, she was guarded and somewhat defensive, but she seemed to be retreating more and more to her room on the pretext of studying. We never saw her anymore. It was true that she was super bright and with her extra top up lessons to make up for her limited township education, she had started to flourish academically. She read voraciously, in English. But her shape had changed, she appeared a bit more mature now and even started to develop a little chubbiness on her face, her body seemed bulky somehow and her gait slow and laboured at times. I'm not a body shamer, so I complimented her on her curviness but every time she caught me looking at her, she would quickly make a beeline for her room and bang the door rudely. Maybe she had a boyfriend, I didn't know anything about her, I just knew that at school, she was always surrounded by her friends and they fell into a hushed silence as soon as I passed by, so I gave her the space she craved and focused on my own healing. In the early days, I had tried so hard to reach out, we had had sisterly sleepovers in my bedroom, pool parties, barbeques with our joint friends. But she had thrown it all in my face by constructing this shroud of secrecy around her. With what *I* had to deal with, it became too frustrating just trying to decode it all. I felt exhausted.

i was broken, now I Am

Marnie's advice was sinking in slowly as I listened repeatedly to the tape on my Walkman. Each week, I had a session now and each time I felt healthier and more aware of myself. Zubbie and I had become friends, we met for coffee every week and her story was so extreme that it made me physically sick, to understand it, I painted it then hid the canvasses so that I didn't have to confront the pain in them.

CHAPTER 10: ZUBBIE

High risk pickpocket area. Keep handbags, purses and wallets safe.

I'm sitting in a coffee shop on the top floor of the mall, reading the signs posted every few metres. Security guards amble around largely ignored by the well -dressed clientele, this is an upmarket suburb and there is a quiet plushness about the mall. Drifts of air conditioning and light music hit me while I scan the entrance looking for Zubbie. Suddenly, she is here. She reminds me of a fragile flower that could disintegrate upon touch, her white shirt hangs down to her knees, underneath she is wearing jeans and flat, sensible shoes.

i was broken, now I Am

When we hug tightly, I feel her bony frame, her shoulder blades stick out and I am sure I remembered a narrow, skeletal back crisscrossed with belt marks, fresh and raw. I shudder and still hold onto her, cupping her beautiful, gaunt face in my hands. She has lost weight since I last saw her, her make up free face appears haggard, the cheekbones prominent. I stroke her hair which hangs down in a high pony tail, it's as soft as a horse's tail. Rarely have I had the chance to connect with such a fragile creature. I'm tearing up and she notices, reaching out across the table to comfort me.

It is what it is my friend.

Let it go.

No. I can't.

There is an unspoken, sisterly silence between us. My broken bird. I want to protect her, put her in cotton wool and guard her.

Then the waiter breaks the moment. She wants me to order for us, so I get baked vanilla cheesecakes and lattes.

'You look amazing,' she says brightly. I'm feeling decadent and overdressed now, it's not my usual style to be dressed up, I'm a shorts and T shirt kind of girl. But today, I was excited to see Zubbie. Besides, Marnie had given me a pep talk about using colour to celebrate life. I'm wearing a turquoise maxi dress in a fitted lycra like fabric, the top is a halter neck and the dress is backless. I've plaited my hair and coiled it in a bun at the top, placing silly turquoise butterfly clips randomly all over to match my dangly silver butterfly earrings, my silver bangles and my flat, silver sandals. This morning, I felt playful and frivolous, but now, I see that it is an excessive display of confidence and youth. Zubbie's warmth spills over the table and envelops me in its embrace, I can't stop tearing and she hands me a scented tissue. She is kind to me, telling me that I look like something out of a magazine, my eyes matching my dress. I'd always thought that they were dad's eyes, limpid, light blue. But now she is saying that they are deep turquoise. Mum's eyes.

Body dysmorphia is another term that Marnie has taught me. My tendency to see myself as flawed, to constantly put myself down as I perceived myself to be ugly. Everyone, everyone seemed slimmer, prettier and better than me.

i was broken, now I Am

'How have you been?' I dread saying it, knowing, by looking into her stricken eyes, that things are not okay. While picking at the food, she tells me her full story.

Zubbie has had a conservative, religious upbringing, she was an only daughter and at sixteen, she had an arranged marriage to an older, wealthy businessman. I'd seen her drive away from Marnie's office in a burnished gold BMW with dark tinted windows. She says that she lived in the lap of luxury and didn't have to work or cook. Her mother- in -law who lived with them did all the cooking, a servant did the cleaning. She was not allowed in the kitchen, even to make snacks for her four young sons. She should be happy with her affluent lifestyle except that this was not what she had dreamed of. Zubbie had wanted to study, like her brothers. But her parents would not hear of it. Now, she was trapped, married to a violent man who never took her out or spent time with the family. He left early and returned at night to eat and be fussed over by his mother. Then, in bed, he would ask her to do degrading things and when she complained, he would beat her with a belt and still have sex with her afterwards.

She was sickened, she tells me, by his collection of porn movies that he kept hidden away. She'd gone into his home office during the day and found them. One evening, she'd gone in to talk to him and found him chatting to a naked woman lying on a sofa with her legs apart. That night he whipped her so hard that she fled with her bleeding wounds to her mother- in -law's room, only to be told coldly that she had to go back and respect her husband.

She is only twenty-five. Six years older than me.

I can't eat anything. Instead, I want ten vodka shots and a Glock 9 mm pistol. It is small enough to conceal in my bag, all I have to do is point, pull the trigger and shoot, I've done my research. I'd hold it to his temple and take pleasure in seeing the wide- eyed shocked expression, then relish in the short, sharp bang as he flew backwards. Of course, I'd follow that with the next, crucial shot to the groin. There's nothing like the sweet pleasure of violently taking the life of an abuser. Die Bitch! I don't even know what he looked like, but I pictured a heavy, middle aged man with a corpulent body and a loose, lecherous mouth. No wait, that was dad. I have been picturing dad all this time.

Breathe in. And out.

Whoooooooooo.

i was broken, now I Am

The mother in law would have to be taken out too.
Which woman puts another woman in that situation?

He beat me black and blue. I'm frightened.

Go back, that's my son. It's your life now.

Please.

Get out of here. Go back to my son. You're talking rubbish!

Worthless piece of shit, you were nothing when he met you.

Look at my back. I'm bleeding.

So? Is it too much to please him in bed? You don't have to cook, you don't have to clean. All you have to do is open your legs.

You don't understand, it's more than that. I can't go to the loo properly, can't control my bowels. He wants it from behind. Always from behind.

He's my son, you give him whatever he needs, you hear me! Now get out bitch!

'You have a faraway look,' she says, a glimmer of a smile now.

'Sorry, I have a habit of zoning out. What will you do now? You can't carry on there, surely not.'

I offer to help with anything possible, cash, a safe haven, transport, if she wants to leave her car there. I will even go to her house and walk out with her and her boys. Get the police involved. Or not. The South African police are famous for bungling things up, you have to payroll them if you want results and even then, you can never be sure about the outcome. But she resists all help. It was pointless, he'd asked her to leave before, but minus her sons. And that was something that she could not do. Her parents would send her back to him, her brothers would do the same. It was part of the culture, she says bitterly, in her soft, faltering voice. Even other women who suffer similar fates will not come forward and talk about it. It is the most hush hush topic of all.

What happens in the bedroom stays in the bedroom.

Zubbie says that just pouring her heart out to Marnie and now me, is enough.

We met three more times.

The fourth time, she did not pitch. I called her repeatedly but felt like I was intruding so I left it. But after a few days an uneasy feeling started to well up in me. I asked Marnie about her on my next visit and there was a long pause before she could meet my eyes. Zubbie had been found hanging in her son's bedroom.

She had been pronounced dead. The police officer who had contacted Marnie said that her business card had been found amongst Zubbie' s things and he wanted to ask routine questions.

Her husband, in laws and parents had been distraught by their loss of this beloved wife and mother that they had all cared about so very deeply.

A new image flashed before my bitter, broken eyes. An old man flanked by his elderly, doting mother at his next wedding. The new bride, a fresh young thing, almost a child herself, would be perfect to bring up his four sons and still be fertile enough to have children of her own. A perfect ending.

CHAPTER 11: THE FARM

One Thursday, mum announced that she wanted
to go to the farm for a long weekend, leaving early the
next day. I knew that before she had me, dad had
coaxed her into living in the city, but her heart was in
the large, colourful house in the Drakensberg that she
had painted in bright, ice cream colours: pistachio,
raspberry pink, mango yellow, bubblegum blue. She
was quick to reel off the names of the paints that she
had lovingly sourced for the old house that she'd
insisted on keeping as she had saved up and bought it
with the proceeds of her work, sometimes she said that

she was only herself when she was there alone. But I also had an affinity for the place and in many ways, I had grown up there. Ever since I was a child, I'd spent every holiday there with mum, sometimes dad visited, sometimes not. My bedroom there was my favourite as it was the all-white, silent space that I craved when I needed to rest. When we were not there, our housekeeper Connie who lived for free in a little cottage on the periphery, looked after things, her children Sara and Jacob being my close friends too. And then there was Anton.

Mum spoke about her plans, packing quickly in that decisive way that signalled that she would not be talked out of going. Boxes were produced, the drinks cabinet was ransacked, and bottles of Scotch and wine loaded into them with Happiness's help. This was a familiar routine for Happiness as mum did the two hour drive up several times a month. She would load the car with anything that she couldn't procure in the rural village shops outside the farm, there'd be milk tarts, biltong strips, boerewors, pre-marinated chops, fish steaks and whole chickens that were cleaned and gutted.

For us South Africans, the jorl or party revolves around one thing: the braai. This time honoured tradition is upheld by all South Africans, perhaps it's the one single thing that we share in this colourful rainbow nation. Put simply, it involves slapping meat, chicken and/or fish that has been marinated in various combination of spices, on hot coals to be barbequed.

I'm told that this smoke infused food is carcinogenic or cancer inducing but nevertheless, the delicious flavours permeating the food cooked in this way is irresistible to us, especially served with the variety of salads that are not just palate cleansers but crucial accompaniments to the main event. This is washed down by a drink or 'dop': ice cold beer for me, brandy and Coke for others, or whiskey. Mum was getting things ready for a weekend of braais, dopping and chilling with her local friends. I knew that this would mean Johan. We didn't need to invite Johan, our neighbour, as he flocked to mum's side whenever she was around. And maybe Anton, his son would be there too. I'm shy when I talk about Anton, Johan's only son who I have had a crush on ever since I can remember.

Johan is this sweet and gentle older man with skin tanned the colour of leather and kind, amber eyes. Poor Johan, he had issues of his own. He nurses a deep and profound grief as fifteen years ago, his wife was

violently pulled out of her car by Black thugs who
proceeded to rape and assault her in front of their ten -
year old son Anton, finally shooting her dead when
they finished with her. Poor Anton! He had to watch
his mother being gang raped, then her corpse being
flung out onto the dusty, dirt track. He had run for his
life as they were coming after him. How do you bounce
back after something like that? It broke both Johan and
his son, relatives from Holland flew in for the funeral
and insisted on taking Anton back to Holland to be
looked after by his aunt where he had to have therapy
for years. Meanwhile Johan soldiered on, quietly
regaining his strength to run his farm. There was a time
when haunted by the past, he'd left the place to fall into
ruin as he struggled to pick up the pace of life again but
mum, his best friend and childhood sweetheart had
stepped up and rescued him. Sometimes she would do
the two -hour drive to the farm just to cook dinner for
him. Then, they would sit on the wrap around veranda
drinking whiskey in the candlelight and talking until the
morning. Together, they made a tight knit duo, leaving
me wondering why she couldn't be like this, with dad,
the man she had married.

My mind racing, picturing mum with Johan alone at the farm, I suddenly had a brainwave. Mum and I would drive up there together for some much-needed bonding, and later, dad could join us after his meeting with his editor as he was about to publish a new book. We would then leave mum to work while we explored the village, and, in the evening, we would invite Johan and light the braai, that way, we could all be together.

How children try desperately but misguidedly sometimes to knit their families together! Harmony. It's what we all yearn for. Frowning at the thought of not having that alone time that she seemed to crave sometimes daily, she agreed reluctantly.

So, we drove together, the two of us, early on Friday. I was bunking from school, but the mock exams were over, and I wanted to relax and celebrate. Mum lovingly joked that this was meant to be her weekend away alone, so I promised her that we would give her space to work all day. We stopped for lunch and petrol, laughing and joking all the time. I drove, showing off with my newfound confidence, with mum squeezed into the back of my tiny new car. It was cute, seeing my mother like this, usually she would glide out of the driveway in her silver car, looking regal and beautiful as always. But that day, she looked like a girl again in her white shorts, red checked shirt and white flat sandals. She had no make- up on, and with her slim figure, long tanned legs and dark, cropped hair she looked much younger than she was. In fact, seeing her in the back seat singing along to silly pop music, I suddenly felt a pang of sadness for her life, she was rarely this abandoned at home in the city, was it dad's presence that upset her? He had put on a lot of weight over the years and with his large, pale blue eyes and bald head I imagined that it must have been difficult for someone as beautiful and as perfect as mum. I knew that things had changed for them, they seemed like brother and sister at times but without the closeness, like two siblings inhabiting a common space because they lived there, not out of choice but out of necessity.

I knew that mum needed a man who loved her in a deeper way compared to dad. Maybe then, mum would not have developed her carefully disguised eating disorder. Nobody can tell me that they would prefer to chew ice cubes to eating food! At her worst, she was gaunt and skinny, her breasts ironing board flat in her concave chest cavity. Oh, she fitted into her little cocktail dresses perfectly, but I saw past these outer trappings, picturing a bony, bird like frame in a coffin because she was not destined for longevity, not with *her* issues. No one could help her. She hid behind make up, perfume and champagne, barking savagely at dad when he recommended certain dishes or held out a slice of something delicious for her to try. Salads were her refuge, the bright greens giving her scope to push bits around playfully so that she effectively scattered them around the plate instead of eating anything. I am and will always be, keenly observant. I knew. Yet she ate well when she was on the farm. I shuddered to think what this yo-yo effect had on her digestive system. Clearly, she associated wellbeing with the farm, our city life was something that she saw as a walk on part, performed through gritted teeth.

Suddenly we turned a corner of the dirt track and there it was, nestling in the hills like a forgotten secret, the farm, looking cozy and inviting with its newly painted exterior and bright flowers planted all around. Funny, Johan had neglected his own farm, but he had made our house his project, lovingly spending his time on repairs and decorating. Occasionally, he even bought pieces of antique furniture that he thought mum would love, such was the bond between them.

Mum gawped and choked back tears, she did this every time we rounded that corner and the house came into view. We both felt like crying that day, the memories held there sat preciously as in tissue paper, as fragrant as old rose petals. There was such a sense of peace and tranquility there, the banana yellow house, the reddish mountains in the distance fringing the horizon, wild flowers in uncontrolled abandon, ablaze with colour, the little blue car. That scene was etched in my mind, never to be forgotten. Time stood still there, in that haven of peace, it felt sacred to me. There was wisdom there, a rhythm and a sense of purpose. I understood why it was the only place that mum came to when she wanted to paint, reflect or to unwind completely. She could be present there.

Johan saw the car immediately and came rushing over with a basket filled with flowers, fruits and vegetables from his garden, no doubt there was a bottle of whiskey nestling at the bottom of the basket too! There were long stemmed crimson roses with velvety petals, fresh raspberries and baby potatoes that would crisp up perfectly on the braai. And the sudden transformation in mum! It made me nervous and shy to see it, to face the truth that I had known in my heart all along. Strange how she metamorphosed into this smiley person, full of hugs and kisses, greeting him like he was more than the best friend that he was.

Embarrassed by the deep love unfolding before my teenage eyes, I greeted him, then left them to explore the house and the farm yard. I missed Anton and couldn't wait for him to arrive. Dear Connie, our housekeeper who looked after us there, would also want me to check in with her, I imagined that she would be frantically getting the place prepared for us.

Her fresh, home -made bread and rolls were legendary and there was always a delicious cold spread or banquet ready when we arrived. This adorable Coloured lady had been another mother to me ever since I was little, she'd lived rent free in the cottage on the periphery ever since mum bought the farm and she was like a sister to mum. Her son Jacob, Anton and I hung out and I knew that they were both sweet on me.

That day, all our lives changed forever.

i was broken, now I Am

CHAPTER 12: ANTON

How do I start, in describing Anton? Maybe the
best place would be to share what happened twelve
years ago, when I was six and Anton thirteen. Oh, he
was a good- looking boy even then, with his large, gold
flecked, sage green eyes, his deeply tanned skin the
colour of pale caramel, his honey blonde hair that he
liked to wear in a cropped style. But his most adorable
feature is his slightly crooked front teeth that gives him
a lopsided, boyish look when he smiles, a look that has
melted the hearts of almost every person he comes
across. At thirteen, Anton was approaching a hundred

and seventy -two centimetres in height, later, he shot up like a giraffe, ending up being well over a hundred and eighty -two centimetres. He's a true Dutchman, my Anton. A man who loves the earth, the bush, his passion for nature running in his blood like his dad Johan. A gentle giant, they call him.

We were on the farm, playing together as we usually did when we were all together. Anton was on his annual holiday from his aunt's care in Holland. Our housekeeper's children Sara and Jacob were approaching Anton's age and then there was little me, a scraggy six -year old, with long blonde hair in plaits and fierce blue eyes. 'Let's play House!' squealed Sara, it was her favourite game after football. It required pinching bits of food from the kitchen, my own toy kitchen set, blankets and our veranda where we would set up a simulated home.

'I wanna be the baby!' she screamed excitedly, stuffing her thumb into her mouth and curling up in a ball on the floor.

'You can be *my* baby,' I suggested. But Jacob liked to have all the fundamentals settled first.

'You have to have a husband,' he remarked, 'it has to be Anton because I wanna be a visitor who gets to be served food.'

'Okay,' agreed Anton smiling, 'let's get married.'

'You have to ask her silly.' Jacob again.

So, on one knee planted in the red sand gritty with stones, smiling that disarming smile, he asked me to marry him. Sara found wild flowers for my hair and Anton found a small strip of dried grass which he fashioned into a ring. Afterwards, I had to simulate birthing Sara and our visitor left feeling sated having feasted on Connie's koeksisters and slices of lemon sponge cake. On the low wall outside the kitchen, Anton carved our names using a penknife: 'Anton loves Zoe. Always and Forever.' Afterwards, when I had to run in for bath time, I felt awkward and shy leaving him. It was as if we had created a bond that would hover over us forever.

The next morning, he waited for me outside the kitchen in our spot. 'You still wearing the ring,' he commented, suddenly shy too. 'Of course,' I said, 'I love you.'

'I love you too,' he whispered. 'I'm gonna wait for you to grow up. Then, I'm really going to marry you.'

Fast forward a few years. Every year, he would return from Holland for a two -month holiday and every visit involved seeing each other all day, Saturday to Sunday. Of course, Johan and mum loved us hanging out, it meant that they too had an excuse to schedule family events together: fishing, braais, picnics, swimming in the river, visits to the village, lunches in the beer garden at the local hotel, even supermarket trips became communal and a reason to join forces. At the back of my mind, I knew that Anton was just like a brother to me and comforted by this thought, I gladly clung to his side, like a burr sticking to my clothing when I walked brazenly barefoot through bushes. For years, we repeated this summer routine until one day, at the age of thirteen, I stopped going to the farm. No one could work out why. I started stuttering, painting wildly, and adopted a reclusive lifestyle. I threw Anton's letters in the trash saying that I hated boys, started wearing makeup and developed an affinity for smoking cannabis, or 'zorl' as we call it.

Then, at fifteen I returned. At twenty-two now, Anton had become a game warden and was stationed in the Kruger National Park, a large game reserve with lodge style accommodation in the northeast of South Africa. He still holidayed several times a year at his family's farm in the Drakensberg, but his working life was spent in the outdoors, patrolling the perimeter, tracking 'spoor' or animal scents and organizing sundowners and expeditions for tourists on safari eager to view 'the big five'. This meant, as he explained, lions, leopards, buffalo, rhinos and elephants.

When I saw him, I was taken aback by how rugged he was, how he had grown. He was a man now. I was a teenager, with long hair, breasts and curves. The electricity between us fizzed and sparked as we spoke animatedly in our first catch up session. He told me all about the spectacular beauty of safari, saying that after returning from Holland, he had fallen in love with South Africa all over again. There was no mention of the crime against his mother that had embittered him in the past, he had come home for good, wanting a fresh start. He ran his eyes repeatedly over my body fascinated with the young woman that I had become, wanting to touch, asking if I had a boyfriend and what was life like in the city. What he couldn't see, was the deadness in my blue eyes, eyes that now saw only pain and humiliation.

I had been burned. James and Tarryn had seen to that. I flinched when he touched me, recoiling dramatically enough for him to feel hurt and confused. We stood staring at our spot, the words of love an embarrassing testimony to our childhood games, silence hanging thickly between us now. 'Will you marry me?' he asked again, knowing the answer already but trying anyway.

'I have to go inside,' I blurted awkwardly, 'mum's calling me.'

'She's not!' he said hissing playfully, and pulling me on top of him, he kissed me. Strange sensations flooded me all at once, my love for him, guilt and shame at sharing my private parts, and a sharp reminder of the psychological pain I experienced with James. But slowly I let him in. I forced myself to give in, telling myself that this would be different and that I needed to move on, let the past be just that, the past.

My therapist who had treated me for the stutter, not the rape, had told me that new beginnings required something in the past to end. I'd also heard somewhere someone say that if you love someone then lock him down, especially if he's a keeper like Anton. What a naive fifteen- year old I made! With all these conflicting ideas racing around in my head, I allowed Anton to make love to me. What a different experience this was, compared to James! He was a gentle and passionate lover, making me feel unique and special. Love bubbled between us, frothy and sweet, stirring up the sensual pleasure that I knew was addictive to me. We wanted more and more, finding rooms to hide in, his house, my house.

But when he reminded me of what he had said years ago, that he would wait for me to grow up to marry me, I pictured being a young Boer or Dutchman's wife living on a game reserve, churning out baby after baby with no educational qualifications behind me, and I couldn't reconcile this image with what my parents wanted for me. What would my liberal, progressive dad say if he knew that I was marrying an Afrikaner, his hated enemy, known for their extreme right- wing views? To have them as cherished friends on the farm was one thing, as an only child marrying them, was an entirely different matter.

In many ways, thinking about dad's stereotypical views of Afrikaans speaking people, angered me. They were *not* all the same. In fact, I had witnessed deplorable habits in dad himself, how dare he judge others? He made us live in that mansion, to start with. And that made me feel awkward when people spoke about White privilege. Why would a family of three need a house with eight bedrooms and four reception rooms? Why would we need so many cars when others went without? He had preached endlessly about the racist Afrikaners, but he himself was racist in appropriating an estate as large as ours, when he could have been an agent of change and opted for a scaled down house with one car. He had spoken about decolonization at cocktail parties while swigging the finest Scotch and eating gourmet food. What a hypocrite! And no one had had the balls to take him to task over his actions! He was off limits, why? Because he had written books about the need for political change. Cringe. I hadn't even read one!

I knew what I knew. Both Anton and Johan were warm, considerate people with no care about the colour or class of people that they interacted with. I knew that we had misunderstood the argument about race and that we needed to look beyond simple stereotypes. That's essentially what a 'rainbow nation' meant right? But of course, no one listens to me. And they would never approve of an Afrikaner husband for me. Dad would be vehemently against it, and mum would follow, like an ice cube chewing sheep.

And I certainly couldn't share these anxieties with poor Anton. After his ordeal, he didn't deserve that!

It seemed like we were all privately nursing wounds from different perceptions, ordeals and violations, all of us locked into inner torment and putting brave faces on for the sake of resuming our daily lives. This is truly representative of life in South Africa. Have you ever wondered why masses of South Africans migrate to the UK or Australia? It is not because we hate our country, the opposite is true. South Africa will always be in my blood, in *our* blood, as a collective, and there are things that expats crave every day. The warm weather, the unparalleled high quality of food and wine, the surf, rugby, the beach, the focus on family, national celebrations enjoyed in communities, the outdoors, braais, safari, the spectacular, dramatic sunsets and sunrises, are but a few aspects of South African culture that are cherished. But we choose to write our own endings and fear of each other, fear of the possibility of what could happen, even if it didn't happen yet, makes us flee. Stereotypical thinking, like dad's, is the curse that contaminates people's minds.

It poisoned *my* mind. I chose badly that day. I chose *not* to end up marrying young and ending up with someone that dad wouldn't approve of.

I chose my Art and an opportunity to develop and progress myself, to please dad.

And I hurt Anton.

A few months after returning to Durban, I met Deon, ironically another Dutchman, and was catapulted into a new world of drug fuelled sex. My voice on the phone to Anton was lackluster, I explained that I had fallen in love and that I could not be with him again. In response to his disbelieving questions, I firmly told him to move on. I knew that I had broken his heart forever. Whether I ever really loved Deon, I will never know. If he hadn't paved the way by offering me drugs to escape my pain, maybe I would have seen him for the narcissist that he was.

But the uncomfortable truth, is that Anton and I never stopped being lovers. Every time we met at the farm which was roughly about every two months, we hooked up. I hate saying it like this. A hook up. It sounds casual and careless. It wasn't. Deep inside, I craved Anton, came alive when he was around, ran to find him when I got to the farm. We were inseparable. Everyone but mum and dad knew what we were doing, we had been caught out lots of times as we lay together in the long grass, in his house, our house. But I couldn't reconcile the fact that he was such an earnest young man and dad saw all Afrikaners as right- wing racists. Deon was one. But with Deon there were added extras, he took me away from the pain. Anton wouldn't. He'd drill down into it, forcing me to go clean and confront some unspeakable truths. And he was a wild creature, comfortable only in the bush, amongst game, raw African skies, mud huts with thatched roofs, braais. Could I settle for that life? With my Art, the city beckoned. I needed a studio, exhibition space, networks. I wanted to do outreach work with children. I was filled with dreams of how Art could heal. How could I achieve this in the bush? I couldn't, and I wouldn't take Anton away from what he loved either. I was torn. Sexually, psychologically and emotionally bonded to him like a fly to jam, a magnet to iron filings. We were fused together, from the start. But...

And he had had his fair share of beautiful women with whom he tormented me, by bringing them to the farm, brandishing them in front of everyone like a trophy hunter showing off. I could see that he was getting his fixes from all sides, there was the constant promise of me, and there were others when I was not around. A sexual predator, unlike Deon.

No. I couldn't be with him. But I craved him. And I gave in.

Even on that day, the day that I will never forget, he had someone by his side. Bastard! I was single, we could have talked about a future if he'd wanted. But no. There he was, emerging from his father's house broad shouldered, muscly and all cheeky smiles, in tow, a young woman with a pleasant face and curly brown hair. Did he grab onto those curls when he mounted her from behind? I hated him at that point. How my heart lurched at the sight of him! But I took hold of myself and greeted them warmly, inviting both to the braai at our place that evening. As if he needed an invitation! He would come anyway, I knew. Her name was Clare. He had met her through the wife of another game warden. He looked nervous around me, constantly checking me out but mostly he hung out with the others, going into deep detail about how peaceful life was on the reserve, how the Black rhino was becoming extinct and how mesmerized foreign tourists were by the safari experience. I wished that I'd worn something more interesting than shorts and a tee shirt, wished that my hair was styled differently instead of falling straight down to my back getting in the way of everything when the breeze picked up. Clare had on smart jeans and a white jacket that accentuated her darkly tanned skin, she clung onto him throughout and made sure that we all knew. He was taken.

But I still found time to be alone with him. I knew that I could click my fingers and he'd come running.

Zoe and Anton sitting in a tree

K-I-S-S-I-N-G

First comes love

Then comes marriage

Then comes a baby

In a baby carriage

CHAPTER 13: DAD

Mercifully, a sky blue Range Rover pulled up. Finally, dad had arrived. At first, I pinched myself thinking that I was dreaming, but there it was as clear as day. He had brought Bongi along to our family farm for the weekend, a time when we had all committed to bonding and spending quality time together, just as a nuclear family, with our friends. Why did he do that to us, I kept asking myself. He just seemed hellbent to destroy every function, by bringing her along. Did he feel so guilty about leaving her behind with her mum that he had to drag her around everywhere? Surely, she had not agreed, surely, she knew that she would not be welcomed at our gathering, surely, she wanted sometimes to go to see *her* family too?

I braced myself at the unpleasant thought of talking politics again, raking over the old coals of wanting democracy and the end of apartheid. He would roll Bongi out as a shining example of the scourge of apartheid, it had created this disadvantaged underclass. White privilege again, from a man who epitomized it in every sense. He had driven his Range Rover to the farm. His designer clothes were pieces that he had sourced, abroad. I'd heard it all. I'd been savouring Anton's eloquent descriptions of life at Kruger, it had brought such a welcome change for me but now here was dad again, with her!

Rudely, I rolled my eyes at mum and dashed inside to finish unpacking and to pour a stiff drink. At eighteen, I was allowed now, not that it had stopped me before. I could see that she felt excluded, but I did little to help, after all we had been reaching out to connect with her from the word go and her consistently cold, aloof response had alienated me from her. In fact, given that she had successfully taken over dad's affections, I positively detested her! I scrutinized her unflattering, baggy clothes and wondered where she was stashing dad's generous allowances, why was she getting so fat, where were the new smart fashionable outfits that mum had picked out, why did she decide to turn up here, in my safe space? Questions and overthinking. My mind has a will of its own sometimes, so I stilled the constant internal chatter in my brain by pouring larger and larger dops, starting with beer then graduating to vodka. The more I mixed the drinks, the merrier I felt. Anton, a willing drinking partner now, joined me on the back porch outside the kitchen where all but Bongi gathered now. Clare seemed keen to help Connie with the braai preparations and the others started to drink seriously too, while helping themselves to the starters that Connie effortlessly produced. Music blared out of the hi-fi in the kitchen. The party had started, in earnest.

I didn't notice that dad had disappeared until half way into the braai. The lamb chops, his favourite, were ready and a platter piled high was handed around. Clare had joined the drinking party by now and was busy regaling us with stories of how she first met Anton. Even with her, he had been serious and committed right at the outset. Every now and then our eyes would meet, and we would glance at the words in our spot, clearly visible now that Connie had cleaned the outside walls in preparation for our visit. The magic was still there, I was sure that Clare could feel it too, despite the odd kisses that he would give her when he knew that I was watching. But I turned away deliberately and announced that I would walk around the veranda that effectively wrapped around the circumference of the house. I was in search of dad I said, he would not want to miss out on the succulent and juicy lamb chops. There was so much going on that evening at our little soiree! Mum and Johan could barely keep their eyes off each other, he kept tempting her with bits of charred, peri-peri chicken, flakes of foil wrapped fish, even a butternut squash had been cooked on the fire and its flesh creamed with butter, cinnamon and feta cheese. And lo and behold, she was eating every bit! I had to stare in pleasant surprise, where was the skinny ironing board who played with her salad and gulped her champagne?

They all wanted to join me, and we formed a very tipsy group when we walked around together, marvelling at the full moon in that velvety sky and the eerily silent countryside. We wanted to surprise dad knowing that he'd taken a bottle of Scotch with him, was he lying on the terracotta tiled floor of the front steps, too inebriated to move? So, we walked in tiptoe, breaking out, every now and again in giggles and whispers. But even at the front of the house, there was no dad to be seen. The platter was getting heavy by now, I wanted to set it down on the tiles. Then, we heard it. Low voices coming from the front bedroom, they were arguing. 'Shush,' mum commanded holding her forefinger to her lips, 'what's going on in there?'

The room was curtainless and stark. It had not been used by any one of us and we had not decorated it with the same care as the other rooms. But, against the simple backdrop, what we saw through the window, will remain firmly planted in my mind forever. It still disturbs me now, cropping up every now and then when I least expect it. Bongi, stark naked, with a hugely swollen belly, on all fours on the double bed, dad with his trousers rolled down to his ankles, penetrating her from behind, we couldn't see whether she was moaning with pleasure or swatting him away. What disturbed me most was the sight of my father, caressing and cradling her engorged breasts, running his hands over her belly. If he wore a wedding band, it would have glinted incompatibly as he touched her dark skin. But his fat, pork sausage fingers were ringless. Funny, how out of shock, I chose to reflect on that. For a moment, we froze. Rabbits caught in headlights. Flight or fight?

Mum emerged out of her reverie first, screaming out in anger and attacking the bedroom door in her efforts to barge in. And once in, she hit and punched, savagely swinging at both dad and Bongi in her fury. She was hysterical.

She's your daughter. Your biological child!

Hold up, she's your adopted daughter mum. Isn't she? It doesn't excuse anything but still, I'm sorry.

Paedophile. I hate you! She's his daughter. You hear me Zo? Him and Happiness! Years back they go. All I ever wanted was to keep you safe from their secret. But now...

You mean. How? Why? Nobody tells me anything!

You have a sister. It's her. And now he's gone and fucked her. His own child.

No!!!!! No!!!! Aaaaaaaaagh. Everything is so wrong. Why me?

Paedophile! I'll kill you!

Words can hurt you so badly, they can dent your soul.

The razor, where was it? Fuck, where was it? Were there razors on this damn farm? Even a kitchen knife would do. I needed something. Quick!

Within minutes, dad tried to regain his composure and pulled out of her, doing his trousers up, desperate to get out of the room now, but I blocked his way snarling and scratching at him like a wild animal. The names that rolled effortlessly off my tongue that evening! It didn't feel like I was aiming them at a parent but at an enemy which is what he had now become. 'Your filthy whore!' I spat, disgustedly at him. 'How could you?' A volley of dirty swear words reserved for lowlifes was aimed at him, delivered with a mixture of sadness for the parent that I had lost and for putting mum through the pain of this terrible scene. Anton tried unsuccessfully to restrain me, but I escaped and slapped and kicked my own father. Mum had gone into full blown hysteria, attacking Bongi by raining blows on her naked body in a screaming fit, until Johan pulled her back and urged her softly to go back to his house. In the end he had to carry her off, and Anton escorted me back with Clare following in confusion. Connie had retired to bed a long time ago, so the remains of that delicious braai food sat there, waiting for the cats and dogs to have their fill.

I vowed sobbing that night, that I never wanted to see dad ever again. I would never refer to him as my father, he was 'that thing' instead. To think that I had based my whole life around what he would think and say! And yet, there he was doing unspeakable things, hiding secrets that no one could forgive, or forget. I didn't want to process it all, his journey with Bongi, that deplorable story. So, she was my sister! And I hadn't had a chance to properly know her! No! I couldn't get my head around it all. Toby Ellis was dead to me forever. And Nature seemed to listen.

Karma catches up with the most illustrious of people. Celebrities, privileged liberals, politicians, beggars, thieves, we're all the same inside really. He didn't die that night. He died six months later, in a bleak one bedroom flat in lower Morningside, from a heart attack, his bloated body had grown blue and cold as he had been undiscovered for a whole week. If his brother from the UK had not arrived to rescue him, he would have lain there forever, stinking and crawling with maggots.

CHAPTER 14: CAPE TOWN

I never returned to the farmhouse. Anton took his long leave that he had been accumulating for years and moved into a flat opposite school in Durban, with me. I did my final exams and received my acceptance letter from the University of Cape Town. One morning, we headed down to the Cape with some of my stuff that he had salvaged from the house. The rest was in storage as the house was going to be sold. Anton had taken care of everything. The staff had all been given generous final salary cheques and released from employment with us. Estate agents were marketing the property and were updating him daily. He was always

on the phone it seemed. Mum was still in the
Drakensberg, in Johan's care now. She had had to be
hospitalized for stress and exhaustion but slowly, very
slowly, she was recovering. Clare had stormed off in a
huff to wherever she came from. No one knew what
happened to Bongi as she had disappeared completely.
It had been kind and considerate Anton who went
looking for her in our farmhouse the next morning, to
find dad passed out drunkenly on the sofa and Bongi
gone, vanished into thin air. How long did she have
before the birth of the child? We were clueless. He'd
insisted on driving around for hours, trying to find her,
to help her, but I refused to accompany him. She too
was dead to me.

Whatever happened between her and dad was
something that I did not want to mull over, that's for
sure! It was not the most cheering prospect to work out
what had been going on and for how long, though
sometimes my mind tried to go there to piece together
the puzzle. It all made sense now. The clothes, the
skulking in the shadows, their closeness, the muffled
sounds in her room, her regular visits to the annexe,
their dates. *She had dated dad.* I'd seen it with my own
eyes. The trips out, the preparations, their mounting

445

excitement. No wonder they hadn't wanted me to tag along! They must have done it all over the house, the annexe for sure as it was his private space, now I was sure that they'd done it in her bedroom too. Maybe even in the Mercedes with its generous leather seats. That image of him buried deep inside her from behind, was enough to put me off sex for a long time.

My father was a paedophile! Which daughter wants to dwell on that? Not me. I didn't have the strength to process it, so I tried to block it all out. I yearned to cut. But Marnie's words came through for me and I didn't. I just psychologically stepped over the threshold, moved forward so to speak. A new world beckoned. Varsity, endless Art. A new city. A fresh start.

Anton and I, well, we never did it again in Durban. I reached out to him several times before we left for Cape Town, especially as we had developed a kind of co-dependency that was comforting and soothing. Who knows what I would have done without him by my side? But he refused to touch me, insisting that I wore pyjamas when I slept next to him. It was not the right time, I knew. He was happy to hold me tightly all night even, he cooked, cleaned and ran around sorting out my family's mess but he flatly refused to go near me in that way. He never gave a reason, so after a while, I decided that he just didn't fancy me anymore. I stopped trying and focused on the next leg of my journey: varsity!

Picture a luminous yellow campervan kitted out with everything that resembled a home. That was us, on our way to the Cape. He'd bought it especially for the trip and had taken pains to make it comfortable for me, choosing my favourite pop songs in audio cassette form for the music player and filling it with snacks, blankets for the bed, coffee and alcohol. I have my driving license, but I was in no mood to do the six or seven-hour drive, so he drove while I entertained him with banter. Sometimes, I'd sing along to the songs and he'd look over at me, amused by my dancing in my seat. I hadn't escaped what happened, I'm not so shallow that something like that could just be forgotten in a few months. Instead, I was focusing hard, really hard on varsity and life on the famous or infamous Cape Town campus. It gave me something to look forward to, it was a fresh beginning. Anton's promise to mum was that he would settle me into varsity and then return to Kruger Park, to his own life. It seemed like a good deal to me.

That evening, we arrived and checked into a hotel close to the Art school, which was separate to the rest of the campus. Just the sight of the majestic Table Mountain with its curiously flattened top was enough to make me cry. The university is mum's alma mater, many lecturers knew her there. I was desperate to follow in her footsteps by studying Fine Art, but I knew too that I would bring my own style to the course, customize it to suit me, so to say. After all, I was an artist in my own right by now, the acceptance letter had read that they would be honoured to have me studying there. I was determined to excel in all aspects, I couldn't possibly let mum down now.

But, at the back of my mind, the worry loomed. I had that stubborn, independent streak that some mistakenly took for arrogance. I was not arrogant though. Call it shyness, social awkwardness or defensiveness maybe. Would I be accepted by the other students? Would dad's actions be made public enough to humiliate me? The daughter of a paedo! We had kept the story out of the media, but what if it got out somehow? Where was Bongi and the baby? What if she did a tell all? I couldn't bear it.

After all, I'm a rape victim.

The next few weeks flew by. I looked at several flat shares but they all lacked studio space, house shares seemed full. Anton considered renting a whole house for me, but I was determined to not look like a spoilt, rich brat. White privilege is embarrassing, I was trying to make a name for myself with as little help as possible. I wanted to blend in.

There was such a welcomed mixture of students on campus, it seemed truly multicultural compared with Durban. Some were on bursaries and scholarships, some paid the hefty fees. Anton settled my fees easily, updating mum each day with news of how much was needed and for what. He even found me studio space on campus itself, securing a light and airy room near the library for a low rent. Books were purchased, art equipment set up. Anton had become overnight, my mother, father and brother rolled into one. It was only by chatting to other students that he learned about the convent for ladies, about an easy ten- minute walk across from the campus and he took me there one afternoon to check it out, after making an appointment with Sister Mary.

It was a nunnery called the Villa of Peace. Gentlemen were not allowed to enter its cool, dark interior but luckily the office was located at the entrance, on the side of which a small visitor's lounge, decorated sparsely with wicker chairs and pale cushions, announced that it was the only venue to entertain male visitors in the place. Statues of Jesus on the cross, Mother Mary and rosy cheeked angels filled every conceivable space on the pale walls, but the signage was typed in bold, black letters. 'Gentlemen stop here. You are not permitted to enter this ladies-only convent and place of worship.' I had to take the tour alone, hiding behind Sister Mary's long, dove grey, A line skirts as I had never visited a convent and didn't know what to expect.

I had grown up in a house full of whispers, secrets and trapped fulfillment, little did I know that I would find the same, there. The silence was noticeable and felt eerie, especially given the size of the building, and the number of inhabitants who ranged from young women to shrivelled old ladies. Some wore the iconic nun's habit, some were in everyday clothes even though this seemed unfashionable and often unflattering. Time had stood still there. Everyone moved around apologetically, eyes were fixed on the ground, even their backs seemed hunched in deference. And the statues were everywhere, from the dining room to the bathroom, it seemed like you could never escape the watchful eyes of Jesus wherever you went. My room on the first floor was small, cool and satisfyingly dark, the simple furniture heavy and reassuring. It was opposite a communal bathroom and I accepted it at once. Anton paid the rent in advance and I said that I would move in the next day.

The next morning, our last, we bid a tearful goodbye and I moved into the convent. Lectures would start later that week and I wanted to prepare.

CHAPTER 15: MOVING ON

I'd always thought of Durban as being the jorl capital of South Africa. In Cape Town, I saw that I had been mistaken. With its cosmopolitan culture, variety of beaches including a nudist one that I started to frequent, array of bars and jazz dens, it was a magnet for pleasure seekers of all shapes, sizes, races and cultures. And I hit the party scene hard. There was no one to supervise my furtive activities or to cast moral judgements about what choices I was making, so I rode that bitch of a pleasure wave hard! If only Marnie fucking Marie could see me now, I thought when I was buzzed out of my head. At parties, I got nicknamed the

'Snow Queen', the tip of my nose seemed to have a dusting of flour or icing sugar every few hours, then some guy would lick it off and pull me into a bedroom or toilet. I had no shame. Sometimes, I took off my panties before hitting the party just to be ready. Oh, I loved sex! Marnie had said something once about hypersexuality in victims of rape, this was where you developed a kind of sex addiction or promiscuity often accompanied by a lack of feeling. But here's the thing. I absolutely loved it! I mean I could orgasm just from someone touching my nipples. In bed, I was feisty and demanding, wanting more and more and more. I didn't crave food, I just wanted to fuck, the dirtier the better. Before long, I developed a name for myself as being 'the easy nymphomaniac,' but I didn't care. Men lined up to try me out. I did threesomes, groups and one on one.

I had become unrecognizably wild. It was like I was exorcising the great burden that I'd been carrying around with me. Durban is a restrained, post -colonial throwback to the British empire, certainly compared to cosmopolitan Cape Town where literally everything was on full display with no one blinking an eye about it. At Art school, lesbians and gays paraded in flamboyant abandon, unfettered by judgy parents and relatives. And why not? It was normal. Interracial couples made out openly on the grass banks without the fear of stigma or reprisal. Again, it made perfect sense. Lecturers and students walked hand in hand with each other in carefree abandon, everyone was screwing each other. To think that all of this had previously been outlawed by the government seemed insane, ridiculous even. Here, fun was the norm. I loved everything about the new normal. I hurled myself into my new life.

The work itself was easy. I melted into assignments and projects effortlessly, earning the best grades consistently. The Art community was carefree, intellectual and addictive. I'd yearned for that kind of cerebral dialogue and debate for years, they were different to the seemingly stream of consciousness rants that we had at home. All over campus, you would see knots of students embroiled passionately in conversation, each cluster containing a true mixture of racial and cultural groups. So, the rainbow nation *was* working here. I'd never felt so alive! There are so many areas of life where, under the umbrellas of liberalism, multiculturalism and diversity, we are muzzled from speaking our divergent truths and bullied into singing from the same hymn sheet as it were, as though we were quoting a prescribed script or mantra. In Cape

Town, it was different. We actively grappled with topics from alternative realities and viewpoints and engaged in penetrating conversations about issues without coming to conclusions, which helped me feed ideas into my work. It fascinated me to listen to students of different races speaking their truths, what a diversity of cultures we had, on campus. It was a privilege just to rub shoulders with such a staggering variety of people. I was producing subtle, softer, more thoughtful pieces now. The anger that I had bottled inside me for so long, seemed to have dissipated. I was growing up.

Sitting on the campus grounds in a straw hat, torn shorts, a borrowed bikini top and someone's string vest, I pulled hard on the proffered joint one day, thinking, as I looked around the knot of new party animal friends that I had now acquired, that Cape Town was the coolest place on earth. The Art school shared a campus with the Drama school and the shared parties were epic with promiscuous divas, dancers and fine artists living life to the max. In the near distance, loomed the iconic Table Mountain. You could see it pretty much everywhere you went, and it truly was breathtaking. When I got stoned, I loved to lie back and take it all in, the way the fog swirled around it like trails of cream making its descent from the top of a treacle coloured Christmas pudding. I loved my luscious, new life.

Years passed in studying, partying and working on a host of fresh themes in my little studio. In between, I visited mum and Johan, now a married couple. Nobody mentioned dad or Bongi now. The houses on the farm and the Berea had long been sold, Johan too had sold his huge estate. Partly due to their love of the beach and partly due to wanting to keep a check on me, mum and Johan had settled into a little rented cottage in Strand, a coastal town in the Cape of unbelievable tranquility and beauty. It meant that I had somewhere to go at weekends, where I would meet Anton on his weekends off. Mum and Johan, an openly loved up couple now, kept pressing us to commit to an engagement or even a relationship but we kept tight lipped. Even we didn't know what we had going. We just knew that it was there, an invisible thread that had attached itself to both our hearts, connecting us forever. And so, the clock ticked on.

Then, another turning point.

Grahamstown is a little town in the Eastern Cape, it's a few hours away from Cape Town and the university there had the best reputation for its journalism course. In June every year, the town hosted the largest arts festival in South Africa, in fact in the continent. People from all over flocked to the town with its colonial buildings with Georgian facades, its wide, central boulevard, its many bars and arty shops. That year, I had been asked to give a talk on the 'Healing Power of Art' but I had been too late to book flights or hotels, so I went up in a shared car, with four other students. I took thick, woollen tops, jeans, thermal socks and a sleeping bag as I was joining my friends on the floor of some student digs, in the middle of winter.

We left at the crack of dawn and arrived in the afternoon. It was such a strange little town, quintessentially South African. For where else would you find, on the hilltops fringing the town, an imperial looking building that was the famous Rhodes University on one end, and a straggly row of makeshift houses that comprised the shantytown where squatters lived, on the other? In the town centre, which was the dip in between, we walked around, greeting long lost friends, trying to spot celebrities and marvelling at the crowds and the posters advertising a bewildering array of shows and events. No one mentioned the presence of the squatters, on the horizon. I'm sure they watched us from their cramped, improvised dwellings made of sheets of rusty tin and cardboard. I'm sure they wondered what it would feel like to float around looking for bars and restaurants instead of shivering in the freezing cold thinking of lack, of futility and of the steady ebbing away of their lives.

Winter in Grahamstown can be cruel, especially without heaters. It was five degrees that night and my friend Thandi and I huddled together in the student digs, moving our sleeping bags right next to each other for bodily warmth. The room had been split into two by an archway and on both side, rucksacks and sleeping bags littered the floor, such was the demand for cheap student accommodation. All night, people were trickling in from bars, parties, late night events and the constant interruptions, coupled by the cold biting into me, were not conducive to sleep. I tossed and turned, wishing that I had brought thicker socks, a warmer jacket. Suddenly, I heard it. It was on the opposite side of the archway, but it was so unmistakable even after all the years, that I had to sit up to get a better look.

Deon.

I'd recognize that voice anywhere.

What was he doing here in this arty haven? He could barely read or write having left high school

458

without finishing, something about being kicked out for selling drugs. Then I remembered, his parents lived in the Cape, I hadn't asked which part, it must be the Eastern Cape. Maybe he was a local. He was speaking rather loudly in that slurry voice that told me that he was drunk. Memories washed over me, taking me first to the magical times that we had together. Dimly lit rooms, flickering candles, the rotten cheesy stench of weed, a mattress on the floor, the smell of his alpha male sweat, sweet and earthy, a pair of huge green eyes, and a muscly, taut body enveloping me, making me feel like a queen, like nothing outside could ever hurt us, that together, welded together in this intense love, we would get through everything. Deon had been my first love and now, dismayed to the point of sobbing silently into my woollen scarf, I knew that I would never stop having a thing for him. Just the sound of his voice was enough for me to rush over and give myself over to him, give him everything I had, such was my need for him. I wanted to give everything just to recreate those precious moments with him.

In those few minutes, I realized why strong, intelligent women like me went to mush over uneducated alpha males. I flitted to the Lady

Chatterley's lover story where a classy, sophisticated woman risked everything, including her marriage to be with the gamekeeper. That novel had always been compelling for me. I knew now that other women had the same craving for alphas, and that Deon's hypnotic manliness was something that, if I had married him, I would have to share with needy women desperate for a hit of super-testosterone fuelled sex. He knew it, he had always known it. It was the reason for his swagger, his total lack of concern for education or training or qualification or money. A man like Deon, with that inherent nugget of confidence that all alpha men have, that biological awareness that he could have anything and everyone that he wanted just by being himself, in the raw, was addictive. It was what I wanted. And needed. I didn't get raped under his watch. I didn't get mugged or attacked. Come to think of it, the years with him were the best years of my life. He hadn't hit me or hurt me physically, unlike the stereotype of the drug dealer image that my friends kept reminded me about. Only I understood what I had gained out of that relationship, he had saved me from myself.

I had a need for him that went far beyond the need for drugs or alcohol, I could see that now. I couldn't ever imagine Deon without drugs or alcohol. But I couldn't imagine a life without him. I had cleverly and successfully blocked out how he'd hurt me by not getting in touch, by ending things so suddenly, for no reason. But I would give myself to him now.

Even as I lifted my sleeping bag and walked over in the dim light to where he was, an image popped into my head. The sacrificial lamb. I was offering myself to him.

He was propped against the wall, hammered out of his head and doing a line of cocaine, using the arts festival brochure to cut it. A young guy sat next to him, chatting. There was the initial surprise to see me, especially after all those years, the summary of what we had been up to or the catch up, edited carefully of course to not cloud the sensuality of the moment, the sharing of his coke and then, he kissed me passionately, turned me around and entered me, doggy style. It was so cold that we kept our clothes on, just removing what was necessary. I couldn't see a thing by now, the darkness had descended for the night. That night, after several rounds, we slept in each other's arms. My dreams were in technicolor, heightened by the drugs. A grim reaper with his death mask stood over me, threatening to take me to the place where the night was endless, and fire torched my very soul in a limitless loop of despair.

It was only in the morning that I heard it. I had woken alone; any presence of Deon and all the drug paraphernalia had disappeared. For a minute, I thought that it had all been a dream then I saw my underwear bunched up at the foot of the sleeping bag and knew that it was not. Thud, thud, thud. There was a fierce pounding in my head. I ached for coffee and carbs. A grilled cheese and tomato sandwich on granary bread, was what I craved, it was my go to after a heavy night partying. Or a soft, scrambled egg with sliced avocado, also on granary bread. I had to find food. Caffeine. My talk was scheduled for around lunchtime but thankfully, I had prepped it days before. Then, just as I was peeling back the sleeping bag to emerge, I heard his voice again, he seemed to be at the front of the house, on the narrow veranda, Deon's voice had always been loud. This time, he was crying. I stood up, feeling a cold, clammy hand reach into me and pull on my insides.

I shouldn't have done it, man what was I thinking?

Why? You love her, right? That's the babe you keep banging on about, the love of your life you said.

i was broken, now I Am

He was talking to that guy from last night. I went close to the window backing onto the veranda to eavesdrop. I could scarcely breathe. I'm not psychic but something had soured the air, I knew that what was coming was not pretty.

I never told you why I came back home. My fucking tail between my legs.

Man don't cry, you're scaring me now. Have a cold beer.

Fuck beer. My baby in there, my baby. What I did to her, no one will forgive me for that. It's fucking beyond forgiveness. And you know what? She didn't deserve that. Okay, I got a bit bored in the end, she's a kid man. Fucking years younger than me, knows nothing about life. Or about me. I used to go behind her back all the fucking time. I deserved it, but she, she was innocent. Have you seen her properly? Most beautiful woman I have ever seen. I used to want to keep her with me covered up always, by my side. You know like those women who cover their faces and bodies walking behind their husbands? Well I wanted her next to me, covered and reserved just for me. My angel.

He was properly sobbing now.

D what the fuck did you do man? You gonna have to spit it out.

Pull up my shirt. Look yourself. Go on, it won't bite you.

Pause. Then a low whistle.

What the fuck?

And check out my back, top half.

I couldn't see a thing, if I went and opened the curtains to look he would have seen me, I didn't want that. Not until I'd heard it all.

Is it what I think it is? I wondered why you looked so ill all the time, the constant tiredness.

Man, I came home to fucking die. Can you just imagine my parents' faces when I told them! I had to beg their forgiveness. But I never thought I'd meet her and pass it onto her, a whore yes but not my baby.

You need to tell her D, she's fucking still inside man. She must go get a blood test and get checked out. Now!

Shhhhh no! Don't fucking do anything that stupid. If she knew that I'd passed Aids onto her, shit, I can't bear to think of what she'll do. She's sensitive. Been through enough shit in her life. And now, this.

There was more talk, and more crying, but I only picked up a few drips of it, I had zoned out.

It's not as bad as you think. You may only have passed her a virus man.

i was broken, now I Am

A virus that she will have for life now. HIV Aids.

You sure you've got full blown Aids man? You could get medicine if it's in the early stages.

Trust me, I know. I had flu that wouldn't go away, thrush, fucking herpes, lesions on my skin as you saw. I can't eat, I'm just tired all the time man. Just so tired. Look at me.

I hadn't been able to see him in the dark. I hadn't had a chance to notice anything. And now, I knew that I had signed my death warrant.

Like a robot on autopilot, I delivered my presentation to the people who had crammed themselves into the little hall. I took questions from the floor in the end and smiled appropriately as people took photographs with me afterwards. Inside, my guts were churning. I craved my white bedroom on the farm, that Glock nine-millimeter that I had fantasized about, and silence.

I was lucky that I found a lift back that afternoon. I'd aborted my stay, pleading fatigue. I slept on the way back and woke up when the familiar and reassuring sight of Table Mountain came into view.

I knew what I had to do.

CHAPTER 16: FINAL DESTINATION

Ordinary people *can* do extraordinary things.

But *I* hadn't done anything extraordinary, in fact I'd fucked up my life. Other people envied what I had, I knew. Good looks, rich parents, all the opportunities a girl could ask for. And I had thrown it all away. Maybe people had a right to be angry. Maybe seeing us throwing away everything that they coveted and yearned for made them pissed enough to want to hurt us. I could imagine a little Black girl kneeling in supplication, her little hands clasped together: Please God let me go to school. Please God, let me be safe today. Please God, let me eat today. Please God, keep

me warm today. Please God, make my mother and
father come home safe today.

I had taken my life for granted, sneered at the
concept of privilege, heckled others who had pointed
out that I was a spoilt White brat. But the
uncomfortable truth was that I had consistently thrown
away every opportunity to thrive. And now, I had
kissed goodbye to my life.

In South Africa there's a lot that you can get away
with. You could say that you shot someone for
example, and the other person would forgive you if it
was in revenge. They'd still sit at the table with you, still
have a drink with you, share ideas, even joke. But two
words, no, it's strictly three syllables and one word that
are guaranteed to clear the table, not just the table, the
room, the building, the country.

HIV. And Aids.

Just the mention of these words gives people the
shivers. Just reading the words in a newspaper, makes
people want to roll up the paper and burn it in case the
words jumped out and crawled into their flesh. The
topic was a non -starter. A non- negotiable at any

function. If the R word was taboo, can you imagine what impact the H or A word had?

I didn't go for a blood test straight away. What I did was jump on a plane and head for the Kruger Park in the province of Gauteng where Anton was a game ranger. I'd called him to say that I was coming over and he collected me from the airport. I was finished with my course. In a few months, I would graduate with a bachelor's degree. Life had become empty and meaningless. I hadn't started cutting again, but I was scared to pick up the phone to call Marnie let alone see her to explain how I had fucked up. I hadn't spoken to mum or anyone. It was Anton, only Anton that I needed now.

What a crybaby! Always fucking up then running to Anton! An evil demon had taken residence inside me now. It kept jeering and mocking me at every turn. Inwardly, I had punched and slapped myself. Just desserts, yes, I was to blame, no one could sugar coat it for me. Was it a tokoloshe that Happiness had taken pains to protect me from? Should I have elevated my bed at the villa? Maybe if I had done this, dark things wouldn't have happened. That was it. I'd strayed away from everything that my second mother had taught me. Stupid, stupid girl. Worthless piece of shit. That was me. Dirty, disgusting, soiled. I was an oxygen thief, polluting the very air that others were breathing in.

Where was that Glock? Why hadn't I invested in one? I could have looked hard to find one on the black market. Instead, I had been cowardly in pushing those thoughts out of my head. My thoughts flitted to Zubbie, my poor friend who had died for nothing. Now here I was doing the kind of shit I had despised in others, sleeping around with random strangers, having unprotected sex, going at it like an animal behind Anton's back, unbeknown to mum. And the drugs had been part of it, like one big demonic package. I disgusted myself, could barely eat or drink anymore. Why would I put good food into my diseased body? Instead, I starved it. I gave away the food that the villa served me to random beggars, surprising some who had been habituated to lack, by my sheer generosity.

Maybe, if I starved my body, I would just waste away and perish, I thought. But another thought struck me. Would I go to heaven or hell, if there were such places? No, I knew the answer already.

God wouldn't want me.

No one did.

I had to say goodbye to Anton, he deserved it after all.

I scanned the faces at the airport but could see no Anton, maybe he knew already and decided against ever seeing me again. Then I saw a bouquet of raspberry red roses, my favourite flower, and someone behind it struggling to see from behind it. He had come after all.

I'm not a religious person. Dad being a Marxist would never have allowed me to dip into religion no matter which one I chose. But when I saw beautiful, kind Anton with his innocent soul and cheeky smile baring crooked teeth, something in me clicked and I grasped onto the one thing that could save me. My wild card. Please God save me. Please God help me. My soul cried out for one last chance to make things right.

In my English Literature class, I had been fascinated by the story of Dr Faustus by Christopher Marlowe, how he had sold his soul to the devil. The doctor had enjoyed super powers until an allotted time when an emissary from the devil had come to collect him. In those final seconds, Faustus had regretted the agreement that he had made, in despair, he had called out to God to save him. I felt this now.

i was broken, now I Am

Throughout the car journey I fell silent, Anton thought that I was tired and urged me to nap but I was praying silently.

I wanted to live free from HIV or Aids.

I wanted another chance. Just one. A life with the man on my side. A boring, everyday life with the man that I had loved since my childhood. I wanted everything with him. Even a family. Bring on vomit, dirty nappies and sleepless nights, I begged God. Bring on stretch marks, a saggy belly, floppy boobs and housewifely chores. Dirty dishes, endless cooking and baking, barefoot and pregnant. I wanted it.

Please, please, please God let me live! Let me have a future!

At the hotel where we were staying overnight before leaving for the park the next day, I told Anton everything over a few bottles of wine.

CHAPTER 17: HOLLAND

I was a dead woman walking when we got to
Holland. I'd wanted a tiny wedding ceremony at the
safari park, but Maddie, Indira, mum and Johan refused
to let that happen. Even Anton's best friends and
colleagues colluded to surprise me. Sibusiso, the
Michelin starred head chef at Kruger Park rustled up a
banquet that had my eyes popping out, the boys behind
this wonderful gesture had called it a wedding present
to us. The marquee was open, the view of the
waterhole breathtaking as we took our vows. I hadn't
seen Anton in a suit before and we both teared when

we clapped eyes on each other. My dress was simple, long, sleeveless, high necked in the front and backless with thin, cross back spaghetti straps. My skin is tanned now, I insisted on just light make up and Grecian style braids studded with cream rosebuds. 'My Goddess,' Anton murmured when he got to kiss me. A sick goddess, I thought. I was trying like I promised him, to put it all behind me.

We feasted and took our champagne and sundowners into the bush for a private tour, all thirty of us. That day wasn't just the cliched most memorable day of my life. It was more. I had married my childhood sweetheart. Watching the game quietly, marvelling at the seamless way in which the game melted into the landscape, that unforgettable, panoramic sunset. It felt like the heavens had opened and God was painting the sky in magenta, orange and gold for me. For us. It was a blessing that I would never have recognized or acknowledged if I hadn't been through the many traumas in my life, especially the recent one.

For that was how Anton asked me to perceive it. In his fumbling, simple but profound way he said that shit happened to everyone. It was how we moved forward afterwards, that counted. Our honeymoon consisted of one night in our bush lodge, a thatched hut with an open, viewing area along a river, we made love carefully and talked over our plans all night. Mum and Johan had been over in the Hague in Holland for a few months already, it was where Johan's brother and sister were based, and they had bought a little cottage near an art gallery where mum worked part time. Johan had retired after a long battle with arthritis. I was happy to go to Holland with Anton as, second to South Africa, this was where he had grown up. We both needed a fresh start. But I hadn't taken my blood test yet. And no one else knew.

Then, we got to Amsterdam and it was a game changer. Suddenly I didn't want to settle near mum in the Hague as planned. I wanted to live in vibrant, culturally explosive Amsterdam. The tulips, those charming canals, the tree lined avenues, the brashness and honesty of the red -light district, of course the lure of the coffeeshops although I was aware that I could easily descend into what I was trying to run away from now. The Hague was driving distance to us, we could see our family whenever we wanted. The blood tests came back, we poured every bit of our funds into our new project with some help from Anton's cousins and

i was broken, now I Am

Johan, and eight months later, our sustainable, self-build house was finished. With my new heaviness and alarming girth, I felt like a cow blundering around but Anton kissed me and gave me the, 'You're not fat, you're pregnant,' speech.

Maddie flew over from Edinburgh, Scotland where she shared a flat with her girlfriend, and rescued me. With Anton at work doing property maintenance for a leasing company, I'd been sitting at home staring at the walls and getting paranoid. Maddie was doing her medical training in Scotland, she had come out as a lesbian soon after winning her scholarship to study there. She knows my story fully now and calls it a 'journey, not just some narrative.' Along with Indira who is doing her medical training in London, they are still my BFF. Who flies over to pamper a pregnant woman with presents for the baby even before the birth? Well, I should say babies really. I blame Anton for that. It's his family that has a history of twins not mine. He wants me to rest. I'm not allowed to do anything but read and eat.

I did an Art therapy course so that is all I'm into these days. It's a fascinating and rewarding cross over from my days as a practising artist, but I'm fine with that, doing Art has no more interest for me. Along with a lot of baggage from the past, I threw it over the proverbial cliff and refuse to touch it these days. I want to work with communities, I want to reach out, give back.

I'm only twenty-seven years old. Maddie says I've been very lucky. 'You did the crime, you should have done the time,' she says sternly, 'but you got away.' She hands me a fresh, non- alcoholic watermelon margarita, accompanied by a lentil burger with sweet potato fries and baby beetroot. The dinner she's rustling up is crispy kale with walnuts, curried cauliflower and brown rice. 'I love you Mad,' I complain, 'but ever since you became vegan, I'm suffering with flatulence!'

'So why don't you do a bit of research?' she lectures, 'look up the water footprint of animal husbandry? Check out how we're polluting the planet by eating meat! Check out how animals that we eat are slaughtered! Check out why we're getting diseases! You have to detoxify yourself.'

Geez, I regret complaining, she gets animated and loud when she is on her vegan high horse. Still, she's passionate about issues and I get what she is saying. I respect everything about her and I'm docile when she hands me the delicious food. I'll eat anything that's safe for our babies. They *have* to come first.

I know I'm on a tight leash from all sides. I know that they're looking after me during this delicate pregnancy. But I can't help feeling like they're monitoring me too. When Maddie leaves, Indira and her new man will come to stay. Mum and Johan come every weekend without fail, we thought they were joking when they made us build them their own bedroom in this big, bespoke house. But I don't mind all this attention.

You see, I now recognize it for what it is. Love. The love of family and friends. It's easily the most precious thing that we have. The money comes and goes. We gave chunks of it away to charities before we left South Africa for good: orphaned children due to parents dying of Aids, homeless people, women escaping domestic violence and living in refuge shelters. We helped set up structures and resources. Using our good reputations, we helped to forge partnerships between impoverished communities and big businesses. And when we left, we didn't just bow out. Using my new-found friend, a laptop, I'm still there, in South Africa, using my name to do everything I can to help. And that too, is love. When my tests came back negative, I knew I'd been given a second chance. And I saw this as a blessing, a hug if you like, from the Universe. Almost overnight I've changed and become attuned to ancient wisdoms. I'm no longer the little White brat. I've been saved.

Love *is* the answer, the common denominator in every situation. I'm not interested in corrupt governments, in dysfunctional politics, corrupt cops and impotent law courts. To me, it's about giving young people the life chances to thrive and to live well. I don't want a Nobel prize either. People have said that my dad, dead now, would be proud of me as I am continuing his charity work. But I'm not. I'm not a political activist. Or a label. I don't want to be shoehorned into being on the left or on the right. I'm just a wife, a soon to be mother and a person like everyone else on this planet.

Just spreading a bit of love.

Talking about love, there's just one more act of love that I have been planning on for a long time. It was a germ of an idea, but it grew and grew. The baby that Bongi and dad had. My half-sister I suppose. I'm going to find her. No matter what it takes. I can't move forward until she's found.

Blood. It's thicker than water. And I will love her and her mother, my sister Bongi, no matter what.

Carrie

MOTHER, THIS IS FOR YOU

i was broken, now I Am

CHAPTER 1: GOODBYE

London 2005

'What do you do when an old man wants to marry your eleven year -old daughter?'

The woman, a parent, beseeches me with dark, pleading eyes. She wants help. Pinching at her brown cheek, she reaches out and pinches mine in a pathetic gesture of sisterhood, that ethnic bond that us 'non - Whites' have or are supposed to have. Then, she clasps her hands together, beseeching me, desperation etched in every wrinkle on her face. What indeed could I do?

I'm so helpless, I'm just a bottom feeder. I'm supposed to say, 'My hands are tied but I'll refer it to the Safeguarding officer.' Fat lot of good that will do! I can't imagine her sitting down with a load of paperwork thrust in front of her and be forced to repeat the story again and again only for him to repeat what I could have told her in two minutes. 'We've referred it to the relevant authorities but for now, our hands are tied. There's a time factor here, they take a while to process it, if it gets to that level in the first place. Sometimes, they won't intervene if it's a cultural or community matter. If anything changes, please let us know.' (Like if the girl kills herself in protest at the forced marriage looming ahead of her. We would need to update the records then, close the case. The case that was never even opened.)

She doesn't trust the other staff. Who would? Some put their heads down when they clock her approaching, then shuffle away pretending to be busy. No one wants more paperwork. The system's done this to us, no one has the time to care. They make snide remarks about her broken, faltering English and she knows, she can sense these things acutely, can read expressions and body language. Some even turn their noses away, an aversion to the smell of spices still lingering on her long, black robe, her turmeric stained fingers. She's been coming upstairs regularly to talk to staff recently, some parents just pick up at the gates. I'm touched by her attempts to reach out.

'I want her to get education. Like the other girls. Please!'

'She *is* getting an education, she's attending school. She's such a lovely, polite young girl,' I say smiling.

'No! You no understand. My husband, he wants, he wants her to get married. His family, they arrange it all. The old man he pay a lot of money, she's a virgin.'

'We can't get involved in cultural situations, so just refer it all to the Safeguarding officer,' the other teachers advise when I approach them directly. I want so desperately to support her, I would take all these vulnerable kids home if I could. Your heart bleeds sometimes.

'Bloody immigrants!' one teacher says nastily. 'Why can't they go back to where they came from?'

This is London. The place is heaving with immigrants. As soon as they come in to sign the admission forms there's eye rolling and sighs from staff. 'More paperwork! More hassle!'

They mutter about the Principal's inclusive approach where all students are valued and given opportunities to thrive.

'He's not doing the work, we are!' they complain. 'These kids just pull the school down! Can't he see that they're impacting negatively on other students? How can we optimize their achievement if we're too busy focusing on immigrants?'

I'm an immigrant myself, I want to say but don't. Most of the staff are White British, there's just a sprinkling of people of colour. I cringe when I hear them talk. Their stream of throw away comments, is spiteful and ineffectual, they don't solve the problems. All they do is help the speaker to vent. Verbal diarrhoea.

These thoughtscapes plague me even outside of school. I can't sleep, I can't focus. I'm as jittery as a cat on cocaine. I'm cerebral, I know, some may say *intensely* cerebral. I never stop analyzing, chewing things over. Overthinking is a curse, but how to switch off? My mates sit there with joints in their hands after our yoga workouts. 'Be mindful,' they remind me. 'Smell the fresh air. Breathe. Be present. Drop into your heart space.' But I *can't* stop processing these images. My mind is a tangled ball of images and ideas, relentlessly going around and around like a hamster trapped in its wheel. I'm attracted to pain like flies to shit.

In London, it's incessant, the pain we witness every damn day. Homelessness, hunger, poverty, people drifting along looking for what was promised by hearsay, literature, websites and traffickers. Streets paved in gold. In my heart, I know I won't see the woman or the child again. She'll disappear into nothingness, be forced by her community or cultural guilt to send the child abroad to be married and only see her when she returned pregnant and beaten, her snarling, self -righteous husband in tow. A prize-winning trophy hunter. By then it will be too late. Trapped into submission, brainwashed into believing that sickening and deadening statement: 'It is what it is,' or 'think about the baby, you can't leave him *now*.' Futile to protest. We're women, we all *have* to do it. Just put one foot forward and soldier on. Women's issues they call them. Pain is a constant, sometimes the only damn constant in our lives.

I am sitting on the toilet having a miscarriage and still I can't shut out the memories of school. As I peer into the toilet bowl through parted thighs, crimson clots of blood splat into cloudy water causing splashes around the bowl, sometimes it's clumps of liver, sometimes just a piss of blood. The meaty smell makes me want to hurl but I hold myself back. The undeniable remains of my baby, the child that never was. Meanwhile the cramps come and go with a vengeance and I hug myself protectively, as if this will bring her back or dull the pain. This is the right thing, I know. Nature's way of reprimanding me for wanting a second baby with that joke of a man. Still, tears course down my cheeks, a mixture of heavy sadness for the life being lost, the shooting pains in my belly, a realization that cords will be cut with him forever now. No going back. I know, I know. I have said this, many times. So, shoot me for wanting a life with my son's father!

Maybe this second child was just too cheeky. A stab in the dark. What if I told you I was pregnant again? Would you stay with me then? Would you hold me again? What if I lost the weight? Had a boob job? I'll go as big as you want, it's all for you baby. Botox? Enhanced my butt? Hymen repair surgery? You once said that you wanted me tighter. What if I paid for that cruise holiday you've always wanted? Would you want me *then?* Whose desperate now? Me. *What if I turned a blind eye to all the shit that you get up to right in front of me and behind my back…would you stay with me then?*

Why do successful women get reduced to simpering leeches when abusive partners threaten to leave? Why do we constantly condone bad behaviour, in partners? A friend says that it's all about wanting to tame a man's fundamental feral instincts, but really? Vanessa is a stunning brunette, highly qualified and successful. Her hubby goes on 'boys' trips to Amsterdam while she relishes in being able to knuckle down to spring cleaning the house just to please him when he gets back. We all want to be loved, no matter where we get it from and how strong or diluted it is, we all crave it. But how much of ourselves do we give away in the process? How many of us are faithful to ourselves? I've never been able to worship the goddess in me. I'm the most disconnected and fragmented person I know.

What would you say if I shared that with you Mother? Welcome to the club?

A gush of tears now. I'm a crybaby too. *Mother, where are you? I need you. No, not your money or a room in your home.*

No, I'm not a drug addict. All I wish is that you were there on the other side of the phone, just to talk to.

'Going to get mum flowers on Mother's Day,' friends say. I'm silent.

'Planning on ringing mum tonight for our weekly chat,' they say. I'm silent.

'Saw this amazing jacket, will get it for mum's birthday.' I'm silent.

'Taking mum out this weekend for high tea.' I'm silent.

'Having a mother and daughter pamper session at the spa.' I'm crying.

I don't have a mum. Or a dad. Or a boyfriend, now. Just fucking voices in my head. Is it any surprise that I don't like going out with friends? I have nothing to talk about. No one wants to listen to my shit. Apparently, it's all negative energy and bad karma. Everyone gives me a wide berth. So, I make up my own internal dialogues. Oh yes, Mother and I, we communicate all day long. I can't stop it. Why do we fixate on what we don't have?

Fuck that bastard you can do better, yes Carrie you can, believe in yourself! Look how highly educated you are! What has he got? Nothing! Just looks and charm. Oh, he can charm the pants off any girl, surely you can see that, clever girl like you. But anyone can give you that! Look around, it's raining men! Now dry your tears and be a proper mother to your baby son. Look at him Carrie, he's such a lost soul, how can you treat him like that?

Lost soul? That's funny Mother, that's what I am, no I'm not a survivor, I hate it when people say that I'm strong. I'm weak. Forever searching, searching.

They say that it's not you who finds a house, the house finds you. I never used to believe in all that crap, this includes auras, energy fields, blah blah. But since this house found me well, I'm a convert. See I've always been a highly sensitive person or HSP, I'm gifted and extremely sensitive to colour. That last place nearly killed me with stress, all those conflicting colours, it was like living inside a rainbow salad! I couldn't sleep or think. I even stopped writing, which saddened me, as I love writing with a passion. Must be my father in me. I can't relate to people, well not all the time. Pointless, mindless conversations about nothing aka small talk does nothing for me. I want deep, intense, drill down to the core, cut the crap. And people are frightened of that, who wants to do soul searching every time they fancy a natter over a cup of tea and a hobnob? So, when people steer clear from me, especially dull teachers with their invariably droll conversations, I don't care! I'd rather be a lone ranger than participate in mind numbing conversations about the best way to mow the lawn. I have my writing, I'm good.

See, I'm like a cat with fur balls inside me, I need to vomit them out. I've nurtured narratives inside me for so long, it's like I've housed these stories, nourished them like my own offspring, fed them ideas, exploring possibilities, twists, turns and when they're fully developed, they want to be birthed. Hence the frenzied urge to write. I have so much to say, I almost attack the keyboard when I type. This maisonette was a fluke find, I'd wanted a fresh start and was gazing in the window of the local estate agent, just on the off chance that something new would be available. It sounded too good to be true, I was the first to view and of course I wanted to take it straight away, it was dirt cheap for what it was! Okay maybe the young agent fancied me and fast tracked the paperwork as soon as I'd rearranged my push up bra, plumped up my breasts and reapplied three-dimensional lip gloss in sultry nude. Just a teasing pout from those wet, shiny, hydrated lips got him going. Poor chap, he got increasingly flustered by the minute! When I leaned over the counter and smiled sweetly, whispering that I planned to invite him for a glass of Prosecco or two to say thank you, I knew I had it in the bag. It was empty, I moved in the next day.

The whole place is in different shades of white, even this bathroom, it feels like I'm living in milky silence. It's so eerily peaceful too, especially given the proximity to the shops. I said to myself, 'Carrie it's a sign all the white, it's time for you to step into the Light now. Leave all that darkness behind.' It made sense. That's when I realized that I was converted. My writing has come on in leaps and bounds in the house, it gives me such satisfaction! Any day now, I'll be ready to send the manuscript to the agent. Well, once I can stop tinkering.

Even my bedroom has been tastefully done, my friend says it reminds her of coffee and cream but then she's a caffeine addict, it's always on her mind, where can she go to find her next hit? She's constantly searching up new cafes, new varieties and types. Columbian, Java, mocha, espresso, latte, macchiato. It's like liquid gold to her. Her recent obsession is coffee made from the shit of civet cats. I'm happy with a Starbucks coconut latte thank you very much. No, I don't see coffee associations in my room, I prefer to see it as having earthy mushroom tones, cave like and comforting, I half expect to see bats hanging from stalactites on the ceiling.

My friend, a Feng- Shui expert, says that I'll never kick start my love life here. According to her, it needs hints of Valentine's Day red, soft textures, a his and hers mentality, for example matching bedside lamps, space for him in the closet. I have to act as if I am in a relationship to attract a mate, even though technically, I'm not. I must process this, I'm not changing anything about this place yet. It even comes tastefully furnished, what a bonus! The large living area has a fat, comfy three- seater sofa in sage, the floors are dark walnut throughout. It's the most therapeutic living environment I have ever seen, and I haven't had the heart to confuse the colours, so I just got rid of a lot of my own stuff. Even the sculptural indoor plants come with it, there's the ubiquitous yucca, a few orchids, a thriving money plant, some cacti. What more can a girl ask for? There's even a penis shaped one, tantalizingly big enough to make you want to sit on it, if you had a few drinks and felt a masochistic urge coming on. Imagine what those prickles would do to your insides?

No, that's for other people to try. I like to chill out. I put on spa music: sounds of the ocean or the rainforest and straightaway I'm in another world.

The truth is, there's no substitute for a man. A real man, not a blow -up doll or a Ken robot, even if he had artificial intelligence and could clean the house and cook you a roast dinner after giving you one.

Michael. It was all about you baby. Just you. I'm lost without you...

A shrill piercing ringing...it's my landline. Fuck. If I get up I take blood balls into the living room, can't risk it. There is no way I am *not* getting my deposit back. I know your game Mister Landlord. Whip a deep pile, cream rug on the floor just when you know that your tenant's a single mother with a young son, then complain that it's been stained and whisk away all the deposit money. *It's not just any rug, we're talking hand tufted, super shag in cream wool.* No, I'm not wrangling about my hefty deposit post moving out and I don't care whether you can shag the rug or shag on it. That deposit took a chunk of my savings, I'm getting it back. Still, I won't risk anything in this house. It still reminds me of a museum, everything carefully in its place, beautifully preserved. After a few rings the phone stops.

Breathe deeply Carrie. Feel it in your gut.

Exhale. It's gone. Now, you can carry on having your miscarriage. Carry on Carrie. Ha! Funny girl.

Then, another startling sound. A melody now, close to me. My mobile phone, a fancy flip version, set to the annoying default ring tone. Someone's keen to get hold of me. I fumble around on the floor trying to find it amongst my miscarriage paraphernalia: packets of sanitary pads, paracetamols, tampons, cigarettes. Eventually I answer, screwing up my eyes as another thunderbolt of pain rips into my belly, pulling on my insides. Who said that killing a baby was this painful? Well it was not intentional. I wanted this baby so deeply.

'Hello?'

'Hello. I would like to speak to Miss Bryant please?'

'Speaking.'

'Oh, hello there, it's the Child Support Agency. Is it ok to talk?'

(Well I am having a miscarriage right now so if you don't mind I would like to carry on in peace thank you very much.)

494

i was broken, now I Am

'Um, yes…carry on…'

'Before we start, could you tell me your reference number?'

'What????' *I mean wtf? I'm crying now, sobbing audibly.*

'Your reference number, it's a twelve-digit number on the right- hand side of the letters we sent you.'

'I don't know where it is…'

'Well, as I've just said, it's on the right- hand side of the letters we sent you.'

'Oh! I *can* tell the difference between right and left, it's just that now is not a good time. Sorry!' I've tried to keep it together. but I can't anymore, the pain is killing me. It's like tying an already tight belt tighter and tighter around my tummy. I burst into sobs.

'Oh, I am sorry, however that does not help your case. If you can't remember your reference number, we cannot proceed as you have not passed security.'

Just tell me have you been able to get my ex to pay something for his son? As you know in the two years since Zane's birth, he has contributed next to nothing.'

Pain makes me impatient. *Just spit it out love? Is it a yes or is it a no?* My voice is rising, I am angry now. Shouty.

The woman is coldly patient and polite. Obligatory politeness, a friend said once, in summing up the English. So true. 'Well as I have just explained, I cannot give out that information without that reference number. Why don't you call us back when you are ready with it and we can proceed to discuss this case?'

You mean spend half a frigging day on the phone waiting for you to pick up? No! I don't have phone credit to waste on that.

'Ok! Just give me one second!' *Fuck. Why now?*

I have been waiting for this call for a while now, I need to know the answer, my financial stability is riding on this. But in the recesses of my mind another question pops up, *'Is it just about money Carrie, or do you want to find out what that scumbag is up to these days?'* Still sitting on the loo, I empty the contents of my fake designer handbag on the bathroom floor, eventually fishing out several crumpled letters most of them demands for payment. I sort through them, find what I'm looking for and give her the damned number.

'Thank you,' she says. 'Now I can confirm that Mr Mike West has been contacted about the outstanding Child Support payments for your son and he is in the

496

process of making a calculation of how much he can afford especially given his new circumstances.'

'New circumstances?'

'Strictly speaking, I shouldn't really be sharing this with you but, well, Mr West is in another relationship currently and will soon be a father again. Therefore, he is trying to work out how much he can afford. As you can appreciate, this changes things somewhat for you and for him.'

'Wait, whaaaaattt???'

A dad again? Another relationship? When? Laughter, not pain now, from me. I am hysterical with derision and disbelief. He was never a dad to Zane in the first place and now, he goes and makes another baby with someone else? Meanwhile, I am having a miscarriage, his daughter is in my toilet! The absurdity of the situation. Don't go to a comedy show, there's comedy right here. Right effing here, in this house!

'As you can appreciate Miss Bryant, this is a sensitive issue and it's not my place to comment. We will be in touch as soon as Mr West contacts us about his financial situation. I am sorry we could not have helped you more.'

Are you serious! Helped me? When has anyone ever done that?

'*Well,* the situation is absolutely ridiculous if you ask me! I've been trying to get hold of you people for ages, hoping for some answers as to why he has not paid in two years, now you tell me that he's going to be a dad again! What about the two years of payments that he's missed? What are you doing about that? Do you have any clue about how much I have spent in phone credit just in trying to call you guys? I've been put through to department after department and I've not had answers. It is just ridiculous. Why have a Child Support Agency if it doesn't function effectively? Why give us this illusion of some agency out there helping us lone parents when, in fact, there's absolutely nothing?' I am irate now. I'm sitting on the toilet shouting and sobbing at the same time.

I thought he was the love of my life! What had I done wrong but give myself to him completely, turn a blind eye to his many faults. And now this bull about a new relationship, a new child, maybe he'd propose to this one. I wasn't good enough, but she is.

i was broken, now I Am

'Miss Bryant…Carrie if I may call you that,' her voice had softened now sensing hysteria, 'we *have* indeed been attempting to contact Mr West for some time now. However, it seems that he has not *wanted* to be contacted. The number that you gave us changed several times as did his addresses. He's quite a tricky one to pin down. Please understand that we really *are* trying to be as supportive to yourself as much as possible, it's hard, I know. I'm a mum myself.'

I'm listening hard now, for once, she's trying to reach out to me.

'Rest assured that we will do everything to try to help you, but in the meantime, why don't you join a support group? There are so many ideas on our website, have you had a chance to look through them?'

Oh of course! I spend all my non- existent free time perusing your crappy website! I don't know if she gets sarcasm, 'I will check it out,' I smile through gritted teeth. *Just as soon as I finish having this miscarriage!*

I'm lightheaded now.

'If there's anything else that we could assist you with, otherwise have a nice day Miss Bryant.'

Sure, you too! I'll have a super- duper day and thanks for fucking NOTHING!

I flip the cover, close the phone, stand up shakily, place a thick pad normally reserved for a heavy night flow in between my legs and flush my daughter away.

Phoebe. Goodbye Phoebes, I whisper. Call it a mother's instinct, I just know it's a little girl. Well, was. Zane looks like his dad, Phoebes would have looked like me. Just something for me. I wanted her so badly, loved this pregnancy from day one. Okay, I know I'm sad and desperate, shoot me for wanting a family, my own tribe. No, not a case of nine kids and living off benefits, just two of each, then I'm done. But it was not to happen, fate again. *I wanted her, she didn't want me. I wanted him, he didn't want me. It's as simple as that.*

A handful of strong painkillers, a glug of vodka, big knickers reserved for periods, not miscarriages, and I am ready to hit the sack. Sleep Zane, please sleep I pray. I need to rest. He is safe in his cot, I check quickly, then tiptoe out of his room. It is late afternoon, but I turn off the lamps and lie down heavily, sobbing into my pillow, my bat cave of a room enveloping me in an earthy embrace.

i was broken, now I Am

CHAPTER 2: DURBAN

Who calls their kid Caramel? It's a strange name for a child. India maybe, or Whisper, Rain, Journey. Even Chrysalis would be understandable from New Age hippie parents. Chardonnay would have been perfect, that would have summed me up at once. The 'Ch' would be pronounced as 'Sh' of course and I can just see it: Char this and Char that. But Caramel, from a Black woman? Makes me feel like a piece of confectionery, it's just so unimaginative. And a tiny bit racist. Look, I know I'm a half and half, a Coloured, mixed race or biracial. So many names to describe us depending on the latest trends. I didn't *ask* to be born. But don't rub it in my face...calling me Caramel like I'm some sort of ice cream flavour or a syrup to lift a boring cappuccino. I guess you can say that I had absurdity from the day I was born...conceived even. Oh yes Mother, I know all your little secrets, I am quite the detective really. Who wouldn't have started investigating?

One look at my so- called parents with their poker straight White hair and blue eyes, light, UK skins tanned somewhat now in the South African sun. Funny, they'd both arrived in Durban as children although why anyone sane would want to leave their cushy lives in the UK and settle in Durban beats me, especially with young families. They met and married in their twenties, Joe worked at the harbour as a manager what else? The snowy White Boss from overseas with his team of Black 'boys' sorting out cargo. Of course, he just gave instructions, *they* did all the hard work! She stayed at home, trying and trying for the baby that was never to be. Can you imagine me with them? Me, with a head full of wormy black curls and skin the colour of toffee. A wide nose and thick lips. I didn't belong there. First, I so wanted to be their little girl, to make up for the child they never had, but it was not to happen. Fate. I was pulled towards you.

i was broken, now I Am

When I discovered the secret, I wanted you, only you Mother. Not my father. Just you. Not to get anything from you my dear, God forbid that you would give *me, the devil's spawn,* anything! I just wanted to hold you close, smell your scent, examine your features, familiarize myself with the person who held me albeit reluctantly for nine months. Then, I wanted just to sit with you, hear your version of the story from your own lips. Maybe we could share a warming masala chai, I'm not judging you Mother, I'm comforting you. I heard that you were raped.

Of course, I read all about him, the famous writer blah blah blah, hey I could have milked the situation, demanded money even, he's super rich! But let me tell you something, there's no glory in being a by-product of a rape. In fact, for most of my life I've wanted to hide just from the shame of it. I was an unwanted baby. A blip in your lives. Sperm ejaculated in lust meets unwilling egg and voila! Life! How distasteful this is, even I cringe in disgust thinking about it. And unsurprisingly, both of you got swallowed up back into your lives afterwards. His was one of middle class White comfort, he probably drowned his sorrows in a bottle of brandy. Or a case. His wife would have forgiven him after a few days of sulking and slowly they would be busy healing their fractured relationship. There'd be no place for someone like me, a constant reminder of how he'd strayed outside the marriage, maybe that would be the Ts and Cs of their renewed marriage contract, *cut out that bitch forever and I will stand by you.* 'It's too costly to connect with you,' he'd say to me, 'I have to focus on my wife and real daughter, the pure White one. Sorry but that's the way it is. What I did with *your* mother, well it was a big mistake okay? It was her fault anyway, strutting around my home like she owned it! Practically gave it away on a platter! I was stupid! Putting my family in jeopardy like that! Never again. Now voetsak! Bugger off or I'll call the police!'

There's a whole tribe of us out there, biracial, mixed, Coloured, halves. Not wholes. By products of lustful, erotic encounters, White on Black, Black on White. Embarrassing reminders of people's depraved, biological needs. We come in varying shades. Some edge on the milk chocolate side, some are almost taupe or mushroom. For some of us, our acceptance or success is directly proportional to how light we are, our proximity to the desired White. Colourism is cruel Mother. I know you know.

I can just see it. Gossip magazines would post carefully retouched pictures of daddy holding his wife protectively with the headline: 'Toby and Wendy Ellis

Renew their Vows.' How predictable, this ritual of
atonement.

A small but exclusive, select crowd in a five -star
hotel along the golden mile of beach, a mile-long row
of glittering hotels reserved for Durban's elite. Decor in
muted champagne and antique rose, celebs arriving in
limousines, walking up the red carpet, discreet pouting
poses, his Missus keeping a beady eye on him the
whole evening in case he strayed again.

Once you go Black you can't go back!

'Oh, but you can! I've proved it!' he'd say. 'I'm back
with her and I'm happy. What was I thinking?
Everyone makes mistakes, you were just that. A blip on
my professional and personal landscape. Almost cost
me my marriage, my career. Who'd want to read books
from someone who strayed like me? No! I had to let
you go, my dear. Exorcise those memories of what
your mother and I did, amputate that side of my brain
like chopping off a diseased limb. I must not go with
servants anymore.'

Oh, I can see it clear as day. Paparazzi clicking away,
security armed with weaponry buzzing around
authoritatively, keeping out the scum, the knots of

feral, homeless Black children that own the city after dark. This was no place for them, oh no. In fact, the whole area would be screened off from their prying, attack dogs at the ready. This is Durban after all, heightened security is paramount in those posh functions. Light music from a live orchestra would mask the underlying paranoia about crime, Black on White, vengeful and spiteful. Payback for White privilege. White jacketed waiters carrying trays of fluted champagne glasses full of golden bubbly, husbands with hands around their ironing board, trophy wives, toasting, nuzzling ear lobes, examining existing wedding bands, considering upgrades. Whose turn would it be to renew *their* vows next?

Weddings are not a place for mistresses, even dazzling evening functions. No, in Durban, girlfriends and secret lovers are reserved for after parties, the dusk to dawn events when wives are dropped off home to look after the kids or because they have had too much excitement for one night. People sleep early in Durban. Especially wives with early breakfasts to prepare. The jocks congregate after dark sans wives, then, ties can be loosened, drinks are shorts: whiskey, brandy, tequila. A joint or line of coke may be produced, conversation turns to pussy and the posse head for the nearest red-light district which in Durban, is never far away from wherever you are. Some head for apartment blocks on the beach where mistresses live, closeted away, trussed up like sexual prey, waiting their lives away for their alpha predators to drop in for a bit of spice on the side.

You? You are a piece of work. Couldn't wait to exit our shores, could you? I dragged the truth out of Niall bit by bit like extracting teeth with pliers. He wanted to cover for you at first, couldn't stop singing your praises, how beautiful you were, intelligent, classy. Seemed like he'd taken a shine to you Mother. You seem to gravitate towards old White guys, like a moth to a flame. Must be that Zulu magic, was it muti that you put into their food?

Something had hardened your heart, or were you always this cold? In fact, you didn't even want to feed or hold me when I was born. Niall said it made him sad to see that, after all the whole bonding process between mother and baby depends on those crucial first minutes, I know, I've done my research. It's all documented. And I had a baby too Mother, so I know firsthand. But then you'd been defiled, he understood. Your mother worked in that household, you said, and the boss took advantage of you, raped you. Then, when your baby was born, you wanted to hot foot it out of there. Abandon me to be adopted by people you didn't even know. How cruel Mother! Just think! You could have been selling me into the hands of paedophiles. You didn't go through an agency, you didn't care to vet my new parents. That's the most insulting act in this whole sorry saga.

But it's fine, it has all worked out nicely. Do you know the adage Mother, 'what goes around comes around?' Karma will find you one day. That's a certainty, it's a non- negotiable or universal truth. And you'll get your comeuppance. You see, Uncle Niall had plenty of money in the pot. That old codger sat on money from his properties, seems like he owned half of Durban. What would he do with all his money after all? It was just the drink and whores that kept him going, I guess. He looked after me well, I was his spoilt little niece from the get go. In the end though, he couldn't even bear to come with me, to leave me in England. It's the cold Mother, he doesn't like it now that he's used to the warm, African sun. I had to say goodbye to Mary and Joe, I'm not going to call them mum and dad because we all know that they are not my real parents. Sorry I don't class adoptive parents as real, not when they look different and act different to you. Everything was wrong in that house. They slept in the day and drank at night. The ubiquitous, luxurious expat lifestyle. Big house and car, servants to clean and cook, the best food and drink. Epicurean tastes. Of course, they lounged around getting pissed. Did you know this Mother? How could you and Uncle Niall have placed me there? Oh yes sorry, I forgot. Niall was thinking of his childless sister Mary. He just forgot that she was an alcoholic. Besides:

You didn't want a mixed -race child.

You did not want a child.

You wanted a new identity.

That's why you fled to London.

That's where the party is. London.

Look, I get that you were raped. I get that you were young, Black and terrified. But then to add insult to injury, you just left me and disappeared? No birthday cards, no letters explaining the situation, no photos of you, no invitations for me to visit? Just nothing! And you think I'm messed up for nothing?

They were ready to take anything. Became desperate she did, maybe even ill with longing. Well, maybe if they had both cleaned up their acts and sobered up, Fate would have stepped in earlier. I know that she prayed. And suddenly, this miracle, Niall, bringing them this bundle of joy, barely a few hours old, their very own child at last. Documents were produced. Or is manufactured the right word? Niall, with his finger in every pie. Pardon the pun. Suddenly, I was *their* child. And the family was complete.

Except that *I* was not complete. I kept noticing eyes all around us staring, people slyly comparing them and me, clucking noises of sympathy, was I abandoned? Did they take me in out of charity? What a good deed that was! Healing the planet by taking me in, offering me the home I had never had. Did I have Aids? Everyone was doing it, in fact it was all the rage. Whites adopting children of colour. Call it out for whatever it was: middle class guilt, White privilege, the phony side of Liberalism. That Good Samaritan act is convincing! Everywhere we went people looked at us, playgroup, shopping malls, the beach. A smart White couple and their Coloured child. Of course, *they* never took any notice of people, but I started to see it, felt prying eyes on me. And after a while I couldn't take it, call me sensitive, oversensitive or fucked up, whatever you like. I *had* to get out of there. Even at school, the White kids whispered, 'Coloured! Half caste!' Sometimes they'd tug at my curls and run away. So, I hung out with the Black kids until they spotted Mary and Joe picking me up after school, then even *they* would look at me strangely as if I was unusual or weird. After a while, I stopped wanting friends Mother. This is your fault, *you* did this to me! I didn't even play out with friends anymore, can you imagine how lonely and dark my world became, especially as a young child? No one could understand it, no one. I'm surprised they didn't think to put me in therapy. Mary, she encouraged me to play out, wanted me to be normal. But I buried myself in the world of books, I could travel to every corner of the globe then, and no one could hurt me Mother. Lovingly, she'd call me a bookworm, ruffling my curls tenderly, but I saw it more as an escape.

Stop the world I want to get off!

Where's my real mother, Uncle Niall? I want my real mother!

Hush child, what do you mean??

You know uncle, you know! Stop pretending it's boring.

'What? You don't want to be speaking like that little one! It's hurtful to Mary and Joe. They've done so much for you! They love you child! Adore you! Don't you like your designer bedroom? Your toys? All those books we got you? The school? The school fees are killing us, but we willingly pay every month. We care! What's wrong? Just settle now!'

'No! You can't just make this go away, just like those Black whores who creep out of your house every morning! I know, I see everything!'

Anger does terrible things, plays tricks with the mind. At first there is incomprehension and denial, but I can see that under this, he is relieved, the truth is out. He sighs but there is a twinkle in his Irish eyes.

'Besides, I have evidence. I found this diary, well it's more of a scrapbook uncle. You see, Mary used to have great penmanship in her odd, sober moments, she wrote it all down here. See? It's the story of my life. Just as you told her when you handed me over. I pored over the excerpts like a historian going over old documents, then looked again at the photo albums, piecing it all together. She'd kept everything dear Mary, my first hair ribbon, a hibiscus flower we pressed together, photos of me as a baby, even my first dress. I had a lot of time dear uncle, when Mary hit the bottle, she hit it hard. So, I became a sort of child detective, a super sleuth.'

i was broken, now I Am

'*Oh* sherbet. This was not meant to be revealed to you like this. Why did you have to go opening Pandora's box? Why now?'

'Well, it's done now. And, I know.'

The moment when the penny dropped! It all made so much sense. And I want to go to England too, to see the Queen, maybe I will bump into my mother too, you never know! Maybe I'll say, 'Hi Mother it's me, remember Caramel? Well I've deleted the Mel bit now and even tweaked the Cara bit. Sorry, I'm not a fucking joke! How are you Mother and what are you up to these days? Any more relationships with old White men? Maybe there's a few more mixed-race kids kicking around. Or have you gotten rid of them too? Or was it just me that you had to give away?'

Then I'd blow her brains out. Bitch. How could she do this to me?

CHAPTER 3: FREEDOM

They say that your present, adult life is dominated by patterns you created in childhood and that your relationships are shaped by relationships you had with your parents. Growing up, I never felt safe. Even on the odd day when I let my guard down and relaxed, there was still that inner tiger, alert and aware, ready to spring. At my worst, I would shut myself up inside me like being psychologically holed up, asking nothing of others, relying only on myself. Humans are meant to be sociable, only those who have completely lost their trust in humanity choose to hibernate.

i was broken, now I Am

For the first few years of my life, paralyzed by the
knowledge that I had about the rape of my mother, I
was in psychic shock. The foetus can experience higher
levels of trauma in the intrauterine environment than
we know. I'm sure that that is how I miscarried *my*
baby. Foetal distress. Her soul must have sensed
something sour and putrid in the air and she found a
small courage to abort herself. I was a late developer, a
child who was late to walk and talk. But inside me, I
was biding my time. With vestiges of the traumatic
memories passed down from my mother who had been
systematically raped, to me, her baby, trust me, walking
and talking were on the back burner for me. Sitting in
that pushchair, I observed Mary's pat reply to anyone
who enquired with dispassion. 'She's special, my little
one. But I love her.' But. Always a 'but'.

Then at three years of age, she happened to take me
to the public library in Durban, a massive, grand, sand
coloured building fronted by giant, baroque angels and
flanked by tall, Grecian pillars. In the cool of the black
and white tiled lobby, a sign pointed to the lending
library on the right and the national museum upstairs.
The whole place was a revelation and I felt something
dormant stirring in me, my soul or spirit was stirring, I

had finally come home. Joy, no ecstasy filled me with a furious, fantastical energy! The smell of books and printed paper, the sight of thousands of colourful spines all with delicious new worlds within, the sobering silence, the coolness of the interior, a welcome respite from the oppressive mugginess outside. Then upstairs, the recaptured scenes of animals in the African bush: lions, gigantic elephants, giraffes with gloriously patterned skins…African tribes in huts, the minutiae of their lives preserved meticulously by the taxidermists' skills. I was mesmerized. I realized then that I was finally free to unfurl and participate in the world, *this* world of books and art and stories.

Almost overnight I started walking and babbling, then my first full words, then the rest is history as they say. I was a sponge, soaking up literacy and numeracy skills effortlessly at kindergarten, as soon as I could immerse myself in the alternate reality that books provided, I was off on my own adventures, I had found a way to escape. To this day, I am turned on by books, libraries and museums. I cannot go into either of those places without having an orgasm, caffeinated coffee prior to the visit makes me so horny that I can have multiple orgasms just by rubbing my thighs together so that the milky, fishy juices run down my thighs in streaks.

At the tender age of eleven, I started menstruating. No one warned me that I would become a hotbed of lust, with sexual urges searing up in me unashamedly daily. One minute my body was plain, flat and boring. The next, I had become three dimensional so to speak. My new pointy breasts with their big, dark areolas poked out of my tops, I had dense, dark pubic hair and a pronounced, rounded bum and shapely legs. Men openly leered at me as I did the twenty-minute walk to school and back, I was convinced that they could smell the new smells of sweat and sex on me no matter how often I showered or doused myself in deodorant.

Around us, sex was everywhere. It was as if someone had pried open the skin covering my eyes and I could see everything in technicolor. In the Sunday papers, the back pages were full of models in skimpy bikinis, Joe would stare and stare, arranging then rearranging his balls until Mary would ask tartly if his eyeballs had fallen off yet. I started to notice the women emerging secretively from Niall's outbuilding every morning doing the walk of shame. In the news,

517

they reported that a White woman had married a Black tribal king and pictures of her bare breasted dressed in animal skins were all over the papers with the nipples blacked out of course. In the columns about overseas news, older, husbandless White women passed their prime, were paying dark skinned, foreign men who spoke no English, to marry them, saying that they could save on childminding as the men could care for the kids in exchange for a passport and a free home. Everyone seemed to be 'doing it' no matter how they packaged it. From princes to pop stars, everyone but me.

And I had become horny. All I had to do was brush over my nipples with my fingertips and the juices came flooding out of me, my body going into spasms of pleasure. Later, I learned how to touch myself. We are hard wired to feel sexual arousal, for me it was addictive. At thirteen, I used to fantasize about caretakers, teachers, singers, actors, guys on the street, everyone really! But disappointingly, nobody asked me to be their girlfriend. At school, I had my sights on a pale skinned biracial boy in my class, he had beautiful green eyes and dark curly hair like mine. But when someone whispered my little secret to him he became condescending, spitting on me in the playground and hissing that he did not 'go with dark girls who were adopted.' Oh, the shame! I clammed up immediately needing solitude and space away from the taunts of other students.

A couple of years of this boring, dull existence and I realized how unexciting my life was, the pleasant flatlining had become unpleasantly dreary. Every day was the same as the next, I read in a book that I had a 'vanilla' life meaning bland and predictable, the very opposite that I had read about in romantic fiction. So, I decided to change the routine a bit, I wanted to experience sex.

Every morning and afternoon a much older, dark skinned Indian man would wait for me outside his shoe shop which was situated in a parade of seemingly discrepant shops equidistant between my school and home. He'd pretend to be doing something constructive like arrange and rearrange the racks of shoes that were stacked up outside, but I knew what his eyes told me, they travelled up and down my body and a slow smile would light up his face as I approached. First, he would offer me money for sweets and expect nothing in return, over time he lured me into his shop in the afternoons, promising to find me the perfect pair of sandals for my 'beautiful feet.' Once again, as in the library and museum, I was mesmerized, I liked him, loved the matte, smooth, chocolate of his skin, the sudden contrast with his cropped, grey hair, his compact body, the grey white tufts of hair on his chest. I allowed him to slip off my school shoes and measure my feet, then he went on to touch my legs, marvelling at the softness of my skin. As I wore a short school skirt every day, I knew what he *wanted*, I could see the fire in his eyes, the desire in the sudden bulge in his trousers. Bit by bit, day by day, he was building up to something, I could tell.

One day he brought the racks inside, closed the doors and latched them and pulled down the blinds. The golden sandals he had sweetened me up with, lay on the table next to the till, ready for me to collect on my way home. Usually, we sat on the long bench for only fifteen minutes at a time, not that I had to rush home as Mary was always asleep and I would let myself in to a seemingly empty house. This time, he led me to the back room where he kept all the stock, walking through a parted wall of long beads. It felt symbolically like I was entering a realm that was deliciously dangerous and opening the doors to another world.

If my compliance fascinated him, he was too excited to show it. With his eyes shining, he asked me to lie back on a narrow, makeshift bed on the side of the stockroom, a sink and tea making facilities were on the other side. As I did, he slipped off my shoes and socks, taking in my white school girl panties with its wet spot where moistness was gathering. I closed my eyes and lay back. First, I felt his tongue taking in my toes one by one, licking and sucking as if they were some sweet fruit. Then, he ran said tongue up and down my smooth, hairless legs. When he started kissing me on top of my panties, I could hardly hold myself together. It was I who pulled them off and it was I who allowed him to taste me down below. I must have had orgasm after orgasm, my back was arched, my head thrown back, the sounds I was making seemed guttural and strange. Then he unzipped himself and entered me, it was only then that he kissed me on my mouth. It felt like I was kissing my own sex, but I couldn't take my mouth away from him. It was difficult to part company from him in the end, but I had to. My overriding and all -consuming thought was that I would see him the next day as he worked alone in his shoe shop six days a week. If he was married, he never said.

We became lovers, seeing each other every afternoon in a relationship that lasted three months. In that time, he became familiar with every undulating curve of my body, his tongue navigating the curves tasting, teasing. And I became an expert in how to please him. Once a week, we stayed together all night. I would explain to a drunken Mary that there was a sleepover and she would give me her blessing without a thought. His name was Dev. He was sixty years old.

No! Don't look at me with those horrified eyes, I'm not just looking for you, Mother. It's my father that I need too. I don't understand it myself, these feelings that come over me sometimes. I'm a walking ball of shame Mother. There's no upside or downside to be an adopted by product of rape. Every breath is a humiliation. I have no place on this planet, no right to be here. I wasn't planned or predicted. Even unwelcome Christmas presents get sent to charity shops to be rehomed. I was sent to a place where I was not wanted. It was a struggle to fill my time with anything meaningful.

Dev's friend lived in a small flat around the corner and when we stayed together they would swop for the night, we would use the flat and he would sleep on the stockroom bed. He even obtained birth control pills for me so that he never had to use a condom. He liked to feel me, he said. I was fifteen.

i was broken, now I Am

In some ways, I was an immature teenager. Green, unformed about the world around me. Well relatively. I mean look at my close contacts. Mary, Joe, Niall were my so- called family. They were all alcoholics. We didn't go on holidays, just shopping, the beach and back home to open a fresh bottle and start a new party. Then there was school where I didn't want any friends. Before Dev, I'd kept myself going, running on autopilot, just floating around, trying to be invisible, taking in everything around me in my own quiet way as you can expect from a child in my shoes. With Dev in my life, I did not morally unravel. Instead, I was conducting an experiment, testing and probing the edges of social acceptability, teasing boundaries. Older man, young girl. Dark and light. Work and school. I was just biding my time and this exercise filled in the yawning gaps of time between morning and night.

In many ways, Leela saved me.

'Hey!' a slim, middle aged Indian woman ran after me one afternoon as I passed a pharmacy just two doors from Dev's shoe shop. This was the bit of the parade that I loved and hated the most. There was the large, modern pharmacy with its white coated staff and reassuring smells of disinfectant, then a butcher shop next door and then Dev's shop. I'd always been fascinated but repulsed by the butcher shop. Take, for instance those trays with their pyramids of cow's heads, the doe eyes deadened now but still staring, those slack, blackened tongues poking out on one side, the sickening smell of the place, the sight of congealed fat, velvety ears and groups of flesh flies hovering and settling over lumps of exposed blood and meat. The high pitched, crazed buzzing always triggered a gag instinct in me especially when they transferred their attention onto me, my eyes, nose, lips. I'm not usually morbid but this, this was writer's gold! I'd linger there, feasting my senses, then hurry on to Dev or school, later, I'd write poem after poem as an ode to the cows.

I didn't like strangers, I hadn't wanted to talk to this Leela with her white pharmacist coat.

'How old are you?' she pounced on me as she caught up.

'Why?' Suddenly, I was on my guard.

'I want to talk to you,' she said softly. We were outside the butcher shop now, it was early afternoon. Out of the corner of my eye, I noticed that most of the cow's heads had been replaced on the tray, by clumps of dirty wash cloths and a few bloody hooves. Had they been sold already? She caught me looking.

'Offal, it's delicious with broad beans,' she smiled suddenly showing bright white teeth.

'Offal?' The word sounded a bit like 'awful.'

'Yes, come I'll show you darling. Look,' she had her arm around me and was pointing at the tray, 'That's a sheep's stomach. We chop it up and put it in a curry. Yummy!' That made me laugh, cleared the air. Leela convinced me to cross over the road to a sweet shop where she bought me a cold drink and a packet of toffees.

Then she started on me.

'What you're doing is wrong, if your parents came to know, they'd be very angry. I know about you and that old man, it's wrong, it's very wrong. I've seen you there in the shop. You must stop. Where's your sense of pride in yourself huh?'

To my feigned incomprehension slash deep embarrassment, she continued in a scolding tone now.

'He's how old fifty? sixty? You're fifteen! Darling, he's using you. Do you know what grooming means?

That's what he's doing. Who wouldn't want a beautiful young girl like you? He may be married with kids, even grandkids maybe! How can you carry on like that so brazenly? You need hobbies, friends your own age, sport. You shouldn't be going around with paedophiles!'

I wanted Dev. He helped me to stop thinking about Mary, Joe and Niall.

'No!' she insisted as if she had read my thoughts. 'You're like a daughter to me, I'm going to nip this in the bud right now. You're never going back there! Do you hear me? Just wait until I finish my shift then I'll drop you off home, I'll drop you every day if you like but I'm *not* letting you do this.'

Leela burst into our lives that day, like a ray of curried sunshine. Poor Dev, he must have waited in vain for me every day, but he never saw me again. Instead, I spent all my free time with Leela. She introduced herself to Mary who took an instant liking to her warm personality, soon she was bringing their prescriptions home, demonstrating how to cook the ubiquitous Durban curry and taking me away to her house for weekends. I started looking forward to helping to babysit her young son, soon my shyness wore off and I even found that I could speak to her husband without stuttering with shyness.

i was broken, now I Am

Sometimes, she would take me with her to cultural events. I loved visiting the Indian temple where peafowl foraged in the lush, surrounding gardens. 'Did you know that it's the national bird of India?' Leela was always trying to enhance my general knowledge and talked me through the prayer rituals in detail and depth. 'Us Hindus burn camphor to spread positivity,' she droned. 'We place it in a muslin bag around children's necks to alleviate colds in children, we also use it in prayer. It's very powerful in purifying the home. That's why we take it into each room in the house. When you burn camphor, you symbolically burn away ego.' It was a lot to take in, even for me. One day, I should go on a spiritual pilgrimage to India, she recommended. She could see that I needed a profound experience. In fact, she had seen some missing link deep inside of me from day one. Resisting her intense scrutiny, I knelt at the sacred stone that she pointed out, clasped my hands together in a namaste, allowed her to place a thumbprint of holy ashes onto my forehead and made a beeline for the sanctuary of the garden hoping to hear the wild cries that signalled the presence of the peafowl.

What a magical place that was! The peahens would stare accusingly at me as if I'd wronged them by attributing colour only to the males. Then the glorious and extravagant show off gestures by the peacocks, those fans of brilliant tail feathers, the iridescence of the turquoise on their bodies. Those images have stayed with me. The rustic bench under the sacred tree, with its rings of fresh and old cotton threads, placed there by girls looking to marry and needing luck, the broken coconuts at its base, the sprinkling of turmeric and ash, the deep silence save for the calls of the birds and the gong beats delivered, intermittently, by the priest. That was the most memorable experience of Durban for me. A truly enchanting and luminous experience, close to bliss.

Then, the visitors came.

Uncle Niall's and Mary's relatives had come to visit from the UK. We took them to rugby matches, the beach, the malls and the flea markets. In the evenings, we sat in the back and braaied chicken, fish and lamb chops. Mary made her salads: avocado and pine nuts, mango and feta cheese, potato and parsley, cherry tomatoes and tuna. 'This is food paradise!' our visitors would say. Of course, they washed it all down with wine and beer. They had never seen such hospitality! Uncle Stephen had missed his little sister, missed Niall too. He'd grown up in Durban too but left as a child with his dad when his parents' marriage had come apart, the others had stayed on. Now, childless and on his second marriage, he kept talking about how Durban had changed for the better and how he was ready to embrace the changes. Behind his back, the family had described him as suffering from nostalgia with a side of guilt, he had chosen to leave with his father after all. When his mother had passed, he stubbornly refused to attend the funeral saying that he was a 'conscientious objector' to the racist White government. But now, the races were mingling, opportunities had opened for Black people, the government had changed. It was time to embrace the place where he had grown up. To this Mary had piped up, 'Hey you don't have to embrace anything! You'll be on your way home soon. It's us, we have to live here, and it's not easy!'

'Then why do you *choose* to stay?' It was funny to hear Auntie Debbie speak, she still had a soft, musical, Irish accent, I couldn't believe that she'd lived in London for ages, she spoke differently to uncle. I sensed a warmth in her, she'd make us stop on the roadside and give money to beggars even though Joe warned that stopping the car was dangerous, she kept saying that it was so sad. She teared when she saw mothers and toddlers begging together. She wanted to see the townships, can you imagine that Mother? She kept repeating that that was what she had come to see. When could we take her? Why couldn't we go on a day trip to the townships? Mary had rolled her eyes at Uncle Stephen and shaken her head, 'No way,' she'd exclaimed. 'They'll pull us out of the BMW and blow our brains out before speeding off with the car. You need to wake up and smell the coffee Debs!' We all laughed except Auntie Debs, I joined them too but inside I too wanted to go to the townships. Why couldn't Mary just take us? Durban was such a huge province, but we'd only seen a small part of it, I had never even seen the other parts of South Africa.

Joe rarely spoke even to visitors. Mostly, he would plonk his now wizened body into a deckchair and smoke and drink continuously, it seemed like he was always high or drunk. With his heart problems and skinny frame, he looked fragile. But when the topic of people choosing to remain in South Africa came up, he became animated, like a puppet springing to life. Of course, this was another topic on everyone's lips, as the only child in the house, I'd grown up with this kind of adult talk.

'Listen!' he hissed sitting forward. 'I'm not leaving to go anywhere. This is home. I came here when I was twenty, I'm sixty now. Forty years of working, saving, paying off my mortgage. I've put a lot into this country, it's not easy just to get up and run overseas. That cold weather and those dour Brits, nah, it's not for me! I'll die here on South African soil. I've told Mary she must go, but I'm not budging.'

'So, don't complain about crime!' retorted Debs. 'You want to continue to live in this beautiful country and enjoy your elite lifestyle, you have to accept the crime too, I guess. You've taken a lot from the native people, enjoyed a lot of privileges. Servants, swimming pool, gardener. How many of us ordinary British people live like that?'

I thought that he would slap her, his face looked as dark as thunder. Everyone looked nervous.

'So why did you come here on holiday?' he demanded. 'This is an affluent area, you are being wined and dined daily at our expense. You're getting a free holiday, I don't see you dipping your hands in your pockets! You're accusing me of living the dream at the expense of the disadvantaged, do you know how much we do for charity? Do you know how well we treat our staff? You know nothing, sitting in your liberal British armchair making soothing noises about how we should help people when you haven't helped anyone in your life!' Then he shuffled indoors muttering under his breath.

I felt like I had to smooth things over.

The reality was that in Durban we were all living in a kind of a prison, we had heavy, metallic, burglar bars on the windows and security gates at the front and back, signs posted on our front wall proudly announced that our house was protected by a well - known security company, the image showed a man with a rifle. Everywhere we went we had to do a risk assessment beforehand, were there police on standby? If we parked the car, were there car guards to help us protect the car from being stolen? What kind of area was it? Did it have a reputation for being dangerous? Of course, the newspapers and media were chock full of stories of how people were getting attacked day and night, and news often provoked hysterical reactions in people.

The debate of whether to be poor and free in another country or wealthy and a sitting duck for criminals in South Africa was a common one, it was all everyone talked about. Mary, ever loyal to Joe, had become firm and tight lipped with the visitors, she put an immediate end to the questions, saying that certain areas were 'no go' areas, maybe Debs could go back home and see it all on the internet. That was better, you could watch it all on the net these days, that way you didn't have to go there and get yourself killed. I kept laughing seeing Debbie's smiley face turn sour as she kept repeating, 'No go areas? What's a no -go area?' The atmosphere had become decidedly sour but a few hours later, with the drinks flowing, the party was on again.

Meanwhile, ever waiting and watching, I hatched a plan. Every day in their company, listening to those clipped British tones, bonding with them jokingly, but planning behind the scenes. Eventually, it all came out.

I steered the conversation one lazy Saturday, while they were busy getting pissed in the garden. 'Hey people!' Mary had slipped on shorts and flip flops, 'As my family is here, I'm getting legless today!' It was ten o' clock in the morning. Poor Joe was drinking himself into an early grave and ever since the visitors came he had become worse, knocking back hard liquor with no dash even early in the morning. Vodka, brandy,

anything. His wrinkled torso had become thin and
wasted, his skin sagged. As usual, his eyes were
bloodshot, so he covered them up with dark glasses.
He wore shorts but no top, a floppy hat covered his
liver spotted, balding head. 'And I'm having a hair of
the dog!' he announced, holding up a cold beer. He was
tossing fat pork sausages on the braai, his hands
trembling. Earlier he'd slipped out to buy fresh bread
rolls from the Portuguese bakery. Niall had made
caramelized onions and placed mustard and ketchup on
the side, next to the plates and napkins. I had to put on
Joe's country and western music and turn up the
volume, so they could hear it outside, then I had to
pour tequila into tiny shot glasses, next I had to pour
whiskey with a dash of Coke into large glasses, ready
for the following round. It would be one of those lazy
but dangerous Saturdays, anything could happen.
Crates of booze stood ready on one side, the acrid
smell of cannabis filled the air as Niall lit up a pipe and
passed it around. They cheered each other, and
conversation flowed, I clutched my orange juice and
monitored everything.

'You guys live the life of Riley here!' Uncle Stephen.
'We don't have anything like this, do we babes?' He
was nuzzling Auntie Debs's ear. Every now and then,
he'd give her nipples a playful tug too, she really had

the biggest breasts I had ever seen, they practically jumped out of her white bikini top.

'Too right!' quipped Mary and Joe in unison, 'we just love it here. The weather, the food, the jorl.' They shared a long kiss. Uncle had to explain what 'jorl' meant to auntie. 'You mean life here is a permanent party?' she asked, 'I wonder if *everyone* in South Africa is partying like you. I'm sure most people live in abject poverty. You're just a good example of the privileged few,' she said bitterly, sipping her drink. 'It's not right.'

For a moment everything went embarrassingly silent. I tried not to stare at her skin which was turning lobster pink in the intense Durban heat.

'Oh well! Someone's gotta do it! Have a joint and take a fucking chill pill doll. Don't start that shit again! You're always lecturing us, have a drink or go home!' Mary was slurring now, she hadn't even touched her food. I felt like something was about to explode. Joe muttered darkly about Whites having done their bit for the country, Niall, buzzed out of his head, sat staring into space. Uncle Stephen tried to whisper something placating in auntie's ear, but she would not back down.

I had to change the subject, I didn't want World War three again.

What's London like then? Is it different to Durban? What food did they eat? What was the education like? I'd heard that it was free unlike South Africa. Did they have good healthcare? It was free as well, I'd heard. What were the teenagers wearing? What was their music like? What was it like to watch a show in the West End? Did they go shopping in Harrods? *Did they know of a Black woman who arrived fifteen years ago fleeing rape? Sibongile was her name.*

'Come and visit when you're older.' The words flew out of auntie's mouth.

'How sweet of you, auntie! Would you like me to rub tanning lotion on your back? I'd love to come now…you know, when you go back.' Silence from Mary, Joe, Niall.

'Why not?' Uncle was a bit tipsy now, I think he liked my tequila shots, I'd given him generous ones. I went for the hard sell. They wouldn't have to pay for anything, I had a year to go then I'd turn sixteen and would be independent, I could work part time, help out. I was a good student, always getting top marks, look how helpful I was around the house. To my shocked family it seemed insane, but my arguments made sense. It would be a better education for me in any case, no one boycotted school there or toy toyed in the town squares. I would be getting a better future all round; didn't I deserve that after the ropey start I'd had? Everyone but everyone was moving to London, it was literally the 'go to' place if you were pissed off with South African politics or if you wanted to see the world. I too would go sooner or later, why not now? I was stubborn, I *wanted* to go. I nagged and then begged until they got tired.

We lived in a mediocre suburb of Durban, just over the bridge from the prestigious Berea, where all the movers and shakers had their mansions. Our area was rapidly going downhill as a multicultural community had moved in. Uncle Niall didn't complain, after all it was a fertile hunting ground for sex workers and dodgy bars that didn't just serve up alcohol. But to a teenager sensing the menacing atmosphere and seeing mountains of filth piling up on the streets, it seemed like the gateway to hell. All the decent people had deserted us, it was becoming a ghost town. As I tried to convince them to set me free, Uncle Niall stared at me with his soft, drunken Irish eyes. He knew what I knew, but he didn't let on. They couldn't keep me there, they were not managing as it was, with Joe's deteriorating condition and the impending threat of being murdered in cold blood. I would come back and visit later, I promised, they could visit too.

But Joe and Mary looked at each other and silence lay heavily between us. I was so anxious, my freedom sat in their hands. I wanted to be sick. In anger, I grabbed the remaining sausages and hurled them into the pool where they floated like fully formed turds, much to auntie's disgust. In the kitchen, Mary was seething.

'You are a bitter and angry young person!' she spat the words out as she dug her nails into my wrist. How dare you humiliate us in public? We're the only family you have!'

'Family, what a joke!'

I marched into my room, pulled out her diary and flung it onto the kitchen table. When she realized what it was, there was a sharp intake of breath and she seemed to fold. I turned away, giving her the space to flick through it, looking at all the notes that she had made from the moment she first held me, to when I was about ten.

She hadn't told me that I was adopted.

Still, she had the chance then, she could have put it right. I was at the window, watching the visitors trying to fish out the sausages using pool nets, the minutes ticked by. I'd known that the diary was a game changer. It's not that I didn't love them or that I wasn't grateful to them for saving my life.

I was hungry Mother. So hungry. I wanted to be with you. And my tribe. I am a cultural person Mother, is it too hard to comprehend that I wanted to experience that side too? Maybe if I found you, you could show me.

Moving forward.

'Here's what's going to happen,' I said. 'I'm going to London to find my mother. It's up to you, if you want to explain that to your family, but I need this opportunity.' Then, seeing the tears in her eyes, I went over and hugged her. 'Hopefully, I'll make something of myself there. I heard that the streets are paved with gold.'

Then we both giggled.

'You'll hate the grim weather, the narrow houses,' she said, 'but I know that this place is not good for a young person. We'll visit you, don't worry. Hopefully this won't break Joe.' More tears, from both of us now.

We both knew that they would never go back to the UK.

Paperwork was rushed but ready just in time, money greases palms. Tearful goodbyes were said. Leela sobbed as if I was her own child and pushed a parcel of fragrant Indian spices in my hand, all bubble wrapped and ready for my suitcase. 'In case you want to cook a curry,' she said, clutching me tightly.

'You'll have to leave that here,' Mary said shrewdly, eyeing up the package. 'You can't take that stuff onto the plane.' I could see her work out her menu for the next week. Beef curry then chicken followed by lamb then pork then back to beef. It was her favourite food.

Soon enough, another brand-new life awaited me.

They lived in a quiet, leafy suburb in London with a huge park right opposite. There was a lake with ducks, swans and geese; everything was so green and clean it took my breath away, I felt like I'd found Emerald City at last! People seemed gentle, polite, peaceful, Mary would call it 'well behaved.' The all girls' school that they'd picked out was a mere ten- minute walk. It was perfect. Talk about not wanting to upset the apple cart, I was no trouble really, I passed my exams easily, didn't bring unsavoury friends' home, slept early and left before breakfast. All my efforts were about not letting even a whisper of a breeze ruffle their lives. I was invisible in that house. But I was on borrowed time.

Later, I was to learn that despite our efforts at trying to control situations, life sometimes has other plans for us.

When I'd stepped off the plane, I had been preparing for an Arctic blast, after all the talk about the winters in Britain. But I found that the cold air was so invigorating I actually welcomed it into my soul so to speak. It helped me to forget, temporarily at least. It's the reason why I love Winter so much. When you concentrate on keeping warm you can't think about the past. I still love those icy blasts, they blast out pain and I seem to be always in need of that! London had been a change all right. Everyone was so pleasant, they just left you alone to get on with it. You were free to colour your hair blue, wear outrageous clothing or sit in the park smoking a fag while gazing at the lake. Of course, I never did any of these things. The provincial, conservative South African mentality, drilled into me from childhood, put the brakes on any kind of wild behaviour. Still, I relished that spirit of being totally free. Whether your skin colour was milk chocolate, dark chocolate, mahogany, cappuccino, vanilla, olive green, yellow or bubblegum pink, you were free to walk anywhere and do anything you wanted. I was experiencing the Rainbow Nation at last! Funny, I'd left a country that had branded itself as a 'rainbow nation' where the race and culture of each citizen was supposed to be celebrated in the true spirit of diversity, yet there was little evidence of this on the streets or anywhere for that matter. In fact, ironically, the very opposite was true!

We had lived under threat constantly. There was the threat of being raped or murdered or robbed or burgled and the sickening justification for this, from some circles was that it was right to target affluent people in the spirit of payback. An eye for an eye. You took our land, now we take your life. It was such a major part of daily life there that often such hateful crimes did not get the press coverage that they deserved. As a child, growing up with these issues as a daily backdrop, I'd become habituated to violence. Now, I was seeing a 'rainbow nation' for the first time, in an 'un-rainbow' country and I wanted to cry with relief. Normal now had a brand- new meaning. I'd heard the saying, 'You can't put a price on freedom' so many times. Now, I could feel in my bones and blood

i was broken, now I Am

physically and psychologically what this meant. Yes, I
was finally free.

CHAPTER 4: WHERE DO I BELONG?

Aunt Debbie had been a supply teacher, the kind that stood in for a teacher who was absent. She worked all over London wherever there was a need for her, a job was a job she said. Except that gradually, the pleasure in teaching unruly, non- compliant London teenagers had worn off and she did not want to do it anymore.

One evening, huddled in a threadbare armchair clutching a bottle of Jamieson's whiskey, she howled and sobbed for what seemed like hours about the job getting under her skin. In between swigs of drink, she said that the kids had thrown food all over the classroom floor and she'd been expected to clean it all up.

'Baguettes!' she howled. 'Pieces of pizza, pepperoni clinging onto chair legs! I had to go down on my hands and knees to scrape it all off from the floor. How did you think I felt?' She was addressing uncle who had tried unsuccessfully to stroke her hair by way of offering comfort. She had simply batted his hands away, screaming that, as she was not prepared to get up from the chair, he could cook his own dinner that night. Of course, uncle sent me off to the chippy to get fish and chips, partly so that I did not have to see her disintegrate.

I knew that he had loved her deeply and would do everything possible to make her happy. What I didn't know was that they were only renting the house and the lease was up for renewal.

'I'm not doing it ANYMORE!' She shouted. 'Not for one fucking minute of my life! Nothing,' she hissed, 'Nothing is worth this! Not even you! They're animals! They don't want to learn! Don't care about teachers or teacher assistants. These are not humans! British education! My fucking big arse.'

Each time she swore, uncle flinched as if the words were physically hurting him. 'You've got a great arse,' he said nuzzling her face. 'It's not you, it's them.

'I'll get a transfer,' he said gently and softly. 'We'll move to the countryside near your sister. You like it there, don't you?'

'No!!' She continued to scream. 'You've been fobbing me off with that crap for fucking years now and I totally fucking believed you. Then, you have the cheek to bring *her* to live here, knowing our financial situation, knowing that that would be another stone around our fucking necks dragging us down. I'm not having it! I'm going to stay with my sister! I'm leaving at the weekend.'

I've become an expert at reading body language, must be something about living with alcoholics, you never knew what to expect so best be prepared. When I saw uncle kick the door shut and heard him whisper soothingly to her, I knew that my time there was over. As I peeped in through the glass pane of the door, he was on his knees before her in complete submission, he had grasped her knees and no doubt shot a good few looks at her pendulous breasts that she made more pronounced by wearing clingy satin shirts and lacy bras. He was a bland looking older man with a paunch, she was young and pretty, with those breasts, she was in the driving seat.

For the next few days, I tiptoed around, not daring to ask for lunch money, not daring to be visible in that house. Then, when I woke up after a lie in on Saturday, I noticed that they had left. Their clothes were gone, some of the trinkets on the mantelpiece had gone. Remarkably and eerily, everything else stayed intact.

Frozen in shock, I stayed in bed not knowing what to do and how to process it all. I had three months to go until I turned sixteen and could qualify for financial aid from the government. I had four months to go until my final exam at secondary school. Then, I could attend college and later, university. But now, with only a few notes that I had clung onto from the stash that Mary and Niall gave me, I was in panic. Where would I live? How would I survive here, in this strange place with nobody to call my true friend or family? I saw suddenly how impulsive and immature my decision to come here to find my mother had been. The UK was a big place, what were my chances of ever finding her? Questions with no answers. I sobbed and sobbed for a few days, mooching about in that house. Of course, I didn't bother going to school, what was the point in that when I was going to be homeless. One day I slipped out to the shop to buy bread and ham, hopefully if I made sandwiches they could last me a few days and I could stretch the money. By the time I returned, a TO LET sign was plastered on the front wall and a note pushed into the letterbox by the estate agent announced that cleaners were arriving at nine a.m. the next morning to strip and clean the place to get it ready for the rental market.

I needed to get out.

i was broken, now I Am

CHAPTER 5: HOMELESS

Homelessness in the London summer conjures up images of knots of rebellious teenagers chilling in parks wearing shorts and cropped tops. Cold beers and joints are passed around, there are jokes and laughter as they swop stories. Docile dogs lie on the sides and a spirit of camaraderie knits the group together, they share sleeping bags and food, some couple. It's the spirit of Glastonbury or the V festival, Reading. Any music festival. There's a looseness and a lack of concern for the judgmental stares of passersby, some might say that they flaunt their one finger up to conformity. But in the harsh winter, something different happens. Driven by hunger, illness and the bitter cold they feel adrift, disconnected from creature comforts like family, food and warmth, at this time, the fight for resources intensifies and the realization that they are misfits, unwanted, out of place, rejected, cuts to the core like the sharp stab of a new blade. Braziers are a luxury, many have nowhere to warm themselves and sit huddled and morose in between shop windows, needing the residual heat from buildings. They cling onto dogs, sheets of cardboard, steal bales of newspapers. Anything to stop shivering.

I was homeless at the beginning of February, the coldest month of the year. I wished I had asked Santa for a sleeping bag and an extra thick coat because it would have been the perfect resource for a life on the streets. All I had was bread, my usual hooded jacket, and a few clothes in my rucksack. I felt dirty. Not as in depraved. I hadn't washed or used deodorant since I left the house. And munching away reluctantly at my carb fest, I was keenly aware that there were no toilets in sight, if there were, I would have willingly slept in them just to get away from the penetrating stares of people. I've always been socially awkward. Just because I haven't cut myself or swallowed bleach doesn't mean

that I'm some uber confident, supremely popular alpha
girl. I'm not even a challenge- to -the- authorities beta
girl. I'm the underdog, quiet and passive, I eat last. I've
been tormented and taunted so obviously my eyes are
downcast, all I crave is a strong alpha to protect me and
to fill my life with wonder. I believe, I'm called the
Omega girl.

At school, they teased me about my heavy South
African accent and unruly curls. Curls were not
fashionable. I had no iron to force them to become
poker straight, and my little money didn't stretch to
make up so once again, I was on the edge of groups,
invisible to all. At parties, they laughed and jeered. Only
the misfits gravitated towards me. But I wanted to wear
the badge of loneliness with honour, teachers took me
out of lessons for an extra boost of revision as I'd
joined the school so late in the year, exams were
looming. So even though I wanted the solitary
confinement of working alone in the corner of the
library, comforted by the books, I had to sit with
assistants who went over the revision material again
and again. And even the assistants floundered about
trying to navigate their way around my accent. 'Are you

Australian?' they'd ask rolling their eyes in exasperation, knowing that I was South African.

So, I've always been wary of people. The social pathologies that they are embedded in, their covert games. When men approached me for sex while I sat huddled in my homeless cave in an alleyway, I was shocked. I was unclean, I had not made the required effort to look shaggable. After the bread, I felt lumpy and constipated. Yet they came at me, young ones, old ones, down and out ones, confident ones in smart power suits. I couldn't bear it, could picture Mary, Joe and Niall's faces, disbelief etched in every pore. After two days, I crawled back to the house one night, found the loose windowpane in the back room, and somehow got myself in. It was rented furnished, bizarrely, everything was intact. I found my school uniform in the bins outside, went back to school and pretended that everything was normal.

When the young estate agent found me out, she was not impressed. A neighbour had seen me coming and going through the back window and had alerted the agency. She was annoyed that she had this shit on her hands now, she'd thought that the house was ready to show to prospective tenants. I liked Breanna immediately. 'Call me Bree,' she said when she had calmed down. First, I had blubbed like a baby. I didn't want to be on the streets. I was starving. I had come to the UK to get an education; my relatives had callously abandoned me. I didn't want to get social services involved and I did not want to live in a care home under a care plan. I'd heard about carers and care homes, the houses were grim, abuse of all kinds was rife, ironically, no one gave a shit about you once you were in the system. From the point of entry into the care system to your exit and forever after, you fitted into one category. A failure. You were destined to be on welfare all your miserable life. I wasn't that. I didn't have grandiose aspirations to be better than others, I didn't judge or turn my back on the vulnerable and fragile. I'm socially inept. I can't do big institutions where you were force fed friends and a socialization programme.

Also, I didn't want to be abused. I'm fucked up as it is.

So, Bree, listening to me rant over egg and mayo sandwiches and a hot chocolate in a café, suggested that I live with her in her little apartment that she shared with her boyfriend. She had a little back room that needed to be cleaned out, as soon as I turned sixteen, I would have to work part time and repay her. She had been adopted herself. She liked me.

In no time, I turned sixteen, got a job in a fast food outlet, finished my final exams and applied to colleges to do 'A' levels. I chose to study Law, English and Psychology. When I passed with flying colours, I chose a university in a different part of London. I'd grown to treasure Bree, but I knew that she had craved her space and was planning a celebratory party after I'd left. At least now, she could orgasm as loudly as she liked.

i was broken, now I Am

CHAPTER 6: THE PATHOLOGICAL LIAR

'I'm your mother and your father now,' he said, *'You'll never want or need for anything, you'll never walk alone. Do you give yourself to me?'*

'I do.'

'Then, I give myself to you. Mind, body and soul.'

The curtain lifts. Enter Michael James West. I fold into him, like I've been searching for him all my life. He is not just a soulmate, he's more than that, much more. He's an essential part of my chemistry, the part that completed me, made me whole again, made me feel loved and rounded and real. He made me see and experience wonder and enchantment for the very first time. I loved him from the minute I saw him. I know it seems surreal how it happened, but it's true.

But what no one told me was that with Michael, I was inviting pain, more pain into my life. Ferocious, belly cramping, vomit inducing pain. And fear. He was addictive.

Convergence in relationships usually takes a long time to embed. If you're compatible, you slowly start to finish each -others' sentences, your body rhythms become similar, you like the same things, you know what each other is thinking. We converge emotionally and sexually. We talk about 'getting' each other, even in bed. Convergence is demonstrated in our physical appearance too, when we dress the same way. Body shapes become synchronized when there is harmony.

Michael and I experienced this ultra -intense level of connectedness and synchrony that I later found to be convergence, right from the get go. At least I thought it was convergence. Who wants to think about their lovers as narcissistic bastards, just playing a role like a stage performer, trying to impress you to get a booty call and later, strip you of everything once he'd gotten

hold of the strings that controlled you. Mike the great
puppet master. Pulling at my strings. His whole life, a
fabrication. It was my first experience of narcissistic
manipulation.

I had just turned twenty-two. At university, I was
the quiet one, burying myself in books and reading
endlessly. I feasted on words, ate them for breakfast,
lunch and dinner. When I wasn't reading, I wrote, short
stories mainly. Somedays I just woke up, made a pot of
tea, dandelion was my favourite, and churned out story
after story. Anything inspired me. A piece of velvet
ribbon on someone's hair, the sight of a beggar,
homeless people comatose in the park, empty cans by
their side. And kids, I wrote a lot about them. Children
birthing children, what a common sight in London.
Skinny young girls with blonde ponytails pushing
prams, shifty eyed lads with hoodies, hanging around
street corners peddling drugs. I noticed everything and
wrote furiously, I have my father's blood in me, I see it
now.

Ruby, my roommate, complained that I was
unsociable, she couldn't understand how I could go
without food for so long. She was loudly jealous of my

body. 'How can you be long and skinny yet have a curvy bottom?' She moaned. She was a beautiful, busty womanly woman with extra-long legs, but her life seemed to revolve around diets and binge eating. Disregarding my pleas for privacy, she spent a lot of her time trying to pair me up with various young men saying that I was wasting my beautiful body in the pursuit of academia and exasperated, I would tune her out. That night as usual, she insisted that we go down the Nag's Head for a few jars. I knew that she was on the pull since her break up, Ruby didn't hang around for long with that 'Life is short' mantra of hers. It was my main reason *not* to go out, what watch some drop dead gorgeous, leggy girl get shit faced and make out with half the guys in the pub while I stood in the corner wishing I was somewhere else?

As a South African girl in London, I hated my accent. Even though I'd lost some of it, the remnants were still there. 'Where are you from?' potential dates would ask during the ice breaking first few minutes of meeting and I would freeze, who wants to talk about South Africa in London? The politics and anecdotes about the crime, oh no not that again. Please, change the CD, turn the page, quick! I didn't want to be called a Saffa babe. All I wanted was to blend in. Be a wallflower. So, I had no agenda that night of my twenty second birthday other than a few forced drinks to please Ruby and we proceeded to the pub across the road from the college.

Rubes pulled straight away, he came at her flashing money and buying us drink after drink, all the while locking eyes with her. I had become bored of watching this sexual conquest and chose a seat in the corner instead, where I entertained myself by looking down at my beer watching the bubbles pop and subside, thinking about my new story about a wallflower turned Miss Popular. Or a country bumpkin turned porn star, wouldn't that be funny? Suddenly a smooth voice, husky from smoking, interrupted this reverie.

It was Mike. Ruby had found a guy who was wasted, and she'd urged him to chat me up as a birthday present from her. A hook up as a gift! He was handsome, I could see straight away, in a super skinny, blonde hair, grey eyes kind of way. I liked skinny guys. They reminded me of rock stars, especially if their hair flopped onto their faces. That was Mike's appeal. What an evening! We drank beer after beer, talking and laughing. He ignited something youthful and fun in the recesses of my soul. Our eyes never left each other's, the chemistry fizzed and popped, even Ruby felt like an intruder when she approached me to ask whether I wanted to go to a party or go back to the room. Without even glancing in her direction, he led me out of the pub, clutching my hand tightly. Wordlessly, we walked to my room. A cocoon made of soft cotton had enveloped us. Like the cocoons of silk worms that we kept as children, in shoe boxes with the lids pierced. They were a safe haven for budding moths. Ruby never made it back that night and we didn't morph into moths. We stayed ensconced in that cocoon for as long as our relationship lasted.

I shape shifted that night from a brooding loner into every man's sexual fantasy. Mike was, no is, a first -class lover. He was gentle and generous, patient and energetic. I am all that too, and more, I discovered. That night, I made up for years of carnal deprivation, wanting more, demanding constantly but surrendering and submitting, too. My orgasms must have rung out in the outside corridor, but I couldn't care less if the whole university heard me. I *needed* this. To me they sounded primal and debauched, my whole body seemed to release a deep- seated emotion. Was it pain? Fear? Maybe it was just a longing to be loved, I think. I couldn't put my finger on it and I didn't want to overthink it. I just wanted to be.

I am love. I am joy. I am.

That was the place that Mike had taken me. *Nirvana.*

It wasn't a hook up. It was love.

There is a hollow around his shoulder blade where I can snuggle perfectly, after. But the whole night, I could barely breathe for fear of losing the moment. As he slept I sneaked a look at him, savouring the youthful beauty of his face, the lack of care and purity that I found there. He seemed so peaceful. If only I could stop time, if only we could hold each other there forever. But time rolls on regardless and reveals ugly truths. Morning breath. Smudged make up. Cellulite. Were my boobs pert enough? My butt big enough? My tummy flat enough for him? What torture we put ourselves through for people that we love. Eventually, I shut off my mind and just enjoyed being intertwined with this beautiful man and in the morning, we woke to find that we were still wrapped around each other.

Everything had suddenly taken on a new meaning for me, even the meaningless minutiae of my morning rituals had become strangely intense and oozing with colour and magic. I washed my face, not daring to shower for fear of washing him off, and in the mirror, I noticed that my eyes were sparkling. Had they been so alive before? They looked now like they had little glints of light. My lips felt bruised and raw from the lovemaking but the colour of my mouth had changed to a deep, sensuous red.

Over scrambled eggs, avocado and coffee that I rustled up in our dormitory kitchen, I pulled out some of my work and read some of my pieces to him. This was the beta test of how connected we were and he sailed through it, listening attentively and actively. In fact, he couldn't stop praising my efforts and encouraged me to find a literary agent. He wanted me to read a story every time we met. *That* was the turning point for me. *He got me. He really got me.* Finally, I had found someone who didn't just want me in the bedroom, he actually connected with me on a visceral level. We spent days like this, I read my pieces out loud and he listened, beer and fag in hand. He even gave me feedback, maybe I could add this or consider that, was that a suitable way to represent the character? He told me that he loved me and wanted us to get our own place together, his job in retail sales paid him an average wage and he wanted to use it to pay the rent on a bedsit for us, at nineteen, he was three years younger than me but had always lived off friends and family sleeping on couches. He wanted to settle down now.

No alarm bells rang at that point, how could they? I was utterly head over heels in love.

I had just finished my teaching practice and had final exams to go in a few weeks. I wanted to get this over with before committing to Mike. In my mind, that made sense as I wanted to give my all to this wonderful man. But Mike was adamant. He would look for a place immediately, he couldn't live without me, my exams could take second place, he had to come first. He left reluctantly, before lunch. That evening when he returned, Ruby was at the door.

'She's studying for her final exam. Can you call next time?'

'Fuck off, I want to see my girlfriend.'

'Girlfriend? You only met last night! Now stop harassing her or I'll call security!'

'I want to see her now!'

I was in the library. 'Babe,' I said, 'if I don't get my qualification, I will never be able to get a teaching job and I won't be able to contribute to our place together. You have to let me study, it's only for four weeks.'

But over the next intensive weeks when the tensions rose for every student on my course, he pouted, sulked and bullied me into sleeping with him every night. We did it in my room when Ruby was out, in the park toilets when Ruby was in, anywhere. I realized, with alarm, that sex was becoming an addiction. Sometimes he would start and then withhold himself until I promised to do something like see him the next day. Sometimes he would bite me on my face so that I would have to endure the disapproving gaze of other students over the next few days. But I liked him being in control. The truth was that I was tired of being on my own. That glimpse into being lovestruck had sucked me in. I couldn't imagine a life without Mike.

Somehow, I wrote my exams and passed. I now had to apply for teaching jobs. The day after my last paper, we moved in to this tiny apartment that he had found. I couldn't see how he could have held down a job as he had been nosing around my university ever since he met me, during the day and night. Also, he had promised to pay for the place but in the end, he pleaded that he was out of funds and I stumped up the cash after taking a loan from the ever-reluctant Ruby. A month later, Zane was conceived, and I guess it's true to say that everything changed after.

Did he *want* the baby? Mike pretty much railroaded me into getting pregnant. He had repeatedly started talking about how perfect it would be to have a baby together to cement the relationship, he said. He found my birth control pills and dropped them one by one into the loo, then started rooting around for spare packs. 'Don't you want my baby inside you darlin'?' he'd ask. 'Imagine how beautiful he or she would be with the combination of you and me.' Every time I said, 'I love you,' to him, he would respond by saying, 'then why don't you want a baby with me?' or, 'Prove it.'

Once, Ruby made an impromptu visit and he lost it, demanding that she leave when she remarked that the place was a dump and that I looked haggard. That night he was resolute. 'That's it! You're getting pregnant and I'm tying you down forever! We will be bonded, and no one will be able to break us.'

Even those words seemed like music to me, everything he uttered was a kind of poetry. I didn't care if he never worked, so what if we were poor, so what if I wasn't eating much, so what if we didn't have the designer apartment that us students would fantasize about when we talked about getting our salary pay cheques? I had something much, much more precious. I had love. An intense flood of love from a beautiful man that I was sure everyone coveted. I would see girls staring at him and think, *he's all mine. He only wants me!*

He had fallen for me too. He couldn't get enough of my body, he wanted sex several times a day and night, clinging onto me, breathing me in, even crying on me saying how much he needed me. Wow! What a closeness we had. No one could penetrate that bond! We were in a trance. Everywhere we went he'd introduce me as his 'beautiful woman', he announced to the world how talented I was at writing and how proud he was of me. For the first time I felt desirable, I couldn't think or focus on anything else but him, what he ate and drank, what he was doing in the hours that I didn't see him. I *needed* him. I physically craved his presence. When he sat near me, the electricity charge in the atmosphere was so palpable that it made the hairs on my arms stand up. Eventually, everything that I had held up as important, diminished. Food, creature comforts, nice clothes, friends, even my writing, in the end. For the first month, I didn't write or look in the mirror. I would start looking when he let me.

Then, the pregnancy set in. At first, we were in glow mode, bursting with adoration and passion for each other and our child that we had made with our love. Then the discomfort started with me, morning sickness, soreness, tiredness. I felt drained all the time and soon lost the will to make love as frequently as before, much to his disgust. He'd started to mock me, asking sarcastically whether I had the proverbial 'headache', in bed. The change had not been slow, gradual or expected, it was sudden, overnight almost. Sometimes I lay there reeling from the transformation in him.

He started becoming abusive when I wouldn't give in to his sexual demands, sometimes forcing himself on me especially after a few drinks which clearly, *I* was not allowed to have anymore. He wanted it day and night like it was his hobby, whether I consented or not was irrelevant. I took it all in my stride, excusing his mood swings as jealousy as now I had something different to focus on, the baby. Perhaps after the birth, things would go back to normal. We had talked frequently about marriage before and I knew that I wanted a future with him. I lost all my close friends while he gathered more, sometimes bringing them back in the late hours to continue drinking and partying while I tried to rest. He couldn't bear academic talk and detested teacher talk. He had to give in though as we needed the money. I took a job as an English teacher at a secondary school not far away.

A few gruelling weeks in, and I arranged to meet Ruby to pay off the loan and because I had started to miss her. When she walked into Costas and saw how overwhelmed I was with stress and anxiety, she kicked off, calling him an 'insensitive bastard,' because he should be more supportive of me now that I was pregnant and working, especially in a new job. I hated it when she disrespected him, so I told him what she had said, that night.

I should have kept my mouth shut. He had been rolling a joint, the place was in a mess as usual. Dishes were stacked up in the sink awaiting my return. Druggie paraphernalia was everywhere, I had known that he was a recreational user, but I had no clue that it would get as bad as it was. Maybe he was stressed about the baby? Maybe it was over the lack of sex? There had to be a reason and it had to be my fault. As I shared Ruby's comments, there was a sudden change in him, first, I could see his facial muscles twitch. Then, he flew into a rage, lashing out so that his tin of weed emptied its contents everywhere. That was the trigger for his first ever attack on me and I shall never forget it, nobody had hit me like that before. He literally flew at me, a wild, manic streak in his eyes. Where was the kind, gentle Mike that I had fallen in love with? This devilish young boy would never have attracted my attention, ever. He kicked and hit me despite my screams, pleading with him to stop. I held out my hands to protect my face, but I need not have bothered, he went for my stomach, my head, my back and torso. Later, he said that facial bruising could trigger a police visit, if the bruising was anywhere else, no one would notice.

My love bubble had become tinged with fear.

What do you do as a professional woman when you are in the unquestionable grip of narcissistic manipulation? Of course, you blame yourself. After all, no one forced you to go with him in the first place! You chose him! I kept reminding myself of this as I tried to mark the students' books, as I tried to prepare lesson plans. It was not his fault, he was off the hook. I hadn't experienced a harrowing ordeal, no. I had mismanaged a potentially explosive situation, I should have read him better, his pent -up anxiety, the lack of sex, the constant criticism from my friends who were tuned in to only one issue: what did he do for a living? We hadn't seen any signs of him working. He had stopped going out. All he did now was play video games and smoke weed. I knew what the answer was.

I needed to give him space. Then, everything would get better.

We had the best make up sex and everything *was* better.

Weeks passed.

One day, I arrived home exhausted after a day of back to back lessons and the bubble finally burst. His eyes were glazed, and he seemed to be chewing on his lips and cheeks. When he saw me, he threw himself on me and almost ripped my cotton dress off, spreading me on the bed roughly and taking me without my consent several times until my crying stopped him. I was used to this by now, but it hurt. Then the apologies and excuses, he was stressed about finances, how could we afford a baby? He had lost his job, what were we thinking? He could hardly keep himself let alone a girlfriend and a baby. We had become weights around his skinny neck, dragging him down. Mike does not do reality. And the drugs, he needed them now that he was going through a stressful patch, they helped to get him by. If I didn't like it, maybe it was best to part company. They were here to stay. Non -negotiables, he called them.

His change of attitude was a cruel blow. Just literally a few months back it had been him who had begged me to come off the pill, pleaded even. Now, replete after several hours in bed with me, he lit a cigarette and shakily informed me that he felt that he was too young to have a baby and that I could have the child by myself or abort even though I was too far gone. He greeted my incredulity with shrugs then asked if he could borrow money to score some exciting new drug that was reputed to make me feel as if I'd been flying. Now, my pregnancy was a case of 'giving birth to that thing.' He urged me to drug with him and drink to excess.

My tears fell on deaf ears. Intermittently, I cried and plotted. That night, I showered and sat alone in the dark porch, reflecting on the last few months, the highs and lows, thinking about my options. Uncle Niall had set me up with some money in a savings account, ready for a rainy day. Well, the day had arrived. Clearly, I was about to become a single mother and there was nothing that I could do about it. I let the tears flow but underneath, a quiet resolve had set in. I was not angry with Mike, just deeply disappointed with myself that I had been taken in so easily by what seemed now like a trickster, a joker, an arsehole. Later, I learned the proper term for him: narcissistic sociopath. Ruby who had studied Psychology had pointed out the word when I'd confided in her and I'd looked it up, the words sending chills down my spine. It was Mike to a 'T'. The writer spoke about the lack of a conscience, and the person becoming increasingly antisocial, aggressive, impulsive, consistently irresponsible, showing a lack of remorse, even deceitfulness. I wanted to add sexually predatory behavior to the mix.

I cringed. *I had chosen this man.*

'*Own* your choices Carrie,' Ruby explained sighing. 'Just accept what has happened. You invited this into your life, now take responsibility.' She thrust a book into my hands, *Women who Love Too Much*. 'Read,' she instructed, 'you need to understand yourself.'

So, while lying in bed, resting in the last trimester of my pregnancy, feeling large, sore and clumsy, I read the book from cover to cover. A new consciousness had set in, the scales were starting to lift.

That week, he moved out. He waited for an excuse, any one would do as he had packed his things already, I'd noticed. The cheeky bastard! In the end he asked to borrow more money and when I refused, he said that he couldn't bear to be with a mean and miserable older woman like me, maybe he should stick to young, tight, fresh things. He shot a withering look at my baby bump, grabbed his bag and walked out. Later, I discovered that he had cleaned me out of my emergency housekeeping money that I kept in a jug in the kitchen.

I felt numb. For days after, I went about as if I was on tranquillizers. I had a new issue to beat myself over.

I had totally lost my confidence.

Where had that come from? I had never been a social butterfly, but I felt certain that I was attractive as lots of boys had asked me out and I had had a few dalliances in the past. I was intelligent as I cruised easily through school and university. My friends had liked my sense of focus and my insistence on remaining true to my identity, I was never a sheep. I knew that I could please a lover in bed as Mike had loved that side of me. So why the loss of my confidence so suddenly? I couldn't process it all. My world had become dark and lifeless. All the music seemed to have gone out with Mike. I looked around the apartment, remembering places where we had made love, things that we had done together in the different spaces. In the end, I curled up in a foetal ball on the bed and stayed there for days, taking a leave of absence from work due to my illness. My Principal called it a breakdown.

Then slowly, it lifted, thanks to my friends who had come back to me. Never compromise friendships! One by one, they rescued me and brought food, tea and baby clothes. In fact, they went the extra mile in completely redecorating and reorganizing the apartment for me. One friend even 'blessed' the place by wafting burning sage in every corner to ward off evil spirits and I knew that she meant Mike. They painted the place pale cream, bought a cot as a housewarming present and raided charity shops around for cushions, curtains, plants and a changing unit in light green. The baby would sleep in a cot in the corner, in the other corner was the white two -seater sofa and then my bed in the middle. Outside was a tiny kitchenette and bathroom, it was perfect. I would have the baby, go on maternity leave then find a childminder nearby to have the baby when I went back to work. In fact, I was so busy that I had temporary lapses when I would totally forget Mike. Then one morning there was a knock on the door.

I was in my last trimester. My breasts had become swollen and engorged, I leaked milk all the time now and hated going out. I felt self -consciously bulky and fat. Reluctantly, I opened the door a fraction to find a slim, posh, middle aged woman with her hair in a blonde bob. She introduced herself as Michael's mother, she wanted to come in for a chat.

What happened next seemed unreal, it was the stuff of nightmares, I kept thinking that it was a hoax, even at the end, after she'd left. First, I tried to cover my surprise by offering her some tea and biscuits, no she did not want that. She took everything in all right, the size of my belly, the tiny nursery set up in the corner, my hospital bag which was clearly packed and ready. I tried to lighten the mood by joking about my appearance as you do, I reminded myself of a cow, a hippo, an elephant, I was so unexpectedly large. But she refused to laugh. In the middle of my joke, she rudely interrupted, asking me whether it was her turn to speak. 'My name is Mrs West,' she said coldly, 'I'd heard that you were,' she indicated my stomach and struggled to find the words.

'Pregnant?' I tried.

'Don't get clever with me!' She had turned cold. You could have cut the atmosphere with a knife. Her eyes were razor sharp. 'Someone told me that you had trapped my son!' she spat. 'My only son! My baby! Do you know what that feels like? We had high hopes for him, his dad and I, we thought at least that he'd make something of himself, you know, be somebody one day. We are a *very* close- knit family, we do everything together. We've always supported him, his sport, his schoolwork, his aspirations.'

'Aspirations? That's just what *I* wanted for him all along!' I gushed, 'I love Mike! I'm sure it was just a misunderstanding, I'm so glad I got to meet you now! Better late than never!' I'm Carrie, I reached out my hand.

'Oh no!' she wrinkled her mouth in disgust and gave a little laugh. 'I didn't mean that I wanted him to have a future with...' she glared at me and indicated my stomach, 'you!'

'Oh, ok then! Thanks.' Tears had started to roll down my cheeks. This humiliation was uncalled for, I could see why Mike was so fucked up, why he needed the drugs. She was an iceberg! Cold, unrelenting, snobby. I wasn't with Mike anyway.

'You see, you may feel triumphant that you managed to ensnare him, but you will never get Michael. Never! As long as there's life left in my body! Michael is recovering from a terrible tragedy, it happened only a few months before you two must have met. He had a girlfriend that we all loved, what an amazing bash we threw them! But then she was an amazing girl! Platinum blonde, cornflower blue eyes...' she wasn't talking to me, she seemed to be gazing into the distance as if delivering some great monologue.

'They met at school, fell in love they did. We were all surprised by how serious and committed they both were. They wanted to do a course in hotel management together so that they could open a hotel together on the coast. Phillip and I were thrilled, we even offered to stump up some of the money and Amy's parents would help too. And boy did they do well in their studies! Put their hearts and souls into their homework they did! God they were inseparable! Studied together, went on holidays together. Amy, well, she became part of the family. Even the ring, it was Michael's idea, he saved up for it, picked it out carefully with his dad, waited to go on holiday with her to Devon, and then gave it to her just to cement the relationship you know, they were so young.'

I dared not move. I felt numb. I had wanted to ask several times why she was telling me this when in fact I was not even with Mike, but I decided to hear her out. I felt scared of her, those cold eyes, that thin, nervous, boob-less body.

'And then the party! Well, some said it was the party of the year, she looked so stunning! She could have modelled any day, those legs! She was perfect.'

I looked down at my thick, swollen ankles, I was getting tired of this, I wanted her to go. She could go, find fucking Amy and put them back together wherever he was, I didn't care anymore! We had broken up as in never to be with each other again. When she paused, I quickly got up from where I was sitting, opposite her. 'I understand, you don't like me, you want Amy for Mike! Okay, I got it now. Is that all?'

i was broken, now I Am

'Ohh you don't get to talk about Amy like that you…you immigrant!' Slap!!! She hit me so hard across the face that I reeled in shock, falling onto the side of the bed. Then, she stood over me while I cowered in genuine fear, still on the bed. She shouted, 'I can't bring her back, I can't! I want to with all my heart, but I can't! She died in that car, went out one day to get me a Mother's Day present and a stupid, stupid driver hit her full on. She died in his arms, in hospital. Can you imagine what that has done to him? To us? Can you?'

She'd backed off a bit and I took the opportunity to stand up too. 'Oh my God, I'm so sorry,' I managed, 'he didn't say anything!'

'Of course, he wouldn't say, he's in deep pain, we can't reach him. Those drugs you see him doing, they're just an expression of how bad it is for him! We're so surprised that he's not suicidal! He didn't speak to anyone at first, didn't eat or sleep…then someone told me that he was seen with this girl, we just ignored it, put it down to the shock of it all. But when we heard that you were pregnant! I mean how can you abuse him like that? Take advantage of a good, decent boy like that? A White, British boy? He had his whole life before him! Now, you've taken it away with that…thing you're carrying!'

'So, this is about race?' I had regained my confidence. I'd gone to the kitchen area to make tea, if she attacked me again, I swore I'd stab her, I had a few, sharp knives ready.

'Look,' she said with a kind of placatory smile, 'your kind and us, we're different correct? Where are you from? Africa? I thought so. I mean you're welcome to come to our country to study, we understand that. We have a lot of Africans here. But to get pregnant with my son's child? That's taking things to a whole new level. That will NEVER be my grandchild! Do you understand me?'

I had thought I would be prepared but I wasn't. She came at me, grabbing me by my long, loose hair and pushed me up against a wall. First, she slapped me hard on my face, then, unexpectedly and cruelly, she delivered a series of kicks to my stomach. I was in so much shock that I could feel no pain.

'There!' she spat proudly, as I lay on the floor in pain, 'I hope that the Almighty would step in and kill that thing inside you. And I never ever want to see you with my son again, do you understand me?' Slowly, through a haze of tears, I nodded.

i was broken, now I Am

'Fucking immigrant!' she barked before storming out.

CHAPTER 7: THE BABY

I haven't mentioned this before Mother but during my first few days in London, I cried non-stop, all in secret of course. For here, for the very first time, was the Rainbow Nation in all its glory, no one gave a flying fish what your race or culture was, the fact that you were born in another country just seemed to fuel their curiosity and interest. Here, I thought, was a truly inclusive society and I wanted to live here forever. You know in Durban, I didn't even want a boyfriend because of all the obsession with race. Imagine what his parents would ask. 'Oh, so you're Coloured or mixed race. So which parent was Black, which was White? Some boys there wouldn't even touch me because of my parentage, we were all racist there, Mother! Even Coloureds would judge you according to how light skinned you were or how dark. Of course, after the transformation, after Mandela's release, it was more fashionable to be dark. As a Black woman or person of colour, you lucked out by running away from your country Mother. You could have cashed in on all the new opportunities reserved only for Blacks.

With Whites they would go with you if they wanted to make a statement, hold a finger up to the establishment, that kind of thing. And then some would just blank you altogether, like you didn't exist. And not all Blacks would accept you, it wasn't like they had been oppressed so now they were open and tolerant overnight, ohhh no! They blamed it on latent anger about the past, tribalism, affirmative action blah blah. The simple and painful truth as you showed clearly in abandoning me, is that racism and territoriality is part of how we are hard wired, deep down its back to Darwin and sticking with our own familiar tribes. I had thought that London was the ideal role model in promoting inclusion, but Mike's mother showed me clearly that I was wrong, that behind the pretense of middle class liberalism of equal opportunities and integration, we were back to square one.

Go back to where you came from. No dogs, no Irish, no Blacks.

After she left, I felt like a sledgehammer had hit me and it wasn't just because of a dull pain in my stomach. I lay in bed tossing everything round and round in my head, like dressing a salad. I couldn't sleep. I didn't want to eat or drink anything. The phone rang repeatedly and then the battery died. Two days later, I found a patch of blood on my underwear. I remembered from my antenatal classes they called it a 'show' and said that it signalled the impending birth of the baby. In this case, I hoped desperately that the thing, as his mum had called it, had heeded her warning, the words of its paternal grandmother, and sabotaged its own life.

I was wrong again. It was my neighbour who called the ambulance and accompanied me to the hospital, carrying my hospital bag. Zane was two weeks early but emerged intact and stunningly healthy after only four hours of labour. The midwife prattled on endlessly about nothing, but I could see her look at me and then back at the baby, he was the spitting image of his dad. I had only delivered a Caucasian baby. The room resounded with her bitterness and I could picture Mike's mother's face too. Suddenly, I could hear and feel you Mother, how you must have felt to birth me, someone who was so alien to your culture, your fears about questions, whispers, funny looks. For once, I got you, Mother.

It was only the next day that I felt well enough to walk around, shower etc. and the first thing I did Mother, was something familiar to your dear heart. I checked the whereabouts of the exits of course, just in case I needed to do that runner. You want to ask me why I didn't want to walk down the street with that White baby and I will say, 'Don't be cheeky Mother, you *know* why.' Case closed. But then Fate plays its hand again. For just as I was about to edge towards the door of the ward under the guise of looking for the vending machine, in walked Mr Fucking Father of the Year, replete with a huge bouquet of white roses, a White teddy bear, (was there some symbolism in the colour I wondered cynically), and a huge card saying, 'It's a Boy!'

'Who keeps pumping you with news?' I challenged when he tried to kiss me tenderly. 'I haven't told anyone! And I never wanted *you* to know!'

'Hey, hey, hey! Of course, I keep tracks on my lovely,' he tried, pulling me gently to sit on his lap, on the bed. He'd closed the curtains around us and was piling on the charm now. 'You've given me the greatest gift of all,' he whispered, 'my own son. My first child. I've never loved you more! I've been irresponsible, I know. Karma will get me for how I've treated you, but now that my son is here, I want to turn over a brand-new leaf. I want us to be a family, my name on the birth certificate. Will you marry me baby?'

He seemed overcome when he saw the little pink bundle wrapped in a sky- blue blanket in the crib next to me. Tears flowed down his cheeks. 'I've been such a fool,' he repeated. 'Everything I've ever wanted is right here.'

My stomach had done a somersault when he'd walked in, he had had a sharp hair -cut, shaved, and put on new, smart clothes. He had doused himself in some sexy aftershave. The nurses and female patients had started drooling when he walked in. Why couldn't he have brought droopy, petrol station flowers? Why couldn't he have appeared drunk and drugged up as I'd seen him before? Clearly his mother had not seen or spoken to him, he seemed to know nothing about our little chat. He helped me gently into my nursing pyjamas, undid the top buttons, and supported the baby while he latched on to my breast, it was all so picture - perfect. 'Zane Michael West,' he said before I could interject. 'He literally is the spitting image of me babes, please let me name him.'

Memories came flooding back to the few months we had together, I knew that I still adored him...but was adoration love? If you put someone on a pedestal you haven't really connected with him, right? And that amazing book, 'Women who Love too Much' had opened my eyes now, not just about him but about me, the reason that I chose this type of man in the first place...I was looking at Mike with a whole new awareness. His mother's monologue, theatrically delivered, a constant soundtrack in my head. But I am weak, no Mother, I'm not strong. I'm such a spineless, fragmented soul really, I don't have that centre, that grounding. After all, I'm the by-product of rape, *say no more! Messed up, pathetic, always defining myself based on what other people think, always searching but never finding.*

Within a few hours, the book with all its teachings was pushed to the recesses of my mind. Mike had the script worked out…he had no money as he had given up his job to be a full- time house husband/ daddy, could he come live with me and the baby? He had realized the moment he had walked out that he truly loved me, he had just not been ready for responsibilities at the time, but since then he had grown up. With my support, he could be the best father! The sex was amazing, was *that* not enough for us to try again? Didn't I want a father for Zane? A biological father not someone else raising his child just like the rest of London? Blah, blah blah, he went on and on.

The prospect of my working and earning well as a teacher energized him too, wouldn't a stay at home dad be preferable to a stranger looking after our love child? We had a family hug with the baby in the middle, and a few hours later, I left the hospital with Mike carrying the baby in a car seat that my friend had bought. Of course, he did not own a car, we had to flag down a cab, but hey we were in a love bubble, we didn't care! Take two I can hear you comment drily Mother, miming a clipboard on a film set.

Again, the first few days were special.

We had the glow back. He was every bit the man that I had fallen in love with. He cooked healthy meals and served up huge portions so that I could get my strength back. He cleaned, making the apartment spotless, took care of the baby like he'd read every manual on how to be the perfect parent, and seemed to have cleaned up his act. We didn't mention drugs or alcohol and it seemed that the past was well behind us.

Mike was a proud father, he took Zane to see his family while I stayed at home on the pretext of having time to myself. Apparently, they were thrilled to bits to see that Zane looked just like their son, he came back with bags bulging with presents for the baby.

Then one day, he took me to see his grandmother who lived out in Essex. When the door first opened, she looked startled to see me, then she noticed that I was with Mike and she quickly recovered. But, even inside, she kept shooting Mike a 'why didn't you tell us that she was Black /Mixed race' looks. Remarks about my so called gorgeous dark hair and skin followed and questions about what I liked to eat, was it difficult to get my type of food in London, how did I manage with the cold weather? Was I not used to the subtropical conditions back in Africa? I bit back the urge to retort that I was not a hothouse flower in Kew Gardens. I had not stepped out of a film set of 'Roots.' Indignantly, I reminded her that I had lived in London for almost eight years. I realized that sometimes it's *people* who don't allow you to forget, who stop you from integrating. It's convenient for them to keep you at arm's length, forcing you to do constant comparing and contrasting, the merits of London vs Your Country. Yet when she saw the baby, she didn't hide her relief that he looked White. I let all this wash over me, merely smiling and gritting my teeth while she fussed over Zane. It was important to me that our son had an identity, a proper family unlike me.

I couldn't remember much about the episode with Mike's mother. Sometimes, while in the glow, I wondered whether it really happened, was it a figment of my imagination? A sign that my tendency to overthink and over analyze was sending me over the edge, making me mentally ill. I vowed to get myself checked out when I felt better and then I let it all wash over me like a tidal wave, whoosh! It never occurred to me that I was in denial.

Shame on Mike, what a piece of work! He never fought for me! Each Sunday his parents would invite him and the baby for a roast dinner, he insisted that it was good for me to have 'alone time,' to do whatever I liked, like see friends or go shopping. When I'd feebly suggest that we all go out together somewhere, he'd say that he had family obligations, they had a routine of having the family over every Sunday. He never explained why *I* was not invited and he never ever disrespected his parents by questioning their judgement. Like a sheep, I went along with it all but unsurprisingly, I came home one day, and he was gone, the honeymoon lasting six months this time. The telly was gone and so was my posh camera that I'd saved up for, my stereo and weirdly, Zane's pushchair. The biggest sadness was seeing Zane alone, lying on the floor in a shitty diaper that had become stuck to his bottom it had been on for so long. The place reeked of excrement and sadness. Mike had abandoned us again. This time I had his number and I messaged him with 'Where the fuck *are* you, you dog? Where's my stuff?'

No reply.

A few days later I got this, 'Please understand, I needed the money, I will pay it back. You know I'm not right in the head, sorry baby!'

In our local Cash Converters one day I found some of the missing items and had to pay to get everything back. I had not been angry really. Just very bitter at being used yet again.

i was broken, now I Am

CHAPTER 8: ROSEMARY

At work, they changed my timetable. I had had a
lesson observation by Rosemary, my head of
department and her verdict was that I was a crap
teacher. In fact, I was so bad that she had to rescue all
the good students, the ones with potential. It was
immoral for them to be exposed to a creature like me,
no way. They would be taken away and fed a diet of
well, Rosemary. She would have to teach them, adding
to her list of tasks in the school, this made her furious.
I've never seen Rosemary smile. At most, she moves
her face into a grimace, but she ends up looking like a
hamster with food in its cheeks, her eyes never light up,

they look as lifeless as the eyes of dead fish. So, she had moved things around and assigned all the low ability kids to work with me, they were not going anywhere anyway so why not have the worst teacher to teach them?

Rosemary was at a conference for 'very important people', on the day that the Principal hired me. If she had been part of the selection committee, she would never have touched me with a bargepole. She was only introduced to me five days later, when she returned and quickly, I realized that my new team leader frowned upon anyone departing from the 'Rosemary model' of teaching. Maybe, by hiring me, the Principal inadvertently threw me under the bus and set me up to fail. He must have known that I was a creative, headstrong, intelligent young woman, and not the lap dog type that Rosemary wanted in her team. Unquestionable loyalty to her, was what kept you sane, at the school. She detested me, so my time there can be described as a series of obstacles that I had to constantly navigate around.

The first, was that they had assigned me a dark and depressing classroom, at the back of the dinner hall whereas all the other English teachers had rooms on the top floor overlooking lush, green fields. But I didn't complain. I was pregnant when I started there, and my clothes tended to be appropriately loose and mumsy.

One day, I was arranging books on a large, low bookcase that the Principal had gifted me from his office, he was redesigning his space and wanted to throw it out. Suddenly I spun around to see a scrawny woman with a stricken expression and a pronounced tic on one cheek, her purple hair was so short that it looked like it had been painted onto her skull, the curl in front looking totally incompatible with the rest of her. Her long, flowing dress and haughty expression completed the look that shouted, 'Person on the edge of a nervous breakdown!' Once she had looked me over she looked around disappointedly.

I had come in on the weekend to spice up the room. I needed the space to look appealing to the kids, we already had the smells of fat and cheap meat from the dinner hall to contend with and the dark atmosphere did not lend itself to the niceties of plants and bowls of goldfish. So, having denied my kids this, I set about painting the room in a soft peach. I put up colourful posters of new and old theatre productions in London's West End. One wall was prepped and ready to mount the students' work and the new bookcase was full of discarded books that the librarian had binned, coupled with a terracotta rug from a charity shop and an armchair nicked from the staffroom, it made a cozy reading corner. She looked confused as she potted around checking it out until I explained that I had done this, for the students.

Compliments are not part of Rosemary's toolkit. And I knew what went through her mind when she shot that look at me. Troublemaker. She doesn't just accept things the way they are, she creates change, ripples. Rosemary sat me down trying to smile but grimacing instead. After the introductions, she explained that, as she was so very important, she had many courses and conferences to attend. As the newbie, it was my responsibility to stand in for her every time she was away, it would be good for me as well, to have a chance at teaching the top students in the school which obviously she had as she was the head of department. She expected me to attend a weekly English team meeting and to be ready for the constant program of lesson observations that she would do in my class, they were part of my professional review. As she floated out, she reminded me that where teachers were found to be suboptimal, they were customarily sacked.

i was broken, now I Am

When I returned from maternity leave, fresh and desperate for solace, succor and stimulation, Rosemary seemed hell bent on securing my disintegration. This time, I was so exhausted from the trials of being a single parent that I couldn't take her viciousness any longer. I felt like I'd started out juggling several balls in the air but that they'd all fallen and smashed. I've read somewhere that it's a great advantage to start from a position of being shattered, then you can collect the broken pieces and build. And one day, at the peak of your achievement, you can reflect on how far you came.

Really? Really? This was not the case for me. I had become so crushed by Rosemary's constant belittling of me, by the indifference and lack of support in the English department, that I started to believe that the fault was in me. The fault *was* me. Rosemary had won. The vestiges of functionality that I had been clinging onto started to slip away and I started to question everything, even the point of my existence.

When we hear of seemingly ordinary people doing outrageous things like picking up a machine gun and obliterating a class or a school full of kids, we cluck with concern or dismay saying that these extreme actions are not acceptable in modern society. And we are right, they are not. It's the same when we hear about fifty -year old virgins or people who refuse to leave their homes or others who cut themselves or even take their own lives. There is a collective sense of sadness here, maybe, just maybe these people have been failed in some way. What we don't embrace is the possibility that as a society, we are responsible for each other, that we are indeed one big global village and if we focused more on the core values of say community, love, acceptance and respect maybe we could give our people something to live for. Liberals have truly messed up the planet. Everything is about lip service. Nothing is heartfelt. In our English department office, a large poster above the coffee station says:

Feeling Suicidal? No need. Feeling depressed? Don't worry. We are here to support you. Call this number and speak to an advisor for free. Lines are open 24/7

And it is here in this very same office where I experienced the most compelling example of exclusion. I'd walk in to make a coffee and suddenly, the knot of people speaking in low voices would disband and look around at me, suddenly everyone would stop talking. If someone forgot the drill and continued, someone else would whisper 'Shush' or, more unambiguously, 'She's here.' Then everyone would do the fake smiles and shuffle about on the pretext of doing something. How can I not feel excluded when this is the context that I work in? And its invariably, Rosemary who is at the centre of the group.

'My daughter has straight, red hair. It's gorgeous and glossy, lucky girl. It hangs down her back, swishing as she moves.'

I love my afro.

'Your hair is so frizzy; do you ever iron it with straighteners?'

'I don't want to damage my hair with heat. I love my afro, it expresses my identity.'

'Oh, just trying to help you look smart. That's all.'

'We're going out for a drink as a team. We know that you can't come as you're a single parent. It's okay'

'Must be so hard.'

Being Black, a single mum and a crap teacher that no one likes.

I keep reframing these situations trying to see them in a new, positive ways. These people suffer from collective xenophobia. They haven't been exposed to people of different cultures, they don't know, it's not their fault. They're ultra-provincial. They haven't travelled, some don't even have passports, I can't expect them to have tolerance or respect because they haven't been anywhere, they've done nothing but work within the narrow confines of the English office in this school where the endless demands on teachers suck out your soul. They can't be expected to demonstrate humanitarian values, they deal with aggression day by day. These things get into your psyche, morph you somehow, you lose perspective, it's understandable. Work is a microcosm especially when it is mentally and physically draining. You give and give and then are expected to give even more of yourself. And when you are not living purposefully, you lose your sense of humanity.

But the truth is that there's no excuse for bullying and excluding others. We all have a right to be on this planet. Even if there were ideological differences between us, professional etiquette dictates that we demonstrate tolerance, respect and empathy towards others. Ganging up on individuals, singling them out, dropping your voice when someone enters the room is bullying. Workplace bullying is rife amongst teachers, ironically, we're supposed to be champions of tolerance, guardians of democracy. Well that's what we preach to kids anyway. In reality, teachers take the moral high ground but they're the ones who need to interrogate their own motives, search their own hearts. Many are bitter, vacuous hypocrites, never practicing what they preach.

The job was becoming joyless and unbearable. And it wasn't the students. It went back to the myth of multiculturalism, teachers were not trained or aware or awake enough to embrace diversity in its real sense. White, straight, non-religious was good, anything that deviated from this was bad.

Over the months, I could feel my grip on things slipping. I didn't have that work life balance, that ratio went out the window a long time ago. In a desperate bid to please, I gave too much of myself away. I ran clubs after school every day: Homework Club, Reading Club, Debating Club, Film Appreciation Club. One afternoon a week, we held our team meeting. Each day I'd finish later than others and head straight to the child minders to pick up Zane, then we'd come home and plonk in front of the telly. Except that I didn't factor in how much I'd miss Mike. At first, a glass of wine or two took the edges of the day away. Naughty kids that bad mouthed me to my face faded into nothingness, the growing pile of books to be marked became invisible, my anxiety about being a single mum dissipating. Rosemary's tic distorted face and floaty dresses dissolved into nothingness. Then it became a bottle a night and slowly it grew into two. Why do bottles of wine finish so damn quickly? Evenings became blurry and mornings slurry, I started taking time off just to get through my hangovers. And the baby? Well, I was never a great cook anyway, a sandwich and salad were my type of dinner, okay not the salad, maybe just some toast on some days with peanut butter slapped on. When Zane got to be weaned off his bottles of milk, he liked what I gave him: biscuits, bread, crisps. Sometimes if he was extra good chicken nuggets and fizzy drinks which is what he really liked. Anything quick. I never went the extra mile with cooking complicated food, it just wasn't my thing. We were both fine I kept telling myself, sure I was battered and bruised inside but who was to know?

When they called me in for a formal meeting to discuss my 'performance' I knew that my days were numbered. I muttered positive responses to their probing questions about my life and promised that things would be better. I had to commit to a few goals:

1. The students' work would be marked (Work?
    Most of the time we were embroiled in
    constant arguments about the seating plan, '*I'm
    not sitting next to that waste of space!*' After that it
    was a case of pleading with them to take out
    their books and pens, '*What books? We lost them,
    and our parents don't buy us pens!*' so they didn't
    produce much.)

2. Homework would be set (what was the point,
they didn't do it?)

3. Detentions would be given more regularly to
enforce the Behaviour Policy. (Have you tried detaining
aggressive and low ability kids? I don't *want* to see them
after a full work day thank you very much!) Basically,
the Behaviour policy meant that senior managers of the
school who were paid a small fortune, did not have to
deal with unruly students. Often, they walked by with
their noses in the air, pretending not to notice, after
blatantly seeing the class teacher in an altercation with
an aggressive student. No, 'very important people'
didn't sully their hands dealing with behaviour! That
was the job of the class teacher. Bottom feeders like

me. We all felt alone but the system rendered you voiceless. If you asked for support, you were weak. Substandard. I constantly felt like I'd been conned into believing that teaching was a respectable and worthwhile profession, an altruistic, humanitarian one even. All that crap about helping others achieve their hopes and dreams. Well, the job was certainly crushing me. And with Rosemary's beady eyes on me, it was a wonder that I kept it together.

I felt so low that I focused on Rosemary's tics for the entire meeting, I could barely meet the Principal's eyes, I liked him. Of course, Rosemary said that she was committed to supporting me on my journey towards being a good teacher. As part of that commitment, she would drop in to monitor my lessons even more frequently and even check my lesson planning to give me so called constructive feedback. This was the same team leader who had whisked away all the easiest groups from the rest of the team, leaving us struggling with violent bullies, stoners, slags in mini - skirts and thugs carrying knives in their socks. She kept reminding us in meetings that the school 'was on the up.' I wanted to check her definitions, I was certain that the Oxford English Dictionary did not class 'up' as a war zone!

i was broken, now I Am

The rest of the team in the English department had navigated their way through the difficult weeks by adopting various strategies. There was Nick, a young, newly married teacher who sat at his desk texting on his phone the whole day, he gave the kids simple worksheets to finish in every lesson and ignored poor behaviour. But he was a loyal Rosemary supporter, so he escaped scrutiny.

There was a large lady Sandy, who munched her way through lessons and tried to steer the kids into talking and writing about food. Funny how I detested her at first but later, we bonded over a box of custard cream doughnuts and a bottle of Sangria. She only came alive at the mention of food so when I started my salad diet, I became boring to her. She too escaped Rosemary's wrath as she was the department's daily snack provider, supplying the team with a never-ending hoard of budget biscuits and cookies.

Then, there was a greying, shabby, older man who was close to retirement, so the school was powerless to discipline him. He'd shuffle in wearing the same smelly suit every day, stinking of weed, he kept his head down always but was a cool teacher with his 'anarchy rules' approach. Students threw things at each other in his class and other staff were constantly called to sort out fights, yet he insisted that 'structured chaos' was the best educational environment. I think he fancied me a little. Every time I saw him, he called me in to compliment me on my perfect derriere and invite me around to his place to get stoned. Rosemary didn't dare to boss him around as he had age, experience and an irreverent attitude on his side.

There were other teachers in the department, nondescript busybodies who crept around in silence, cowering when they saw senior management, too scared to laugh, chat or fart. I called them the joyless society. I wanted to put their cheerless faces on giant billboards with the words, 'What to become a teacher? This is what we look like.'

So, we had all these different people in the department, each bringing different skills, experiences, and incompetence's to the table, yet it was only *me* that would be monitored. Ohkay! I got the message, loud and clear. Suck up to Frau Rosemary or be damned! Unsurprisingly, no one backed me up at any stage during her obvious mistreatment of me, instead, everyone kept their heads down at team meetings, she had successfully whipped them into submission. No one was interested in sticking their head above the parapet. Not for me.

The next few months went quickly, term times melting into long stretches of holiday. I stayed home, rested and saved money eating the basics: jacket potatoes and butter, toast, chips. I worked on lesson plans too. I had to. As the sole breadwinner, I knew that I could not afford to mess things up. *I'm not stupid Mother! I can jump through hoops!*

I became the model teacher. I arrived early at school and left late, I put myself on every training course out there, paying my own way of course, I was too unimportant to be selected for free training! As a result, I learned how to create lessons that would reach these disengaged students, I learned what secured an 'outstanding' grading during government inspections. Soon the students were eating out of my hands and, when inspectors descended on the school, I got my 'outstanding' grade as the students were being exemplary just for me. My Principal was in awe, he gave me consistently glowing reports and soon I was off the radar. But he had conveniently bypassed Rosemary and she had her heckles u

CHAPTER 9: THE CHILDMINDER

Zane had turned three and the lone cake on the kitchen table surrounded by clown cups of cola looked uneventful and lame. Well, my first cup was full of chardonnay. Next, I had a mojito. He didn't want a lot of cake and pushed me away when I tried to kiss him, so it wasn't such a great party. I couldn't concentrate in any case, because inside, I was seething! Who the fuck gave childminders the right to judge us single parents? I had found this woman through word of mouth and would never have chosen her, but I was desperate, my old childminder was emigrating to Australia to live with her daughter.

If Zane was sad about saying goodbye, he did not show it, in fact he was expressionless a lot and there was nothing I could do to liven him up. Maybe I should have had him tested to see if he had Special Educational Needs. At the back of my head was a voice that screamed, '*It is I who has special needs…I have a need and it's special. I need to see my mother! I can't mother if I haven't been mothered.*'

Well the new childminder, Miss Know it All Psychology Expert said that she was concerned. At three years and a few months, Zane was 'listless' and 'woeful.' Woeful indeed. So, I looked it up just to be sure of what she was accusing me of.

Woeful is an adjective meaning gloomy, downcast, grief stricken.

So, if he was born with turned down eyes, if he had that kind of face anyway, how was it my fault? I knew that she was blaming me, I could see the way in which she looked at me when I lit up a ciggie around Zane, I am an adult, I will smoke whenever and wherever I want! She kept asking questions and narrowing her eyes when she looked at me, taking in everything about me.

When did he eat last?

What sort of meals did I cook?

When did I take him to the GP for a check last?

How much exercise did he get?

Did he have access to his father and wider family?

They were all valid questions. Maybe if his mother had not been abandoned at birth by a cold and careless person, aka you Mother, and given to people who were totally unsuitable, aka my adoptive, alcoholic parents, hold up hold up, let's not forget, maybe if my father, a wealthy married man, had not raped his servant's daughter and made her pregnant, then Zane would have had a different future, maybe if I had been loved and nurtured and properly cared for then things would be better for all involved. Maybe if there's a big, bold sign on the foreheads of narcissists saying, 'Stay Away All Decent Potential Partners, this Person is Not a Good Option,' then Zane would be an upbeat, energetic, happy go lucky little sod. Not someone who looked like he was at a funeral twenty- four seven.

I do *not* accept her judgements of me. She is young and highly trained she tells me. Is this why she is charging almost double what the old childminder charged? How do you think I feel when I visit her house to drop and collect him? Her plasma TV is so big that it covers one whole wall. She's had her floors laminated and is always shopping when she is free, she shows me her new clothes and shoes, 'Handbags are my thing!' she says breezily, 'I like to have a matching one for every outfit. And I don't do fakes! It's strictly designer for me!'

Well, *bills* are my thing! Okay, so I was funding her flash lifestyle and she still had the cheek to make nasty remarks about my ability to parent! Charming!

'Social Services take a dim view of neglect,' she said one day, 'not that I'm talking about you.'

Really?

Her smile did not reach her eyes. I grabbed my child and left hastily, I had decided not to linger around her too much during the drop off and collecting process, she was trouble. The other niggling problem was that she kept looking hard at me as if she was trying to penetrate me through my skin. Her eyes skimmed over my body and face and I would squirm uncomfortably. This happened mainly when her husband was out.

'You've got a gorgeous colour,' she said one day when, in the heat of the British summer I appeared wearing a fitted camel coloured skirt and matching silk blouse and stilettos. I had smartened up my act for work. I could see the Principal warming to me each time I tried, I needed an ally.

'I wouldn't mind having an arse like that! You slay in that skirt!'

'I'm African,' I said smiling, 'it's in my genes.'

'Lucky you, lucky Zane,' she said. 'I'm just plain old White English.'

Oh, so it was Compliment Day. I had smartened up Zane too, something in her expression had been unnerving me so I had taken him shopping. He was kitted out in a white T shirt, blue shorts, blue sandals and a denim jacket which he shrugged off. I even included in his bag a sun hat, sun cream and a beaker of water. *I'm covered bitch.* Gone are the days when I dropped him off in his pyjamas or clothes that he had been wearing for a few days. I even invested in a new changing bag for Zane, but he refused to be fully toilet trained so we still used diapers. But hey that's my fault again. *Right.*

Something had come over her, she looked fragile like she'd been crying. I was a bit early, so I listened to her at the door for a few minutes. She suggested that we went out for a drink sometime.

'Maybe we can help each other,' she said smiling weakly, 'You help me, I help you. After all, what are friends for?'

Excuse me? Friends? Suddenly I was off the radar as far as Social Services were concerned, and my child would now not be taken from me because she wanted to be friends. I could not afford to piss this woman off.

'Help each other? How?' I asked trembling slightly, not wanting to think about what was in store for me.

'Well, let's go out and talk,' she said a bit too playfully, all that early sadness gone. Let me know when you are free, we can get someone to babysit.'

'Okay, I will, have to run now,' I muttered and blew Zane a kiss instead of planting my lipsticked mouth on his little face as I didn't want to ruin my make- up.

Then as I turned to leave, a strange thing happened. 'Damn', she exclaimed and slapped me hard on my behind. I turned to look at her wondering what that was all about, she was leaning against the front door smiling cheekily, even flirtatiously at me, I couldn't bear it. As I walked, I could still feel her hands on me through my linen skirt.

CHAPTER 10: THE DETECTIVE

I've got news for you, Mother. I'm saving to pay
for a private detective, I found one whose fees did not
require me to take out a bank loan. But still, I need to
save. I've even cut down on ciggies and booze because
this investment is so worth it. You see, I am hellbent
on finding you Mother and I've been told that you are
here, in London somewhere. The feeling of being in
the same city as you, excites me so much that I tingle
just thinking about it. I roll over the image of us
meeting for the first time, in my mind. This picture is
my constant companion: in slow motion, we would
run towards each other and clasp each other in a never-

ending hug, the soundtrack for this is something dramatic like Pavarotti's 'Nessun Dorma'. Sometimes, I would tune out of everything and just think about this, mentally adjusting this image until it felt like I was rolling it around on my tongue, prodding it and tasting it with the tip. It was delicious. Better than any food. I know that you regret giving me up, I mean any mother would, right? I could never give up Zane no matter what the scenario was. I dare not entertain the idea that you are not here any longer, that you have left these shores. I need to find you, I'm not living in limbo like this, it's the ultimate cruelty. And no, I'm not throwing my name away by going on Jeremy Kyle, pleading for help in finding you. I can just imagine that lie detector test. Knowing me, I'd probably fail it even though I've done nothing wrong! The kids at school would have a field day, 'Miss, you don't have a mother! Dustbin baby! Your daddy raped your mum. You were never wanted!' And then it would be all over social media. No! Not going to happen. I'm not giving Rosemary the satisfaction.

The detective has told me that I would need photos of you, possible addresses even of friends and relatives (*why would I need him if I already had this?*) and an entry date into the UK. But how was I to find this? It's been years since you left me, twenty-six years ago to be exact. I am the Coloured child that you rejected mother! Apart from snippets of information from Uncle Niall about an entry date, there isn't much information on you. I do have your name, it's a Zulu name: Sibongile. I looked it up, it means, 'We are grateful.' *You* might be grateful, I've nothing to be grateful for. Caramel, you gave me a throwaway name and escaped.

So, you were/are a Zulu, a member of the largest native tribe in South Africa. Why didn't you give *me* a special Zulu name? I would have loved to be part of something. As a child growing up in Durban, I loved to watch the Zulu dance shows, the gumboot dance was my best, all that frenetic energy and muscly men wearing skins of animals. Again, disappointment and emptiness fill me up and I feel lost. Alcohol helps, but suddenly half way through swigging a bottle of whiskey, I bring up images of Joe and Mary, sitting in the living room playing Bingo and gradually working their way through bottle after bottle of drink until they would pass out, comatose. In the morning, the stench of their breath as I picked them up from the floor or sofa and dragged them into their beds, often they were urine soaked and smeared with vomit. Oh yes, they saw me coming. I became the official carer at the age of six or seven. Where was uncle? Cavorting with whores he was, I was not so naïve that I couldn't pick up what was going on in that little granny flat of his at the back of our house. He too, would end up drunk and naked and there would always be a Black woman by his side, naked or partially clothed. He would try any excuse when I visited and asked uncomfortable questions. She was a cleaner, oh no wait, she was selling something, (yes, her bits), a friend (excuse me old White men did not have young Black girls as friends in racist South Africa.)

I often wondered hopefully, as I loved uncle and wanted the best possible explanation for the scenes that I had often witnessed in his house, whether he had fallen in love with someone decent and she had broken his heart. After this, it seemed plausible that he would seek comfort in the arms of whores. But no, this was not the case or, so Mary told me. He was just not the relationship type. Just seemed to love the drink and a taste of whores. *In fact, that was how he had met you Mother, is that not true? He had been seeing a lady friend of yours and she had mentioned your delicate situation. He wanted to keep his lady happy, so he had pulled out all the stops to help you. Which involved allowing you to leave the country and abandon me. Thanks uncle. Nice one. Were you a whore too Mother? You can*

i was broken, now I Am

tell me, I'd still love you. They're called sex workers now Mother, in some countries, they pay taxes too. A job is a job.

I end this reverie by putting down the bottle and sinking into bed. It's ugly when you do it in your bedroom, seeing the empty bottle on the side in the morning, the place starting to stink already, me wanting to heave but still trying to avoid it going on the duvet. I had a bucket in the corner instead, but sometimes I never made that. Rosemary said that drinking alcohol to excess was a kind of self- harm. A type of self-flagellation she said, in her posh voice with her big, impressive words.

What does she know, is she a by-product of rape? Is she a single parent? Has she been adopted? No? Thought so. Interfering so and so. I bet she hit the bottle every now and again, how would she be so authoritative on the subject otherwise? She wasn't perfect, I could tell. No balanced, mindful person has nervous tics like hers. Some days, I didn't know where to look.

Sad. My ugly, sad life. A neglectful mother to my little boy, maybe the dead child chose well not to want to grow in my womb. I feel tired constantly. It's a deep exhaustion that I have felt all my life. Depression leaves you depleted.

i was broken, now I Am

CHAPTER 11: THE SOCIAL WORKER

There's a plus size woman in my kitchen. She's sitting at the little table that I now regret placing in the centre, every time I go to the fridge or the cooker, she can see what I'm doing, and I know she's looking. Every now and then she makes notes in her little book and closes it strategically when I approach. Trembling, I cut open a bag of oven chips, remove a frozen clump and drop them into the oven tray. Next, I open a tin of spaghetti hoops and place the contents in a saucepan on the cooker.

'Your dinner?' she smiles disarmingly but I can sense the toxic nature of her, I know her agenda.

'No, I eat at school. In the canteen. I'm a teacher. English. There was a nice lasagna today,' I smile. *I'm a decent mother now get out of my house!*

' That was lunch, what about tonight?' she asks still smiling but I can see it's getting stiffer now. She's a large lady, the chrome chair under her seems to be buckling under her.

'Just toast will do,' I say back. 'And a bottle of whatever's going'.

'A bottle?' Her eyes narrow.

'Of water! Love water, don't you?' Obviously not.

She's a social worker, come to assess my suitability to be Zane's mother. I want her out of here, what does she know about me? Who's monitoring *her?* There should be a rule, if you're an exemplary parent as judged by an independent panel then and only then should you have the right to pass judgement on others. My life has been all about struggle, let downs, put downs, deception, rejection. So how am I supposed to bounce back after all that? If I knew I wouldn't be doing my job, I'd put it in a bottle or a book and milk it. Half the world is messed up, no one's perfect, not

even her Miss Uppity Social Worker come to pass
judgement on me. She wants to see Zane.

'He's asleep,' I say.

'Oh. It's six p.m.'

Thanks, I can tell the time.

More notes. Is that a crime now? That he's sleeping?
I didn't get him addicted to Calpol, he just likes it. He'd
drink the whole bottle if he could!

She starts the interrogation. What is this, twenty
questions? No, more like fifty. She searches my face
trying to read something but I'm inscrutable. Half way
through I get up and put the laundry on, I could see
from the corner of my eye that the wash basket was
overflowing. I tidy up pretending that this is what I do
every day. As if. She wants to check the fridge, open
cupboards, see Zane's room. Well, she can do whatever
she wants, there's nothing amiss, the landlord has gifted
us with good décor here, his room is white, his cot bed
pine wood, his toys are stacked in the corner, his
unread books sit neatly on a shelf, what more is there?
No! There're no knives lying around, I'm not *that*
stupid! So, if you want to take my son, you better have
some hard evidence.

She goes at last and I pour myself the biggest wine ever. Imagine if she comes back on the pretext of having left something behind! I'd have to open the door drunk.

I'm waiting for that report. Trust me, I'll challenge every damn point in it.

At work, Rosemary is in a bad mood. Some VIP visitors had come to the school and the Principal brought them straight to my room. I'd worn a sharp, charcoal pencil skirt and killer heels with a silk shirt in letterbox red, he'd been full of compliments, telling me that I was the best dressed teacher of all the staff. I wished he didn't keep staring like that. Especially not in front of visitors. They'd loved my room straight away saying that it was the ideal space to learn English. My students are low ability. Everyone expects them to be hanging from the ceiling or climbing up the walls. Instead, my students were doing different activities that day. Some were acting out scenes from 'Romeo and Juliet.' Others were on the bean bags in the reading corner engrossed in books. Two were preparing a display on their favourite quotes from the text. I was sitting next to a student talking through my feedback on an assignment.

'What a wonderful, constructive atmosphere!' someone remarked.

'Makes me want to be a kid again.'

'And Miss here decorated this room all by herself! She's such a credit to us. Runs the Debating Club, the Homework Club, and many more don't you Miss.'

'Oh, I loved debating at school. This is just wonderful. So different from the rather dry lessons that we watched upstairs.'

'I wish I had a teacher like this, when I was at school!'

Applause please. I was pumped!

My credibility with the Principal is growing by the day. He must have cautioned Rottweiler Rosemary and asked her to leave me alone, I was safe! She seems more standoffish around me which gives me breathing space. Anyway, I don't care what Miss Misery-guts thinks anymore! I have something else to think about.

My childminder.

Keep your friends close but keep your enemies closer. I can't allow her to take my son from me.

CHAPTER 12: THE CLUB

I couldn't help jigging to the rousing techno beat of the house music. It was a Saturday night and Pam, my childminder and I, were out 'on the town.' We had ended up in some nightclub and were trying to talk over the loud music, ciggies in one hand, double vodkas and mixers in the other. She looked amazing, sexy even, I was ashamed to admit. Her leather dress sculpted her slim body, her legs were in fishnets. I on the other hand had opted for hot pants in dark red satin, this and a fitted silver, lycra, cropped top. I had

long stiletto boots and had left my hair loose so that it
hung like a halo around my head. My hair does not
hang straight down, it's more like a wormy ball around
my head but I like being different and, my afro gets me
compliments. We were both covered in make-up and,
since we had been drinking since the afternoon, (pre-
clubbing nerves), were feeling merry. We gyrated to the
music blaring out and tried to focus in the colourful,
flashing light. Young men openly stared at us and some
approached us asking for a dance. To my irritation,
Pam chased them off like a matriarch attacking
predatory animals that were circling around her young.
Some were so hot that I had started salivating. A lean,
beautiful Black guy kept giving me the eye.

   'Whooaaaaa', I said, 'he's smoking hot!!! I want
him! It's been a while since, you know.'

   'Well you don't need to do it with that car crash!'
she yelled over the music. 'Just stick with me.' More
gyrating. She knocked her buttocks against mine, then
her tits bumped into mine. 'Don't you love the bump
dance?' she shouted smiling, her teeth looking strange
in the purple fluorescent lights, it was like dancing with
someone from a horror movie.

'Hmmm,' I said, tired and a bit pissed, 'Can we sit down for a bit? Talk, like you wanted?'

First, she had to get a round of drinks in and while her back was turned, I pretended to walk towards the toilet, brushing past Mr Handsome on the way. Quickly, we swopped phone numbers and then I casually sat down, my phone hidden in my handbag again.

When she returned with two lagers, we staggered towards a round table with four seats. A young man sat on one seat with a teenage girl on his lap, her arms were around his neck. They were in the middle of a wet snog, their lips never leaving each -other's. For a moment, we watched mesmerised and a little jealous, while his hands fumbled under her skirt and she rolled her eyes moaning with pleasure.

'Get a room,' Pam muttered and pulled me to sit down as we occupied the remaining seats on the opposite end.

'Well?' I asked, 'what's up?' I was really drunk by now and intermittently, the room had started to spin around me, I was so grateful for the seat. In the back of my mind was the image of my bed, Zane, the babysitter that I still needed to pay.

i was broken, now I Am

'It's a bit embarrassing for me to say this. So, I'll just come out with it. It's you, you are just so, so beautiful!' she blurted out suddenly, 'I can't get over your body, you're so…curvy,' she gushed staring hard at me now, 'I like your skin colour, your arse, everything. You're so hot I can't focus on anything. I want you. I've wanted you for a while now.'

I was hammered but I knew when someone was hitting on me.

'You have your hubby,' I said leaning back to get the full support of the backrest. It was always the married ones!

'Him?' she sneered, 'Oh! fuck him! Fat twat! I'm going to ask him for a divorce. He just doesn't do it for me no more. Farting and burping, who wants that in bed? That marriage died a sorry death a while ago now. I want something different to that.' White teeth smiled at me, grey eyes bore into me as if looking for a spark.

No, no, no, no, no! I wanted to tell her something badly.

'But you…' she moved closer to me. Desperate to articulate the words, I turned to watch the couple again, the girl had undone his flies and was giving him a hand -job inside his trousers, I couldn't hear anything over the noise, but I could see the rhythmic pumping of her hands and the sweat on his brow. I wondered how long it would be until he came, I wanted to stay to watch his cum face, I was owed that as a front row spectator. He was blonde, slim and hot, my type. She was skinny and very young. Still, he was lost in the moment and their heavy petting had aroused me. Now, Pam put her arms around me and redirected my attention by cupping my face in her hands.

'Can I be honest?' she confessed.

I knew what was coming. She'd been honest enough already. The truth was that no matter what, I couldn't go with her. She'd stabbed me in the back over that fiasco with the social worker. I never got the report, when I contacted her, she said that the case was closed. I'd never forgive Pam.

Fuck.

'I think I love you,' she said softly. 'I fancy you. I want you, want to turn for you, have wanted it for a while now.' And then she kissed me. Her lips were unexpectedly soft and yielding, I tried to submit, looking for something substantial to tug onto but it wasn't to be, and I didn't feel good. She tried to poke her tongue in and out of mine, but I couldn't move my tongue to reciprocate.

'Stop!' I said. 'I need to be sick!' We looked around wildly as if a sick bucket would magically appear out of nowhere. The guy must have cum by now as they were less frenzied. Fuck! I'd missed it! I noticed that they'd rearranged themselves and that she was sitting next to him now, both clutched drinks and stared in some amusement at us. There was something vaguely familiar about him though and I kept trying to think where I'd seen him before? Was he a student of mine? He looked skinny and young enough.

Then, the shame of it. I put my hand out to catch the stream of vomit, but the projectile seemed to shoot out everywhere catching Pam's and my hair and clothes, the small bits of red and brown looking suspiciously like peppers and mushrooms from the pizza I had for dinner at Pizza Inn. I could see the bouncer approaching, frowning. He would be wanting me out of there sharpish. Fuck how embarrassing! Just when I was having my first lesbian kiss.

Then, 'Leave her alone! I'll take her home,' a familiar voice. It was the guy. The blonde student look a-like.

'Wot?' Pam was wrinkling her nose at the smell and desperately dabbing her hair and cheek at the same time with a tissue from her tiny clutch bag. 'She's *my* friend and I'm fine to take her,' she screeched. 'Now fuck off and concentrate on your little girly-friend over there!' Things seemed blurry to me, I was going to pass out. I swayed heavily seeing stars.

'Get lost, you dirty lezzie!' I heard. 'She's my Baby-mummy. I'm taking her home.'

I knew that voice. Slowly I opened my eyes trying to match the voice with the person. Mike. It was him all along. The same Mike who had abandoned us, not seen his child for a year, and hadn't bothered with Child Maintenance. Now, here he was fingering a teenager and getting a hand-job in a nightclub. I closed my eyes and fell heavily against the table. Everything was going to be okay, my baby was back. I must have collapsed smiling. 'I love you baby,' I whispered, and then everything went black.

i was broken, now I Am

CHAPTER 13: LESSONS IN LOVE

Zane is growing quickly now, he just looks heavy.
Not that he wants to move around much. Mostly, he
just sleeps so I leave him in his pram. He is safe there,
all strapped in. Today is the most exciting day of my
life! The detective has given me some details, he says
it's a very long shot, but I know it's the real thing. We
are on a bus coming to visit you Mother. *Yes Mother, I'm
coming to get you!* I want to sing, scream, cry, laugh all at
once. I'm trembling with anticipation. Every now and

then I glance at the paper in my hand, it has an address scrawled on it. It's an unfamiliar area about an hour's bus ride from where we live, still who cares? I've taken a sickie as it's a school day, honestly, I don't give a flying f**** about work, if I'd waited until after work I would have been a bag of nerves anyway and not been able to function.

Pam? Well I never saw her properly after that night. I just visited her soon after to say sorry about the vomit and to pay her what I owed. Mike and I had got back together that night, or should I say the next morning as apparently, I was comatose that night and he had put me to bed and slept in Zane's cot bed, hugging his son the whole night. For a minute when I heard this, I wondered if he had washed away the smell of fish from his fingers when he embraced our sleeping son, I saw where his hands had been. In the morning of course, he had climbed into my bed and given me a good seeing to. I had heard all about how he had missed me but couldn't face me after all the bad things that he had done. So, he just stayed away. Agreed, he had not paid anything towards Zane, but didn't I receive Child Benefit? Wasn't I working? He on the other hand was not able to pay anything blah blah blah.

i was broken, now I Am

For two blissful weeks we stayed together, Mike looked after Zane in the day and I went to work, rushing home eagerly in the afternoons to spend time with my family. He made me feel complete. We made love, took long walks, cooked together and drank a lot. Sure, there were a fair few sickies on days when I couldn't bear to leave them, but I just didn't care. Love has a habit of putting you in a bubble.

Talking about love. I have knocked on about thirty doors so far, just looking for you Mother. Once, I would have had the energy to knock on a hundred more. But I think I'm getting disheartened. It's been going on for so long, this fruitless search. Each time, I get my hopes up, only to be let down again. The door is opened by some woman who hasn't heard of Sibongile, she's Sindiswa and I am embarrassed. *All Blacks look alike.* I swear at the detective under my breath. She feels pity for me though as we have travelled a fair distance, invites me in for delicious carrot cake and a cup of mint tea. I try to pick her brain but it's no use, I leave feeling deflated.

I visit five more addresses. Nothing. I'm persistent but there's a voice in my head telling me that maybe the search is useless.

But deep inside me the ache is still there. It is a kind of yearning. I want to see you Mother before you know, before it's too late. Sometimes, I don't know whether I'll kill you or cherish you. And maybe after I find you, I will go in search of my father, sure I knew that he'd raped you, but still, I wanted to experience daddy-ness for myself. Is that too ambitious Mother? *Didn't everyone have that right?* Maybe, just maybe *he* had wanted the child. Maybe you could have handed me over to him and then left. He was a wealthy and influential man after all, a writer and political activist, I would have had a different life. I wouldn't have cared that he was White and old, he was still my father. What about my grandparents, my wider family? I know that you grew up in the township and that your family were rat poor. I don't care about that Mother. But at least it would have given me a sense of place, of belongingness. Reference points. Don't we all deserve this? Adopted children suffer the greatest losses. Their inner worlds are just vacuums. I have no culture, no tribe and I'm telling you Mother, I need this.

i was broken, now I Am

I feel like I'm clutching at straws here. All these maybes.

What do I hear you say Mother? My father, my grandparents, they wouldn't have wanted a Coloured or mixed-race child, how would that have worked in a country like South Africa? Don't be stupid child, wake up and smell the roses, people like us we will always be down just like they will always be up. It's how things work, just accept it, accept. I don't know Mother, sometimes I don't believe you, sometimes I feel sure that they would have loved to have a chance to know me. Did you tell them that you were abandoning me Mother? Did you? Is it you or is it me speaking Mother? Sometimes it gets so confusing, I wish I could make the voices stop.

I drink to shut them out.

But the next day they are there again. I need to stop speaking to you Mother. I need to start living. Can you let me go?

Of course, Mike was gone when I returned from work one afternoon. This time, he left a note saying that he was sorry, he just needed to borrow my bank card for a few days and he would return all the money. He must have extricated it from my wallet when I wasn't looking. I had trouble deciphering the note, his spelling was so poor. I called the bank straight away and reported it as stolen, so they could stop it. Then, I called the police and reported it as a theft. I gave them all Mike's details, his parents' address, everything. I wanted him charged. I was growing up, finally! I could smell the coffee and the roses now! He was not getting away with this! Still, the whole yo-yo nature of the relationship left me feeling depleted.

Depression is a savage animal, once it takes up residence inside you, everything around seems bleak, raw and ugly.

I'd been in this fug since childhood, I'd put on a brave face, but I was suffering. Every time there was a where are-you-from, who-are-you question, I clammed up. I'd really thought that having children would solve it all, create my own tribe so to speak, and live forever in a bubble of love. It was not to be. Of course, I had some sort of happy place, didn't we all? How else would we survive this cruel world? Mine was an image of a little girl playing on the beach, she's flanked by a mummy and daddy who look like her and who love her dearly. They are all building that proverbial sandcastle together, mushing their hands in the wet sand and slapping pats of it on the gritty mound, their silliness and laughter rings out on that deserted beach, the ocean in front is stretched out, glittering and shimmering under the golden sun.

I've become so good at accessing this happy place, I can almost summon it whenever and wherever I am. That day, however, I couldn't reach that place even though I tried. I'd not seen Mike for ages and that alone had been painful, but I hadn't anticipated that he would continue to steal, cheat, lie yet embrace me in a love bubble each time as though we were long lost souls with an unbreakable bond. I didn't respect him anymore.

No. That's a lie.

I didn't respect myself anymore. Each time I took him back, never calling him out, never asking him to account for his actions. Why should he change? He knew he had a good thing in stupid, naïve me! I was the sucker that delivered each time he gave his award - winning performances. I drank up his words, salivated at the thought of his nether regions and submitted. I'm no reiki master, but this time after the nightclub incident, I could almost see a black aura around him, like he had become so toxic that you could sense it from afar. How many girlfriends did he have now? He always seemed flush for drink and drugs. That clearly came first, yet Zane never received any presents from him, not even on his birthday. Poor little boy! He even looked like his father with his big grey eyes, his blonde, floppy hair.

Something had to change. I couldn't go on getting drunk and ignoring my son. I had to break the cycle and stop hankering after Mike. He was not mine anymore. I had to let him go. It was time. Time for me to grow up, time to stop wanting anything to do with him, a second child for example, what was I thinking?

I was an embarrassment to the sisterhood that's what. To think how far we'd come in being self -reliant and then to see myself choosing to take us right back to a regressive time when we walked submissively, behind caveman, waiting for scraps of attention. I was a limpet, a lame, pathetic figure, clinging to the hope that he would change.

My bad. I needed to make some changes.

i was broken, now I Am

CHAPTER 14: THE LANDLORD

There's a man in the garden. Well, it's more of a
courtyard with a shed at the far end. Still, I never gave
anyone permission to live in my shed. To my horror, I
would never have known that he was there in the first
place, I leave early and get home late. But the lady who
lives upstairs noticed something wrong and nipped
down last night to tell me, she can see everything from
her upstairs window of course. Get this, apparently, he

uses my washing line when I'm not at home, even invites friends over and has a barbeque in the yard! The cheek of it! I'm paying the rent here and he's just squatting! I never realised the shed was big enough! Some people are animals, they don't care where they live! How long has he been tapping into my electricity? My wifi? Using my water? No wonder the bills have shot up! He's got to go today!

In desperation, I call the estate agency. I could go there, it's just around the corner, but it's Saturday, my day off and I'm taking time off to relax, after all I'm allowed to. I'm a teacher *and* a single parent. It's mid - morning but I've already made significant inroads on the Pinot Grigio and a packet of fags. There is a bottle lying empty on the side and I don't give a monkey's. Despite the threat posed by the bloke out there, I'm feeling quite merry.

I've put on a very short, silver and black tie-dye dress that ends in a flared skirt, I've got silver sequined flip flops on and I've curled my hair into long, loopy, ringlets. A bit of smoky eye shadow and some silver hoop earrings and I'm done. Zane loves it when I'm in a colourful mood, he tries to wrest the bottle of silver nail polish from me and I turn on him and paint his fingernails while trying to blow raspberries on his tummy. When our nails have dried, we do silly dances to pop songs on the radio and laugh until we collapse on the sofa.

Laughter is healing they say and truth be told, we have come a long way, he will start school in a few months, in reception, and I think that this will signal an upward rise in our fortunes. No wildly expensive childminders after that. I can put him in after school club and collect him when I'm done teaching for the day. He's such a fussy child, I've given up. Hopefully he can get his dinner at school and his tea at the after-school club, that way I don't have to do much in the evening.

A knock at the door and I abandon Zane who I had been cuddling on the floor. Hercules Poirot stands there in posh designer jeans, a dark leather jacket and a V neck cashmere jumper underneath, in baby pink. I love men in pink, men who can embrace their inner goddesses. It must be that yin yang balancing thing. He smells powerfully of sandalwood and leather, I want to breathe him in, I absolutely love these smells. Once I followed a man home from the bus, just because I had fallen in love with his aftershave. Okay he was hot too.

I'm not a stalker, just really into nice smells especially on men

'Hello,' I say, 'where have you been all my life?'
I sing this line with a straight face, but he starts smiling, it's a disarming smile showing rows of even, dazzling, white teeth. His dimples are charming. I'm in love. He's carrying some letter headed paper from the agency in his hand. As I make way for him to enter the living room, he is still looking at me intently, giving me the eye, I think. Then he surprises me. He sings:

'Where have you been all *my* life? I've been looking everywhere for a girl like you.'

He looks at Zane still showing those delightful dimples.

We both giggle. We've successfully broken the ice.

'Awright mate!' Then to me, 'You must be Carrie. I'm Neil, I own the agency. And the maisonette as it happens. One of my best investments.' He looks around.

'Spacious innit!'

'Have you come to sort out the man in the shed?' I ask. 'I'm not comfortable until he's gone. Just turf him out I don't care where,' I say, 'the cheek! Camping out in someone's shed! Who does he think he is? He's lucky I haven't called the police!'

He has his hands up now as if to say hold on.

'It's all sorted don't stress,' he says, 'I went in via the side gate and had a word. Put him in a taxi headed for an organization I know that helps homeless people, I know he'll get the support there.'

'Really? Really?' I'm in a wild mood today, I do not find this funny. 'I suppose you gave him money too, did you? And lunch? What about a plane ticket to Bali? A well -deserved holiday on the beach? Bloody ridiculous!' I hiss.

'Whoa! Someone's in a bad mood!' He grins while sitting down and holding his hands out to Zane. 'I asked the cafe next door to serve him up a cooked breakfast before he left. Can you just imagine how desperate he must have been living in that tiny box of a shed?' he shudders. 'What some people have to do to live hey?'

'Who was your mother? Mother Theresa?' The bitterness, it's there, a common thread in *everything* I say and do, it seems. I can hear myself, but I still do it, I'm a walking ball of hate.

He sighs and smiles, 'One day hopefully, I'll tell you about my mother. In the meantime, all I can say is that it's my nature. I like to help wherever I can.'

'Great, you can help me. I need help too.'

'Okay! No problem. Do you mind if I take off my jacket?'

'Make yourself comfortable, I'll make you a cup of tea,' I say, 'or would you like a glass of wine? I've had a few already,' I smile indicating the empty bottle.

It was so bizarre, but nice bizarre. I went to the kitchen to get the last bottle and two glasses, I even found some crisps and threw them into a bowl. By the time I'd come back after replenishing my make-up, blusher, nude lipstick, that kind of thing, he was sitting on the floor with Zane in his lap doing a wooden jigsaw puzzle. I was dumbstruck! The biggest surprise being Zane, he seemed much more animated than when I played with him, much more alert and focused.

i was broken, now I Am

'You have such a beautiful son,' he said ruffling his fair hair. 'A beautiful woman with a beautiful son! What gorgeous grey eyes. I hope you don't mind me holding him. I love kids.'

'Oh no, go for it, you can keep the compliments coming, it's earning you brownie points,' I say, sinking onto the sofa next to him. 'He likes cuddles. Only I can't give them to him all the time.'

'Why not?' he asks sipping his wine.

'Why not?' I laugh but it has a hollow ring to it. 'How long is a piece of string? Because I'm tired that's what. Being a teacher, it's not easy you know, all that aggro from students and staff at school. Then you come home to marking and parenting. Don't get me wrong, I love my child. But when things went wrong between me and his dad...' my voice tailed off, I could feel tears stinging my eyes, I gulped down more wine. Why did he have to pry? I had been in a fun mood before he arrived.

'Listen,' he was on the sofa next to me now, 'I don't mean to be nosy, you can tell me to get lost, I would understand. But I want to help you, I can see that you need a bit of support.'

'You think?' I say tearful and angry, staring into my wine glass, watching the wine swirl round and round. He puts his arm around my shoulder.

'I don't want to pry,' he says, 'but I'm here for you.'

I'm here for you.

I'm here for you.

You know Mother, I've never heard anyone say that to me? Ever. I want to record him saying it, I want to play it again and again after he fucks me and leaves me, just like everyone else.

'I've brought some paperwork for you to sign,' he says softly, 'but we don't have to do it now. Just chill okay? I'm here.' This makes me cry more, proper tears now rolling down my eyes. God, I'm such a mess! He strokes my hair and brings my head towards his chest which is comforting as he smells so good. I give in to him and lie there for a bit feeling the anger and bitterness subside slowly. I wonder if he will kiss me, I want him to. It's been a long, long time since I was intimate with someone and I've missed it. I look up hopefully, realizing that my make-up has smudged. He puts his fingers over my lips, tracing the outlines,

staring softly at me, I open my mouth and lick his
fingers. I can sense his excitement, feel him stiffen
before I can even touch him there. We kiss. It's a long,
deep kiss. A foreplay kiss. I want to take him straight to
my bedroom, that smell…dammit!

Zane has made his way to us, he stares at us
entwined together like this, he looks at me and then at
Neil. He has never seen me with anyone other than his
father. The landlord is a surprise to him, come to think
of it, he's a surprise to me too. If I'd known how hot
he was, I'd have rung the agency a long time ago.
Funny, I had been popping in every month to pay the
rent, but I hadn't seen this lovely creature of a man.
Now that he was here, I don't want to let him go. My
son is whimpering and puts his hands up to be carried.

'Has he eaten?' says the landlord, picking him up?

'No, he doesn't eat much,' I say, resenting this
intrusion. 'He had some crisps.'

'Really?' He has carried Zane to the kitchen now
much to his delight, I can't do that kind of thing, he's
way too heavy for me. I sit feeling horny and drunk.
Neil has opened cupboards and is talking to Zane non-

stop. I'm sulking, I had hoped to be carried into the bedroom for a bit of pampering. But now we're playing mummies and daddies. Yawn.

'Let's see what we can rustle up for you mate okay! Don't worry, we'll sort you out in no time.' Then, 'do you mind if we nip out to the Co-op across the street?' he asks. 'We won't be long.'

Mind? Why would I mind? That would give me a few minutes to rearrange myself, which is what I badly needed.

'Go for it,' I say, 'get some more wine while you're at it. I'm going to take a bath, can you let yourself in?'

A bubble bath. One of my favourite things that I have not been able to do in a while. Half of the time, I'm worried about where Zane is and what he is doing, is he safe or doing something dangerous? I can't relax. I'm a bag of nerves. Different story if he liked to come in with me but he is a wriggler the little sod. Doesn't like soap in his eyes, starts to go mad. So, I just resign myself to a quick shower. Wine and fags are the only things that keep me going, fuck food. I lie back, close my eyes and immerse myself in the suds. It feels absurd to be bathing after putting all that make up on, that dress, but I needed this, need to reflect too, it's all happening so quickly. I feel like I'm falling for this Neil. It feels ridiculous really, I've literally only just met him. I need to check myself, I'm so sick of meeting the wrong person and getting hurt. I just can't do that to myself anymore. And yet, I must do something to erase the memory of Mike. I want to delete it but that's impossible, maybe if I got with someone else it would just fade away. I need to play my cards carefully, anyone can see that Neil's a diamond in the haystack.

Then, the safeguarding training drummed into us at school kicks in. What if he's a paedo? What if it isn't the landlord but someone off the street pretending? Shit Carrie! Sort yourself out! I'm talking to no one. I get out of the bath.

By now, my fingers and toes are wrinkled like prunes from the water. Then I hear the sounds. The activity in the kitchen is in full flow. I have a towel around me and my hair is in the familiar wormy curls and piled high off my face now, my face scrubbed clean of make -up. If he doesn't like me au naturel, oh well. He has bought groceries, lots. Is there a message here somewhere? *Bad mother who does not look after herself let alone her baby son!*

'What's he eating?' I'm incredulous. My son is sitting at the table with a plate of finger sandwiches in brown bread no less! With me he only eats white bread! I make a mental note to try this. Neil has put sliced bananas and chocolate spread in the sandwiches, he has poured milk into his non- spill beaker and Zane is drinking happily. I nick one of the sandwiches, it's delicious.

'My, my! Quite the daddy, are you? I can't get over this,' I indicate Zane and the groceries. 'I don't bother cos he's different with me. Only likes his bottle with juice in it. That and crisps, chicken nuggets sometimes. Or bits of burger. He's so fussy I gave up.' He's cut cheese into small squares and Zane eats this too. In the frying pan, Neil has some sort of spinach omelette going. There are salad leaves in a bowl. I open the fridge, there are four bottles of expensive white wine nestling amongst a ton of fresh vegetables and cartons of coconut water and juice. I'm impressed, very. Who is this man and where has he been all my life? 'Do you eat spicy food?' he asks. 'I'm making an egg roti roll. It's an omelette rolled inside a roti just cut into fancy bits and placed on a bed of salad. Okay?'

'Bring it on, I'm starving!' I laugh reaching for more wine, this man with his generous spirit is making me nervous. Doesn't he have any place to go? People to see? He says that he owns the agency. Surely, he must be busy. But then I remember, he spoke about paperwork, was I in trouble? That familiar knot of anxiety inside me, growling now. Later, while Zane naps, we eat and talk about nothing. Then, he approaches me, takes my clothes off wordlessly, cheeky sod! He's so beautiful, I give in sans protest and we make love slowly and mindfully. Afterwards, I find a new place to lay my head, it's on his chest. I don't know anything about this man, yet I'm spending my whole Saturday with him.

'You're my landlord, I don't want a relationship with you,' I whisper after the third round. 'This was a big mistake!' He smiles and starts talking softly.

CHAPTER 15: LOVE

Neil tells me a few things about himself, but I want
to know more. I keep interrogating him. He has
produced a joint ready rolled from a tin in his jacket
pocket and we smoke in bed together, it's his place not
mine. He has disabled the smoke alarm and brought a
cup to serve as an ash tray, into the bedroom. He tells
me that he loves my curves and that I am stunningly
beautiful. He keeps running his manicured fingers over
me and I do not protest. He says that my skin is as soft

as silk. Well, he has to say that, he can't exactly call me ugly after all that love -making, can he?

He's in the tail end of a relationship, he says softly while I lie against him and stroke his dark moustache. He used to love her but stopped when she started cheating. He starts getting upset while he talks so I hand the joint back to him and he drags on it deeply looking instantly composed again. He says that he's tried everything to help her, but she continued to cheat behind his back, in his block of flats he was a laughing stock. Men came and went openly to see her so most times he avoided being there, spending evenings and weekends away with friends or in his sister's house where he was a regular occupant. He had a security camera outside his place which picked up all the comings and goings, he watched the tapes with his sister, horrified.

'So why didn't you leave?' I ask furious now that this dear, sweet, handsome man would have been treated like that. It sounded so absurd, why would anyone in their right mind put up with that? She sounded wrong for him anyway, but I could just picture her, I knew the type, an animal, a man eater we called them. Someone with no respect for herself let alone her boyfriend.

He sighs heavily and is silent for a while. I give him space to formulate his response.

'You need to see her to understand,' he says finally. 'She's here in London all alone, she's got no one. Her family are all abroad. She doesn't take well to other people, doesn't have friends. She bitches about her work colleagues and refuses to accept social invitations. I used to be worried sick about her and her mental health that's why I stayed close, even when I knew that she was, well, you know,' he shrugged. I could see how painful all this was to talk about. He'd brought another bottle of wine in from the kitchen and we were swigging it from the bottle. A pleasant warmth and increased horniness spread through me. I wanted this to last forever.

'But all those wasted years!' I blurt out. I'm feeling protective now, how dare she do this? What about Neil? Who takes care of him? 'You can't simply give and give without it draining you.'

'Well, all that negativity, it just dragged me down really,' he says, 'for a time it was an eye for an eye, I too played away just thinking about how she'd disrespected me. In the end, it all got so tedious, I just wanted a safe space to go home to. And I certainly couldn't go there, it didn't feel like home anymore. So, I used any excuse *not* to go home. What gets me, is that we were very happy for a long time. I loved her. Thought that she was the One. Then it all went pear shaped.' His shoulders slump in resignation. I hate her already.

He tells me that before her, he had been married to a Russian beauty. That had lasted a few years until one day, unexpectedly and unpredictably, she had run away with their daughter and cleaned out his bank account. He had grieved for the marriage and his child, alone, for a long time until he met this man eater. It seemed like he was just trying to avoid loneliness, but I didn't say anything. His parents had died in a car crash when he was a young boy. I guessed that he had a taste of loneliness and didn't like it.

I looked at him carefully. I had never dated an older man like him before. He was very handsome for an older, middle aged man, those magnetic, hazel, long fringed eyes that reminded me of a horse. And brilliant in the sack too. Different from Mike, more patient, giving. But equally energetic and a tad more experimental. I wondered what he saw in me. My battered and bruised psyche, my constant whingeing about being single, my self -indulgent search for a mother that I had little hope in finding. How could I have naively expected to find her through just a name? There must be hundreds of women here with her name. Besides, it was most likely that she had changed her name by now, I changed mine via deed poll. Everyone here seemed to abbreviate their original names, as if a monosyllable was all they could muster. Deena became Deen, Prakash Prak, Joanna Jo, Andile Dee, Sandile San and so on. Was she Sib? And the UK was so huge, she could be anywhere, not just London. She could have gone abroad, she could have died. And maybe, just maybe she didn't want to be found, after all she'd given me away and made no contact! How presumptuous of me that she'd want this big fat reunion! I felt awash with shame, embarrassment. All that time spent on searching for her, I could have done something else, publish my book, done another degree, gone on holiday! Instead, I'd spent precious money on a useless detective who had rinsed me properly.

The truth staring at me in the face now was that I already *had* a mother and father, they were my adoptive parents in Durban who had showered me with love. It had been me who had turned away from that. Why?

i was broken, now I Am

No reason but this obstinate and misguided wish to see my real mother! How stupid I had been, rejecting the people who really *did* love me! How lonely they must have felt without the child that they'd lovingly brought up. Even Niall used to say that I was the 'apple of his eye!' Used to bring me a chocolate every-day. And Joe, he'd stop at the bakery after work and get me a cake: a pink snowball dusted in white coconut, a custard cream, a chocolate éclair. I loved sweet things, no wonder I was a little chubber! It was their way of showing love, and I had turned my back on this. Silly, silly me! Maybe it was time to count my blessings, get back in touch with my family, and invite them to London to see Zane. Christmas would be a good time.

Compared to Neil, I was blessed. I had family, some money, talent as a writer. Maybe one day I would publish my book and be famous. I had youth too, and a son of course, my precious son. A child that I'd neglected, from birth. There were no words to express how deeply ashamed I felt about being a shitty, irresponsible parent. I needed to change things up now! What did Neil have? A business and money. A sister but one who was also busy running *her* business, so no one was there for him.

Weed makes me think profound thoughts. Feeling suddenly energized and comforted by these epiphanies, I make my way to the bathroom, fishing out, en route, the new address on the slip of paper that the detective had given me. It would not be her anyway, I know. I am sick of these long shots that lead nowhere. I screw it up and bin it.

'I want to spend this weekend with you,' he says, 'I hardly know you, but I'm drawn to you. Can we do that? Just you, me and Zane?'

'I told you I don't want a relationship,' I say adamantly, 'been there, done that. But hey if you want to hang, you know, then cool by me!' *Shit, what I meant was, let's get married. Just go do it now! Anywhere, Vegas even. Let's never let go of this magic.*

'Brilliant,' he says, 'Because I have nowhere to go really! You're in my spot!'

'Spot?'

i was broken, now I Am

CHAPTER 16: WELLNESS

'I believe that life is chaotic, a jumble of accidents, ambitions, misconceptions, bold intentions, lazy happenstances, and unintended consequences, yet I also believe that there are connections that illuminate our world, revealing its endless mystery and wonder.'

David Maraniss

Neil tells me cautiously that the agency had made a major screw up. He had bought the garden maisonette a few weeks before I'd seen it, it was meant to be the place that he'd move into when he left her. He says that he'd hunted and hunted for the right place and eventually found this mancave. But somehow, the details got mixed up in other paperwork from other properties that he'd owned and let out, he'd disappeared to the north to open a new branch and a new, young agent had thought that this apartment was to be let. He hadn't even consulted Neil about pricing, if he had it would have not been in my budget. Of course, I'd taken it on the same day that it was advertised, and the agent clearly took a shine to me, I asked him to push it through quickly, I was so paranoid that I would lose it for that price! 'Sure Madam, I will expedite the lease!' he'd said politely while giving me the once over.

Neil had returned to find that his apartment had been rented for peanuts and he now had to wait for two more months to turf me out. I'd signed a twelve-month lease with a six- month break clause either way. I guess he wanted to give me notice that he wanted the place back as I'd been there for a glorious four months. My heart sank. Move again? I didn't like the idea of creating upheaval for Zane, even a change of childminder had knocked him for six. And the primary schools in the area were good, I'd put his name on the waiting lists and had settled into the idea of living there for a while. Of course, I could have gotten a mortgage and bought a small place of my own, I had enough for a deposit, but I had really, really fallen in love with the place.

What was the solution? I couldn't possibly ask Neil to wait two months or continue to sleep on his sister's sofa. Going back to their shared apartment was out of the question too, besides, he had sold that flat, it was all going through quickly.

'Let's have a modern-day arrangement?' I suggested brightly, 'move in here.'

'Sleep where?' he laughed.

With me. Everyday. Hold me tight, never let me go.

'The sofa opens out to a sleeper couch, right? And when you're here you'll mainly be in the living areas. Then in two months, we can see. Maybe it's time I bought somewhere myself.' I was trying to come to a compromise. I didn't want him to be homeless, I didn't want to move just yet. And I'd hatched a plan to pay a reduced rent now, if we shared. Bigger deposit for me in the end! Talk about win win! 'I'm sorry you can't move in with me,' I said, 'I told you, I don't do relationships. And I love sleeping alone.' Even though strictly speaking, the king size bed was his.

He loved the idea and started moving his bags in bit by bit using the large cupboard in the alcove and the spare chest in my room. Within hours he transformed the space. I didn't mind either way, as long as I had my space. His aftershave (posh, expensive) and toothbrush (fancy, electric next to my budget cheapie) sat in the bathroom cabinet, making me feel tingly and sexy for some reason, after all we were *not* cohabiting. Not.

That weekend we went for a long drive into the countryside and found a sweet village where we stopped to feed the ducks with Zane, later we had a delicious pub lunch. There was colour in Zane's cheeks when we got back, we had all laughed a lot and done plenty of walking. I couldn't believe how much he had started to eat, 'Hey piggy!' I teased, after he finished all his fish and chips then went on to apple pie and custard. We made love constantly too, we agreed to start our new living arrangement from Monday, the next day. So that Sunday, we made the most of our time in that huge king size bed.

I'd stopped talking to my mother in my head. Every so often I so wanted to say, 'See Mother see! I *am* capable of happiness without you! I'm moving forward Mother, I've thrown that address away and now we both go our separate ways!'

But I didn't.

At work they'd started a new Wellness Programme for teachers, I doubted that it was motivated by a burning desire to actually *help* the staff, maybe it was part of the recruitment drive. I'd heard that London was struggling to recruit staff as the salaries were mediocre and the students' bad behaviour just escalated year by year. That, or a finger up to existing staff to say, 'You can stop taking sickies due to stress, we have wellness under control here!' Anyway, as part of this, we each had to choose an element that we wanted to participate in, I chose the Counsellor. I had to sit on the couch and spill all in confidence of course, but at least I got to have period four and five off on Fridays.

'You need to put a total stop to this talking to your mother business!' she said in faltering immigrant English. I wasn't interested in where she came from, just how I could get better.

'It's not healthy! You need to find real people to interact with. And the drinking, it looks like it needs to go!'

'Oh no, no, no,' I said quickly in panic, 'it's under control.'

'No!' she said firmly, banging her fist on the coffee table in the office allocated to her for the one day that she was in school. 'It seems like it makes it worse! I want you to try something,' she continued, 'try not speaking to her at all, try cutting down on drinking, spend time with your son, walking in the Nature if possible.'

'Okay, okay,' she'd hit a raw nerve there including Zane in my wellness. I would spend more time with him, but I was not hugging bloody trees.

Coward that I am, that night that I first met Neil, I'd had a panic attack. I'd tip toed out of bed when he was asleep and rushed to the kitchen bin where I searched in the trash for the address the detective had given me, the address that I'd binned. I had to try just one more time. Eventually I found the curled- up slip of paper, stinky now with bits of eggshell and onion on it. I scribbled it down on new paper and threw the original away.

Days passed uneventfully and in no time, we slipped into a routine. I dropped Zane off at the childminder's and went to work each day, after work I'd fetch him and rush home in anticipation of seeing Neil. Neil for his part, had cut back his hours drastically. When I teased him that this was down to Zane and me, he totally denied it saying that he'd intended this all along, it was his age and him wanting quality time to pursue other things like fitness and travel. He said that this was why he had managers to run his offices, besides everything was virtual nowadays.

Part of the deliciousness of Neil was that often he worked in the evenings and he encouraged me to work too unlike Mike who had resented it. Often when Zane was tucked up in bed we would open a bottle of wine and just sit quietly on our laptops, working. My book was coming on, in fact I was growing in literary confidence and wanted to find the right agent. Most of the stories were about South Africa. I'd told Neil a bit about how everything there was politicised, I'd even shared a little about my parents and my fruitless search for my biological mother. He'd not said much except that it was my choice what I wanted to do and that he'd support me whatever decision I made. In turn, he shared stories about India, his birth country that he was determined to take me to. So, between Mamma Africa and Mother India, I had rich, unlimited fodder for my stories. Social media too helped, some of the people with their eccentric and absurd requests became protagonists in the narratives that I churned out.

Take 'Swami Douchebag' for instance. It was the story of a predatory Swami who was known far and wide for his powers of healing. Sick people who couldn't afford the medical route came to his ashram daily, forming straggly queues, waiting for his blessing. One day, he took a young, disabled girl into his quarters, later she told her parents that he had violated her. I'd written many stories that referenced different contexts and cultures. Forced marriages, female genital mutilation, homelessness, human trafficking, poverty. It was all there. But given Neil's anecdotes about how Swamis were revered and respected in India, that story struck me as being particularly poignant. I spent ages reflecting on how that vulnerable, sick child would feel in the presence of the Swami. First, there'd be awe. An offering of sorts: fruit, milk, fresh flowers. Next, complete trust in his integrity and ability to heal. So much so that despite her disability which was a partial immobility on one side of her body, she felt comfortable enough to be alone with him, leaving her parents outside to wait and pray. Their naive belief that prayers would expedite her healing was a key element too. They had delivered their precious only child into a paedophile's hands, unthinkingly. The things we do for love! And then, the toe curling moment when he would reveal himself to her by parting his dhoti, her inability to move swiftly rendering her voiceless, his descent on her and lastly, the threats to keep the secret hidden, or else….he probably guilted her out by pointing out, in true patriarchal style, that it was her sins that had led up to this, that she, a child tainted by disability, was destined to suffer. And if she disclosed, what a curse would afflict the entire family!

On social media which was rapidly sucking me in, many people who had tried to befriend me turned out to be fakes. It was called 'catfishing.' Their personalities and fake stories fuelled my imagination; others who in-boxed me with pictures of their body parts: penises, vaginas, etc met with a similar fate. They became immortalised in my fictional tales. A very real flesh and blood Swami tried to contact me once. He said that he had selected me out of everyone else, as he sensed that I needed his spiritual intervention. In blind faith, like the girl, I believed it, felt flattered even. But when, via private messenger, he outlined what he would like to do to my naked body and then accompanied this by sending me photos of his hirsute body and underwhelming genitalia, I felt like I'd been played by a pervert. My story was based on him, in fact the collection was called Swami Douchebag and Other Stories. I had finally awakened to the realisation that contemptible, hypocritical people lurked in every corner of the globe virtually and physically, life sometimes felt like a giant obstacle course where swerving to avoid them was a prerequisite part of survival.

Mike and his family, my mother, uncle and auntie, Rosemary were all part of the douchebag tribe. Oh, they were dressed up to masquerade as professional, spiritual, humanitarian, decent. But once you were awakened enough to whip off their disguises, you could see them for what they actually were. Evil personified.

i was broken, now I Am

Yes, evil existed, it needed to be identified and labelled for what it was.

That meant that Good existed too.

Finally.

I was coming home, to the Light. A moth finding its pathway to the flame.

CHAPTER 17: NOT MY MOTHER

Time eases pain. It softens things. Just a year ago I had such a horrible, horrible experience, I shudder now just thinking about it. I haven't told Neil and I'm not going to, I will only feel deeply embarrassed and ashamed. I visited the address on the slip of paper. We had finished school early as it was the half term holiday, Zane was at school and would go to aftercare straight after. Neil was spending a few days in his office in the north. Ever since I'd started to heed that counsellor's advice, I'd felt better all round, but that address that was in my coat pocket still felt like I had one stone that was unturned. So, I drove there after school. It was easy enough to find, my satellite navigation toy was a useful present from Neil.

The block was nice enough, the plants and level of tidiness in the foyer attesting to an effective association that was managing the building well. Neil had taught me well. I'd found the third floor easily and knocked on the door, my heart in my mouth as you do when you are searching for your biological mother. But the knocking came to nothing, there'd been this silence. In desperation, I had called out, 'Sibongile!' Crikey, I can see now how strange this would have sounded and how disrespectful to the other occupants of the building to disturb them like that. In despair, I'd turned to walk away, when the door adjacent to the apartment had opened a fraction, the curtain had twitched vigorously a while before, but now the door had opened fully. It was the neighbour. I'd been parched. Over a cup of tea and a plate of samosas, she had explained that the woman who lived next door to her was not African, no she had categorically heard her partner mention that she was from Jamaica. She had not spoken about having had a child, she was, in fact, not a good neighbour and everyone wanted to see her leave the block, she was what you could call a bad influence.

I'd sighed heavily, once again, I'd been barking up the wrong tree. Impressed by the old woman's hospitality, I'd thanked her and turned to go. Then, once outside the door again, I'd given a final knock in full view of the neighbour. Imagine my total surprise when strangely, a window opened a fraction, a brown face poked out, I couldn't see much but I could hear her and to this day I don't know if I was overwrought and imagined it all or whether it was real.

'Caramel? Is that you?' she asked in a hesitant, small voice. Then repeatedly, 'Caramel? Caramel?' I'd totally forgotten that name, that absurd name. Her voice was slurry and soft. I had to strain to hear it. Did she really say, 'Caramel? Or just Caaaaa?' I couldn't hear her properly.

'Yes Mother, it's me Caramel!'

'I'm coming! Just wait Caramel, I'm coming! Don't go! Wait!'

'Pardon? Sorry I can't hear you properly. Could you repeat that?'

i was broken, now I Am

I'm waiting Mother. I've waited all my life to see you.

'You're wasting your time,' said the neighbour, she'd emerged fully now, dressed colourfully in an Indian suit in peacock blue and silver, her grey hair in a dignified topknot.

'It's okay, I want to talk to her, I think she's my mother,' I said desperately, stupidly, wanting to believe, wanting Topknot to go away and leave me to it.

'She doesn't have a daughter, she told me herself. She's from Jamaica. Sorry to say, she's a sort of prostitute.'

'Sorry, do you mind? I need to talk to her.'

'She doesn't deserve a daughter!' she spat. 'What I wouldn't do to see *my* children again! But they hardly come visit me, maybe birthdays, Mother's Day, then you never see them anymore. My house is falling apart and there's no one to help me.'

'I'm sorry.'

I heard sounds inside. I dared not breathe. Maybe if I did, she would go away. Or I would wake up and it would be all a dream. The front door was being opened, I could hear her fumbling heavily. Why the delay? She'd closed the window now, I couldn't even go and open it to check what was going on. It seemed like she was taking ages.

My heart was in my mouth.

'See? I'm never wrong!' spat Topknot, 'why don't you come visit me? She's not anyone's mother, I know.'

Eventually, the door opened, and a woman stood there, garish in a snowy white nightie and make up smeared all over her face. For a minute, we looked at each other, then, her face and body crumpled like a concertina and she went down. I could smell alcohol strongly, was she on drugs too? I knew something for sure. She was not my mother. There was absolutely no resemblance there, zero. Not the face or the body, just nothing. There should be something right?

With a heavy heart I called for an ambulance and waited with Topknot outside while the paramedics arrived. I didn't feel like intruding, it felt rude. Yes, she was a Black woman but not all Black women would be my mother! How stupid and naive I felt. This woman was ill, I could see that. And the name she'd called out, did I hear it properly? Faith and anticipation do silly

things, I had imagined so many things, but this had
been no Nessun Dorma moment of flying into each
other's arms and rekindling those blood bonds.

Nevertheless, I stayed. It was the right thing to do.
Even when they arrived and announced that she was
barely conscious, I stayed. I drove off only once the
team told me which hospital she would be admitted to,
I wanted to follow through. To Topknot's earnest
appeals for more visits, I promised that I would swing
by every now and then. I never did. But I noted the
phone number of her son and back in my car, I called
him to explain that his mother needed support, care
and attention. He seemed embarrassed that she'd been
so needy that she was willing to cling onto me. Step up,
I thought. Do your bit! He mumbled an apology and
promised to check in on her.

About a month later, again in secret only because
Neil would have laughed, I drove to the hospital and
explained that I was there to see her. I called her my
mother and said that we had lost contact. I didn't have
a clue what she was calling herself by now, so I avoided
names. A cute young guy in a nurse's uniform tracked
down the details by the date that she was admitted,

apparently, she'd been in Intensive Care for a few weeks but had recently been moved to Psychiatrics. He said he'd give me ten minutes only as it was only close family who could see her. As I could not verify her date of birth or name, I would be treated as suspicious. 'I was adopted,' I'd said angrily.

'Tell that to Jeremy Kyle,' he'd said, 'I'm only letting you in the unit because you have a nice body.'

'Hey!' But we'd both collapsed giggling.

He took me to a unit upstairs saying, 'PSYCHIATRIC,' in big, colourful letters outside. Inside, after peering into a large TV lounge in which patients of all ages and colours flopped heavily on leather armchairs, ('wipe clean in case of accidents,' he narrated,) he shook his head and led me to another quieter area where only two patients sat on wheelchairs overlooking the wide windows with their thick bars across. One was the woman. I recognized her straight away. She was talking to herself. 'My baby's like a baby doll. I rock her day and night, puts her to sleep that does. *Hush a bye baby on the tree tops*,' and she repeated this over and over again, singing alternating with slurred speech, her jaw, slack on her chest, looking at nothing. I stood watching intently looking for a sign, of what I did not know. I checked out her fingers, facial features, body shape. Nothing. I stood in front of her. Nothing. She didn't even see me.

It was then, right there, that I decided to end the search and get on with my life. Enough was enough, the pain of building myself up only to be let down constantly. I couldn't bear it anymore. I turned and walked towards the exit. 'Hey, you promised me your number!' the guy shouted. I kept walking until I reached the car park.

CHAPTER 18: DREAMS AND REALITY

'I want to show you a house!' Neil was practically dancing around the kitchen. 'I'm in love!' he shouted to Zane who was giggling now, seeing a middle -aged man jiggle around.

'What house? You mean for me to invest in?' I asked, pouring champagne carefully so as not to waste it, its golden fizz pouring over the sides of the elegant glasses. It was Friday evening, celebration time!

'Well you don't have to, but you might want to when you see it,' he said more carefully now.

i was broken, now I Am

'You want to buy a house with me,' I teased smiling. I welcomed the idea. We had outgrown the maisonette. The concrete yard outside with its structured shrubbery, was not a garden, and the whole arrangement was not working anymore. Zane's stuff was everywhere. He was reading now, and his books and Lego bricks took up all the space. Neil too, had become messy.

'That big, pink house on the hill has just come on the market,' he said, 'it's a four -bedroom detached with a hundred and eighty-foot garden.'

'Have you seen it already?' I asked annoyed.

'I'm sorry darling,' he said, 'I had to see it as it was *moi* who had to take it on our books. Told her it would sell quickly. And as it happens, I've made an appointment for us to see it tomorrow morning first thing. Just so you know, I have a cash deposit and I know exactly how much she'll take. Downsizing she is, going into a one bedroom. It's perfect for us!'

For a few weeks, I had something that I'd been too nervous to show him. I'd done the test myself in Sainsbury's toilets straight after work, it was not like me to miss a period. He'd been asking for ages, 'when are you coming off the pill? Please come off, please, please, pretty please!'

'When I'm good and ready!' I'd announced sharply, but I'd come off that night.

The blue line came through almost immediately and my heart lurched. Then I remembered that miscarriage and how it had ripped through me, not just the physical pain which was bad enough but the vacuum inside, the ache. Now, this chance to start a brand- new life altogether with my love. I'd finally found 'The One' and this, it was just such a blessing. I had not opened the champagne for nothing, the slim white tube lay in its nest of pale tissue in a gift bag that I'd bought in a rush of excitement, tears pouring down my cheeks. I could imagine his face, his excitement. It was what we'd both wanted now that Zane was growing up so fast. I'd not seen Mike since that last time and recently Neil had been talking about adopting Zane which I welcomed. A new start for all of us.

I will never forget a story that one of my teacher mates had told me once on a girls' night out. She'd come from a very poor background, a township, in South Africa. She had to earn scholarships just to afford to attend university, in fact, her whole teenage

i was broken, now I Am

life had been buried in study just to secure scholarships. Once at university, she'd enrolled to study Drama and Acting which had been her dream. During evenings and weekends, she took up a waitressing job in a local café. One evening, a distinguished, elderly gentleman walked in and she happened to serve him. They made an instant connection, he fell in love with her theatrically trained voice and she was charmed by his manners and general demeanour. She was a stunner as well, a tall Black girl with beautiful features and glistening, straight hair flowing down her back. Each evening, he would swing by asking for her to serve him, each time he'd leave a tip so generous that often it was way more than the light meal he'd order. One day, he had a proposition: he owned a luxury hotel and private villa in Spain somewhere, he wanted her to accompany him to Spain to be his companion. Exactly what this meant, she had no idea, but she pointed out to me that he was a man in his eighties possibly, it seemed like he just wanted her to amuse him with talk. He'd give her three days to think about the offer, then he'd be gone forever.

She'd had a boyfriend at the time, it was the proverbial on off relationship that we all seem to experience and come out on the other side damaged in some way. For days she pondered over the idea of leaving everything behind and starting anew, she could still study, he'd promised, she could do whatever she wanted. At the end of the three days, he'd returned wearing a sharp, silver suit and a navy cashmere coat, his chauffeur was standing outside the car. Tearfully, she'd refused to go, citing the commitment that she'd made to the scholarship, her studies, her boyfriend. And equally tearfully, he'd bade her farewell and sped off. A week later, she discovered that her boyfriend had been cheating, so they broke up. Her job ended a few weeks after this as the owner was selling up. She finished her studies successfully and ended up as a Drama teacher in London, as she couldn't get acting roles. She lived in a shared house in an area where drug dealing children lurked in every corner. There'd been numerous knife crimes and three teenagers had lost their lives.

She was miserable.

Infused with alcohol, she'd cried that night as she narrated the story, telling me that not a day went by that she didn't think about that offer and what her life could have been like if she had only removed her apron that evening, grabbed her bag and passport and jumped in the car.

She'd fucked up her 'Carpe Diem' moment.

Now, *I* had met my 'elderly gent', except that Neil was not elderly just more mature. He was a keeper and I was not going to throw away *my* chance. I knew that he had money and a heart of gold, he could give Zane and me the best life ever. Above all, we had come to love and care for each other deeply. He'd hinted that there was no need for me to work and maybe it was time I had a break to focus on our son, my writing and this precious bubble of life inside me. I was going to accept his offer. 'It's a yes from me, my love, it's a big, fat yes!'

The bag with its snowy white tube lay on the table. I'd resisted the urge to write 'DADDY,' in big letters on it even though Zane had started calling him that already. It just said, 'To Neil. My Best Friend and My Love.' He'd find it any minute as he was preparing dinner. Better down as much champers as possible before he went funny and stopped me from drinking for nine whole months!

It was a warm evening, so I wondered outside in the courtyard. The stars were out already. In a few weeks we could be out of here, in our new house. It was still close enough, so Zane would not have to move schools, he and the baby could have their own rooms. Our two children! It was what I'd craved so much. I'd stop work and write, maybe paint too. Neil would garden, cook. He'd always wanted a chef's kitchen. It was his sort of thing. It was all going to be okay, at last, I knew it.

And then shouts from inside, screams and whoops of joy. He'd found it. A lightning bolt of pure joy shot through me.

Let the love in, Carrie. Quit resisting. Open yourself and let it in. There's so much love waiting to come to you. Accept. Think with your heart. Everything is going to be okay. The universe has your back. You're safe.

It had been a blissful evening. After that memorable angel hair pasta with lobster that Neil had cooked and served in the garden we had sat in semi silence, just cuddling, watching the twinkling tea light candles and soft, recessed lights illuminating the trees that fringed the garden. Every now and then, he would kiss my stomach and shed a few tears. What a cry baby! Still, he was *my* cry baby. I loved him more than ever. Finally, finally, we were heading somewhere together. What a journey though, to get here! Of course, he had never used the sofa bed, he had never left our bedroom. I wouldn't let him. It felt right, our love. You know it in your bones when it's right. That night, we hardly slept. Instead we lay in each other's arms the whole night and talked into the morning. He wanted to get married straight away, we would buy the pink house, he would sell the businesses, start an organic garden, cook more, start enjoying being older and being a full- time dad. I wanted to promote my writing. Plans, plans, plans. Life enhancing stuff with wellbeing at the core. In the early dawn, we drifted off, wrapped around each other.

But there was one more thing that I had to do. In my handbag, I had a clutch of adoption papers that my solicitor had drawn up. I knew that Mike would sign in a heartbeat especially if I took him a bottle of something and a packet of fags. I wanted to surprise Neil with it and present it at our celebratory breakfast in a hotel by the seaside that he had picked out. It was only a forty-five-minute drive away, but Zane would love the walk along the sand afterwards. We were so sure that our offer on the house would be accepted. And there was so much to celebrate!

So, I left them sleeping and sneaked out, first thing in the morning. I would only be gone for some forty minutes, I would have enough time to change when I returned. I'd put on that flowery summer dress that he'd bought me, maybe a straw hat, gladiator sandals. I loved dressing up for his appreciative eye.

When I knocked on Mike's door, it was nine -thirty. His parents were early risers, I knew. They liked to do their Tesco shopping early on Saturday to avoid the crowds, I was hoping that they wouldn't be there. But his elderly nan opened the door, she looked dressed to go out. And from the moment I clapped eyes on that evil old bitch, I knew in my belly that I had made the biggest mistake coming here.

'What do you want? We thought we'd never have to see *you* again!' Like I was dirt.

'I just need a few minutes with Mike please.' Polite, respectful as always.

i was broken, now I Am

'Who's that at the door? You're ready to go out Mum?'

'I'm ready, but you need to come and see what the cat's dragged in. And she hasn't brought my grandson as usual. Haven't seen that boy in ages.'

'Who is it? Where are my car keys Beth?'

'Please, is Mike in?'

'Oh, it's you. What are you doing here at my door?'

'Is Mike here?'

'Why do you ask? Scumbag! After how you ruined his life, took away his childhood! Then took away his baby son! We don't want you here okay?'

'Dad! Just leave it! What is it? What do you want? I've just come in.'

'All- night party?'

'What's it to you, what do you need? After you reported me to the fucking cops, they took me in for questioning. I broke up with you but you're still fucking up my life! I only took a tenner!'

Shakily, I told him about the adoption, still standing on his doorstep. Why did I come here alone? I just wanted everything over and done with. Immediately, he reached for the pen and, stony faced, he signed his rights to his son away. But his family wouldn't leave it. And I was getting fed up with their taunts.

'You got the cops to pick *my son* up!' The mother. Cold ran through her veins. 'I could have turned the tables on *you*, told them to pick *you* up!' Her blue doll's eyes were glassy and unfeeling.

'*Me?*' I put the signed forms carefully into my handbag and zipped it. 'I've never harmed a hair on Mike's head. Always wanted to do good by him. Always wanted him to be a good father. I tried so hard, you knew that! How dare you accuse me of anything? I'm a professional, a teacher!'

'So? You should have known better! *You bitch!* Took my son's youth from him!'

'Mum! Just leave it and come inside, it's over.'

'You've been protecting that bitch for ever! No! She needs to know.'

i was broken, now I Am

' This is getting boring. Know what exactly? You've got two seconds then I'm going. Going to buy a huge mansion and get married to my boyfriend. Then you'll never see me again. Cos I will be living on the hill. Far, far, away from you all!'

'You got with my son when he was only fifteen years old! Like them young, do you? Who are you marrying now? A twelve -year -old?'

Blood drained from my face. I felt ill.

'What?' Croaky voice.

'Not so brash, now are we? Yes, I know that he didn't tell you, fancied you rotten he did but I can't see why. You're just a piece of mutton dressed as lamb. My boy, he's tall, just like his dad.'

It was true. Mike's dad was well over six feet tall. In fact, they were like two peas in a pod.

'We could have got you done for statutory rape. But Mike begged us to give you chances. He loved you, loved his son too. But you are a piece of work! Coming here and shooting your mouth off just as we're getting ready to take my mother- in -law out.'

It all made sense. He never had a job. Because he was at school. He'd lied from day one. He must have bunked off all the time that he was with me. But then there were days when he'd disappear. Was this when he went to school? Then the kid in the nightclub. That made sense now. They were the same age. In fact, the place had been full of youngsters. It had only been Pam and I who had been oldies, dancing around our handbags. So, at the age of twenty, Mike now had a five- year -old son! No wonder he couldn't cope with fatherhood. I had put it down to his lack of care, the drugs.

But he was only being a teenager. A kid.

I'd slept with a teenager, under the legal age of sixteen. I could picture my Principal's face as he read about it in the newspaper, as reporters approached him for a comment at the school gates. The distaste. The carefully constructed comment after negotiating with the board of directors.

'She doesn't represent our core values. She's from South Africa. I don't know what they teach them there! It's certainly not our approach to endorse personal relationships between

i was broken, now I Am

students and staff. Our staff are aware of this. But as I have said, she's from South Africa, I can't account for how they train teachers there. She doesn't work here anyway, she was sacked a while ago for being suboptimal.'

Rosemary's triumphant face.

'I knew, I knew that she was trouble. Never doubt me and my judgements. I could just see it in her. The flamboyant clothes, the way she strutted around, that wild hair. I never employed her in the first place!'

Shit, Neil. And Zane. My baby Zane.

I had to get out of there. I climbed shakily into my new Audi convertible. The caramel coloured leather seats that I had lovingly picked out, laughing at the connection to my real name, meant nothing to me now. I had to rush home. Cuddle my son. Hide. Run away, perhaps. There was time. I was crying.

'I'm not done with you bitch! I'll show you, I will! *You'll regret you ever came here! You'll see!'*

How could I live with myself?

*A teacher, a professional. In a sexual relationship with a
student for years! Ran after him she did. Even got pregnant.
Deliberately set out to trap him. A blonde White boy of fifteen.
She deserves that jail sentence. Deserves to be sacked. No- one
wants to publish your work, sorry. We don't represent rapists.*

At home, I put on spa music and changed into my
flowery dress, my hands were shaking but I still applied
light make up even though I was crying so much, and it
would all be smudged anyway. Neil was in the throes of
making coffee and didn't notice my face. The signed
papers lay on the table, for him to pursue. He would
need them now, more than ever. My darling Neil! What
joy he had given me over the course of this glorious
relationship journey. What unbelievable peaks of
happiness life had dealt me through this man, sacred
and sacrosanct almost, in purity. Simple, unadulterated
love. It had drowned out the depths of despair that had
filled my soul since I was born. I was filled with
gratitude for this angel's presence in my life, for the
protection and care that I knew he would give to our
son.

I grabbed Zane up and put him on my lap outside.
For a moment, we sat together on the wooden garden
bench. I liked nuzzling his cheeks, he smelled of baby,

his chubby fingers held onto mine. He'd grown taller, one day he'd be as tall as his father.

Neil's roses had grown a treat. How clever to have intertwined two climbers. They were both old, damask varieties with powerful, perfumed bouquets reminiscent of jasmine. They symbolised us, he had once said, our love. A him and a hers. An ivory white and a deep scarlet. They'd grow to wrap around each other, like Neil and I, always caressing, touching, wanting contact. Our love haze. We'd have to uproot the plants, settle them in the new garden. Neil had invested too much love in them just to abandon them here.

Hold me. Never let me go!

'Why are you crying Mummy?'

'Mummy loves you baby, remember that! Okay? Never forget me!'

What else? What else? Quick, think! I tried to feast my eyes on the flowers, my son, things that I may not see again in a very long time, taking in my fill, like inhaling the last lungfuls of fresh, untainted air before being locked in the tower. Freedom slips through my hands, slippery as quicksand. I want to hold on, don't want to let go. But each second brings judgement day closer and closer.

Please keep us safe. Please, please, please.

The breeze ruffled my curls as I heard the police siren then. Yes, I knew it. Call it a mother's instinct. Gosh, they were quick. They stopped at our door. Neil, cursed, as he spilled espresso over his Polo shirt. Opened the door, thinking it was the postman. But I knew.

'We have a warrant for the arrest of a Carrie Bryant.'

'That would be me officer.' I crept up behind Neil. Zane, sensing something ominous, started to cry. What a sensitive boy our son was! He took after his mother.

'Carrie Bryant, I'm arresting you on suspicion of statutory rape.' Blah blah blah.

I'd been holding my stomach. Now, I held out my hands for the handcuffs.

Face your fears.

Surrender.

i was broken, now I Am

Submit.

Drop into your heart space.

Give love to the thing.

All will be well. Mother is right here with you, everything will be okay.

And I swear that, as I was led away, I saw it. A brilliant light, like a flashbulb. It came from above, and it poured down on me. I didn't need to hold out my hands to collect it. It settled onto my head and seemed to illuminate me. Inside, my heart burst into song. My blood bubbled with joy. And a new calm took over me. This was not how my story would end.

It was going to be okay.

The End

GLOSSARY

'Madiba' is an affectionate term used to refer to Nelson Mandela

'Die Swart gevaar' is Afrikaans for the danger of being overthrown by Black people. This term was used by the White apartheid government to create fear. 'Die Rooi gevaar' refers, similarly, to the threat of a communist takeover, 'rooi' means red, symbolizing communism.

The term 'Coloured' is widely used in South Africa to refer to an interracial ethnic group

'Baleta' refers to the African tradition of carrying a child on one's back, using a blanket as a wrap

'dop' is Afrikaans for an alcoholic drink. The word is widely used by most people, as part of urban slang.

* Zoe Chapter 2: 'slipped on a piece of soap and died' is a line from Chris Van Wyk's poem 'In Detention'. During the apartheid era, when political prisoners died in detention, this was often the reason cited for their death, so it is a tongue in cheek reference.

'Voetsak' is a dismissive Afrikaans word meaning 'Go away!'

'muti' means traditional African, herbal medicine

ACKNOWLEDGEMENTS

I would like to sincerely thank the following:

David Maraniss for allowing me to use his quote;

Jeremy Kyle for allowing me to mention the Jeremy Kyle show;

Tesco for allowing me to use the name of their store;

Chris Van Wyk for the reference to his brilliant poem, 'In Detention';

Country Life Magazine for allowing me to mention the name of the magazine;

Ayn Rand for allowing me to her quote.

I have also used quotes from Lewis Carroll and Rose F. Kennedy.

I would like to thank Sir Elton John for allowing me to refer to 'The Circle of Life' song from The Lion King

AUTHOR BIO

 I was born in Durban, South Africa in 1964, to an Indian family in the heyday of the apartheid regime. I grew up with institutionalized racism oozing out of every pore of the social fabric of life. This impacted where and how we lived, our life opportunities and how others perceived us. In short, the deck was stacked against us right from the start.

As a little girl, my father would take me into the city centre every weekend and being young, I would beg him to let me sit down on the benches on the side of the street. But these were 'Whites Only' benches, and he would shake his head, saying that it was not possible. I never understood it. It felt mean and cruel. Growing up, I saw too much of poverty, strife and discord.

After studying English Literature, Psychology and Drama, I joined the exodus of South Africans heading for a better life in London, leaving behind my immediate family and close knit community, which broke my heart. In the UK, I continued to study

i was broken, now I Am

Psychology and became a teacher, working my way up to the role of Head of Special Educational Needs departments in multiple schools. Currently, I am doing an MA at Goldsmiths University in Social, Therapeutic and Community Studies. This is my second novel.

Sian Bezuidenhout

www.ingramcontent.com/pod-product-compliance
Lightning Source LLC
Chambersburg PA
CBHW031957060726
47497CB00015B/19